St David's Well

Castle Menzies

the River Tay

Aberfeldy

TIME SIGHT

Other Books by Lynne Jonell

The Sign of the Cat
The Secret of Zoom

The Emmy and the Rat series

Emmy and the Incredible Shrinking Rat
Emmy and the Home for Troubled Girls
Emmy and the Rats in the Belfry

Praise for *The Secret of Zoom*

A *School Library Journal* Best Book of the Year
A Junior Library Guild Selection

★ "This exciting tale, with just a touch of fantasy and humor, is a winner."
—*School Library Journal*, **starred review**

Praise for the Emmy and the Rat series

A *School Library Journal* Best Book of the Year
A Junior Library Guild Selection
A *Booklist* Editor's Choice
A Smithsonian Notable Book

★ "A droll fantasy with an old-fashioned sweep
and a positively cinematic cast."
—*Publishers Weekly*, **starred review**

★ "A mystery is cleverly woven into this fun and, at times,
hilarious caper, and children are likely to find themselves
laughing out loud . . . a delightful read."
—*School Library Journal*, **starred review**

★ "Jonell takes readers on a merry, sometimes scary romp [that] turns smoothly on its fanciful premise and fabulous characters. As in so many stories featuring a rat, the sneaky rodent gets the best lines."
—*Booklist,* **starred review**

Praise for *The Sign of the Cat*

Winner of the Judy Lopez Memorial Award for Children's Literature
A Bank Street College Best Book of the Year
A *VOYA* Best Fantasy Book of the Year
A Junior Library Guild Selection

★ "Intriguing, well-drawn characters, evocatively described settings, plenty of action, and touches of humor combine to create an utterly satisfying adventure."
—*Kirkus Reviews,* **starred review**

★ "An engaging story of friendship, high seas adventure, and bravery with themes echoing Harry Potter, *Treasure Island,* and the Warrior cats."
—*VOYA,* **starred review**

TIME SIGHT

LYNNE JONELL

illustrations by Vivien Mildenberger

Christy Ottaviano Books
Henry Holt and Company
New York

Henry Holt and Company, *Publishers since 1866*
Henry Holt® is a registered trademark of Henry Holt and Company, LLC
175 Fifth Avenue, New York, NY 10010
mackids.com

Library of Congress Cataloging-in-Publication Data

Names: Jonell, Lynne, author.
Title: Time sight / Lynne Jonell.
Description: New York : Henry Holt and Company, 2019. | "Christy Ottaviano
  Books." | Summary: After a family emergency sends twelve-year-old Will and
  five-year-old Jamie to Scotland, a Magic Eyeball book takes them and their
  cousin Nan on a journey through their family's violent history.
Identifiers: LCCN 2018039229 | ISBN 978-1-250-11767-0 (hardcover) | ISBN
  978-1-250-11768-7 (ebook)
Subjects: | CYAC: Time travel—Fiction. | Brothers—Fiction. | Cousins—
  Fiction. | Books—Fiction. | Scotland—Fiction. | Scotland—History—Fiction.
Classification: LCC PZ7.J675 Tim 2019 | DDC [Fic]—dc23
LC record available at https://lccn.loc.gov/2018039229

Henry Holt books may be purchased for business or promotional use. For information
on bulk purchases please contact the Macmillan Corporate and Premium Sales
Department at (800) 221-7945 x5442 or by email at specialmarkets@macmillan.com.

First edition, 2019 / Designed by Katie Klimowicz

Printed in the United States of America by LSC Communications,
Harrisonburg, Virginia.

1   3   5   7   9   10   8   6   4   2

To the memory of my beloved grandfather
James David Menzie

CONTENTS

Chapter 1: **Magic Eyeball**   1

Chapter 2: **The Other Side of the Wall**   19

Chapter 3: **Stepping Through**   58

Chapter 4: **Morag**   83

Chapter 5: **Pot Boy and Chambermaid**   106

Chapter 6: **Stewarts' Revenge**   137

Chapter 7: **All Mixed Up**   157

Chapter 8: **Saint David's Well**   192

Chapter 9: **Battle of the Bloody Hands**   215

Chapter 10: **Forward in Time**   244

Chapter 11: **Romans and Picts**   272

Chapter 12: **Cray-tee and Poun-ka**   300

Chapter 13: **Almost Home**   325

Chapter 14: **Garth Castle**   354

Afterword   390

1
MAGIC EYEBALL

WILL WASN'T ENTIRELY SURE WHY he was on a plane to Scotland, with only his little brother and no parents at all. His father had explained, of course, but there hadn't been time for all the questions Will wanted to ask. Everything had happened in a great hurry.

There had been that first phone call in the middle of the night, and then more phone calls to follow, so that Will thought his father's ear might fall off from being pressed so tightly to the receiver. Then Will had been put in charge of packing for himself and his brother, Jamie, one suitcase each, and it had been hard to know what to take and what to leave behind. Jamie still slept with his stuffed bear, but it took up so much room! And they would need underwear and socks and things.

"Pack sweaters, too," Will's father had said in between phone calls, his face pale and his hair still wildly on end from where it had lain on his pillow.

"But it's almost summer, Dad!" said Will.

"The Highlands can be cold any time of the year. Damp, too. Pack rain jackets."

Jamie had fallen asleep in the cab to the airport, a warm huddled bunch against Will's side, clutching his bear in a death grip. Will felt like clutching something, too, only he was twelve and past that sort of thing. He did wish, though, that his father would talk to him, instead of to whoever it was on the other end of the phone.

His father put the phone away long enough to buy them books at the airport. Jamie got something with pictures— *Magic Eyeball*, it was called—and Will hardly noticed what he grabbed. Something thick, to last him for the nine-hour flight. He stuffed it under his arm and looked up at his father.

"You're a good lad, Will," said his father. "I know you'll take care of Jamie. And once you land in Scotland, Cousin Elspeth will take care of you."

"Will you bring Mom home?" It was an effort to push out the words; Will's throat felt strangely tight.

"Of course I will." Will's father spoke heartily. "It's all just a mix-up, I'm sure, but sometimes these things are better handled in person. Don't you worry a bit." He smiled, but the line between his eyebrows deepened, and he blinked twice, his eyes red-rimmed with fatigue. "Now one last hug all round, and then get on your plane. I've got a plane to catch myself. Oh, and here's some spending money—you might want to buy a souvenir at the castle."

ಀ

"Cookies or salty snacks?" The flight attendants were coming down the aisle with their cart. "Coffee, tea, or soda, sir? Cookies or pretzels?"

The white-haired man on Will's left flipped a latch on the seat back ahead of him and pulled down a tray table over his knees. "Coffee, please," the man said, his voice a warm Scottish rumble.

Will copied the old gentleman, pulling down his own tray table and Jamie's, too. "Two root beers, please," he said, just like an experienced traveler. "And cookies. Jamie, stop bouncing on your seat, or you'll knock over the drinks."

"But look, Will! I can see it, I can see the picture! I have the magic eyeball!" Jamie thrust the book across his armrest and bumped the tray table, hard.

The root beer sloshed—the plastic cup rocked. Will lunged for it, but the cup slipped away from his fingers. Brown frothy liquid poured over the tray's edge, soaked his jeans, and splashed all the way to the old gentleman's newspaper.

The man was surprisingly nice about it, but the flight

attendant had to mop up the mess with towels, and the other passengers turned around to stare. Will's ears felt hot, and his legs were damp and sticky.

"Can I have another root beer?" Jamie asked.

"*No,*" said Will.

Jamie kicked his legs a little. Then he kicked them a little more. His foot hit the back of the seat in front of him.

The woman in the seat turned around and gave them both a meaningful glare.

"Hold still!" Will hissed in Jamie's ear.

"I'm boooored," said Jamie.

"Look at your book, then. That's why Dad got it for you."

Jamie's lower lip pushed out. "*You* look at my book. Tell me if you can see the pictures. I bet you can't."

Will rolled his eyes. "Of course I can see the pictures." He opened the Magic Eyeball book and glanced at a page. "See? It's just some random pattern. Why did you want this book, anyway? It's dumb."

"No, look *at* the pictures. My friend Ben has one, and he showed me how. Read the directions." Jamie moved a stubby finger along a line of type. "Method . . . One. Put . . . your . . . nose . . . close . . . to . . . the . . . book," he read aloud.

Will sighed. Jamie had only just finished kindergarten, but he was already reading well, and he loved to show off. "I'll do it if you stop bothering me. Look out the window, why don't you? You asked for the window seat, so get some use out of it."

♋

Jamie had fallen asleep, huddled in the corner of his seat with his cheek pressed against his stuffed bear. Will was still trying to see what his brother had seen in the Magic Eyeball book.

There were apparently pictures hidden in the repeating patterns. If you held the book at a certain distance—or unfocused your eyes just slightly—or somehow looked *past* the page while still looking *at* it, then a whole different picture would appear. The book said to be patient, and relax, and not to try too hard. Will had been patient for what seemed like a very long time, and nothing had happened. It was a stupid book. He slammed it shut.

Outside, the sky had grown dark. Will unbuckled his seat belt, leaned across the armrest, and peered out past Jamie's nose. Behind him, the plane's wing stretched away in sections of gray riveted metal, and a flashing light glowed orange every other second. Far below, he could see pinpricks of lights like fallen stars: ships, sailing on an ocean as black and endless as the sky.

The world seemed all at once far too big and dark. It was a place people could get lost in.

Will leaned back in his seat and tried as hard as he could not to think about his mother. His father was going to her. Surely that meant things would be all right in the end?

The interior of the plane was like a snug cocoon. The cabin lights were dimmed, and most of the passengers were asleep. The old gentleman reached above his head to turn a small knob, and a thin ray of light speared down to pool on the book in his lap. His hand turned the pages with a quiet sound.

Will wished he could sleep. He had been awake since the call in the night, and his eyes were gritty, but his mind was too full of worried thoughts to rest. He shook his head, hard, to clear it. He would read his book.

But it wasn't in his backpack under the seat, and it wasn't in the seat pocket in front of him. He remembered with a pang that he had set it down in the airport, when he'd used both hands to put on his backpack.

"Have you lost something?" the old gentleman asked.

"Just my book." Will shrugged as if it didn't matter. But the book was the last thing his father had given him, and Will had lost it.

The old gentleman was on his feet, rummaging in the overhead compartment. Then he handed down something heavy and rectangular in a plastic bag.

"I meant to give it to my granddaughter in the States," the man said, dropping into his seat again, "but I forgot. You can look at it, if you wish. Do you like history?"

The heavy rectangle turned out to be an illustrated book about Scotland. Will turned the pages slowly, looking at the pictures. There were cave dwellers, and chieftains, and war-riors, and kings. . . .

"Sure," he said, "I like history. Thanks, Mr.—uh—"

"Craig." The old gentleman shook Will's hand. "And your name?"

"Will Menzies."

Mr. Craig's eyes crinkled at the corners as he smiled. "Now, that's an old and honored clan name. Visiting Scotland, are you?"

Will looked at him shyly. "I'm going to live at Castle Menzies. Or close to it, anyway," he amended. "My mother's cousin is the castle manager."

The old gentleman chuckled. "You'll have a grand time, laddie. How long are you staying?"

"I don't know." Will looked past Jamie's sleeping form to the dark outside the window, and curled his fingers around the cold metal of the armrest.

His father had told him not to discuss his mother's situation with strangers—that talking might make things worse if the wrong people overheard. Still, Will wished he could tell someone about it. How his mother had gone off for a few weeks with a medical team, to help children in some poor country that had more than its share of disease, war, and disaster. About the call in the middle of the night, warning that his mother was in some kind of trouble—political trouble, his father had said, hard to explain but nothing for Will to worry about. But the cheerful words had come from lips that had gone hard and thin, and his father's knuckles were pale where they gripped the phone, and in the morning his face had new lines that Will had never seen before, as if ten years had gone by in a single night.

The plane was quiet except for the muffled roar of the engines, steady and monotonous. Will smoothed the pages of the history book on his tray table. It was open to a picture of some sort of warrior. The man had a spear, a sword, and a round leather shield. His body was covered with blue tattoos, and he looked tough enough for any kind of trouble. He looked like the sort of person you would want on your side in a fight, or if you needed to rescue someone in a hurry.

If Will was going to rescue someone, he'd like to have a sword. Or maybe he'd use karate instead—he'd taken lessons, after all—and surprise all the bad guys with his lightning-fast kicks. He drifted into a pleasant daydream where his father took him along to help rescue his mother . . . but then his father fell, wounded, in the street, and it was all up to Will. . . .

Will had single-handedly rescued his mother, and father too, and was at the point where he was receiving the Medal of Freedom from the president when the plane hit a patch of turbulence. Will came out of his dream with a bitter jolt.

He wasn't going to rescue anyone. He was going to babysit a five-year-old.

Of course there was the castle to look forward to . . . if there really was a castle. Will couldn't quite make himself believe in it. Just yesterday he had been living his ordinary life, and today everything had changed. It was as if a strong wind had come and whirled apart the pieces of his life.

The plane juddered again, and Jamie woke with a whimper. "Is the plane falling?" he whispered, his eyes wide.

Will sincerely hoped not. "It's just a patch of bumpy air," he whispered back. "Don't be afraid, I'm here." He saw that Jamie's bear had fallen to the floor; he picked it up and tucked it in his brother's arms.

Jamie's lip trembled. "I want *Mom*," he said, his eyes damp with sudden tears. "Where is she?"

"Dad's going to get her. Shh, now, go to sleep. You can lay your head on my lap, see? I'll pull up the armrest."

The little boy subsided into Will's lap with a gulp and a sniffle. Will patted Jamie's back and stared, unseeing, at the history book. He wanted his mother, too. Why had she left them? Other children needed her, she had said . . . but he and Jamie needed her *more*.

The soldier on the page blurred. Will wiped his cheeks roughly with his sleeve and turned his face away. He closed his eyes.

In the morning Will gave back the history book and switched places with Jamie, who wanted to show the old gentleman his Magic Eyeball pictures. Will was glad to have the window seat as the folded hills of Scotland came into view. The plane flew a curving pattern over the coastline's jagged edge, where green and brown met vivid blue, and the sea spiked into the land in a wide crooked V.

"We're flying over Edinburgh Castle now," intoned a voice on the loudspeaker, pronouncing it "Ed-in-burrow." Will peered down at the sprawling castle on its hill. It looked grayer and more serious, somehow, than the pictures of castles he had seen in books. You could see at once that it was meant for defense. . . . It looked grim, and impossibly strong.

The ground grew closer, and water sparkled beneath them in a million points of reflected light. The landing gear engaged with an audible thump, the airport lights flashed by, the runway rushed up, and with a sudden *bump*, the wheels hit the tarmac and the plane was down.

ৎও

Cousin Elspeth was a warm, brisk, hugging sort of person with wavy brown hair and a quick walk. She looked a little like Mother—enough to make Will feel almost at home and for Jamie to leap up and wrap himself around her. She took them first to the airport bank, where Will changed the dollars his father had given him into Scottish money. Then she herded them to baggage claim and out to the car, talking all the way.

A large, creamy dog bounded from side to side in the back

seat, clearly ecstatic to see them. "Gormlaith! Down, girl!" Cousin Elspeth opened the back door a crack. "Get in quick, boys, before she jumps out. I hope you're not afraid of dogs?"

"I've always wanted a dog!" Jamie climbed in, threw both his arms around the dog's heaving chest, and rubbed his cheek against the soft, pale fur.

"Gormlaith?" said Will, ducking as the dog's plumy tail whapped his cheek.

Cousin Elspeth looked over her shoulder as she backed up the car. "It's an old Scottish name; it means 'Splendid Lady.' And you are splendid, aren't you, Gormly?" she added fondly, putting the car in gear with a jerk.

Splendid was not exactly the word he would have chosen, Will thought as Gormlaith pricked up her floppy ears, sniffed his armpit in a manner that was a little too friendly, and licked Jamie's face from chin to forehead with one swipe of her long pink tongue. *Over-enthusiastic* was closer to the mark.

But Jamie was laughing. Will hadn't heard him laugh for a while now.

Gormlaith turned around, treading heavily on Will's thighs with her big paws, and draped herself across his lap. She laid her head on Jamie's knee and whined softly, looking up with melting brown eyes, and Jamie scratched her behind the ears, grinning.

Will settled in for an uncomfortable ride. His legs might be numb by the time they got there, but if it kept Jamie happy, it was worth it. A dog wasn't much of a substitute for a mother, but it was better than nothing.

Cousin Elspeth drove madly on the left side of the road. Will almost shouted when he saw a truck about to hit them at an intersection, but the truck passed without so much as a toot of the horn, and he realized that, in Scotland, everyone drove on the wrong side.

Of course it wasn't the wrong side to them. Still, he had to shut his eyes because Cousin Elspeth's driving was starting to give him a headache.

"I'm glad you've come, boys," she was saying. "You'll be company for my Nan. She whinges that the castle is too far from her friends. . . . She'll be proper glad to have some young people around the place for once. You'll see her when she gets home from school."

"Whinges?" said Will.

"That just means to complain . . . kind of like whining, you might say. Our Nan has it down to a science." Cousin Elspeth chuckled slightly.

"I'm going to show Nan my Magic Eyeball book!" Jamie announced. "It has hidden pictures, and I can see them but Will can't!"

Will rolled his eyes to keep from whingeing himself. If Jamie didn't shut up about that book soon, Will was strongly tempted to give it to Gormlaith and see if she liked to chew on paper.

Fortunately, the car ride lulled Jamie to sleep, and the dog, too. With a little effort, Will managed to slide the animal down to the floor, where she lay with her paws twitching.

Will yawned. Cousin Elspeth was talking on and on about the Menzies family and how he was related to everyone. . . . He couldn't imagine a more boring topic.

"—so you're a Menzies from both sides, do you see?" Cousin Elspeth took her hands off the steering wheel to gesture wildly. Will gripped the armrest. She had lived this long, driving the way she did; she probably wouldn't crash now. Or so he hoped.

"There isn't one drop of your blood that doesn't come straight down through the ages of the clan!"

Will decided not to tell Cousin Elspeth how little he cared. He quietly picked up the Magic Eyeball book and tried again to see the pictures—he didn't want to look foolish in front of Nan—but it was hopeless. At last he closed his eyes and let Cousin Elspeth's words flow over and around him like a bubbling stream rushing past a rock.

ജ

The car stopped with a jerk, and Will's eyes flew open. In front of him a flock of sheep was crossing the road as if they had all the time in the world. Bells around their necks clanked with a hollow sound.

Outside, the landscape had changed. City buildings had given way to a forest that covered the hills like a bear's pelt. The hills themselves loomed larger, higher, steeper, and their craggy faces were seamed with stone. Far below, a river gleamed in a narrow valley.

"You're in the Highlands now, lad!" Cousin Elspeth gunned the engine to disperse the staring sheep, and the bells clanked more rapidly as the sheep moved off. The car jerked forward, and Will leaned his head back against the seat.

The next time he opened his eyes, the car was bumping through a town filled with buildings made of gray stone. And when he opened them after that, they were at the castle.

It loomed above them, tall and grim, with long square towers and corner turrets, but Will hardly had a chance to look up before he was bundled through the front door, down a cold stone hall, up a narrow stair, and into a small room crammed with trunks, boxes, miscellaneous furniture, and two cots.

Cousin Elspeth laid Jamie, limp as a rag, on one of the cots and turned to Will. "Sorry it's so crowded—we use this room for storage, but you can take a kip in here until my Nan gets out of school. She wants to show you the castle herself, and she'll tell you all about the history. . . ." Cousin Elspeth trailed off uncertainly. "At least, I hope she will. You let me know if you have questions Nan doesn't answer!" She straightened and gave Will's shoulder a brisk pat. "The loo is just down the stairs, and I'll be at the front desk if you need me. If you get lost, follow the sound of the bagpipes— I play a recording for the tourists. Come, Gormly, we'll let the boys get some sleep."

A kip was a nap, Will guessed, and the loo was the bathroom. Or so he hoped. He tumbled onto his cot and kicked off his shoes.

But the dog wouldn't go. She lay between the two cots with her head on her paws and her eyes closed. Cousin Elspeth tugged on her collar, but Gormlaith only shut her eyes tighter and whined.

Cousin Elspeth straightened, frowning. "We never let the dog sleep in anyone's bedroom, and she knows it. I wonder why she's acting like this now?"

"I don't mind," Will said sleepily. "Maybe she wants to guard us."

"Could be. Or maybe she knows you boys are a little sad, and wants to stay close. I told you she was special." Cousin Elspeth shook her finger at the dog, mock sternly. "But just this once!"

‿

When Will woke up, he didn't know where he was. The afternoon sun slanted through a high window to lay long gold bars of light across the opposite wall, and, disoriented, he watched the dust motes swirling. His gaze fell on a small writing desk and Jamie's Magic Eyeball book. He caught a glimpse of a turret through the window, and then all at once he remembered.

Jamie and the big cream-colored dog were still asleep. Will sat up and put on his shoes. When was this Nan going to come and show them around the castle? He didn't want to sit in the storage room forever. He rummaged in the desk for a pen and paper, and carefully printed a short note to Jamie. *I've gone downstairs. Be right back. Will.*

On a whim, he picked up the Magic Eyeball book. He would try one more time. Will tiptoed around Gormlaith, down the narrow stairs, and through the door.

The corridor was long and shadowed. Rough stone walls rose on either side and met overhead in a barrel-shaped arch. Here and there, electric lights shaped like torches burned dimly in iron cages. The windows were narrow, barred with iron, and set deep in walls that had to be three feet thick. Archers had shot arrows from those windows, probably. . . .

At the end of the hall was a door with wood so old it had darkened to black, and Will put his hand on the great iron studs and massive bars. Knights had come through this door. They had hung their swords on those hooks, and clanked down the hall with their heavy boots. For a moment Will almost thought he was back in that time. . . . Faintly, in the distance, he seemed to hear the sound of bagpipes.

He let out his breath in a little snort. Of course he heard bagpipes. That was the recording that Cousin Elspeth played for the tourists.

Grinning at himself, Will sat down with his back to the stone wall, stretched his legs out in front of him, and opened the Magic Eyeball book. This time, he would try the third method. He would focus his eyes on something a short distance away, and then slowly bring the book up within view.

Will concentrated. There! Was something shifting? He thought he had caught a sort of shimmering around the edges of the picture, but he lost it as soon as his focus sharpened. He shut his eyes to rest them before he tried again.

In the distance, the bagpipes droned their peculiar music, both sad and stirring, and Will thought he could hear children laughing. The tourists must have kids with them. . . . He hoped they wouldn't come down this hall, not just yet. He opened his eyes and focused again on a spot in midair, raising the book slowly. There! There was that odd sort of shimmer again, as if a picture was coming clear.

He tried to relax as the book said and not look directly at the place where the picture seemed to be, but *through* it somehow. Except the shimmering was only at the edges of the book—no, it was *outside* the edges. And while the picture in the book remained the same, the air around it seemed to waver, like an image seen through running water.

The children's laughter grew louder, and suddenly the gloomy hall was flooded with light, as if part of the wall in front of him had crumbled—

It *had* crumbled. Or at least it wasn't there anymore. Will's arms sagged down, and the book dropped from nerveless fingers. Before him was daylight, and green grass, and two small children playing a game with something like strings and what looked to be acorns dangling from them. Their laughter filled Will's ears as they swung the acorns and then suddenly one of the nuts hit the other, came loose from its string, and flew toward him. He ducked instinctively and blinked.

The children disappeared, the light was gone, and the wall in front of him was as solid as ever. But rolling toward his feet was a single acorn.

A foot scraped on the flagstone near him. Then a girl plopped down next to him on the floor and curled up her knees. "How did you do *that*?" she asked.

2
THE OTHER SIDE
OF THE WALL

WILL STARED AT HER WILDLY. He had no idea how he had done it—if he *had* done it. And yet there was the acorn, round and hard and perfectly real.

"Was it a magic trick, then?" The girl's cheek dimpled, and her smile showed a space between her front teeth. "You're Will, right? I'm your cousin Nan. I don't know any magic tricks except the sliding rope and finding the ace of spades, and sometimes I can do the pencil-in-the-head. But I'm not very good. I've never seen a cobnut come rolling out of a wall before. Did you find that trick in a book?"

Will blinked at his cousin. She had a freckled nose and straight brows and a tumble of reddish gold hair that had fallen in her eyes. She pushed it back and tapped her foot against the stone floor. "Well? How does it work?"

"It wasn't a trick," Will said. "It was—" He stopped. He didn't know what it was. "An optical illusion?"

"Of course it was an illusion," said Nan with something of the same briskness that Cousin Elspeth had in such abundance. "That's what magic tricks *are*. What I want to know is, how did you make it seem like that cobnut rolled right out of the wall?"

Will was silent. He had no idea how *any* of it had happened.

"You don't talk much, do you?" Nan cocked her head to one side like an inquisitive robin. "Are you a bit daft? Or don't you have anything to say?"

Will glared at her. "I don't blab off at the mouth just for the fun of it, like some people I could mention."

"Eh, I reckoned that would get you talking if nothing else would," Nan said comfortably. "Cut a lad's pride and he'll talk quick enough, if only to tell you you're wrong."

"You don't think much of boys, do you?" Will said, annoyed.

"I don't think about them much at all," Nan said, grinning. "The lads I know are mostly dull as dust. But I'm supposed to be nice to you and young Jamie, so I thought I'd get the preliminaries out of the way first. And now we've had our first fight, we can start off even, right?"

Will found himself grinning back in spite of himself. He had never met anyone quite like Nan before.

20

"So, talk to me. I *saw* that cobnut roll out of the wall. How did you do it?"

"Did you see anything else?" Will asked cautiously. "Did you see the little kids playing their game?"

"What game?"

Will described it.

"Oh, conkers," said Nan. "Don't you play conkers in America? See, you bore a hole through a horse chestnut, and then you push a string through and knot it. That's your conker. You dangle it from the string, and the other person tries to hit it with his conker, and you take turns until one of the nuts breaks, and that one's the loser. We always use horse chestnuts, though—I've never heard of anyone doing it with a cobnut. They're too small."

"I thought it was an acorn."

Nan shook her head. "It's a cobnut. Or you can call it a hazelnut; it's all the same."

Will turned the nut in his hand. Now that he was looking for it, the hole was plain to see. "That's what they were using, though."

"Who?" Nan asked patiently.

Will tossed the nut from hand to hand, watching his cousin's face. "The kids on the other side of the wall."

"Right, now you've lost me." Nan frowned and picked at a scab on her knee. "Look, it's a good trick, that, but if you don't want to tell me how you did it, then just say so."

"It's not that I don't want to tell you," Will said. "It's that you won't believe me."

Nan scratched thoughtfully under her chin. "You're my cousin. You'd not lie to me, now, would you?"

"You'll *think* I'm lying," Will said hopelessly.

Nan gave him a long stare.

"Fine, then." Will looked down, so he wouldn't have to watch her face grow scornful, and told her what had happened. When he looked up again, the dimple in Nan's cheek had disappeared.

"I knew you wouldn't believe me." Will shoved the cobnut in his pocket. He could feel the small round holes where the cord had gone through.

Nan picked up the Magic Eyeball book and turned the pages slowly. "I looked at a book like this once, but I only saw the pictures you're supposed to see. They print them plain in the back of the book in case you can't make them out."

Will relaxed slightly. At least she wasn't making fun of him. "I can't see those pictures at all," he said. "What I saw was outside the edges of the book. The book got in the way of the thing I was seeing, so I dropped it."

Nan's eyes widened. "Maybe you have the Sight."

"What?"

"Second Sight! You've got it!" Nan jumped up. "Plenty of Scots have the Sight, they say. And you're Scottish. Well, more or less."

Will gave her a sidelong look. "I'm American, you dolt."

"Dolt, yourself." Nan tossed her hair out of her eyes. "My mum told me you've got Scottish blood going back practically forever. In your genes, you're all Scot."

Will wrinkled his brow. "Isn't Second Sight about seeing the future? The boys I saw were dressed like they were from the past. The Middle Ages, maybe."

"The Middle Ages!" Nan breathed. "Do it again, so I can see it!"

"I don't know how I did it in the first place," Will said, but he took the Magic Eyeball book and held it at arm's length.

It was hard to concentrate with Nan there. The edges of the book stayed stubbornly sharp and clear, and beyond them the stone wall was as solid as ever.

A bead of sweat formed between Will's eyebrows; the back of his neck ached. He didn't want to let down the American side, but he felt foolish. He let the book fall to his lap.

"Are you giving up *already*?" Nan said.

"Just resting my eyes." Will shut them, by way of emphasis.

Nan scooted closer. "Do what you did before. Do it exactly the same."

"Who made you the boss of the world?" Will said grumpily, but he picked up the book. How *had* he done it, exactly? The book gave different methods, but the first two hadn't worked—

The third. He had focused his eyes on a point beyond the book, and then he had slowly raised the book, like this. . . .

There.

"Can you see it?" Will spoke very low. "A sort of shimmering around the edges?"

There came a tiny noise from down the hall, faint and metallic. Will blinked, and the image fled. The noise came again, sounding like a distant knife scraped on wire, or springs squeaking—

"I think that's your little brother, turning over in his cot," whispered Nan.

The two children looked down the hall toward the stairwell. Will's hand slipped into his pocket, and he gripped the cobnut for luck. There was no way he could concentrate with Jamie around. But a whole minute ticked by with no more noises.

"He's still asleep," whispered Nan at last. "Try it again."

This time, it was easier. The shimmer appeared, as if there were a different sort of light shining behind the book, and Will lowered his arms. It was just the same as before— sunlight, no wall—only the two children had stopped playing conkers and had picked up sticks, instead. As Will watched, they began a mock battle, whacking the sticks against each other as if they were swords.

"Do you see them?" Will whispered.

"I can't see a thing," Nan said.

"Maybe you've got to be looking straight at it. Get behind me, why don't you?"

Nan's chin touched Will's shoulder as she leaned in. Her gasp was loud in his ear.

"It's like a wide-screen telly, only better!" she breathed.

It *was* like television, in a way, only the edges were not nicely squared, but fuzzy and undefined. All around him, Will could vaguely sense the dark loom of the castle hall—but directly in front, where he was looking, a picture more real than any on TV was unfolding.

In the distance, a horse and rider trotted under overhanging trees, and three workmen were doing something with a lever. Closer in, the two children chased after each other, laughing.

A girl with a basket on one arm walked into the picture. Her hair was reddish and tumbled, like Nan's, but she was dirtier, and if she had a dimple, it wasn't showing. She looked straight at Will, frowning.

Will's heart bumped in his chest. But the girl's face kept its bored expression. She walked past them and out of the picture.

Nan's breath tickled Will's ear. "She didn't see us!"

Will nodded. His heart was still racing.

"Try turning your head. I want to see where she's going."

Will turned his head, slowly, and the scene changed. The girl with the basket was still walking, but now there were tall yellow flowers in the foreground and something that looked like a long hammer lying on the turf. Sounds came through, too—voices speaking a language that was almost familiar, yet not quite.

"Can you understand them?" Will asked.

Nan shook her head. "I wonder if they can hear us?"

"They can't see us, so maybe they can't hear us, either."

"We could shout," Nan suggested.

"Don't," said Will forcefully. "If a hazelnut could roll through, then maybe one of *them* could come through, too."

"If it was the boys, we could ask them what year it was," said Nan.

"Yeah, but what if it was that guy?" Will pointed as a huge, hairy man came into the picture, hefted the hammer onto his massive shoulder, and lumbered out of the scene.

Somewhere, a horse whinnied. There was a *clink clink* of tools on metal, a grumble of voices, and a sound of soft footsteps. Will and Nan, intent on the picture, waited to see who would come into view next. . . .

The footsteps grew louder. Jamie pushed in close to his brother. "What are you watching?" His voice was clear and high. "Wow, it looks real!"

Jamie's small hand reached into the picture, grasped the stem of a tall yellow flower, and yanked.

"Wha—?" Nan said.

"Don't!" cried Will at the same time, a half second too late.

Pop! went the stem as it gave way, and Jamie tumbled backward. Will threw out an arm to catch him, and the hallway grew suddenly dark as the picture disappeared. The three children stared at one another, wordless. From down the hall Gormlaith appeared, nails skidding on the stone floor as she rounded the corner with a welcoming bark. Cousin Elspeth's slightly plump figure was close behind.

"Well! Did you have a good sleep, then?" Cousin Elspeth hauled Jamie to his feet and dusted him off. "Let's be off home. It's near suppertime, and I've got Callum at the desk to mind the castle. Do you fancy grilled sausages?"

෴

Jamie babbled in the car about a new kind of TV, where you could put your hand right into the picture. He showed Cousin Elspeth his flower by way of proof.

She glanced at the flower, limp now in Jamie's fist. "It sounds as if you had a good game. Did Nan show you the castle?"

"Jamie slept too long," Nan said from the back seat as she scratched Gormlaith's ears. "But," she added, smiling brilliantly at Will, "I'll show them everything tomorrow. It's Saturday, and I won't have school."

Supper was fat, sizzling sausages, splitting their skins

from the heat, with potatoes that were brown and crisp on the outside and hot and mealy on the inside. Cousin Elspeth called them "bangers and tatties," and Will ate until he felt like a stuffed sausage himself. Even Jamie stopped talking in order to eat.

"I can't finish," Jamie said at last, looking down at a half sausage.

"Eh, well, take it out to the dog—she'll be glad of an extra bite," said Cousin Elspeth. "The kennel is just outside the back door, laddie."

Will rolled onto the couch and wondered if he would ever be hungry again. He felt his stomach tenderly. Nan bounced onto the cushions next to him, and he groaned faintly.

"We've got to find out how it works!" Her whisper was insistent. "Let's try again tonight, after Jamie's in bed."

Will slumped. He had kept his eyes open during supper, but now he felt them closing inexorably. "I'm tired," he said.

Nan looked at the clock. "It's not even nine!"

Cousin Elspeth glanced up from the sink, where she was finishing the last of the dishes. "Will and Jamie had a long flight, and they need their rest." She lifted Jamie, who was draped limply over a chair, and carried him up the stairs. Jamie roused long enough to mumble, "I want my bear," and then his eyes closed again.

The room Will was to share with Jamie looked out over

a stone-fenced yard of pleasant trees and grass—Cousin Elspeth called it a garden—and had a peaked roof, two beds, and a chest of drawers. Will had a vague memory of visiting the bathroom, fending off Nan in the hall ("I'll knock on your door in half an hour, and we can try it again!"), and falling into bed with one sock still on. He sank into sleep like a stone falling into deep water, and if Nan knocked at his door, he didn't hear it.

When Will opened his eyes again, the room was filled with the soft gray light of early dawn. It took him a few seconds to remember where he was through the fog of sleep, and then all at once he was awake. The clock on the dresser said 5:09 A.M.

He was terribly hungry. Would Cousin Elspeth mind if he got himself some cereal? Will pulled on his clothes and tiptoed down the creaking wooden stairs to the kitchen.

The light was growing, and through the open window came a trill of birdsong. Will stepped outside and stood with his hand on the doorknob, entranced.

Across the road was a narrow, stony river, and beyond it, a hill of enormous size swooped up and up. It was strangely scooped, as if a giant had pushed the land up with his thumb. At the very top, it was craggy with rock like a mountain, but Will could climb it, he was sure. It looked as if a person could run straight up to the very top.

A gleam of light from the far end of the valley turned

the somber hillside bright with long swaths and patches of color, yellow and purple and tan and a green so vivid that it looked lit from within. Here and there, white woolly sheep dotted the turf, cropping it close, and the air was full of a sweet scent. Gormlaith emerged from her kennel with a jingle of dog tags and rubbed up against his side, licking his hand.

Will felt suddenly, intensely happy, as if everything was going to be all right.

He would climb the hill. He could be to the top and back before anyone else woke up. It didn't matter about breakfast.

He leaped a stone wall, picked his way across the river on rocks slippery with spray, and strode up the green hill, whistling as the big creamy dog lolloped around him, ears flying.

An hour later, breathing hard, he stopped. The climb was steeper than he had thought. Will looked down into the valley and then up at the peak, measuring the distance with his eyes. He was only a third of the way up, his socks were soaked with dew, and his stomach was like an empty pail.

He threw himself onto a flat gray rock that stuck out of the hill like a sideways tooth. It looked ancient, as if it had been there forever. How many of his ancestors had sat right where he was sitting? Maybe his own mother had sat here when she was a girl.

And just that quickly, his mood shifted. Will clasped his forearms as if to hold in the ache that felt like a brick in his chest every time he thought of his mother.

Gormlaith stopped chasing butterflies and looked at him with concern. Then she padded over clumsily, nudging his leg with her nose.

Will's hand stole out and stroked her smooth, warm head. The dog gazed at him with brown liquid eyes that never left his face.

"She's in some kind of trouble," Will said quietly. Somehow it was easier to talk to a dog. "Bad trouble, I think, and I can't do anything about it."

Gormlaith put a paw on his knee and whined softly.

"Why did she have to go?" Will pressed his face into Gormlaith's furry back. His mother had explained her reasons, of course. She had shown him pictures of the children who needed her—kids who had something wrong with them, who didn't have a doctor to help—and while the pictures made Will feel strangely ashamed, they made him mad, too. Why did it have to be *his* mother who solved all the world's problems? He had still been angry when she had left . . . so angry that he hadn't hugged her and had turned his face aside when she went to kiss him.

If only he could do that part over, just that one part. It wouldn't matter that he didn't agree with her. He would hug his mother and let her kiss him and not care who was watching. . . .

Clang clang . . . *clang clang.* . . .

Will lifted his head, blinking. Far down the slope, across the river, Cousin Elspeth's house was a bright spot against a green field. It looked small and tidy, white with black shutters and a red-painted door. As he watched, a tiny figure moved by the door and the sheep bell rang again.

Cousin Elspeth must be calling him to breakfast. He'd better hurry—Jamie might be afraid if he woke up in a strange place and Will wasn't there.

He headed down the slope, half slithering on the wet turf. Gormlaith raced ahead, with occasional surges off to the side to chase a rabbit (unsuccessfully). Will galloped the last stretch to the river and hopped across the stones. There was a smell of bacon and cinnamon and something nutty, like toasted grain.

"What's this?" Jamie sat at the plain oak table, staring down into a bowl.

"Porridge, you silly!" said Nan through a mouthful of bacon.

Cousin Elspeth chuckled. "I can't believe you've never eaten porridge before, my lad." She picked up an armful of rugs and went outside. Through the open door came a rhythmic *thwap thwap thwap* as she shook them from the step.

"We call it oatmeal in America." Will gave his brother a good-morning bump on the shoulder. "You've eaten it before, Jamie. Don't be rude."

Jamie raised eyes, which looked suspiciously wet. "But there's *butter* on it!"

Will leaned over. A big lump of butter stared up at him from the center of the steaming bowl, melting slowly in the hot cereal. "That's okay," he said. "We're in Scotland, and they make it like this. Just try it. It might be good."

Jamie's mouth pinched up, and he shook his head, looking miserable. "I want it the way *Mom* makes it."

"Here, I'll fix it for you." Will took his spoon, scooped up the butter, and put it on his own oatmeal. It was a little greasy, but he slid the butter to one side and ate from the other, hoping Cousin Elspeth wouldn't notice.

"Have jam on it," Nan suggested.

Jamie cheered up at that idea and took a heaping spoonful from the jam jar, getting predictably sticky. "Are we going to watch the new TV again?" he asked between bites.

Nan choked on her toast. "Don't you want to play in the castle?" She swallowed and smiled winningly, her dimple deep. "You can climb into the turrets on top and shoot the enemy with your arrows!"

"Okay," said Jamie. "And *then* the big TV!"

Cousin Elspeth came in with the rugs. "It's daft to talk about TV when you have a whole castle to explore. Get ready, all of you—it's almost time for me to open up for the tourists. Oh, and Will, your father called late last night. He arrived safely. He'll let us know when he has more news, but he says not to worry if he doesn't call—it just means he's not able to get phone service."

Nan started their tour at ground level, in the castle kitchen. Will had never seen a fireplace so huge that a grown man could stand up in it. Inside, iron kettles and pots hung from hooks, dangling over a massive grate.

Jamie thrust his head into a hollowed space at the side. "What's this hole for?"

"Baking bread." Nan pointed at something that looked like a flat wooden spade. "You put the dough on that, then slide it inside. The stones get hot from the fire, and the bread bakes, and when it's done, you use the wooden peel to get it out again."

"Oh." Jamie turned his head and took in a breath. "*Now* can we watch the big—"

Nan clapped her hands like a kindergarten teacher. "Who wants to see the dungeon?"

"I do! I do!" Jamie ran down the hall in the direction of Nan's pointing finger, his footsteps echoing off the stone.

"That got rid of him," said Nan.

"Not for long," said Will.

Nan waved away this point. "There's one thing I can't

understand. Remember how I couldn't see the picture from the past at first? I had to get behind you."

Will nodded.

"But when Jamie came up, *he* saw it from the side. How did he do that?"

Will shrugged. "You know as much as I do."

"Maybe Jamie has the Sight, too." Nan chewed her lower lip. "Am I the only one who doesn't have it?"

"I don't think Jamie has the Sight," Will said, thinking back. "He looked at that Magic Eyeball book on the plane a lot more than I did, and he never saw anything weird. Anyway, Second Sight is about seeing the future, remember?"

"Call it Far Sight, then," Nan said. "Or Time Sight." She beamed at Will. "Because you can look far back into time, see?"

They passed the gift shop, where Gormlaith lay on the rug with her muzzle on her paws, apparently guarding the display of Scottish books. Cousin Elspeth, at the desk, raised her eyebrows, smiling. "Are you done with the kitchen already? Nan, don't just read off the placards—tell them *more*. This castle has a fascinating history!"

"Yes, Mum," said Nan patiently. "I'm telling them everything they want to know." She steered Will down the hall, glancing back over her shoulder. "Mum's a bit mad about castle history, and she thinks I should be, too. Lucky for you she isn't giving you the tour—she'd bore you silly."

Will turned the corner into the vaulted cellars that might once have been the castle dungeons. Jamie was busy climbing up a tiny, curving staircase that ended in a blank wall, and jumping down. "Did they hang the prisoners from that hook?" he shouted, pointing to the ceiling.

Will blinked. For a moment he could almost see a real body hanging in the room—and then he saw it was only shadows. He turned away, his fingers cold.

Jamie was so little. He thought life was like a cartoon; someone got bashed in the head, saw a few stars, and then popped right up again.

Maybe it was better that way. Maybe it was good that Jamie didn't understand about violence and war, the real kind where people got hurt and sometimes died. Will had been thinking a lot about it lately, more than he wanted to.

Nan spoke behind her hand. "We have to find out how to work that thing that happens. With the book. We have to practice somewhere."

A chill ran between Will's shoulder blades. The past might be safe, but it might not. What if somebody put them in a dungeon? Maybe he should quietly lose the book in the woods.

Nan tapped her fingers together, waiting for his answer.

"I've got to concentrate," Will said. "I can't do it with you-know-who around."

"Leave him to me." Nan rumpled her hair with all ten fingers. "Watch this."

Jamie tore past them and up the winding stone staircase. "I'm going to see everything!"

"And I'll tell you everything," Nan said, with a sideways grin.

She did, too. At first, Will was interested. Who wouldn't be interested in gun ports and arrow slits, a nearly six-foot sword, and big paintings of strange-looking men in skirts?

"They're *kilts*," Nan said. "Scottish men wear them. And the different tartans on the plaids tell what clan they're from."

"They look like skirts to me," said Jamie, yawning. "Can't we see the turrets *yet*?"

Nan pointed to the winding stair, and Jamie's feet pattered up the worn stone steps.

"He's almost done for," Nan said with satisfaction.

"Huh?"

"I've seen it a hundred times." The space between Nan's front teeth showed briefly. "Tourists march around the castle, reading every single card and description until the kids are ready to die from boredom. Before they're halfway through the castle, the kids are asleep on the parents' shoulders, with drool coming out of their mouths."

Will gave a snort of amusement. So Nan *had* been trying

to bore them to death! "Jamie doesn't take naps anymore," he pointed out.

Nan mounted the stairs, talking over her shoulder. "He will after I'm finished with him. I brought the Magic Eyeball book in my school satchel for later, too."

The top of the castle was mostly one huge empty room, with high, rough beams, a scarred wooden floor, corner towers, and turrets. Jamie was already at one of the shot holes, making artillery noises.

Will stepped into the south tower and looked out. From this angle, he could see the front of the castle and a row of high windows with carved stone panels above them. They were all different, but one was triangular and seemed more ornately carved than the rest. There was a carved hand, pointing down to some intertwined initials . . . *I M B S,* they looked like. Below them were letters grouped like words, but the spelling was odd: *IИ OWR TYME.* Will read slowly, sounding the words out.

"Oh, 'in our time'! But the *N* is backward."

"Aye," said Nan. "It makes me feel better about *my* spelling."

"What's it supposed to mean?" Will squinted as he tried to decipher another line at the bottom. "It must be important if they bothered to carve it in that stone thing."

"You mean the pediment," Nan said, with an air of authority. "Right, all I know is what Mum says when she gives the castle tour. Let's see"—she squinted at the triangular pediment—"1577, that's the year they carved it. And the *I* really means a *J*—back then, they switched the two letters all the time. So the initials are for James Menzies and his wife, Barbara somebody, and the ribbon entwines around the letters so you know they were in love, I reckon."

"But what did they mean by 'in our time'?"

Nan shrugged. "I haven't the foggiest. You can ask my mum. Or my dad, when he gets home."

Will had almost forgotten about Nan's father. "Where is he?"

"Off on some business trip for a few days. Actually, Mum's better at Castle Menzies history. Dad's the one you want to ask about Scottish hist—"

"Boo!" said Jamie from behind them.

"Is he always this annoying?" Nan asked. "Or is he being that way just for me?"

Will rolled his eyes. "Sorry—he likes to sneak up on people."

"Mom says I'll grow out of it, but I won't," Jamie added cheerfully.

Will gave him a light whack in the ribs. "It's still rude, Jamie. Nan was trying to tell me something about her dad."

Nan shrugged. "I was only going to say that he's big into digging things up from the past." She took Jamie's hand. "Come on, I haven't shown you Bonnie Prince Charlie's bedroom yet!"

"Bonnie is a girl's name." Jamie dragged his feet after her.

"No, in Scotland, *bonnie* means 'good-looking.' So if you were good-looking, we'd call you Bonnie Jamie."

"Don't," Jamie begged as she tugged him down the stairs.

Nan's voice floated faintly up the winding staircase. Will grinned to himself. By the time he got to the bedroom where (apparently) the prince had slept, Jamie was lying on the floor, feebly kicking one leg.

"I'm tiiiired," Jamie whined.

Nan gave Will a wink. "But don't you want to hear more about Bonnie Prince—"

"No!" cried Jamie.

"How about a biscuit in the tearoom, then? And a lie-down on the cot, after?"

Jamie sniffled. "I don't like tea, and I don't want an old dry biscuit, and I'm too big for naps."

Nan ignored this and pulled Jamie to his feet. "Come along. You'll like *our* biscuits."

Jamie cheered up considerably when he saw that a biscuit

was really a cookie. He put his nose to the glass case and read the small sign next to a large cookie with white icing and a cherry. "Empire biscuit," he read aloud. "I want one of those!"

"You can read already?" Nan was impressed.

Jamie took an enormous bite. "I was the kindergarten reading star," he said thickly through a mouthful of crumbs.

The little boy was less excited about taking a nap. "I need my bear," he announced. "Where is it, Will? It wasn't there when I woke up this morning, either."

Will had not seen Jamie's stuffed bear since . . . oh, no. It must have been left on the plane.

Nan caught Will's pan- icked look. "You're kind of big for a stuffed bear," she said cheerfully. "Wouldn't you rather have a new toy?" She dug in her school satchel and pulled out a small plas- tic figurine. It was a man in a short tunic, with a sword held high.

"An army guy!" said Jamie.

"It's a Highland soldier," Nan said. "Close your eyes, and I'll sing you a song about him."

Jamie curled on his side, clutching the soldier, and let his eyelids droop. He peeked at Nan from under his lashes.

Nan began to sing in a low, soft voice: "O flower of Scotland, when will we see your like again—"

Jamie's eyes popped open. "He's not a *flower*! He's an army guy!"

"Hush," said Nan. "'Flower' just means the best and bravest men of Scotland. Shut your eyes now, or I won't sing any more."

Jamie screwed up his face into a frown. "Teach it to me. *I* want to learn my army guy's song."

Will gave a little snort under his breath and sat down. This was going to take a while. "What are you doing with a plastic soldier, anyway?" he muttered to Nan.

"School diorama," she said. "Some battle or the other. Now quiet, I'm teaching Jamie his song. It's practically the Scottish national anthem—you should learn it, too."

Jamie picked the song up quickly. His voice was high and clear, and Will shut his eyes. The blended voices were sweet; his mother used to sing with Jamie, too, when she put him to bed.

After a while, Jamie's voice faded and Nan's voice went on alone. Ten minutes later, Jamie's eyes were shut for real, and the small fist gripping the plastic Highlander had relaxed. Nan and Will tiptoed out.

"Wow," said Will. "You're good."

"I've had babysitting practice," Nan said, walking briskly down the hall. "Mum," she said as they passed the front desk, "Jamie's taking a kip on his cot, and we're going out to the garden." Then, "No, Gormly," she said as the dog rose alertly, "you stay with Mum."

"Be sure to show Will the walled garden!" Cousin Elspeth called. "And the fruit trees, and don't forget to tell him all about old Archibald Menzies—"

"Brilliant idea, Mum!" Nan called, breaking into a jog as she headed for the door. "We'll see you at lunch!" She pushed the door shut behind them with an air of relief and shook her head. "Mum's a bit mental about history. Fine for the tourists, annoying for me. Come on, I was going to take you to the walled garden, anyway."

"Is this it?" They were passing a big rectangle of grass next to the castle, enclosed by a stone wall.

"No, that's just the old kitchen garden," said Nan. "We want to get farther away if we're going to experiment with your Time Sight."

They went down a path and through a little gate of curling iron that creaked when they opened it. They ran between clipped hedges and under trees that curved overhead like an arch.

45

"This is the garden we want." Nan pushed open two tall gates of wrought iron, and they squeezed through. Beyond the gates, stone steps went up and up a steep hill. After what seemed like hundreds of steps, they came to the top, and Nan paused by a sundial, breathing hard. "Here." She pulled out the Magic Eyeball book.

Will took it, hesitating. "Maybe it only works in the castle."

"We're still on castle grounds," said Nan. "Try it!"

"Why don't you try it?" Will countered.

Nan dimpled. "I did already, last night while you were sacked out," she confessed. "And I think I got something to almost happen—the air in front of me kind of shimmered, you know?"

Will nodded. He knew.

"But it made my head go round and round. I got so dizzy I almost threw up. So I'm not doing it again, see? *You* are."

It was not as easy to concentrate outside. Leaves rustled, birds sang, and when an insect landed on Will's arm and began to bite, he swatted it instinctively and the Magic Eyeball book went flying.

Nan picked it up, frowning. "Maybe it doesn't work outside the castle, after all."

"No, it started to shimmer around the edges that

time." Will scratched the bite on his arm. "Didn't you see?"

Nan hadn't. And even when Will managed to concentrate enough to bring the whole picture of the past into focus, she still couldn't see it, even though she went behind him to have the exact same angle of sight.

Then she brushed against his shoulder accidentally, and the picture sprang into view.

"Ha!" Nan was exultant. "I have to be touching you. That's why Jamie could see it from the side. He was pressed against your arm."

Will's attention was on the picture in front of him. There were no more children playing; there was no mumble of voices and people walking in and out. All he could see were trees and bushes and sky.

"It's not the same picture as before." Nan leaned in closer, peering.

"We're not in the same place as before—that's why." Will looked at the outline of the hills in the distance, sharp and dark against the lowering clouds. The sky was different, and the trees in the foreground were not the same, but the hills seemed to have the same shape. "We're in the same *place* in the past, see? Before, we were on the ground floor of the castle. Now we're on the hill above it. You can tell because the rocks and hills haven't changed."

"But it's later in the day," Nan said suddenly. "See? The light is different."

Will leaned forward, his fear forgotten. It was fascinating, trying to figure out how this worked. It was like an experiment in science class.

"Turn your head more," said Nan. "See if you can find the castle."

He found it almost immediately. Golden in the slanting afternoon light, the castle looked like something out of a fairy tale. But it, too, looked different somehow.

"It's smaller than the one in our time," said Nan at once. "And the roofline isn't the same. Look, it has battlements."

"Those lumpy walls on top, you mean?" Will squinted to see them better, and just like that, he lost the picture. The shimmering afternoon light of the past faded to the dull colors of a cloudy day.

He set the book down and shut his eyes to rest them. It wasn't just his eyes that were tired. His whole brain seemed pulled tight, like a rubber band stretched too far.

Nan turned the book's pages eagerly. "Okay, so we know that Jamie could reach in and pick a flower. And we know a cobnut could roll right out of that time into this." She waved the book in the air. "What if *we* could step through? We could go back in time!"

Nan's eyes were bright, and her tumble of hair seemed wilder than ever, as if each strand were sticking straight out.

Will put a hand to his aching head. "We can't just go into the past."

"Why not?" Nan demanded. "How many people ever get a chance like this? We can't just go back to the castle and ignore it. It's like a scientific breakthrough!"

"*I* could ignore it," said Will.

Nan watched him for a moment, her head tipped to one side. "Ooh, I get it. You're a feartie-cat."

Will scowled. He had never heard the term before, but Nan's meaning was clear enough. "I'm not a feartie-cat, and I'm not a chicken, either. I just think things through. For instance, what if we can't get back?"

Nan shrugged. "That's easy. Just bring the book with you."

"Yeah, but what about when I'm on the other side?" Will argued. "We don't *know* that I can do it from there and get back here."

"You mean, do it from *then* and get back to *now*."

Will leaned forward. "Listen, this thing is powerful. Like electric current. And if we just *play* with it, we're like kids fooling around with high-voltage wires or something. It's dangerous."

"Exactly! That's why we have to keep experimenting! Once we find out how it works, we can stay safe."

"But—" Will began.

"How about this?" Nan pushed the book into his

hands. "You open up the picture with your Time Sight again, and I'll throw my satchel into the past. Then I'll step through and bring it back. That way we'll know people can go back and forth, too."

Will frowned. Something about her logic was bothering him . . . but it was hard to argue with Nan. She was a little like a steamroller when she got going—or maybe a tank. A Scottish tank. With a dimple.

"Oh, come *on*," Nan coaxed, and the dimple showed once more. "Don't be a feartie—or how do you say it? Don't be a chicken. It will only take a minute."

Will lifted the book and held it at arm's length. "All right," he said.

It worked just as Nan had said it would. Will opened up the time window as before; Nan tossed her satchel through. It landed with an audible thump on the turf, and nothing happened to it.

"See?" Nan said brightly. "Now me."

"How are you going to do it?" Will asked. "I can't throw *you*."

"I don't know—put a foot through and then step in?"

Will's stomach was hurting. This was not a good idea.

"Keep it up," said Nan. "Don't lose the picture," and she stepped through.

Will blinked carefully, keeping his focus. "How did it feel?"

Nan did not answer. She stretched her arms out and turned slowly around. "I'm in the past! I really am!"

"Better come back now," said Will.

Nan cocked her head, as if listening.

"Come back *now*," Will repeated, louder.

"Are you there, Will?" Nan reached out in the wrong direction. "I can't see you from this side."

Will slowly put a hand through the time window. It felt as if his hand were pushing through water, or heavy air. He wiggled his fingers.

Nan's forehead smoothed out. "Oh, there you are. Come on through, will you? I want to show you something."

"*You* come *back*!" Will cried.

Nan's frown returned. "If you're talking to me, I can't really hear you. That is, I hear something, but it's kind of whispery, like the wind. Anyway, wait one more minute. I just want to go a little farther—"

"NO!" Will shouted, but she was already moving away through the knee-high ferns. She paused by a large gray boulder on the ridge, looked down for a long moment, and came running back. "Where are you?" she whispered, patting the air.

Will reached his hand through and grabbed her arm. "COME BACK NOW!"

Nan flinched. "You don't have to break my eardrums!"

"You couldn't hear me before," said Will, not letting go.

"I guess we have to be touching for the sound part to work, too."

"Oh. Well, come on through, will you?" Nan was whispering again. "I want to show you something."

Will tightened his grip. "No, you come *here*. I can't keep holding this picture forever."

"Oh, all right," said Nan, stepping through.

Will let his focus go with a sigh of relief. His eyes were tired, his head was swimming, and he was breathing as if he had just run a mile.

Nan grabbed his shirt and tugged him forward. "Let's go to the ridge and look down into the past again. I saw two men and a little boy coming on horses, down the forest track. I want to watch and see if they go to the castle."

"Just watch?" said Will cautiously. "Not go through?" He wasn't sure he could hold his focus so long again.

"Just watch," Nan promised.

They brushed through the bracken, paused by the gray boulder, and looked over the ridge.

"I don't see any track."

Nan pointed. "It comes out of the forest and winds along there . . . see?"

It was the faintest suggestion of a path; it almost looked like a shadow, or a trick of the light. If it was a path, no one had walked there for a very long time.

Will held out the book, steadied it, and took a deep

breath as he focused his eyes on that nebulous space just beyond its pages. The air shimmered, and the path of the past sprang into view, a vivid slash of trodden earth. A smell of horses and human sweat came wafting up the ridge.

The horses had stopped where the path widened, and one man was already on the ground, looping the reins around the knob of an oak tree. His loose shirt was sweat-stained, and his bare legs coated with dust from the trail, but the sword and knife at his side were bright and honed to a killing edge.

The other man, slighter and gray-haired but also armed, swung down from his horse and reached up to pull a little boy off the saddlebow. The older man said something, and the child nodded and said something back.

Will whispered, "How come they aren't speaking English?"

"I don't know. It sounds familiar, though, sort of. . . ." Nan leaned forward, listening. "Maybe he just told the boy to stretch his legs?"

They watched as the men dug in the saddlebags and pulled out fresh clothing. The little boy ran around in the clearing, his light hair lifting and falling in the sun like corn silk. The child glanced up at the ridge, and for a moment, his features were clear.

"He looks like Jamie!" Nan said softly.

He did. It gave Will an odd feeling, that someone so far

back in time could look so much like his little brother. "He's probably some kind of cousin, fifteen times removed," he whispered back.

Across the path, in deeper woods, Will caught a flash as if the sun had glinted off metal. He wanted to look carefully at it, to figure out what exactly it was, but he had already noticed that he couldn't stare too hard at any one thing if he wanted to keep the whole picture in focus.

Nan moved restlessly beside him. "I think the little boy is a higher rank than the men," she said.

The clothes now lying on the grassy bank were indeed brighter and more intricately decorated than the ones the men wore.

"I wonder why they're changing," Nan said.

Will felt a hand press lightly on his back—Nan, he supposed, shifting her weight. "Maybe," he said, "they're going to visit the castle, and they want to make a good first impression?"

"Could be. . . ."

Below, the older man changed his clothes while the stronger-looking man was on guard with his sword out. Were they really so worried about defense, Will wondered, this close to a castle?

The little boy spun around on the grassy knoll, laughing. The gray-haired man stuffed his sweat-stained clothes in the saddlebag, adjusted the pin on his cloak, and took up his sword. The younger man's shoulders relaxed. He hung his sword on the saddlebow and drew his shirt off over his head.

Then the child shouted and the old man turned. Suddenly, from the woods on the far side of the track, the underbrush exploded into a confusion of powerful legs charging forward, thick arms with muscles like ropes, and swords that flashed in the sun. In less time than it took for Will and Nan to draw a deep breath, the two men were spitted, stabbed clear through with hardly a sound but a grunt of surprise and the meaty thunk of bodies falling to the earth.

In an instant the horses were seized, the little boy was caught and thrown over a saddle, and the raiders leaped to their mounts. One of them—the shortest, but clearly the leader—lifted his thin, cruel face like a wolf scenting prey and swept the hillside with a narrow-eyed gaze. For a single heartbeat, he squinted straight at Will with a face of such twisted malice that Will felt the shock of it like a spear. In the next moment, all that could be seen was the hindquarters of the horses fast disappearing down the forest track into green shadow, and then there was nothing at all but the bodies of the dead men, blood pooling beneath them on the turf.

"No!" cried a high, childish voice—and all at once Will realized it wasn't Nan who had touched his back. In the moment between recognition and action, before Will could

make his muscles react to his brain's signal, Jamie leaped through the time window and into the past.

Will lunged for him a half second too late. His focus shifted—the picture disappeared—and, from farther down the hill, Gormlaith barked and Cousin Elspeth's voice called breathlessly.

"Is Jamie with you? He's not on his cot, and I've searched the castle. It's time for lunch."

3
STEPPING THROUGH

NAN LOOKED DESPERATELY AT WILL.

Will jammed his hands in the pockets of his shorts. The cobnut, forgotten since yesterday, was still there, and he gripped it tightly as Cousin Elspeth climbed the rest of the way up the hill.

"Well?" Cousin Elspeth's face was red from the climb, and she did not look happy. "Have you seen him or haven't you?"

Will shifted his weight from leg to leg. How could he explain what had happened?

"We've seen him," said Nan, "but—" She swallowed. "He ran off."

"Jamie!" Cousin Elspeth called. "Jaaaaaammiiiiieeee! Time for lunch!"

A red squirrel chittered at her from the lowest bough of an oak, and Gormlaith barked again. A fitful breeze rustled in the treetops, and from over the ridge came a splash of birdsong. Will nervously took out the cobnut and began to toss it up and down in his hand.

"JAMIE! No nonsense, now!" Cousin Elspeth looked at Will and frowned. "Where did the lad run to, then?"

"He went through a sort of . . ." Will took a breath. "Time window. I know it's hard to believe," he said in a rush.

Cousin Elspeth clicked her tongue against her teeth. "I don't have time for your games now, laddie. Gormlaith, leave that squirrel alone! Heel, girl!"

"It's not a game. I'll show you." Will tossed the cobnut into the woods and picked up the Magic Eyeball book with hands that were not quite steady. He fumbled as he opened it, tearing a page in his hurry, and held the book out at arm's length. "You have to touch me to see it," he said.

Cousin Elspeth sighed and put a hand on his shoulder. "Hurry up, then."

But Will couldn't get the picture. He could not even get the shimmering to start around the edges. He tried until the sweat prickled between his shoulder blades and his jaw ached from clenching. He thought once that he saw a brief flicker, but Gormlaith chose that moment to push in between Cousin Elspeth and him, and he lost it.

Cousin Elspeth took her hand away with a quick, irritated motion. "I'm sure it's a lovely game; I used to play pretend when I was your age, too. But I have a lot to do in the castle, so you'd better hurry up and say your magic words, or go through your time portal, or whatever it is you need to do to get your brother to stop hiding and come out. Bring him down when you find him—it's time for lunch." She snatched Gormlaith's leash and stomped down the hill, the bracken swishing violently where she kicked through it.

"Oh, lovely. Now she's raging," said Nan.

Will stared at the place where Jamie had disappeared. "How are we going to find Jamie if I can't get the picture back?"

"Could be my mum made you nervous," suggested Nan. "Or you were trying too hard." She took the book from his unresisting hands and looked at the directions. "It says you should relax your eyes and not work at it. Try to relax."

"*Relax?*" Will's voice scaled up. "My little brother is hundreds of years in the past, and you want me to *relax*?"

"It will be all right." Nan patted his shoulder awkwardly. "Just think of something happy. Something calm."

Will breathed deeply and gazed into the forest. The shadows were beautiful, dark and green and mysterious, and seemed to invite him in. He took the book and told himself that this one time didn't matter. It was the same thing he told himself when he was at bat and didn't want to tense up, and it worked in baseball.

It worked now, too. The shimmering started, just as before. And, just as before, Will slowly lowered the book when he was sure he had the picture.

But the trees in front of him were no longer green and leafy. They were bare, and the ground before him was covered with snow.

Nan groaned. "It's a different time!"

It *was* a different time from the one Jamie had gone into, and so was the next attempt. Half an hour later, Will had been to any number of times, and he was streaming with sweat. There had been three when the ground was white, two when the leaves were yellow, and five when the bracken was just curling out of the ground. There had even been two in summer, but Nan told him that the first was too late in the season—"Look at the hillside," she said. "The heather is in full bloom." And the second was obviously wrong even to Will, for when he turned slowly around, there was no castle there at all.

"It hasn't been built yet," said Nan, stating the obvious.

Will looked down at the place where, hundreds of years ago, two men had been murdered. "I have to get back to the point where we can see the bodies. Why can't I? The first few times, the window opened on the very same minute, almost."

Nan twisted a lock of hair around her finger. "Something must be different."

"No lie." Will shut his eyes to rest them.

"Let's go over everything we did," Nan suggested. "First, I was standing right here, and then Mum called up the hill to ask if we'd seen Jamie."

Will stood up and faced the slope Cousin Elspeth had climbed. "I dropped the book when she came up. I put my hands in my pockets, like this. . . ."

He stopped.

"What?" said Nan.

"The cobnut." Will swallowed. "It was still in my pocket from the day before. I tossed it up and down. . . ."

Nan looked at him. "The same cobnut? The one from the past?"

Will nodded once, jerkily. His neck felt stiff with dread.

"*That's* what connected you to that time." Nan put her hands on her hips. "And you threw it into the forest."

A cold wave of terror washed through Will from his knees to his chest.

"Do you have any idea where it went?" Nan asked. "Did you see it fall?"

Will shook his head. He felt as if he had lost the ability to speak.

Nan's straight brows seemed to join in the middle. "Right, then. We'll just have to find it."

Will said nothing. One tiny nut, somewhere on the forest floor, under bracken and rotting wood, surrounded by thousands of nuts left over from the year before? They would never find it, never. Some squirrel might have already eaten it for lunch.

Nan tossed her hair back out of her eyes. "I'll go over and look. It's got holes in it, right? You stay here and keep trying."

Will gazed down at the faint forest track without seeing it. He was dimly aware of Nan's crouching figure under the trees, busily pushing aside ferns and digging through the underbrush.

He sat dully on the ridge. Sooner or later, Cousin Elspeth would come back and help them search. After that, she would call the police, or the search-and-rescue team, or whatever they called it in Scotland. Then there would be a nationwide alert, and it would be in all the papers. Dad would have to be called, and Mom—

Will pressed his face into his hands. If only he hadn't tossed the stupid cobnut! He had thrown away the one thing that could anchor him to the particular time in which Jamie had been lost.

Suddenly he pricked to the alert as a thought, faint and elusive, wafted through his brain. There *was* something else that connected him strongly to the past. It was Jamie himself.

Of course Will did not have Jamie in his pocket, like the cobnut. But the fact that Jamie was there, in the past, might act like an anchor, pulling Will back to the very same time. The question was how to go about it.

How did the Magic Eyeball book work, anyway? Will had the feeling that the book itself wasn't the key. It was that, in trying to see the pictures the others could see, Will had somehow focused his eyes on a place *beyond*. Somehow, he could bring the past into focus. Just as a telescope could focus on near or far, depending on how much you turned the dial, so Will could look into different times. He hadn't learned how to fine-tune his Time Sight yet, but maybe he could learn. He would try.

This time, when he picked up the Magic Eyeball book, Will let his mind go slack, soft, loose. He was vaguely aware of the sun on his skin, the quiet drone of insects. He thought of his little brother smiling, with the sun on his hair and a smudge on his cheek.

Jamie, he thought, and let the shimmer build around the edges of the book. But this time Will didn't lower the book right away. He shifted his focus ever so slightly, back and forth. The shimmering took on a different quality, as if the picture behind the book was changing somehow. Will sensed the fine muscles in his eyes contracting, relaxing, contracting, a little farther each time—

Wait. There was something. It was faint, as faint as the

forest track; it was as elusive as a distant radio station that came in crackling and unclear. But something felt familiar. With rising hope, he lowered the book and looked into the past.

The time of year seemed right. The heather was not yet blooming, but a moist scent of bluebells wafted through the time window and reached Will's nose. The sun was low in the sky, and light slanted amber through the trees. "Nan," he said hoarsely.

Nan left her cobnuts and came up behind him. Will turned his head slowly and the castle came into view. It looked exactly as it had before, battlements and all.

Nan swallowed audibly. "You did it!"

"Now to find Jamie." Slowly Will scanned the forest—slowly he brought the picture to bear on the forest track. There was the same big oak where the horses had been tethered. There was the place where the path widened, where two men's bodies had lain. . . .

There were no bodies.

Nan cleared her throat. "Maybe someone came and took the bodies away. Maybe Jamie ran to the castle."

"There's no blood on the ground," Will said. His stomach began to hurt, and with it came a sick feeling, as if he had been punched.

"Coo-eee! Nan! Will!" Cousin Elspeth's voice, faint but clear, floated up the hill. "Did you find him?"

The picture wavered, seeming to fade at the edges. Will beat back a rush of panic and forced himself to concentrate, to ignore Cousin Elspeth's voice, to think of nothing but the view before his eyes. The picture steadied, sharpened, became clear once more. He was so close—if only Jamie would run into view—

Nan said quickly, "I'll just go through and call, all right?"

"Call loud," said Will through numb lips.

Nan stepped through the window and shaded her eyes against the sun. "Jamie!" she called. "Jaaaaammiieeee!"

No answer. Will watched as Nan gazed in all directions; she even tipped back her head to look up into the trees and lowered her chin to look down at the ground. Then, suddenly, she stooped and reached for something in the grass.

"Nan! Where are you?" Cousin Elspeth's voice was coming closer.

Will watched Nan without blinking. Instinctively he felt that if he tried to show Cousin Elspeth the time window again, there would be such a confusion of explanations and disbelief and shock that he would lose the delicate connection, and any hope of finding Jamie would be gone forever. Plus, he would probably lose Nan as well.

He reached carefully through the picture and moved his hand back and forth to show Nan where he was.

Nan came running and reached for his wrist.

"Come on!" Will whispered. "Your mother's almost here!"

"Look." Nan held up something small and lumpy. "I found it on the ground."

"The Highlander toy!" Will breathed.

"Come *on*," said Nan urgently. "Jamie's here. He's got to be."

With his heart beating double time, Will put one foot into the picture, pressing past the thick, wavy air, and then the rest of his body followed, as if he were going through a gap in a fence. Cousin Elspeth's voice stopped abruptly. He was through.

৬৹

At first, the past didn't seem all that different. The rocks and hills were in their usual places, and the river valley stretched out before them, golden and green.

The river itself was much closer to the castle, though, which seemed impossible. "How could the river have just *moved*?" Nan said, frowning.

"I don't know, and I don't care," said Will. "Let's get Jamie and get out." He started down the hill, only to stumble over something soft that looked like a dingy cushion with buckles.

"Ha!" said Will. "There's your school satchel, right where you threw it."

Nan squinted. "That can't be my satchel. Mine is brand-new."

"Oh, right," Will said. "They made satchels exactly like yours hundreds of years ago."

"Don't get stroppy," said Nan. She picked up the satchel with the tips of her fingers and held it far from her. It was faded, and filthy with something lumpy and white that appeared to be bird droppings. "I think it's been here longer than a day."

"It can't have been here too long—it's the same time of year. Here's the book. Come *on*." Will began to jog down the hill. Nan wiped the satchel off on a patch of bracken, tucked the Magic Eyeball book inside, and followed him at a run.

But as they got closer to the castle, their pace slowed. Without any discussion, they found themselves edging closer to the forest and then moving just inside a stand of pines.

The pine forest was so thick that all the lower needles had died, leaving a forest of bare poles with a high, dense canopy. The trees moved and creaked ominously in the slight breeze, and now and then there was a louder crack, as if a branch had suddenly given way.

Will and Nan, watching from the shadowy forest, saw people busy at their tasks in the sunny fields. There were sturdy-looking figures plowing with horned oxen, and big-boned women pounding something in a cauldron with long poles. There were fierce-looking men with hair past their shoulders, all armed with swords and long knives. Even the children looked strong, carrying baskets and bundles of sticks or chasing pigs.

"Now what?" said Nan.

"You go ask if anyone has seen Jamie, I guess." Will leaned against a pine tree and came away again almost instantly, his arm covered with sticky resin.

"Why me?" Nan demanded.

"You could understand them! Remember?"

"It was more like I could *almost* understand." Nan kicked at a pinecone and it skittered ahead. "I probably need more practice."

Will picked gloomily at the globs of pine resin on his arm. "Okay, let's try to get close enough so we can hear them talking."

They walked slowly through the pine forest, keeping the castle in sight. Nan stopped suddenly and lifted her hand in warning. "Listen!"

Will and Nan crept forward, stepping softly on a carpet of pine needles, until they reached the lip of a ridge. Below was a woodland path filled with people walking, carrying pots or bags or baskets covered with napkins. A subdued babble of voices rose, filling their ears with unfamiliar words.

Nan lay flat on her stomach, looking down. Will followed suit and put his mouth to Nan's ear. "Can you understand them now?"

"Not quite." Nan rested her chin on her arms and listened intently, her eyes narrowed in concentration. Another minute went by, and then she smiled triumphantly. "Got it! It's market day, and they're talking about what they're bringing to sell!"

Will frowned. He still couldn't understand a word. "I suppose you're used to Scottish accents," he said.

"No, it's not the accent. I think it might be Gaelic. I heard my dad's friend speak it once. It's a whole different language."

"How can you understand it, then?" Will persisted.

Nan looked blank. "I don't know. . . . It's sort of like trying to adjust my hearing. Like tuning in a radio station when the signal isn't strong. At first it's kind of faint and scratchy, but if you turn the knob exactly right, all of a sudden it comes in clear."

Will twitched, startled. He had had the very same thought just half an hour ago, only then it had been about his vision. "I might have Time Sight," he said slowly, "but I think you have Time Hearing!"

"Ah, well, everyone has their own wee talent," Nan said impatiently. "Quiet now, will you? I want to hear if anyone is talking about Jamie."

Will gazed down at the steady stream of market-goers. Their chatter rose in sudden small spurts, like birds rising. The syllables seemed oddly familiar, as if they were only a tiny bit removed from words he already knew. Or was that just wishful thinking?

He shut his eyes, the better to concentrate, and let the strange, soft language wash over his ears. Just as he had with his Time Sight, he deliberately relaxed, not trying too hard to understand. The voices made a kind of lullaby, a music with a lilt and cadence that felt right, somehow. . . . He stretched, and his wrist touched Nan's elbow. Suddenly, below him, he heard a woman say, "If I don't sell these today, I can always try again next week."

Will's eyes flew open. "I know what they're saying!"

Nan turned her head. "Is it because you're touching me?"

"Yes—I don't know—maybe." Will experimented for several minutes, putting a finger on Nan's arm and then taking it away. At last he said, "It's a lot clearer when I'm touching you, but I'm starting to understand bits even when I'm not. And the more I listen, the more I can understand." He shook his head in wonder. "How can it happen?"

Nan shrugged. "How can you see a picture from the past and step into it? That's just as impossible."

Will sucked in his cheeks, thinking. "Has this ever happened to you before? Understanding a language you never learned?"

Nan let out her breath in a small derisive noise. "Not likely."

"That's how I am with Time Sight, too. I kept looking at the Magic Eyeball book on the plane, but no window ever opened up for me—"

"Good thing," Nan interjected, "since you were thirty thousand feet up."

"It only happened when I got here," Will finished.

"In Scotland?" Nan asked with interest.

Will thought back. "No, just being in Scotland isn't enough. I tried to see the pictures in the car ride from the airport, with no luck. It was only when I was in the castle, or close to it."

Nan clutched Will's arm. "I've got it! It only happens when you're on *Menzies* land. It's like Mum said—it's in your blood!"

"Yours, too." Will grinned. "Okay, here's what we know," he went on, ticking points on his fingers. "One, Time Sight only works on land that's been in the Menzies clan for . . . how long?"

"Ages," Nan said. "I mean, it's not all owned by actual Menzies anymore, but our people have lived around here forever, practically."

"Two. I bet you anything that Time Hearing only works around here, too—"

"But my school is close by, and I had plenty of trouble learning Latin when I started last year."

"Hmm. Okay, maybe it only works when people are speaking a language that our ancestors used to speak?"

Nan raised herself on her elbows in her excitement. "That must be it! Dad told me everyone in the Highlands used to speak Gaelic, before English came along."

"Get down, someone will see you!" Will pressed on her shoulder.

"Oh, sorry. Listen, here's what I think." Nan lay flat once more. "All the Scottish cells and bits come together in you, in just the right way, for you to have Time Sight. I have a bit—I made the air sort of shimmer when I tried it—but it made me so dizzy I had to quit or throw up. So that's more your talent.

"Then, once we travel to the past, all those bits of me that were passed on through however many great-grandparents—well, it's like those bits recognize where we are—"

"More like *when* we are," Will cut in.

"Right. Anyway, something in me already knows the language, see? It just takes a while to remember it. That's my talent. You've got it, too, only it's harder for you, and it takes you longer. I bet Jamie might have something of it, too. It's the Menzies bits in us, connecting to everything that went before."

Will nodded slowly. Here was the place where his and Nan's ties to the past went back for hundreds—maybe thousands—of years. Nan must be right—it was in their blood. Through their fathers, through their mothers, they were linked to every one of their ancestors who had gone before.

Did his mother feel that connection to him? he wondered suddenly. Did it still hold, no matter where she was in the world, or how far he had gone back in time?

Nan nudged him suddenly. "Have you noticed something about the way we're talking?"

"We're whispering," Will said, puzzled.

"Not that. Listen to us! We're speaking Gaelic now!"

"What?" Then Will's eyes widened, for the word that came out of his mouth was not English.

Nan laughed to herself, her cheek dimpling as if poked. "I'm pretty sure we've been speaking it for a while, too."

"I think you're right," said Will, just for the pleasure of hearing the words in Gaelic. When had they switched from speaking English? It had all happened so naturally that he hadn't even noticed. Well, that made things easier.

The crowd on the path thinned, and the scent of pines thickened as the sun beat down through gaps high above. Will's brows curled slightly. Why was it brighter now than when they had first arrived? The castle's shadow, too, was not so long. It was morning, then, not afternoon, as it had been when Jamie went missing. Nan was right; her backpack had been outside for a full day at least.

Where had Jamie been that whole day? He was so small; he would have been frightened. And he wouldn't have even had his stuffed bear for comfort.

The crowd had passed, and the path was empty, dappled with sun and shadow and the marks of many feet. Will scrambled to stand. "I'm not waiting around anymore. We've got to find Jamie."

Nan grabbed his arm. "What are you going to do? Just walk up and knock at the castle door?"

"Do you have a better idea?" Will shook off her hand.

"Well, you could ask *her*." Nan pointed to the path as a girl came into view.

She was older than they were, with a pink face and untidy hair. The end of her plaid was untucked and flapping behind her as she broke into a shambling run.

Will skidded down the slope in a flurry of pine needles. "Excuse me," he called, "but have you seen—"

"Get out of the road, I'm late! I must get these eggs to the castle—" Her gaze swept over Nan and Will, and her eyes widened. "And what in the name of Saint Cuthbert are two lads doing abroad in their underthings? Were you robbed of your clothes?" She stepped forward, peering at Will's shirt. "It's fine fabric, too, though a wee bit strange. What dye did ye use to get such a red?"

"Er," said Will, at the same time that Nan said hotly, "I'm not a lad—"

She stopped. Her face took on an alert, listening look.

After a moment, Will heard it, too—multiple hoofbeats, coming down the path through the trees. The last time he had heard horses coming down a forest track, he had seen murder done.

"Get down! Hide!" Will dragged both girls back with him, off the path and behind a fallen tree. The older girl stumbled and fell into the bracken, and her basket went rolling.

The drumbeat of hooves grew loud; there was a confused impression of powerful muscles bunching under sweaty

flanks and an overpowering smell of horse. The riders flashed past in a blur of plaid and bare legs with a glimmer of steel as their daggers caught the light, and then they were gone, cantering toward the castle, getting smaller and smaller in the distance.

The Scottish girl wailed aloud. "Whatever did you do that for? Now I've broken my eggs and I have nothing to sell! Mam will beat me sore!"

"Maybe they're not all broken," Nan soothed. "We'll help you find the ones that rolled out."

But Will stood rigid. "I saw Jamie!"

"Are you sure?" Nan swiveled her head and shaded her eyes. "I didn't know Jamie could ride a horse."

"I saw his face." Will started toward the castle at a run.

Nan hurriedly looked for unbroken eggs—there weren't any—and took off after Will.

"Hey! Come back!" cried the Scottish girl, hurrying to catch up.

Nan tried to keep Will's red shirt in view, but she stumbled over a tree root; by the time she recovered her balance, Will had disappeared. Ahead, a small crowd gathered near where some women had been boiling clothes clean in a heated cauldron. Nan edged around the muddy, sloppy ground, poked her head past someone's elbow, and saw a red T-shirt.

Will's arm was gripped tightly by a brawny man with

tangled, shoulder-length hair and a nose that looked as if it had been broken once or twice. The man had a cudgel in his belt that looked positively wicked.

"Let me go!" Will's voice was not entirely steady. "That boy on the horse was my brother, Jamie!"

The rough-haired man shook Will by the arm. "Jamie, is it? Just because your head's a little cracked, lad, doesn't mean you shouldn't show proper courtesy for the laird's nephew!"

"The laird's *what*?" Will had lost all sense of caution. "He's my brother, I tell you!"

"He really is," said Nan, stepping forward.

The man turned in her direction and spoke cheerfully to the crowd. "And here's another of them, just as cracked as the first! Whatever possessed you two bairns to run about half-dressed? Where are you from, now? Spies from the Stewarts, I'll be bound!"

"They're a mite small for spies!" cackled someone, and everyone laughed.

The man gave Will a shove. "Be off with you, before I give you a beating to teach you manners!"

Will stepped back, the blood mounting hot and furious to his cheeks. Then a movement beyond the castle caught his eye. The riders were dismounting and handing their horses off to be led into the stables; one little boy was already out of the saddle and walking toward the castle.

"JAMIE!" Will lunged forward, ducking under the man's arm.

The man's foot swept out and caught Will's shin. Will staggered forward, trying to catch himself, but his body was already falling and he landed in the mud puddle, face-first.

Will got up slowly, dripping with ooze. Everyone was laughing except for Nan and the Scottish girl with the basket, who looked as if she was still mad about the eggs.

Will spat mud out of his mouth. "Just *ask* him," he said through his teeth. "Here he comes now. Ask him if he knows me—he'll tell you."

The man laughed shortly. "And if he says no, *then* I'll give you a beating!" He turned, pulled off his hat, and took a few steps toward the boy who looked like Jamie.

In fact the boy looked almost exactly like Jamie, except that he was wearing what looked like a belted shirt with enormous long sleeves, and a checkered cloak thrown over one shoulder and fastened with a silver clasp. "Yes, Ranald? What do you want?"

Ranald indicated Will with a jerk of his head. "This boy says he knows you, Master James."

The boy frowned.

Will wiped his muddy face with his palms. "Jamie, it's me!" He stood up, slipping a little in the muck.

The boy looked uncertain. "Who are you?"

Will thought he might burst from exasperation. "I'm

your brother, you goof! Hurry up, we've got to get out of here." He took a step—and hesitated. Something was wrong. Jamie seemed taller than he should be.

A powerful hand gripped Will's collar. He was jerked back and up and flung through the air like a Frisbee.

He seemed to be in the air a long time: long enough to notice the deep blue of the sky, covering over now with scudding gray clouds, and the dark band of pines at the forest's edge, and to catch a glimpse of Nan's shocked face. Then the earth came rushing up at him, and he smacked it with a jolt that made his teeth click down hard.

Will lay on the ground with the wind knocked out of him, trying to breathe. His tongue was a lump of pain where he had bitten it, and he blinked the wetness from his eyes as the crowd laughed. He was not going to cry, not now, not in front of everyone. . . .

He managed at last to suck in a thin thread of air. Wheezing, he pushed himself up on his hands as the laughing crowd dispersed.

Nan tried to help him stand, but Will shook her off and stalked ahead, back to the forest. He didn't have a plan except to hide in the trees for a while and try to figure out why Jamie had pretended not to know him. Even though Will's face had been covered with mud, Jamie should have known his *brother*.

The Scottish girl followed them, still holding her basket.

"What are *you* doing here?" Will demanded, as soon as he had gotten enough breath in him to speak. His mouth tasted of blood, and he wanted to spit.

"You broke my eggs!" said the girl hotly. "So I have nothing to sell and no coin to bring home to Mam. I want you to come home with me and tell her it was all your fault. Happen I might escape a beating if you do."

Nan made an impatient noise. "There's a lot of beating here, isn't there? Don't people ever get tired of it?"

"*I* get tired of it," said the girl with emphasis.

"It's not much fun for me, either," Will muttered.

The girl put a hand on her hip. "You had to know you'd get in trouble for saying the laird's nephew was your brother. Why'd you do such a daft thing?"

"Because he *is* my brother." Will turned away to scrub at his cheeks. The mud was drying on his face and his skin itched.

"Will's brother ran away on this very hill, just a day ago," Nan explained. "And that boy looked exactly like him."

The girl snorted. "That lad didn't get lost a day ago. He's been here a year, fostering with his uncle, the laird."

Will whipped around. "A *year*?"

Nan's face paled, and her freckles stood out as if her

cheeks had been spattered with paint. "No wonder he didn't recognize you, Will! He was only five, and if a whole year's gone by . . ."

Will stared at Nan. "That's why Jamie was taller. He's six now."

4
MORAG

THE GIRL'S NAME WAS MORAG, and she told them the
laird really did have a nephew, named James. James had
been seven, a year ago—small for his age, but old enough
to be fostered at a noble house, to learn hawking and
hunting and riding and weaponry, and so his parents had
written that they would send him with an armed guard of
three men in midsummer.

"*Three* men?" Nan interrupted.

"There were supposed to be three," said Morag darkly,
"but no one knows what happened to the third. The other
two men were found lying in their blood." She lowered
her voice. "Everyone knows that the Stewart clan did
it. They raid, they murder, they stop at nothing. Soon

enough, they say, the king will have to come and put a halt to it."

"But what about the boy?" Will asked.

Morag shrugged. "Young James was running about like a mad thing, shouting gibberish and only half-clothed. They couldn't get any sense out of him for a long while after. In fact," she said, lowering her voice, "the laird said privately to his lady that he thought the boy had taken a blow to the head, he was so stupid."

Will exchanged a glance with Nan. "If it was in private, how did you hear it?"

Morag tossed her head. "Believe me or not, just as you like. I don't want to answer your questions, anyway. I'm hungry, and I want my dinner."

She sat down on a rock by the trail and took out a small parcel, wrapped in a napkin, from her basket. It was covered in egg and bits of broken shell, and Morag gave Will a reproachful look as she wiped it off with a handful of bracken. She opened the napkin to reveal a round, flat loaf of bread and a lump of cheese, and pulled a sharp knife from her belt. Then she cut thick slices of bread and cheese, clapped them together, and took a huge bite.

Nan swallowed audibly. Will watched Morag's jaws moving up and down, and his stomach made a sound like a gurgling drain. It had been a long time since Cousin Elspeth called them for the lunch they didn't get to eat, and an even longer time since breakfast.

Morag wiped her mouth. "Don't think I'm giving you anything to eat. You already robbed me of the farthing I would have gotten for the eggs, and you're not taking my bread and cheese, too."

"Farthing?" said Will. "What's that?"

Morag tossed her head. "Are you stupid? Where have you come from, that you don't know what a farthing is?"

Will shifted his weight. What was he supposed to say—that he came from the United States, but it wouldn't exist for a few hundred years?

"He comes from across the sea," Nan cut in. "He's my second cousin."

"And don't they use money, across the sea?" Morag said tartly.

Will thought of an answer at last. "Our money is different. We don't have farthings."

"Do you have halfpennies? Pennies? Groats?" Morag took another bite of her lunch.

Will put his hands in his pockets. "Sure, we have pennies."

"Well, then," Morag said through a mouthful of crumbs. "It takes two halfpennies to make a penny, and it takes two farthings to make a halfpenny."

Will would have laughed out loud if he had been in a better mood. So a farthing was a quarter of a penny, and a quarter of a penny could buy a whole basket of eggs? He was rich! He dug among the coins in his pocket and found one he recognized. "Would you give us some bread and cheese for a *whole* penny?" he coaxed, and held one out.

Morag peered at the copper cent on his palm. "That's not a penny," she said with scorn. "That's what we call black money, hereabouts. A real penny is silver. Still," she added, taking a closer look, "it's a fine imprint. Who is that man on it? It's not our King James the Fourth. Is that your king?"

"That's Lincoln," said Will. "He's more of a president."

Morag turned the penny to the light. "What's this writing supposed to say?"

"Read it yourself." Will absently jingled the change in his pockets.

"Do I look like a noble?" Morag demanded. "Or a monk? I can't read, you daft fool. Next you're going to be telling me *you* know how to read—and write, too, no doubt!"

"But I *do*—" Will began, until his toe was pressed firmly by Nan's foot.

"You do what?" Morag looked suspicious.

"He does want to know if the—er—black money will buy us some of your lunch," said Nan. "And I want to know, too."

"Oh, all right." Morag clearly wanted to keep the Lincoln cent. "But you still owe me for the basket of eggs."

Will reached in his pocket again. "You said a penny was silver. Would this pay for the eggs?" He pulled out a small, silvery Scottish coin, about the size of a dime, that said *Five Pence*.

Morag's eyes widened. "Eh, that's a fine bright penny!" She poked at it with her finger, turning it over. "It's foreign money, but that matters none, so long as it's good silver. . . ." She looked at them, considering. "That pays for much more than eggs, though."

"Well, I can't break a coin in half," said Will, irritated.

"What if I could find you some clothes?" Morag gave their shorts and T-shirts a calculating look. "You don't want to walk around in your underthings, do you?"

Nan glanced at Will. "We could use something else to wear. We stand out too much in these."

Will nodded slowly. It would help if they could blend in more. "Maybe that big nasty guy, what's-his-name—"

"Ranald," Morag supplied.

"Right. Maybe Ranald won't recognize us if we look like everyone else."

Morag laughed. "And why would you want to get anywhere near Ranald again? Next time he might not be so gentle!"

Will scratched at his arm where the mud was drying.

"We need to get back to the castle to get Jamie," he said shortly.

Morag cocked her head. "You still think Master James is your brother, when he didn't even know you? That doesn't make sense. And if you were robbed of your clothes, why do you still have coins in your pocket?"

Will looked at Nan helplessly. Where could he possibly start?

"It's hard to explain," said Nan suddenly, laying a hand on Morag's arm. "Please, won't you trust us? We're not Stewart spies, and we aren't going to hurt anyone—we're just two kids."

"Are you truly not spies?" Morag chewed on a fingernail. "The Stewarts, they're terrible ones for spying, but I've never known them to send children before."

"I'm not a Stewart—I'm a Menzies," said Will.

Nan nodded. "Me too."

Morag narrowed her eyes. "Will you swear on the holy rood?"

Will opened his mouth to ask what a rood was.

Nan put an elbow in his ribs before he could speak. "Yes," she said firmly, and smiled up at Morag.

It was the full hundred-watt, dimpled, impossible-to-resist smile, and Will watched Morag's face. It was clear she was feeling the effects of the Dimple.

"Well, all right," said Morag. "I don't suppose even the

Stewarts would send spies that didn't know how to dress. Come home with me, and I'll get you some clothes. You can eat your bread and cheese while we walk, and there's ale in this skin, if you're thirsty."

Will choked. "*Ale?*"

Morag rolled her eyes. "If you'd rather have beer, sorry, I don't have any."

"*Beer?*"

Morag looked at Nan. "Is he deaf, as well as daft?"

"Um," said Nan. "I think he's just not used to kids drinking beer and ale, where he comes from. Across the water, I mean."

Morag hefted the basket so it rested on her hip. "What else would children drink? Wine is too costly for anyone but a noble, and you are not babies, to drink milk, are you?"

"Of course not," said Will hastily, deciding that he wouldn't tell her what he poured on his Cheerios. "But doesn't anybody drink water?"

Morag's eyebrows went up. "Of course, if you can find nothing better, so long as it comes from a pure stream or a good well. But the streams hereabouts smell too strongly of horse. And you don't want to drink water with a meal—it chills the stomach."

"I guess she wouldn't approve of ice cubes," Will muttered to Nan as Morag started off along the trail.

They stopped just off the path to swear on the holy

rood, which turned out to be a carved stone cross. She made them place their hands on the cross and vow that they were true Menzies and not spies. Satisfied, she pulled the stopper from her aleskin and offered a drink all round. David, hot and thirsty, took an experimental swig. The ale was sweetish, thick, and yeasty tasting.

Nan took a swallow and made a face. "I'd rather have a fizzy drink any day." She glanced at Morag's sturdy back and lowered her voice. "Once we get the clothes, what next?"

Will had no clue, but he didn't want to sound feeble. "I'm still thinking." He glanced at the stone cross and hesitated. "You go on with Morag—I'll catch up."

Nan's dimple flitted into sight. "No worries, mate. I'll have to make a trip to the bushes soon, myself."

Will watched until they were out of sight along the path. But he did not go to the bushes to answer a call of nature, as Nan had supposed. Instead, he placed his hand on the holy rood and closed his eyes. Would God be more likely to listen, in this special place? Will didn't know, but he couldn't pass up the chance.

But after he had bowed his head, he didn't know what to say. Everything he wanted rose up in him like a torrent— his longing for his mother, his fear of Ranald, the desperate responsibility to bring Jamie home, his terror of everything that could go wrong. Could God hear a wordless cry?

Will was pretty sure a prayer was supposed to have words. "Please," he croaked at last. "Help me get Jamie home. Keep my mother safe. Make me braver than I am."

✺

Morag's home was small, made of stone, and thatched with straw. A thin, chuckling stream meandered through the clearing and disappeared into the woods on the opposite side. In the yard, clothes flapped lazily on a line stretched between the hut and a tree, two chickens pecked in the yard, and a wisp of smoke curled up from a hole in the roof.

Inside, the house was dark and smelled of goat. Will stood beside the rough wooden door, waiting until his eyes got used to the dimness. In the center of the floor a small fire glowed, and above it an iron pot hung from a chain.

There was a rustling from a bench against the wall and a shadowy figure raised itself on one elbow. "Morag? Who's that with you? Did you sell the eggs?"

The voice was thin and peevish, and Morag went swiftly to the bench. "It's all right, Mam, they just want a plaid each. We have that old one of Da's, and I've another—my second best. You can see they need some decent clothes."

The figure reared up straighter, and a thin finger shook in Morag's face, outlined by the firelight. "Not unless they pay me! Beautifully woven, my plaids are!"

"They'll pay," Morag said hurriedly. "See? Such a fine coin!"

"Let's get out of here," Will muttered to Nan.

The air outside was fresh and clean-smelling, and they took deep breaths. "I can't say I like Morag's mother much," said Nan.

Will nudged her into silence as Morag came outside.

"Don't worry," the girl said. "Mam's been sick since Da died, and it makes her cross, like. But she says you can't have two plaids for just one penny. Do you have another?"

Will reached silently into his pocket and pulled out a handful of change. The coins shone in the sun.

Morag sucked in her breath. "Did you steal it?" she whispered.

"Of course not!" Will threw back his shoulders. "I'm not a thief."

"How did you ever get so much, then?" Morag reached out and touched a coin the size of a quarter. "This one. It's as big as a groat. Is it worth the same? Sixpence?"

"*Ten* pence, actually," said Nan.

"All right," said Morag. "I will give you two plaids, and belts, and a knife. . . . The knife is notched," she added hurriedly, "but it will serve to cut your food."

"Will you help us get to Jamie?" Will asked. "I have to get close enough to talk to him. He's kind of—um— confused."

Morag's thick brows drew together. "He can't be your brother," she reminded Will. "You said your brother just ran away today, and that lad's been here since last summer."

Will and Nan glanced at each other and were silent.

Morag folded her arms. "Come on, then. What is it you're not saying?"

Will groaned aloud. "You won't believe us, not in a million years."

Morag was silent. She tapped her foot.

"Fine, then," Will said, exasperated. "We're from another time. Far into the future. And my brother, Jamie, accidentally went running into this time and got lost. And now we've come to find him. I *told* you that you wouldn't believe us," he added.

The color drained from Morag's face, leaving it pale as winter. "Witchcraft!" she breathed.

Nan glared at Will. "Now look what you've done." She put out a reassuring hand, but the older girl backed away, her eyes wide.

"Wait a minute." Will scratched behind his ear. "You still believe in witches? Like those guys at the Salem witch trials?"

"That happens *later*," Nan hissed under her breath. "And in *America*."

"Sor-*reee*, Miss Perfect History," said Will.

Morag put out her arms on either side of the door and blocked the entrance with her body. "Don't hurt me and Mam," she begged. "I will give you back your silver, see?" She reached into her long, pouched sleeve and pulled out the ten pence coin.

Nan moved toward her. "Come on, don't be like that. We're not really witches."

"*Witches?*" The word sounded as if it had been hissed by a snake. But it came from Morag's mother, her hair wildly tangled and her eyes strangely shiny as she peered around her daughter. "You will burn at the stake for this!"

Nan gasped.

Will's thoughts hurried over one another like tumbling dice. If people in this time still believed in witches, they were in serious danger . . . and he wasn't going to change their minds. Suddenly he had an idea. It might not work, but it was all he could think of. He gripped his hands together to keep them steady. "You're right about the witch-craft," he said, over Nan's fierce whisper. "But *we* aren't the ones doing it. My brother has been—er—bewitched. Yeah. And we've come to save him."

Morag's hands came down, but she still looked wary. "Bewitched?"

Will nodded, thinking fast. "He was bewitched by—um—a powerful enchantment. That's why he didn't recog-nize us. And that's why we thought he'd been gone only a day, when he was actually away for a whole year."

Impossibly, Morag's eyes seemed to grow even wider. "Oh!"

Morag's mother batted her hand at them as if swatting flies. "Don't you trust them, Morag. That little monk was lying the whole time. I could tell."

"Little *monk*?" said Will.

"She means you," Morag said hurriedly. "Because your hair is so short, you see. Men cut their hair short at the monastery. . . . Mam, go back to bed, you're sick," she said, turning her mother around. "I can feel the fever in your skin. Come on, back to bed, and I'll give you a drink of ale."

"But if they're witches, girl?"

"He can't be a witch if he's a monk," Morag explained patiently. "Right, Mam?"

"I don't trust monks, either," muttered the old woman. "And he's all clarty with dirt, head to toe. Doesn't he know how to wash?"

"He was just going to, at the burn." Morag jerked her head toward the little stream with a meaningful look at Will, and led her mother into the hut.

So a burn was what the Scots called a stream. The water was ice cold, but it felt good to get the dried mud off him. Will rubbed and rubbed until his skin was clean, and stood shivering outside the hut as Morag tucked a blanket over her mother. There was a sound of swallowing as Morag tipped up the aleskin; then the girl tiptoed out, her arms full.

"Here," she said hurriedly. "Put these on. The shirt first. Then the plaid—no," she said to Will, "it goes over the shoulder, like this—then you pull this string through the loops to pleat it and tuck it into your belt, like so."

With deft, quick movements, Morag's hands draped and tucked and pleated the long, wide, multicolored piece of cloth until it looked a little like a toga and a little like a kilt. She slid an old, notched knife inside Will's belt and then turned and fixed Nan's plaid as well.

"There, now," Morag said. "Mam's quiet for the moment, but you'd best be gone before she wakes. You said you wanted my help to get close to young Jamie, but I don't know what I can do. It's a pity one of you isn't a girl."

"*I'm* a girl," said Nan pointedly.

"You?" Morag peered at her. "Why are you running about in a boy's underthings, then? And why did you cut your hair?"

Nan frowned. "I haven't cut my hair for a year now. It's past my shoulders."

Morag shook her head. "Girls let theirs grow long enough to sit on, and they put it in a braid. Your hair is boys' length." She glanced at Will. "Or most boys," she amended.

"In any case, I'll have to tie your plaid differently. Hold still."

Nan stood impatiently as Morag tugged and pulled the plaid about. "What did you mean, it was a pity one of us wasn't a girl? How would being a girl help?"

Morag finished and stepped back to view her handiwork. "It's just that I could get you a job at the castle," she said. "My cousin is a chambermaid there—she's the one who overheard what the laird said to his lady about young James—and my cousin says the last new girl they got was hopeless, all thumbs, could hardly sew on a button without pricking her fingers and getting blood all over everything. She wanted me, but I can't leave Mam. Can you sew?"

"Of course," said Nan recklessly. "What's so hard about sewing? Stick the needle in, pull it out, that's all there is to it."

Will gave her a sidelong look.

"And as for you . . ." Morag scanned Will up and down. "What can you do? Do you know how to care for horses?"

Will shook his head.

"Pigs?"

"No," said Will firmly.

"Are you sure?" Morag said. "You don't have to be that smart to be a pig boy."

Nan laughed.

"I'm smart enough," said Will, annoyed. "I got A's in

English and math last year at school. Anyway, I need a job where I have a chance to talk with Jamie. I probably wouldn't see much of him if I was hanging around with porkers."

Morag lifted both her eyebrows. "I thought you said you came from across the sea. How could you go to school with the English? And what do you mean by 'math'?"

"I didn't go to school *with* the English," Will said. "English is just what we call reading and writing. And math is numbers. You know, adding, subtracting, multiplying, fractions, all that."

"Oh." Morag gave Will a slightly more respectful look. "You really do know how to read and write, then? And figure? Did you learn from the monks?"

Will made an indistinct motion with his head and changed the subject. "Would reading and writing get me a job closer to Jamie?"

"Maybe," said Morag, considering. "If you can stay out of Ranald's way. But the laird already has a clerk to write and figure for him. Let's go talk to my cousin and see what she can do about jobs. I'll tell her you're distant relations of mine."

"About five hundred years distant," Nan whispered in Will's ear.

ॐ

The light under the trees grew dimmer as they followed the path back to the castle. By the time they emerged from the forest, the gathering clouds had massed into a sullen shelf overhead and were spitting a thin drizzle. The castle, half-obscured with gray misting rain, showed bleak and forbidding against the dark hills.

Will swallowed hard. His knees felt strangely weak. But Morag was charging across the muddy field, and Nan was close behind; he really had no choice. Besides, Jamie was there.

The gate creaked open, and they shook the wet off themselves inside the entrance, where the gift shop was in their own time. Now it was a larger room with stacked weapons, mounted heads of deer hung on the wall, and two guards on duty. Morag went to talk with them while Will and Nan waited.

From the left came the sound of booted feet and the scrape and clink of metal. From the right came a clash of pots and pans, a high-pitched squeal, and the sound of a full-throated woman in what seemed to be a passionate fury.

All at once a door banged open and a thin, gangling teenager scuttled down the hall toward the entryway. His eyes were wide, his plaid was flapping, and behind him, thumping heavily (but at remarkable speed) was a stout, big woman with red hair, a red face, and something red dripping from a ladle. She was swinging it over her head with what looked like homicidal intent.

The boy ducked as the ladle nearly connected with his head; shoved past Morag, who stood in his way; and spun

out into the rain with a shriek. The big woman stood in the
door, breathing heavily and brandishing the ladle. Bits of
red splattered all around, and one splash landed on Will's
cheek. He wiped it off, hoping it wasn't blood.

"AND DON'T COME BACK!" howled the big
woman as the boy's thin figure diminished in the distance.
"That's the last sauce that clarty lad will ever ruin for me," she

muttered, turning. "Oh, it's you, Morag. Have you ever in all your life seen such a fool of a pot boy?"

"Where did he come from?" Morag asked.

"The monks sent him over—they said he'd been helping them in the brewery, but he must have been as bad at brewing water-of-life as he was at stirring a sauce, for they got rid of him quick enough, didn't they?"

"Water-of-life?" said Nan. "What's that?"

"It's called *uisge*," Morag answered. "Too strong a brew for you, lassie." She nudged Will in the ribs with her elbow. "Go on, lad, tell Cook you're ready to work! She needs a new pot boy, that's clear enough."

Will stared up at the red-haired woman, dismayed.

The woman stared back, frowning. "Is he stupid? The last boy was stupid as a bannock. I had to tell him three times how to do a task, and even then he got it wrong."

"I don't *think* he's stupid," said Morag. "Just a bit tongue-tied." She pushed her elbow harder into Will's ribs.

"It's a job at the castle, anyway!" whispered Nan.

Will got his arm up in time to block Morag's third bruising nudge, and considered his options. He wanted to get close to Jamie, not get hired by someone who would kill him if he made a mistake. But then, with any luck, he wouldn't be on the job long. "I'd like to be your new pot boy," he said, swallowing hard.

The cook looked Will up and down. "Are you a clean lad?"

"Um . . ." Will looked down at himself. Had he missed a spot when he'd washed at the burn?

"My last pot boy was dirty and careless," said Cook. "I can't have that in my kitchen."

Will had a sudden memory of his mother at the kitchen counter, teaching him how to cook. "I always wash my hands before I prepare food," he offered.

The cook chuckled. "Well, you don't have to go *that* far. It will be enough if you don't drop twigs and bark and hunks of dried peat into the kettle, like the last boy."

"Give him a try, Cook," Morag said. "Will's a bit slow with his tongue, but that's good, isn't it? He won't be so pert to answer back. And he's ready to work this instant."

The big woman's face was not so red now, and the ladle was dangling at her side. "You'll vouch for him, Morag? You know him?"

"He's a cousin, of sorts," Morag said promptly.

Cook nodded. "Well, I'll give him a trial. Will, is it? We've the evening meal to prepare and serve, and if you do well enough, I'll keep you on. Come along."

Morag gave Will a little shove. "Go on, follow her. She's a bit crabbit, but she's a bonnie cook. Stay on her good side, and she'll feed you well! As for you," she said to Nan, "come with me."

"Wait!" Will reached for Nan's wrist. "What about Jamie? We can't just split up like this."

"First do your job," said Morag sternly, "or you'll get thrown out of the castle before you even get a chance to speak to him."

"But where are you taking her? We've got to make a plan!"

Morag made an impatient noise deep in her throat. "Hurry now, or Cook will be angry again, and you've seen what *that* looks like. You'll see Nan at supper in the Great Hall, maybe." Morag started up a narrow, curving stair, gripping Nan firmly by the arm. "Come along. I can't spend all day!"

Nan leaned back to wave at Will. "I'll find out what I can," she promised, and then she was gone.

Will trudged toward the kitchen, thinking hard. He was in the castle, with a job. That was good. There was no need to panic.

Except his chest felt fluttery, as if something kept brushing at his ribs. Would Jamie recognize him, now that Will had cleaned the mud off his face? It still seemed crazy that Jamie hadn't known his own brother, but Will supposed that, to a little kid, a year was a long time. And Jamie would have been terribly confused when he first came.

Will tried to recall his own kindergarten year, and could only come up with three or four clear memories. What if *he* had been suddenly picked up out of his world, at that age, and then at once plunked down in another one? Would he have thought his old life was all a dream after a while? Would he have tried to forget?

Maybe he should be slow to approach Jamie. Maybe he should give his little brother time to get used to the idea.

No. He had to get Jamie and Nan back home. How much time was going by for Cousin Elspeth while they were stuck here? If Will could manage to get them all back in time for a late lunch, they might get off with only a scolding. But if they were gone much longer, Cousin Elspeth would be tearing the hillside apart to look for them. She would call in local searchers, and she would call his father. Except his dad was already busy trying to rescue Will's mother.

The hall was long and dark. The narrow windows didn't let in enough light to see clearly, and Will's hand scraped on the rough stone wall. He sucked on his grazed knuckles. How had things gotten this complicated? Only two days ago, his biggest worry was that he might not get his homework done in time to play ball with his friends. And now, because Jamie had gotten that stupid Magic Eyeball book, they were in all kinds of trouble.

He groaned aloud. He had just remembered; Nan still had the Magic Eyeball book in her satchel. He should never have agreed to split up! He had to find Nan, and he had to find Jamie, and they all had to get out of here *now*.

Will turned around in an instant, already running. If he hurried, he could catch up with them on the stairs.

He rammed headfirst into something large and solid. A heavy hand came down on his shoulder, and his chin was wrenched upward.

"You again!" growled Ranald.

5

POT BOY AND CHAMBERMAID

RANALD SHOOK HIM THE WAY a dog might shake a rat it wanted to kill. Will's teeth clicked in his head and his eyes closed as if on hinges. He tried to remember what he had learned in karate class, but it was hopeless when Ranald was lifting him right off his feet. Will had the odd sensation that it was all happening to someone else.

He forced his eyes open and found he was staring up at the rough stone arch overhead. Then his head snapped forward and there was a glimpse of Ranald's lumpy face, brows drawn together in a thick line like a hairy caterpillar, lips twisted in a snarl more angry dog than human.

Abruptly Ranald changed his shaking motion, and

Will's head whipped sideways long enough to catch sight of Cook's face, red and enraged.

"I'll thank you to keep your paws off my pot boy, ye daft bahookie!" Cook's roar was at least the equal of Ranald's.

"He's your *pot boy*?" Ranald's grip loosened; Will twisted violently and freed himself with a jerk.

Cook stomped up until her face was level with Ranald's breastbone. She shook her fist, and Ranald took a step back.

Will rubbed the back of his neck as Cook let loose with a barrage of furious words, her accent growing thicker with her outrage. He made a mental note to ask Nan what *bahookie* meant and gripped his arms in an attempt to stop their sudden trembling. He didn't have time for the shakes, not if he wanted to search for Nan and Jamie.

But there was no getting away from Cook. Will found himself being marched back down the hall to the kitchen. "Would you mind letting go of my ear?" he said as politely as he could through clenched teeth.

"I don't want you lagging," Cook snapped. "We've supper to serve." She released his ear and turned curiously. "Whatever did you do to Ranald to get him so wickit?"

Not surprisingly, Will couldn't think what to say. It didn't matter, because Cook just went on talking.

"Well, it doesn't take much to anger Ranald; he thinks

the worst of everyone. Maybe that's a good thing in a castle guard, but it's a mite annoying to those of us that aren't thieves, murderers, or Stewarts." She cackled, a high crack of laughter. "Of course, if you're a Stewart, you're already a thief *and* a murderer, most likely."

She propelled Will through the kitchen door with a firm hand. "Now, get in and stoke up the fire, and fetch more wood, and after that—well, I'll tell you more when you're done with the wood. If you're like my old pot boy, you won't be able to remember three things together." Cook snorted like a horse. "In fact, he had trouble remembering just the one. But he's gone now, and you're here, so let's see how well you can work."

The kitchen looked familiar, with its massive fireplace and stone walls, but it was no longer the silent, cold room Will had seen in his own time. Now it was ablaze with light and warmth, filled with the good smells of baking bread and roasting meat, and bustling with kitchen helpers rolling out pastry at a long wooden table.

It took him some minutes to locate the wood stacked outside the castle walls, and he made three trips with his arms full before someone took pity on him and pointed to the leather carrier. He could carry more split logs that way, but each load was heavier, too.

Where should he put it? Cook was busy yelling at her

helpers—big girls with sturdy arms—and Will didn't want to interrupt and get yelled at himself. He saw a few pieces of wood stacked along one side of the huge fireplace. The last pot boy had let the woodpile dwindle to almost nothing, and new as he was, Will could still see that whatever was bubbling in the big cauldron—stew, maybe—had to be kept on the boil.

He quickly shoved a few more pieces of wood under the cauldron and arranged them so the fire got plenty of air. He was glad that his dad had taken him camping and shown him how to build a proper fire. The thought of his father was a sudden pang, but Will shoved it quickly into a back corner of his mind. One problem at a time.

It was fun, in a way, to figure out what to do. Will had never stacked wood before, but after two logs rolled onto his foot, he began to see that if he took a moment to adjust each piece of wood slightly, he could fit the logs on the stack so they wouldn't roll.

It was almost a relief to have a clear task ahead of him. He might not be as quick with his tongue as some people, but he could figure things out, and he knew how to work. If he could do the job well enough, Cook would keep Ranald from pounding him into the ground. It was clear that she was a privileged person—that much had become obvious when Ranald had backed down so suddenly. Will had almost laughed aloud when the snarl on Ranald's face had changed to slack-jawed confusion and he had backed away like a whipped puppy.

Of course Ranald would probably try to get even later on. Will told himself that he didn't care. With any luck, he would be safely back in the future by that time.

The afternoon went slowly past as Will worked harder than he ever had before. The only break he took was when he went to the garderobe—which was what they called a toilet—and he didn't stay there long. It was only a hole on a stone pedestal, and it smelled so bad he held his nose the whole time. He looked for a place to wash his hands and found a pitcher of water and a bowl. The bowl was the sink, he realized, and the drab yellow lump at the side was the soap. He poured water into the bowl, washed his hands, and dumped the bowl's contents down the toilet hole. He wasn't sure he'd done it right, but he wasn't staying there any longer; he was ready to gag as it was.

Somewhere between stoking the fire, stirring the stew, and scraping the grates, Will must have proved to Cook that he was a good worker. When one of the kitchen girls went out to draw the ale, Cook put Will in charge of pitting cherries. It was tedious work, but at least he could sit down to do it, and she was in a talkative mood.

Unfortunately, Cook wanted to talk about the Stewarts, especially one she called "the Wolf." Apparently the Wolf liked to get rid of his enemies (he had a lot of these) by hurling them over the battlements of his castle to the rocks a hundred feet below. Rumor had it he'd burned down a cathedral (just because he felt like it) and had a nice deep dungeon especially equipped for torture. Worse yet, he lived in the next glen—close enough to do a night's raid and get back again before dawn. Will was worried at first, until Cook mentioned that the Wolf had lived over a hundred years before.

"But his great-great-great-grandson is chief of the Stewarts now, and he's near as bad as the Wolf, that accursed whelp." Cook measured flour and spices into the largest bowl Will had ever seen, and added honey from a crock. "Neil Gointe Stewart is young yet, and hasn't come into his full measure of wickedness. But you mark my words, he's on his way. Why else do you think they call him 'gointe'?"

Will pitted his last cherry and wiped his fingers on a rag, leaving red streaks. "What does it mean?"

"Bitter and twisted, that's what it means, and you'd know it if you saw him face-to-face—a little runt of a man, with a thin, sour mouth and a nasty squint on him that would do justice to a forest wildcat."

For a moment Will's breath stopped. He remembered, all too clearly, the murders he had seen through the time window—the two men spitted like chickens and lying in their blood, the little boy who looked like Jamie flung onto a horse and taken away. The leader of the raiders had been a small, thin-faced man, with a vicious squint that had seemed to pierce Will like a spear.

Will let out his breath cautiously. "Has he ever murdered anyone?"

"Who?" Cook scraped the pitted cherries into the bowl and stirred vigorously. "Ellen, hurry up with that pastry. Will, mend the fire and stir the stew."

"Neil Gointe. Has he ever murdered anyone?"

Ellen, elbow deep in pastry dough, lifted a plump, pale face. "He's going to be angered enough to murder once he hears about the new charter!"

Cook chuckled richly. "Aye, that he will. It was a good day for Sir Robert when the king granted him those lands about Loch Rannoch."

Ellen giggled. "The Stewarts wanted them, but the Stewarts didn't get them!"

The cook waggled her spoon in the air. "Serves them right, the wicked, ranting lads, they with their cattle stealing and their murd—" Cook stopped, sniffing the air. "Blessed Saint Cuthbert, the bread! Pull it out of the oven before it burns, girl!"

Ellen looked up from the mound of dough. "My hands are all messy!" she wailed.

"You, then, William! Haste ye, now!"

Will couldn't see anything that looked remotely like an

oven. But then he remembered how Nan had taken them on a tour of the castle, and Jamie had run inside the great fireplace to stick his head in a hole in the wall.

Will dashed inside the massive fireplace, avoiding the fire and big pot of bubbling stew in the center, and lifted the long-handled bread peel off its peg on the wall. Carefully, he shoved the flat wooden peel into the baking hole and under the first well-browned loaf, and then the next.

He slid the round, crusty loaves onto the table and went back for more. When he had emptied that oven of bread, he saw another baking hole and emptied it, too.

Cook nodded, her fat face satisfied. "You're a canny lad. Now put the bread in the basket—no, the big one."

Will picked up the warm round loaves and tucked them into the massive basket. "So have the Stewarts murdered anyone lately?" he persisted. "Like, in the last year or so?"

"Och, aye," said Cook, "there've been terrible murders in the last years, and raids, and thieving, and Neil Gointe Stewart behind it all—or so they say."

Ellen thumped the rolling pin onto the pastry. "Under his hair they say he has devil's horns!"

Cook snorted. "That's just your imagination, girl. He's got no devil's horns."

"Well, he acts like twenty devils, ye can't deny that." Ellen waved her rolling pin. "Everyone knows he was the one behind those murders when young Master James first came.

Those two men-at-arms were murdered in cold blood, and young James got such a blow on the head he was half-mad for months."

"Half-mad?" said Will.

Cook shot him a look. "He's fine now, ye understand," she said. "But at first he was out of his head. Thought he was some other boy, from some other place—and kept raving about things that made no sense at all. Carts on wheels that go with no oxen or horse to pull them, and great silver carriages in the sky that fly like birds!"

"Pictures that move and talk, too," Ellen added. "And lamps that light when you push a magic button in the wall!"

"The laird and his lady were that worrit," Cook said, lowering her voice, "they thought of sending for the boy's parents, away off in France. But we had a good leech here, a doctor, who opened a vein and bled him—"

"Nay," Ellen interrupted, "it was after the good monk brought him water from the holy well—"

"And then the folk healer was about to feed him a mouse from a horn spoon, when all of a sudden, young James sat up, said he must have been mistaken, and that it had all been a wild dream when his head was addled. Ever since he's been just fine, except he's forgotten how to speak French."

Will choked slightly. Eating a *mouse*? No wonder Jamie had decided to agree that his memories of life in the future were nothing but crazy dreams. He'd gone along with what everyone told him was true, and after a while, he had even come to believe it. Most five-year-olds probably would, in the end.

But still—wouldn't Jamie remember the truth, at least a little? Especially once he saw his own brother? And what had happened to the real laird's nephew, the little boy who had been taken away by Neil Gointe Stewart?

A sound of tramping feet and the clash of metal filled the long hall, and Cook whirled around. "Get in another two loads of wood, boy—they're about to bar the gates for the night, and I want plenty on hand." She pointed with her ladle. "Scoot!"

Will ran to get the wood, glad to see that the rain had stopped. Still, he scurried past the guards with his head low; he didn't want to catch Ranald's attention. On his second trip, he was stopped to wait outside the castle gate with several other latecomers. The sun was setting over the Tay river valley, peeking out from beneath a curling cloud, and golden light like long fingers lay across the green land.

To Will's surprise, the gangly teenager, Cook's old pot boy, was waiting to be let in as well. The boy stood awkwardly in line, shifting his weight, his gaze flicking to the guard at the door and then down to the ground.

Will moved a step nearer. "Are you going to try for your old job back again? That's okay if you are," he added hastily. "I'm probably leaving soon."

The teenager started, nearly dropping the wooden cask he carried. "N—no."

"Are you working someplace else, then?" Will hoped the boy was getting enough to eat. He looked awfully thin.

The teenager swallowed hard, and his Adam's apple moved convulsively up and down. His eyes seemed to bulge a bit, like a rabbit's, as the guard turned to him.

"And what's your business at Castle Menzies, this late in the day?" The guard was not Ranald, Will was glad to see, and he looked friendly enough.

"I bear a gift for the guardhouse," the teenage boy said rapidly, as if repeating a memorized speech. "My master's heard of the new lands come to the Menzies, an'—an' is well pleased. He wishes that the guards should celebrate as well." The boy lifted the keg in his arms a little, as if to show it off.

"Ho! Water-of-life!" The guard's face split in a wide grin as he reached forward to take the keg. "Who is your master, boy? For we should surely thank him."

"M—Mungo Menzies. But he does not want thanks. He asks only that I return the cask in the morn and that you give me shelter this night, for the sun is almost down."

"That we will, and welcome!"

The teenage boy shuffled over the threshold without a backward glance. And soon enough Will, too, was inside and unloading the wood in the kitchen.

"JANET!" bellowed the cook.

A blowsy-looking girl stuck her head around the corner.

"Tell Dougal to get that ale up now. And you bring the cheese. Ellen, aren't you done with that pastry yet? Bess, hurry up, fill the tureens with that stew—by our Lady, can't you dafties do what's needed without being told every minute?"

"And if we did anything *without* being told," Janet muttered under her breath as she passed Will, staggering under the weight of a large wheel of cheese, "she'd be just as crabbit. Watch out, here comes the steward."

A man with a long nose, high cheekbones, and an air of command entered the kitchen, carrying a ledger.

"I'm getting supper up now," said the cook, her face redder than usual. "Can accounts wait until after?"

"Yes, yes," said the steward, shooting a keen look around the kitchen full of activity. "In fact I came to tell you that it will be some time before I come to do an accounting; the laird has some other business for me, having to do with the new land grant, that will keep me busy for some days. Please keep a list of the stores you use in the kitchen until then." He took a sheet of paper from his ledger and laid down a stick that looked like a squared-off bit of gray, soft stone.

"Keep a list?" The cook snorted. "That's all well enough for those who know how to write. I'll keep the list in my head, where it's always been."

"Ah." The steward looked taken aback. "Well, it might be several days. Can you really remember that long, or shall I send my clerk down to write for you?"

"I can write," said Will without thinking.

Cook stared at him. "You? A pot boy?"

The steward looked at him sidelong. "Let's see you do it, lad. Write this: 'twelve pounds of oaten flour.'"

Will picked up the gray stick, which, as it turned out, was like a piece of pencil lead without the wood around it, and wrote the sentence.

The steward smiled down at him. "The monks taught you, did they? Did they teach you how to figure, as well?"

"Sort of," said Will cautiously.

"Here," said the steward, "try this sum. If I bought an oil cruet for three groats halfpenny, a firkin of soap for a half-angel, and a silver saltbox for two gold nobles, how much would I have spent altogether?"

"Um . . . ," said Will. How was he supposed to know what a half-angel or a noble was worth? And what on earth was a firkin? He scratched his head and said, "I can't add Scottish money."

The steward laughed. "What other coin would you use? Never mind," he added kindly. "Just write down the stores Cook tells you, and how much of each, and I'll do the adding."

"What should I write?" Will asked Cook as the steward disappeared down the hall.

"Nothing *now*, you daftie!" said Cook. "Put that paper away and hurry up, lad, what are you dawdling for? Take the bushel of bread up to the Great Hall, and mind you don't drop it!"

Will folded the paper and stuck it inside his plaid along with the gray lead stick. "Where's the Great—" he began, but Cook pointed at Janet's disappearing backside. Hefting the basket by its withy handles, Will followed the kitchen girl down a hall, through a storeroom, and up a narrow stair he had never noticed before. Then suddenly the noise of voices increased and he was in the Great Hall.

It was different than he remembered. Oil lamps flared and smoked in their hanging cressets, and the great central fireplace blazed with a cheerful crackle. Banners, red and white, hung at intervals, and candles cast a warm glow on the long tables that ran the length of the room. But darkness hung in the corners of the hall and gathered in clots overhead between the heavy oaken beams.

"What are you waiting for?" Janet clumped back from the massive sideboard where she had deposited her cheese.

"Hurry, now, put that bread on the table, and then get back to the kitchen. Don't dawdle, boy!"

Someone had put smaller baskets on the tables, and Will went around to every one, filling them with the round, heavy loaves. He tried to avoid stepping on the dogs that whined underfoot, but someone's foot got in his way and he tripped. Will caught at the basket, but one loaf fell out. It was instantly buried under a swarm of yelping dogs, and Will scrambled to his feet.

"Clumsy, aren't you?" said a sneering voice. "Cook won't keep you on if you throw food on the floor."

Will felt heat rise past his neck. Ranald had tripped him on purpose.

The man stuck his leg wide and waggled his boot. "I'd have thought these were big enough for even you to see, blind as you are."

"I'm not blind," Will said through his teeth. He tried to step around Ranald's foot, but the big man blocked his way again.

"You're blind enough to look at Master James and think he's your brother!" Ranald's brows contracted so they looked like one hairy bar across his forehead. "Keep away from him, you hear? It's my job to protect this family, and by Saint Cuthbert himself, I'm going to do it."

Will set his jaw and brushed past Ranald without

saying a word. The table at the far end still didn't have any bread.

It had chairs instead of benches, made of wood so dark they looked almost black. Will stacked loaves hurriedly in the baskets and had started down the other side when, out of the corner of his eye, he saw a little bustle at the door behind him. He turned to see a tall, lordly man stalk in, sweep the room with a pair of keen eyes, and raise his chin with a slight sideways tilt as he sat down in the high central chair, which was carved like some ancient throne.

It must be the laird. He looked almost familiar—a little like Will's father around the nose and mouth. Were these people his ancestors? The pleasant-faced woman sitting down with a swish of skirts had curly hair like his mother's. Behind the woman came a tall young man, and behind him came—Jamie!

Will almost dropped his basket. He caught it just in time and got very busy about putting the last loaves on the table. But from under his lashes he watched his brother.

Jamie was dressed in some checkered cloth, bright and clashing by modern standards. He didn't fidget at the table or wriggle in his chair, and he had a knife, a big one. For someone who had been allowed to use only blunt kindergarten scissors, the knife looked wickedly sharp—but Jamie was cutting a hunk of bread with casual competence.

"What are you gawking at?" Janet waved a hand in front of his eyes. "Hurry along, Cook wants us in the kitchen. Haven't you ever seen the laird before?"

Will shook his head.

Janet clicked her tongue, turning. "That's Sir Robert Menzies, the clan chief, the laird. The tall boy next to him is his son, and the lady next to the laird is his wife. The little lad next to her is young James, the laird's nephew, sent here for fostering. But he's still a bit touched in the head."

Will trotted after her. "Touched?"

Janet rolled a finger in circles near her temple and gave an expressive wink. "Once a loony, always a loony, I say. Oh, he acts like he's supposed to now—most of the time. But every so often, he says the strangest things!"

They had reached the stairs. "Like what?" Will kept close by Janet's side as she hurried down the curving steps.

Janet snorted. "Once he came down to the kitchen and asked if we had any candy. I said did he mean boiled sweetmeats, and he said no, he wanted a girl bar."

"A *girl* bar?"

"Well, a 'her' bar. Or no, maybe it was a 'she' bar." Janet stopped, frowning. "Or was it a she-her bar? No—"

"A Hershey bar?"

Janet snapped her fingers. "That's it! How did you know?"

Will laughed. "Lucky guess."

"He says stranger things than that," she added, banging open the kitchen door.

Cook was just sliding cherry pies into the bake oven. A crowd of helpers were bringing up tureens of stew and great platters of turnips and pickled onions and lumpy things Will couldn't quite identify. His stomach made a noise like a bear growling.

"Here, you, pot boy! Go up and serve out the ale. Run fast when they call you, and water it for the small ones."

Will wasn't quite sure exactly what she meant, but Janet went up, too, and showed him. He was to stand by the sideboard in the Great Hall and wait until someone called for ale. Then he was to take one of the mugs from the sideboard, fill it from the keg, and bring it to the person who was thirsty. There was a pitcher of water to add to the ale if someone wanted it weaker.

"Don't use the covered cup, that's for the laird and his lady. Whenever someone is finished drinking, bring their mug back to the sideboard so it's ready for the next person."

"What, you keep using them over and over without washing them?"

Janet stared at him. "Why not? It's all good ale, nothing else is going in the mug to dirty it."

"Germs are going in," Will muttered, but Janet had already whisked off to her next task.

He was almost run off his legs. "ALE!" shouted one

after the other, and Will hurried to obey. Why on earth couldn't they each have their own cup? he wondered. But some of the mugs were wonderfully made: silver and enamel, with ornate etchings and beautifully curved handles, and there were drinking bowls, too, with little legs on the bottom so they would stand upright. He was careful to keep far from Ranald, but everyone else blurred into one big mass of noise and laughter and grasping hands, and it was with a shock that he heard Nan's voice at his elbow.

"Can you just get me plain water?" she begged.

The plump girl next to her gasped. "You don't want to do that," she said earnestly. "Water alone is unhealthy. Have ale, it is better for you!"

The woman on the other side looked down her long nose at Nan, her mouth pinched in at the corners. "Maybe that's why your stitches were so crooked today. You're sick from drinking water! Take ale and get a good night's rest, and perhaps tomorrow you can sew a seam that doesn't look like a crooked man limping."

"Yes, Mistress Cullen." Nan waited until the woman looked away, and then rolled her eyes. "Have you talked to Jamie yet?" she whispered.

Will shook his head.

"Well, do it quick, will you? I'm going to die if I have to thread one more stupid needle. Look at my fingers!" She waved them in front of Will's face. "I pricked them so many times, they look like a cheese grater!"

Will bent his head, as if taking her order for ale. "You've still got the Magic Eyeball book, right?"

Nan patted the satchel in her lap.

Will looked over at the head table. Maybe he could bring Jamie some water and use that excuse to talk to him . . . but Jamie's chair was empty.

Nan jerked her chin in the direction of the sideboard. "He's over there. Guzzling ale, probably."

Will hurried over to Jamie's side. "What are you doing?" he demanded. "Mom and Dad would never let you drink ale, no matter what century it is!"

Jamie carefully closed the spigot on the keg and frowned. "I don't know what you're talking about."

Will tried to adopt a more reasonable tone. "Shouldn't you be watering that?"

Jamie flipped the silver lid over the top of the mug in his hand. "It's for the laird," he said. "I'm supposed to serve him—I'm his page." He hesitated, staring at Will. "I've seen you somewhere."

"Oh, come *on*, you've known me your whole—" Will folded his fingers into fists to keep himself from grabbing Jamie by the shoulders and shaking him. "Forget it. Listen, you saw me yesterday. I'm the one Ranald tossed in the mud puddle."

Jamie nodded slowly.

Will lowered his voice. "You knew me before that, though. Remember?"

Jamie shook his head, but his forehead wrinkled above his nose, and his teeth caught at his lower lip.

That was the way Jamie's face always looked when he was worried or unsure. Encouraged, Will pressed on. "We lived together with Mom and Dad, and our address was—"

"Seventy-five twenty-one, Seventeenth Avenue South," Jamie blurted out. Then he clapped a hand to his mouth. Above his fingers, his eyes widened.

Yes! Will felt like pumping his fist in triumph, but he kept his voice calm. "That's right," he said. "In Plymouth, Minnesota. And our zip code is—"

"Five-five-four-four-seven," Jamie whispered through his fingers.

Will grinned. Like every kindergartner, Jamie had memorized his address and practiced it over and over. "You *do* remember!"

Jamie took his hand away from his mouth. "I'm not supposed to remember." He flipped the lid on the silver mug back and forth on its hinge. "None of those things I remember are true. They were just dreams that came after I hit my head. That's what everybody told me," he added, gnawing his lower lip again.

"*I'm* true," said Will quietly. "Don't you know me, Jamie?

Your big brother, Will? Don't you remember Mom and Dad, and the trip on the big plane, where you spilled your root beer?"

Jamie gulped. A shadow loomed above them.

"Master James, is the pot boy bothering you?" growled Ranald.

Jamie shook his head. He snapped the silver lid down and walked quickly away toward the head table.

"ALE!" shrieked Nan, waving her arm, and Will ran over with a mug of water, glad for the excuse to get away.

"I *hate* that guy," Nan whispered, glaring at Ranald.

Will bent close to her ear and pretended to brush crumbs off the table. "Jamie remembered our address! He knows me, too, I'm sure, but he's afraid to admit it. They've told him that everything he remembered from his old life was crazy."

Nan gazed at the head table thoughtfully. "How are we going to get him to meet us? We've got to be together when we go back to our own time."

"I don't know!"

"Can't you think of more things he'll remember? The more you tell him, the more he'll believe you."

Will's mouth twisted. "I can't even get close to him without that stupid Ranald coming over—"

"ALE!" yelled someone at the far end of the table.

Will gave an exasperated grunt and ran back to the

sideboard. By the end of the night he was sick of the smell of ale. When were the pot boys fed, he wondered? After everyone else, apparently. It wasn't until the cherry pies came up from the kitchen that Will was given a dish of stew and told he could eat.

There was a little space not far from the high table, at the end of a bench. Will squeezed himself in and applied himself to his meal. The stew was good, salty and rich with beef, and the bread was chewy and dense, with a flavor of oats. After the first few bites, he slowed down, listening to the conversation around him.

"The Stewarts are lawless, and getting worse—"

"Now that Sir Robert's got the king's authority for those lands, he can clean things up a bit."

"Eh, and how? Neil Gointe and his wild men will never submit to the king, or the laird, either. If we come in force, they'll melt away into the hills and come out again worse than ever when we're gone."

The argument grew louder, and someone bumped Will's elbow. "Shove over," Nan said, sliding onto the edge of the bench. "The Stewarts aren't so bad," she said under her breath. "Isobel Stewart is almost my best friend at school—"

"Quiet, will you?" Will choked on a bite of crumbly pastry and took a swig of water. "Someone will hear you. Besides, I don't want to talk about the Stewarts."

"Why not? Everyone else is."

Will scooped a last bite of cherry pie into his spoon— where were the forks? he wondered; no one seemed to use them here—and with his mouth conveniently full, didn't answer. It made him nervous to think about the Stewarts. He kept seeing the cruel, wolfish face of the man who had murdered two men with such quick and unexpected violence.

Someone banged on the table with his mug. "I say murder the bunch of them! That's what they're trying to do to us!"

"Who speaks of murder in my hall?" It was the laird, and all around Will, the voices quieted to listen.

"It would stop their lawless ways!" said a voice down the table—Ranald's, Will thought.

Sir Robert lifted his chin with the sideways motion Will had noticed before. "And shall we then become lawless ourselves? Shall we become like those we despise?"

"Good point," whispered Nan in Will's ear.

Will shifted uneasily on the bench. "How are we supposed to stop bad guys, then?" he whispered back. "Shake our fingers at them and hope they listen?"

"The police can arrest them," Nan said. "Then a judge can put them in jail."

"There aren't any police or judges here! There's just Sir Robert and his armed men!"

Nan tossed her head. "I don't know why you care. It's not like we're going to stay here long."

"You *hope* we aren't," Will muttered.

Sir Robert was still speaking; his words echoed sternly in the Great Hall. "By the king's grace, the disputed lands are rightfully ours. If the Stewart chief fails to obey, we shall by force bring him to justice in the name of the king. But murder, secret and dishonorable murder, in the dark?" He turned his head, surveying the crowded room, and his eyes gleamed in the candlelight. "Never while I am chief!

Remember our deeds of arms; remember our proud history; remember our motto, 'Will God, I Shall.' Remember!" He pointed to a shield on the wall. "Remember that we are Clan Menzies, and up with the Red and White!"

"MENZIES!" roared a hundred voices, and "Menzies!" cried a high, childish voice, later than the others. Will looked up to see his little brother waving a silver mug in the air.

"There's my brave Jamie!" The laird's stern face was glowing. "Sound in wit once more, and as proud a Menzies as any. Come, lad, give us a song!"

"A song! A song from Master James!" The cry was taken up around the Great Hall, and mugs banged lustily on the wooden tables. Rough hands lifted Jamie and set him, standing, on the head table, his feet between the plates. He stood wide-legged on the table, grinning.

Will winced. Jamie could sing, all right—but he was such a show-off.

"He looks like he's done this before," Nan said.

"It wouldn't surprise me," Will said glumly.

"Sing 'Rose o' the Glen'!" shouted someone from the back of the room.

"Nay, give us 'Langtree'!"

"'Loch Tay'!"

Jamie raised a hand, and the room quieted down. Then Nan cried, "Sing 'Flower of Scotland,' Jamie!"

Jamie blinked in the flaring candlelight.

"What did you do that for?" Will whispered. "Everyone's looking at us."

"Who cares?" Nan hissed back. "It's one more thing that will remind Jamie of his life in the future, see?"

"He won't remember a song you taught him *once*," Will said scornfully.

Nan tossed her head, and her red gold hair went flying past Will's cheek as she stood. "You learned it from me," she called to Jamie. "Remember? It goes like this." She tilted back her head and began:

"O flower of Scotland, when will we see your like again? That fought and died for your wee bit . . ." She paused and looked at Jamie.

He hesitated. "Hill and glen," he quavered at last.

Nan shot Will a triumphant glance. "And stood against him," she sang heartily, and Jamie joined her, his voice growing stronger with each word. "Proud Edward's army, and sent him homeward to think again!" they bellowed together, as the room erupted in shouts and cheers.

"Bravely sung!" Sir Robert said. "I've never heard that song before. Did you truly teach it to him, lass?"

Nan nodded.

"And you know what it's about, of course?"

Nan grinned. "It's Robert the—" She stopped midsentence, her eyes suddenly panicked. "Wait, did Robert the

Bruce come before this time, or after? I can never remember dates!" she hissed to Will.

"You're asking *me*?"

But Sir Robert was smiling. "Speak up, now. Don't be afraid."

"Go big, or go home," Will murmured.

Nan gripped her hands together behind her back. "It's about Robert the Bruce, sir. When he fought King Edward and gave us back our Scotland from the English."

"Well spoken! And though it was many long years ago, it's good to hear that new songs are still being made about it. But there are more verses, surely?"

Nan, sagging with relief, nodded. "I can teach him the rest of the song tonight, sir, if you'll let Jamie come with me." She nudged Will with her foot and gave him the ghost of a wink.

Sir Robert frowned; his chin jerked up and to one side. "That's Master James, to you, lassie—you must not be so pert. As for James, the song can wait—it's time for him to be abed." He ushered his family out by the far door. Jamie had time for just one backward look before he was out of Nan's and Will's sight.

"See?" Nan's dimple was showing. "He *did* remember the song!"

Will was strongly tempted to point out that people who said "I told you so" were annoying to almost everyone. He made an effort and managed to say instead, "Good job trying to get him to meet us."

Nan brushed her hair out of her eyes. "Yeah, but it didn't work."

"We'll think of something," Will said with an optimism he didn't feel. "If we could just find out where—"

"Pert, Sir Robert said, and he was right!" The waspish voice was just above their heads, and they looked up to see Mistress Cullen's pinched and disapproving face. "I can see that I will have to teach you manners as well as sewing! No wonder your stitches were so slapdash today. You must have run off to play with Master James when you were supposed to be setting a seam. And here I thought you were just going to the garderobe."

"I didn't *play*," Nan began, but the woman cut her off.

"Teaching him that song when you were supposed to be about your duties is what *I* call playing. I don't care if it pleased the laird—it's me you've got to please tomorrow, or you'll be out on your ear and good riddance to you!" She sailed off, her nose held high.

The plump girl who trailed after her gave Nan a commiserating look. "Better come up soon," she whispered over her shoulder, "or you won't get your share of the blankets. The other girls hog them all."

At the mention of bed, Will almost split his head with a yawn.

Janet, bustling past, shook her head at him. "Stop that gawping, laddie. You've got pots to scrub and grates to scrape before you can shut your eyes."

Shutting his eyes sounded immensely appealing to Will. "Where do I sleep when I finish?" he asked.

Janet stared at him. "Where do you think? Where pot boys always sleep—on the hearthstone, by the fire. And you'd better bank it well, so some embers are left in the morning, or Cook will eat you for breakfast," she added as she gathered the plates.

Nan scowled as Mistress Cullen's skirts swished out of sight. "I'm getting sick of this. I say we just grab Jamie and go."

"Right. And when he screams and wakes the whole castle, and Ranald pitches us out in the dark or puts us in the lockup, what then?"

Nan twisted a lock of hair moodily around her finger. "Fine. *You* think of an idea. But hurry up, will you? I'm not in the mood to share a bed with a bunch of blanket-hogging girls."

"Yeah, well, I'm not in the mood to sleep on a hard stone floor." Will gnawed on a fingernail. "Listen, do you know which room is Jamie's?"

"Aye. It's just next to the laird's." Nan frowned. "Have you noticed this castle is different? The rooms aren't all the same, and the stair is in a different place, and—"

"Pot boy!" shouted Janet from across the hall. "Get busy!"

Will hurriedly got up and stacked a few bowls. "We've got to make Jamie *want* to come with us," he whispered.

"But how?" Nan added her bowl to his stack with a convincing clatter.

Will jammed his hands inside his plaid, where it bloused out over the belt and made a sort of pocket. He touched something that crinkled like paper. . . .

"I've got an idea." He pulled out the lead stick he had gotten from the steward and hurriedly wrote a few lines. "Jamie can read," he explained to Nan, "and I bet you anything he's kept in practice just to show off. You can tuck this into his hand without anyone noticing."

Nan looked over his shoulder and read:

Meet me in kitchen after all are asleep, to learn
rest of song and find out a secret.

"That ought to do it," said Will, folding the note up small and pressing it into Nan's palm. "Jamie never could resist a secret."

6
STEWARTS' REVENGE

WILL WAS EXHAUSTED. SCRAPING GRATES with the long-handled metal brush was hard work, but it was nothing compared to scrubbing the pots and pans needed to feed so many people. To make it worse, he had to carry the wash water in buckets and heat it before pouring it into the big sink. And the iron pans were dreadfully heavy.

At least he didn't have to wash the mugs; he was only required to dry their insides with a cloth. Now he saw why everyone in the Great Hall had wiped their stew bowls out with pieces of bread and then eaten the bread after. It was a marvelously efficient way of polishing the bowls until they were clean—well, more or less—and though it wasn't exactly hygienic, it made a pot boy's life easier.

Sundown was early this time of year in the Highlands. Gradually the castle quieted as the workers did their final tasks and went off to bed. Some of the guards were still awake, for Will heard their boots pacing the hall, and after a while, snatches of song and rough laughter came faintly to his ears.

Will wasn't in a singing mood, himself. The washing up was too dismally real. He scraped and scrubbed, with only the kitchen fire for light, until his back was sore and his knuckles were raw. When he caught his thumb between a pot and its lid, he stifled a yelp and straightened his back, groaning. Why was he even doing this? He didn't need to finish the job—he'd be gone long before Cook woke up in the morning.

If, that is, Nan managed to pass the note to Jamie. And if he still remembered how to read after all this time. Then *if* Jamie was curious enough to come, and *if* no one saw him on his way down to the kitchen . . .

Will sucked his wrist where he had burned it on the hot kettle and wearily lifted the next pot into the sink. At last, exhausted, he collapsed on the stone hearth, pillowing his head on his arm. He heard one soft *tick* as a burning ember crumbled into ash, and then he slid into sleep as swiftly as a stone dropping into deep water.

After a while he dreamed. His mother was imprisoned

behind a wall, shaking her head in warning, but then he couldn't see her anymore for the towering stack of pots and pans that grew before his eyes and stayed dirty no matter how he scrubbed. All at once, the largest pot reached out to him with iron handles that had somehow become hands, and shook him by the shoulders. "Wake up!" it called, and Will opened his eyes to see Nan's arm vigorously shaking him, and Jamie's eager face, alight with curiosity.

"Did anyone see you?" Will mumbled, blinking the sleep from his eyes.

Nan shook her head. "Not a soul. I slept on a bench in the hall, and when Jamie woke up to use the garderobe, I showed him the note, and he came with me. I think the guards must all be at the other end of the castle."

"I read your letter all by myself!" Jamie plumped himself down on the hearth. "The steward says I read ree-mark-a-ble for my years. What's the secret?"

Will gave his head two shakes and ran his fingers through his hair. "The secret is . . ." He looked at Nan. "Do you have the Magic Eyeball book?"

"Right here." Nan reached inside her satchel.

"Okay." Will sat up and looked Jamie in the eye. "Here's the secret. You know all those things you thought you remembered? That everyone told you were just dreams because you'd hit your head?"

Jamie nodded, looking troubled.

"Well, everything you remembered was true. Nan and I can prove it to you, if you're brave enough."

"I'm braver than you!" Jamie angled his chin up in a not-quite-successful imitation of Sir Robert. "I'm a Menzies, and Sir Robert's nephew! *You're* just a pot boy."

"I'm a Menzies, too, you dumbwit," Will said, nobly resisting the urge to smack his brother.

"I'm not a dumbwit! Anyway, Ranald says you're just a—"

"I'm a Menzies, too," Nan interrupted hastily.

"But I'm *noble*!" Jamie stuck out his chest.

"Yes, you are," Nan added, "and brave, too." She gave Jamie a ravishing smile, complete with dimple. "Here, show me how brave you are. Stand close, like this, touching Will. Now, watch what happens!"

Will noted sourly that the Dimple was having its usual effect. Jamie looked up at Nan like a trusting puppy and put his hand obediently on his brother's back.

The fire was low, and the kitchen was full of shadow. Will could just make out the pattern in the open book. He relaxed his gaze, looked at a place just beyond the book, and waited for the shimmer of light to show around the edges.

It didn't come. Yet something seemed different, in a way he couldn't define.

"What's wrong?" Nan whispered.

"I don't know. It's not working the same way. Maybe I need more light." Will turned slightly, so that the fire's glow shone more brightly on the page.

"This is daft," said Jamie loudly.

"Quiet, now!" Nan said. "He's got to concentrate!"

Will brushed away the thin thread of worry that spun into his mind and focused on the page once more. He knew how to do this, he told himself. He had done it before. . . .

There. He could sense something different now, on the other side of the book. Yet there was no light leaking around the edges. Rather, there was a shimmer of darkness, if such a thing could be. Slowly he lowered his arms.

Before him was a squarish hole in the air: a window in time, perhaps, but a window into total blackness. It showed up clearly against the fire's glow—a largish patch with fuzzy edges, dark where it should have been light, blocking the flickering flames and reflecting no gleam of the moon that showed palely through the high, small window and spilled in a narrow swath of brightness across the flagstone floor.

"Witchcraft!" breathed Jamie, staring.

"No," said Nan swiftly, "not witchcraft. It's more like . . . science. Magical science."

Jamie frowned. "Do you mean alchemy?"

Will heard their voices like a buzzing in the background of his mind. What had he opened a window on? Slowly, carefully, he put out a hand. But his fingers met a barrier, a rough, cold wall that felt almost like—

"Stone," said Nan, touching the darkness. "You opened a window on stone."

Will looked around wildly, and the window disappeared. "But we always go to the same *place* in another time. We're in the middle of the castle kitchen—so why doesn't it open into the castle kitchen in the future?"

Nan's eyebrows twitched down. "It's like I said before; the whole castle is different." Suddenly her brow cleared. "I know! Mum told me once that the castle was destroyed somehow, I don't remember how, and then they built it again. So this must be the first castle. The kitchen must not be in exactly the same place as in our time."

"But then why aren't we just in a different room?"

Nan knew the answer to that, too. "I bet this spot is inside one of the walls. The walls in a castle are thicker," she added. "Sometimes they're three feet—"

"Sir Robert's castle has walls *seven* feet thick!" said Jamie with pride.

"Okay, then, I just have to move over a little, like this." Will stepped a few feet away and tried again. This time there was still darkness, but when Nan put her hand through, she met only air. She stuck her head in carefully and looked around.

"It's dark everywhere," she reported, then—"*Eeeek!*" She

pulled her head back like a shot, shuddering. "There was something moving in there—something *chewing*—"

"Probably just a mouse," Will said.

"Or a rat," Jamie added cheerfully.

"I'm not going in there," Nan said firmly. "That was like a locked closet, or a sealed room, or something. We don't want to get into a place like that. If it was a closet you might not have enough light to do the Magic Eyeball thing, and we'd be locked in there forever, and someday they would find our bones—"

"All right," Will said hastily. "Don't go on and on about it."

"Why did you tell me to come?" Jamie shuffled his feet. "You haven't shown me any secret, just a big dark hole. And you said you were going to teach me the rest of the song," he added, gazing accusingly at Nan. "I want to sing it for Sir Robert tomorrow!"

Will rolled his eyes. "You won't even be here tomorrow, so don't bother—"

He stopped. Jamie's lower lip had gone out in a motion Will knew only too well.

"You teach me the song," said Jamie, sounding suddenly like the laird, "or I'm going to bed and I'll never talk to you again."

Will made an exasperated noise in his throat. He was strongly tempted to grab Jamie and carry him away, out of the castle where he couldn't tattle to the laird. "Fine, then."

Will put his hands behind his back with an effort. "Nan will teach you the song, but you have to promise to stay with us until we get a window open into our own time. You'll see, it will be just like you remember it."

Fifteen minutes later, Jamie knew every word to "Flower of Scotland"—and so did his big brother, much against his will.

But Will had been thinking. It made him increasingly nervous to think of making a time jump inside Castle Menzies. There was too big a chance for someone to suddenly round a corner and see them as they appeared. It would be hard enough if they appeared in front of a bunch of tourists or Cousin Elspeth, but what if he missed his own time entirely? Then they might get taken for witches, and be burned at the stake, or something.

If only they could get outside! The moon was bright enough to see by. But the gates were barred for the night, and there would be guards at the door.

"Those days are past now," warbled Jamie, "and in the past they must remain—"

Will stepped to the door that opened to the hall and glanced down the passageway.

"But we can still rise now, and be the nation again—"

The hall was dimly lit, with torches that had been allowed to burn low. The barrel ceiling loomed like the inside of a tomb, and Will felt a chill at the back of his neck.

"That stood against him," came faintly to his ear. "Proud Edward's army—"

Will peered into the gloom. There were no guards that he could see. Step by careful step, Will moved down the passageway. Jamie started singing his song again, a little louder this time, and Will wished with all his heart that his brother would shut up, just for one minute. There was a sound ahead, a low sort of rumble, coming from the guardroom. He couldn't identify it.

Will neared the gate, the big barred door with its strong iron grating that was called a yett. But no one stood guard there, either. Did they trust their iron bars and wooden door so much? It seemed careless not to have a guard on duty, especially with all the enemies they had running loose.

The rumbling noise grew louder. It sounded like a lawn mower that wouldn't start. He stuck his head cautiously around the corner and choked back a sudden laugh. The guardroom had guards in it all right—but they were snoring. One sprawled against the back wall, under the marks in the stone where soldiers had sharpened their knives. Another, smaller in build, huddled in a corner with his head on his knees. The third guard was at the table. Where his cheek pressed against the wood, a small puddle of drool dampened the surface. None of them was Ranald, Will was glad to see, but every man had a mug near him, and in the center of the table was a small wooden keg that Will had seen once before. Water-of-life, the guard had called it. On the keg's wooden surface was burned an unfamiliar word: *Uisge*.

Will sounded it out under his breath. "Ooo-is-gey," he muttered. It sounded familiar, as if he had heard it somewhere before. Of course, spelling here was quite different from the way he had learned it at home. "Ooo-is-gee . . . ," he tried again, and then suddenly he had it.

Whiskey! They had been drinking whiskey, and they had all passed out! It was stronger than ale; maybe they weren't used to it. He might be able to get outside after all.

Will turned to the castle gate and put his shoulder under the heavy bar. It moved an inch, but no farther. He let it down softly and raced back to the kitchen.

Jamie was still at it. "That fought and died for your wee bit hill and glen—"

"Shut up, will you? The guards are asleep!" Will's whisper was fierce. "Nan, help me open the gate. If we get outside, I can open a time window without any walls getting in the way, and it will be easier to hide if someone comes." He snatched up the Magic Eyeball book and shoved it into Nan's satchel.

Jamie followed them to the door, but balked when he realized what Will was about to do. "You can't open the gate in the middle of the night! Uncle Robert won't allow it!"

"Uncle Robert . . . will never . . . know," Will panted as he heaved at the bar. "Come on, Nan, help!"

"Shh!" Nan laid a warning finger on his wrist. There was a sliding sound behind them, and a soft chink of metal.

The children slipped into the shadows. Will clapped his hand over Jamie's mouth just in case. Jamie wriggled, but Will whispered into his brother's ear. "You don't want Uncle Robert to find you out of bed, do you?"

"He's not *your* uncle," Jamie whispered back hotly, but he stood still.

Someone was moving in the guardroom. A long shadow changed shape as it met the flickering light from the hall torches. A thin, gangling form appeared in the doorway, and Will let out his breath in relief. It was only the old pot boy, the teenager who had brought the whiskey.

The pot boy cast a quick look over his shoulder and went soft-footed to the gate. He pulled out a ring of keys, clinking slightly, and fumbled with the shadowed end of the heavy, iron-reinforced bar across the gate.

Now Will knew why he had been unable to lift the bar more than an inch. He had not noticed the padlock, as wide as a man's fist, that hung beneath one end. With a final chink and a scrape of metal, the teenager unlocked the gate and muscled up the heavy bar. The iron yett creaked, and a swirl of cool night air came gusting in. The dust on the floor stirred, a leaf skittered across the stone, and the boy put his foot on the threshold.

Will stepped from the shadows to the door. "Hey," he whispered.

The pot boy jumped a foot. "I—I was only going for a breath of air," he stammered wildly.

"It's okay," Nan soothed. "We want to go outside, too."

The boy's eyes, darting everywhere, settled on Jamie. "*He* wants to go outside?"

Will frowned in puzzlement. He had expected the teenager to ask their business, and instead the boy seemed scared of *them*. Well, maybe it was because of Jamie. Will had a sudden inspiration and said, "He needs a breath of air, too. He's got . . . you know, breathing trouble—"

"Asthma," Nan said promptly. "He gasps and wheezes like you wouldn't believe." She pushed Jamie forward.

The teenager looked suspiciously at Jamie. "He's not doing any of that now."

"It comes and goes," said Nan.

Jamie, between Nan and Will, gave a gasp and a little start, as if he had been suddenly poked in the ribs from both sides.

"Like that," said Nan, "only worse."

"Much worse," said Will, giving Jamie another quiet dig with his knuckle.

"*Eeeeessp!*" Jamie obliged, sucking in air with a rasping sound. "*Eeeesp! Eeeesp!*"

Will leaned against the heavy door and pushed it open

wider. The hinges creaked, but the snoring from the guard-room continued without a break. The children pressed through and hesitated a moment in the damp cool night.

The teenager turned his head from side to side, as if scanning the darkness for enemies. "All right, he's had his fresh air. You'd better get back to your beds." The boy's Adam's apple bobbed up and down.

"We want to go a little farther." Will pulled at Nan's elbow.

"Yes," said Nan, reaching for Jamie's hand. "We want to go where the air is really fresh. He's still not breathing perfectly well—"

"*Eeeessp!*" Jamie said helpfully.

"We're just going to those bushes." Will pointed to a little rise just past the castle road. "The air is—um, clearer there. More leaves, more oxygen, see?"

The pot boy stared as they walked away. Behind him, the light from the hall's torches streamed out into the darkness, and his gangly form was outlined like a cutout silhouette.

"Is this far enough away?" Nan whispered as they moved behind the bushes.

Will nodded. "He can't tell what we're doing in the dark. But we've got to stay close so he still knows we're here, or he might give the alarm."

Nan fumbled in her satchel for the Magic Eyeball book. Will scanned the surrounding hills, the dark mass of forest, all silver-edged with the moon's light, and willed himself to relax. Everything was quiet; nothing was going to go wrong. "Okay, get behind me, you two, and grab on."

The cold gleam of the moon shone pale on the open book. The pattern wasn't clearly distinguishable, but it wasn't about the pattern anyway, Will thought. It was about focusing his eyes somewhere beyond the pattern. . . . Would it be harder, now that it was dark?

A movement from the figure at the castle gate distracted him.

"He's waving for us to come back," said Jamie.

"Hurry up, Will!" Nan urged.

The pot boy moved his arm again, making a wide, stiff-elbowed sweep from shoulder to shoulder.

Jamie gave a little hop. "He's waving like a windshield wiper!"

Nan's dimple showed in the moonlight. "You remember windshield wipers and cars, do you? Good lad."

"Shh!" Will crouched behind the bushes and tugged at their arms. "Get down."

"What?" Nan knelt and pulled Jamie down beside her.

"I don't think he's waving to us," Will said urgently. "It's more like—"

The pot boy raised his arm again and made a stiff, back-and-forth motion, three times.

"A signal!" Will hissed.

The ground shook lightly, *thump thump thump*, as if a thousand ripe apples were falling to earth at the same time. There was a rustle of bracken and then the dark spaces between the trees suddenly sent out strange hunched shapes that ran with powerful legs. Armed men streamed from the forested hill and moved in a swift flood toward the castle, their long hair flying behind them and their swords glinting in the moon's clear light.

"Stewarts!" Jamie whimpered.

"We've got to warn them at the castle!" Nan said with a sob.

But already the enemy was pouring through the gate the treacherous pot boy held open. There was a sound of metal meeting flesh and bone, and a terrible screaming. Over at the stables, horses whinnied and reared as Stewarts led them out of their boxes. Behind the moving shapes, flames licked at the wooden walls and caught at the thatch.

Jamie was crying.

"Hush, hush," Nan whispered, rocking him. She looked over Jamie's head and caught Will's eye. "Get us home *now*."

Will held out the book. He tried to focus on that still point just beyond the pages, that place where their own time waited. But he could not do it—could not relax his eyes, could not keep his gaze from the castle, now showing a flickering light from its upper windows.

"Look!" Nan gripped Will's arm. "They've lit candles—Sir Robert's awake, he's going to fight back—"

Fear congealed in Will's stomach like a lump of ice. A tongue of fire leaped out from the topmost window—and now there was another. "No," he said, shuddering. "They're burning the castle."

"It's stone," Nan protested. "Stone doesn't burn."

"But there's wood inside—wood beams, and wood floors—"

"There are *people* inside!" Jamie cried. "Uncle Robert, and Aunt Margaret, and Rabbie, and old Angus—"

"They're going to be all right," Nan soothed. "Look, they're coming out."

It was true, Will saw. The unmistakable form of Sir Robert was pushed out the castle gate, his hands tied behind his back and a sword at his throat. Armed Stewarts surrounded him and threw him over a horse like a sack.

"Uncle Robert!" Jamie leaped up.

Nan dragged him back down. "You can't do anything to help him." She grabbed the Magic Eyeball book from the ground where Will had dropped it and thrust it in his face. "Do it *now*!"

Hands shaking, Will held the book at arm's length. Behind it, the castle glowed more fiercely. Dimly he was aware of Stewarts mounting; horses wheeling; of groups of men splitting up, some riding off toward the town of Weem, some galloping down the road toward the place where the children crouched, hidden.

Will never knew how he did it. Perhaps all that practice had helped. Perhaps he was so afraid that he had gone numb. However it happened, he found himself watching as the edges behind the book started to shimmer with light. He did not lose concentration, not even when horses' hooves came thundering very near.

He heard Jamie's panicked whisper—"Stop! They'll see the light!" and Nan's low, "No, they won't. You can only see the light if you're touching Will. Be quiet, now, and when I give you a push, go through!"

Will lowered the book slowly and stared at a patch of bright sunlit field, a little fuzzy around the edges. In the distance he could see the castle of his own time, sturdy and safe, with the cars of tourists in the parking lot and what looked like Cousin Elspeth's car off to one side. "Go," he said urgently. "Go *now*."

Jamie stared, openmouthed, at the scene through the window.

The horses on the road slowed to a trot, then a walk. Will's forehead grew damp; a drop of sweat rolled into an eye, but he forced himself not to blink. Slowly he lowered his gaze, and the window moved down until it was inches off the ground. If Nan and Jamie didn't go through right *now*—

Nan grabbed Jamie and shoved him like a sack of laundry through the opening in time. Then she crawled after him.

The hoofbeats stopped. Will could smell the pungent odor of horse and unwashed men. He held himself perfectly still, his heart beating like a hummingbird's in his throat. Had the riders heard Nan and Jamie moving? What if the men grabbed Will's legs when he was halfway through the time window?

The horses circled, as if the riders had turned for a last look at the burning castle and its wailing inhabitants, now streaming out.

A rough voice spoke out of the darkness, very near. "What are you going to do with him, chief?"

Another voice laughed, softly and low. It was a sound so cruel that Will felt the cold crawling on his skin. He should go through the time window—it was dangerous to wait any longer—but something kept him rooted in place. What *were* they going to do with Sir Robert?

"I'll persuade him," said the smooth, malicious voice. "He's got a king's charter to some lands that are mine by rights. By the time I'm through burning his castle, and the village, too, he'll respect me, or my name isn't Neil Stewart!"

"But what are you going to *do* with him?" asked the other man again.

"Throw him in the dungeon at Garth Castle until he signs the lands over to me," said Neil Gointe Stewart. "He can keep his little nephew company."

No! thought Will, launching himself through the time window. He pulled the Magic Eyeball book in behind him and rolled on earth that felt warm and stubbly. The darkness fled, and all around him was a field of cut hay, its round stacks golden in the sun. Nan and Jamie stared at him from a few feet off, too dazed to speak. A dog barked.

"There you are!" cried Cousin Elspeth, bustling toward them from the castle garden. "Wherever have you been? I've been calling and calling, and it's a good hour past lunchtime!" She stood before them, her face red and her hands on her hips. "And where on earth did you get those clothes?"

7

ALL MIXED UP

JAMIE LOOKED UP AT COUSIN Elspeth, his eyes wide. His chin quivered.

"Now, lad, I didn't mean to frighten you," she said. "It's all right if you were playing dress-up, but I can't think where you got the costumes—out of those old trunks in the storeroom, I suppose. Come, get washed up for lunch, and then you can put your own things on again." She took Jamie's hand in a firm grip and strode back toward the castle.

Jamie trotted beside her obediently. But two silent tears rolled down his cheeks, and then two more.

Cousin Elspeth looked down. "What's this? Surely you aren't upset because I asked about your costumes?"

Jamie shook his head. "They took Sir Robert," he whispered. "And there was a fire . . . and *murder* . . ."

Cousin Elspeth frowned at Will and Nan. "What non-sense have you been filling his head with, now?"

Will hesitated. Should they try again to tell Cousin Elspeth what really happened? Could she even believe it? "It was a sort of window. . . . We traveled back in time," he said helplessly.

Cousin Elspeth's face grew severe. "We've been through this before. There's a time for pretending, and there's a time to tell the truth."

"But it *is*—"

Nan stopped Will with a well-placed elbow to his ribs. "It's my fault, Mum. I was telling Jamie what it was like hundreds of years ago, and we started to play we were living in the castle then, with swords and danger and fires. Jamie must have thought it was all really happening. He's got a big imagination."

Cousin Elspeth made a sound that might have been a suppressed snort. "Jamie, I can see. But you are old enough to know the difference. And, Will, you shouldn't keep on pretending when it worries your little brother."

Nan threw an arm across Will's shoulders. "You know Americans, always so enthusiastic. They just don't know when to quit." She smiled enchantingly.

Will glared at his cousin. He wished for a moment that he had left her back in the past, dimple and all.

"There, there, my lamb, don't you fret!" Cousin Elspeth

gave Jamie's hand a comforting squeeze. "None of it was real, laddie. It was all just pretend, like a dream, don't you see?"

Jamie jerked back as if Cousin Elspeth had slapped him. "A dream?" he cried. "Sir Robert told me *this* was the dream!" He turned an accusing gaze on Will. "It can't all be a dream. You told me the cars and planes and things were real, but the fire was real, too, and I was the laird's nephew, you were *there*—" He rubbed at his eyes with grubby fists.

Cousin Elspeth glared at Nan and Will, picked Jamie up in her arms, and marched off indignantly.

Nan tossed her hair out of her eyes. "He's never going to get it straight now."

Will didn't say anything. He felt too terrible.

The Magic Eyeball book was still in his hand. He flipped open Nan's satchel, still hanging on her back, and stuffed the book down deep, where he wouldn't have to see it again. His hand met something lumpy and hard, and he pulled it out. He looked at the dirty plastic figurine in his palm. Jamie's Highlander.

Will ran after Cousin Elspeth. Jamie's arms were around her neck and his face half hidden. His eyes showed above her shoulder, as round as a baby seal's, and he stared reproachfully at his brother.

"Here," said Will, and he tucked the small action figure into Jamie's grimy hand. "*That's* real."

Jamie's fingers closed around the Highlander as Cousin Elspeth strode past Gormlaith, who had been investigating the burrow of a meadow vole. The creamy dog lifted her head and trotted after them, her forehead puzzled as she kept her eyes on Jamie.

Nan caught up to Will, who gave her a look of scorn.

"Don't get stroppy," she said. "It isn't *my* fault Mum wouldn't believe you."

"You didn't help," Will said bitterly. "Saying all that about Jamie's imagination and how Americans never know when to quit."

Nan grinned. "Well, you don't, do you? You should have stopped trying to get my mum to understand about the time window long ago. Anyone could have seen that she'd never believe you, not if you opened a window and dragged her through it. Once Mum makes up her mind about something, that's that. You know how mothers are."

Will looked down. He knew. Once his own mother had made up her mind to go help in that other country, nothing Will said had made any difference at all. . . .

He kicked at the stubble with every step. It made a light crackling as he walked, almost like the sound of fire. Somewhere, back in time, the castle was still blazing and Sir Robert had been carried off to the Stewart dungeons. Will's mouth twisted at the thought. He had done the right thing, getting Nan and Jamie back to safety—hadn't he?

He cleared his throat. "Do you remember what that man said, right before you went through the window?"

"Who?" asked Nan.

"Neil Gointe Stewart." Will hated the sound of the name. "He was one of the guys on the horses, remember? He was talking with one of his men."

Nan shrugged. "I didn't hear anything. Jamie and I must have gone through the time window before they started talking."

"Oh, right." Will remembered now.

"Was that why it took you so long to come through? What did they say?"

"They said they were going to put Sir Robert in their castle dungeons," Will said slowly, "until he signed a paper that gave them his new lands."

Nan bit her lip.

"And then," Will said, kicking viciously at a particularly stiff bit of stubble, "Neil Gointe Stewart said that Sir Robert could keep his little nephew company."

Nan narrowed her eyes as their feet crunched on the stones of the castle road. "Did he think they were going to capture Jamie, too?"

"That's what I thought at first. But the way he said it—it sounded like he had a boy in his dungeon already." Will picked up a stone and threw it to relieve his feelings. "Don't you remember that kid we saw before? The one who looked like Jamie—the one they carried off on a horse when they murdered his two guards?"

Nan nodded. She looked as if she were going to be sick.

"That's who they must have been talking about. I bet they've had that little guy in one of their dungeons for a whole year now."

The castle door opened, and two tourists walked out, consulting a guidebook. "Should we walk up to Saint David's Well?" the woman asked. "Or is it Saint Cuthbert's well? I never can remember. It's not far, at any rate."

"I'd rather get lunch first," said the man, sounding grumpy.

"Oh, all right. . . ."

Will blinked as the tourists got in their car and slammed the doors. Something in his vision seemed strangely askew, as if he had been a long time at sea and couldn't quite get his balance.

Nan turned to watch as the car drove away. "It's daft. Those tourists, chatting away about ordinary things . . . when right on this spot, just ten minutes ago, men dragged Sir Robert out, with flames everywhere and people crying."

Will nodded. That was it exactly. The fire had been hundreds of years ago, really, but . . . "It feels like it just happened."

"It *did* just happen," Nan pointed out.

"No wonder Jamie's so messed up," Will went on. "If it's this weird for us, after one day in the past, think what it's like for him after a whole year!"

"He'll get used to it." Nan's dimple made a brief appearance as she opened the castle door. "He's a bright lad. Before you know it, he'll be back to normal."

But Jamie just seemed to grow quieter. The next day was Sunday, and he sat politely in church—they called it "kirk"—without wriggling or complaining. His face showed a gleam of interest at the reading from Psalms ("With Your help I can advance against a troop; with my God I can scale a wall"), but lost all expression when he was dismissed with the other children for Sunday school. And after, when Cousin Elspeth asked him what the lesson had been about, he said, "Angels," in a tone of such disinterest that she didn't ask anything else.

He didn't want to play games or run around when they got home, and he avoided Will and Nan. He spent most of Sunday afternoon by himself near the narrow, stony burn, tossing pebbles into the water. Gormlaith came up with a stick, dropping it at his feet in a clear invitation to play fetch, but when Jamie ignored her, the dog flopped down beside him with a gusty sigh, her brown eyes watching him soulfully.

The only time Jamie made a fuss was when Cousin Elspeth tried to take the Highlander away. "Come, now," she coaxed, "you've had it in your hand all day, and it's too clarty to take to bed. I'll clean it up for you while you sleep, and tomorrow you'll have it back, good as new!"

But Jamie put up such resistance that Cousin Elspeth gave up and tucked him into bed with the dirty plastic toy still clutched in his fist.

"Eh, well," she said to Will and Nan as she closed the bedroom door, "I'll pop him in the tub tomorrow, and the toy can get clean at the same time. But he's got me that worried," she added in a low voice. "Does he often get quiet like this, Will?"

Will shifted his weight uncomfortably. "Not often."

"I wouldn't think that game you played yesterday would have had such a lasting effect. Perhaps he's worried about his mother. . . ." Cousin Elspeth shot a look at Will, and adopted a more cheerful air. "Maybe it's just a growth spurt. He's shooting up so fast, it's taking up all his energy. I know it's impossible, but I could swear the lad's gone up an inch in a week!"

Will had a sudden coughing fit.

"It's probably your cooking," said Nan brightly.

Cousin Elspeth laughed. "I will say he's taken a better liking to my porridge! And he asked me this morning for a bannock, bless him. We're going to make a Scotsman of him yet." She chuckled, ruffling Will's hair. "I'll bring you lads with me to Castle Menzies this week while Nan's at school. Perhaps Jamie will enjoy playing in all the rooms. Though," she added sternly, "no more telling stories to frighten him, you two."

Will didn't tell Jamie any stories that week at the castle.
ear things up for his little brother. "It all
Will told him on Monday, "Sir Robert
it, but it happened in the past, see? Like
ry."

he plastic Highlander out of his pocket
a talisman. "Go away!"

nie, just try to understand—"

Jamie p   fingers in his ears and ran out of the castle kitchen. "La la la la, I can't hear you!" His voice echoed in the stone hallway and up the stone stairs.

Will trudged up the stairs after him, frowning. There had to be a way to explain things to Jamie. But when he caught sight of his brother running from room to room, peering around corners as if hoping to see someone he knew, something in Will's chest twisted like a cord knotting around his heart, and he walked slowly down again without saying anything.

His mother would have known how to make Jamie feel better. But she wasn't here. Will sank down on the wide stone steps and leaned against the curving wall. He wasn't Jamie's parent; he was only a kid. It wasn't fair that he had to deal with all this on his own.

And what happened to Mom, was that fair? countered a small voice inside his head.

Maybe not, Will answered, but *she* had made the choice that got her into trouble. He had not had any choice at all.

Something snuffled at his elbow, and Will lifted his face to see Gormlaith's long nose and anxious brown eyes.

"Good old girl." Will rubbed the dog gently behind the ears. Gormlaith drooled on his knee and nudged his arm with her wet black nose. Then she looked up the stairs and whined uneasily.

"Go ahead, Gormly," Will said quietly. "Maybe he needs a dog more than a brother. If he even believes I *am* his brother," he added under his breath.

Gormlaith barked softly, licked his hand, and padded up the spiraling tower steps with an air of purpose.

Will watched her fringed tail disappear around the corner. Did the dog really know how sad Jamie was? It seemed so. "Splendid Lady," Will murmured, remembering the meaning of Gormlaith's name. He had once thought it a stupid description for the clumsy, floppy-eared animal, but he didn't anymore.

An hour later, when he saw Jamie walking with his hand on the dog's back, Will felt an easing of the cord around his heart. Maybe it would be all right, after all.

Tuesday, Will brought along some of his spending money and offered to treat his little brother at the castle tearoom. Jamie came warily, lagging two steps behind, but his eyes brightened at the sight of the sweets in the display case.

The little boy was deep into a bowl of sticky toffee pudding when Will gave it another try. "Hey," he said casually, "about Sir Robert and those guys—"

Jamie scraped back his chair and picked up his bowl and spoon. "I'm going to sit at another table," he announced loudly.

The tearoom attendant glanced curiously at Will.

Will's cheeks turned hot. He grimly put a fork into his cake—it looked like a checkerboard, but he wasn't in the mood to appreciate it—and watched under his lashes as Jamie got predictably sticky.

Mom would want you to wipe his face, came the voice in his head.

Will rolled his eyes. Jamie didn't want his help.

And his hands, the voice went on remorselessly. *You promised to take care of him.*

Sighing, Will dampened a napkin in his water glass and went over to wipe Jamie's face, but the little boy ducked under his hand and ran out of the room.

Will gritted his teeth. Fine, then. If Jamie wanted to run off alone, Will wasn't going to stop him. Let him run around looking for Sir Robert and anyone else he missed, for all the good it would do him.

Grumpily, Will stalked off to the gift shop. At least Cousin Elspeth would talk to him. Or maybe Gormlaith would be up for a game of fetch.

But Cousin Elspeth was talking to tourists, and Gormlaith was napping under the desk. Will browsed aimlessly through the display rack of books, trying to feel an interest and failing miserably. His thoughts, as always, drifted to his mother, the way a tongue went to the space where a tooth had been. Where was she now? What was happening to her? It wouldn't seem so awful if only he could *do* something.

Suddenly he blinked at the book open in his hands. Where had he seen that picture before? A warrior with blue tattoos and a round leather shield looked sternly up from the page as if challenging him.

It was the same book that the old gentleman on the plane had let him look at! Will flipped through the pages with mounting excitement. Here were pictures of all different time periods. Maybe it would be easier to explain things to Jamie with pictures?

He looked at the price, did a mental calculation of pounds to dollars in his head, and winced. It would take nearly all the spending money he had left. No more visits to the tearoom, if he bought it. And he had wanted to try the sticky toffee pudding, too.

Slowly his hand went to his pocket and came out with a

fistful of pound notes. "I'd like to buy this book, please," he told Cousin Elspeth.

Her face glowed with delight. "Do you like history, then, laddie? Perhaps you can get my Nan to take an interest!" She rang up the purchase, talking all the while. "You'll have to show her the page about the Romans. She visited an old Roman fort with her school class! But she didn't seem overly excited about it," the woman added sadly. "Such an opportunity, too."

When Nan came in after school, Will told her his plan. And on the drive from the castle to the house that afternoon, Will pulled the book out of its bag. "Look, Nan," he said, making sure that Jamie could see the pages, "I got this book so we could see what people dressed like when you go back in time. Hey, here's King James the Fourth! He lived, what? Five hundred years ago, or so?"

Jamie paled, shot one startled glance at the book, and then went scarlet with fury. He glared at Will and slid as close to the back door as he could get, turning his whole body to face the window.

Nan slid her eyes sideways. "That worked out well."

"Show her the Romans, Will!"

Cousin Elspeth chirped from the driver's seat. "You'll be interested, Nan—you just had a field trip to Pinnata Castra! Or Inchtuthil, as we call it. In fact, some scholars think that might have been the original Pictish name—" She went on for some time.

Will had to admit he'd wasted his money; his brilliant idea had only made things worse. The minute the car stopped, Jamie stalked off without a word. And he spent the rest of the evening sitting by the burn with his arm around Gormlaith, staring into the distance as if waiting for someone to come riding over the hills.

By Thursday, Jamie had turned sullen. At supper, he said nothing at all, and his face looked so miserable that Cousin Elspeth told Will she thought he was going to be sick.

That night, Will went to his room five minutes after Jamie had been put to bed, but his little brother lay still with his face turned to the wall, his eyes shut tight.

Will got into his pajamas and under the covers. "I know you're awake," he said quietly.

Jamie did not stir.

"You can talk to me, you know," said Will. "I'm your *brother*."

Jamie said nothing.

"I know Mom and Dad aren't here," Will went on doggedly. "But Dad told me to take care of you, and I'm trying my best, really I am. I'm sorry you miss Sir Robert so much. I'm sorry about everything."

Will listened until it seemed he could hear the dust fall and a spider spinning its web in a high corner. He breathed shallowly, waiting for a response, but it never came. After a while he closed his eyes.

He woke to a muffled sound he couldn't identify. His eyes went to the clock on the dresser; it was after midnight. The moon had risen, and a cold pale light streamed through the narrow window.

The sound came again, and this time he recognized it: a sob, smothered in a pillow.

Will pushed back the covers and sat on Jamie's bed, his throat aching with pity.

The small body stiffened, and the sobs ceased with a gulp. Will laid his hand on Jamie's hair, stroking it as he had seen his mother do, slowly and gently.

The silence grew. Just when Will was thinking of going back to bed, Jamie spoke.

"What?" Will leaned close. "I didn't hear—"

Jamie rolled over, showing a crumpled face. "Gormly," he whispered again.

The moon's light caught the wispy ends of Jamie's hair, standing up in sweaty tufts. His eyes were shadowed, but the pleading in them was unmistakable.

Of course they weren't supposed to let the dog up into their bedroom. Nan's mother had been very clear about that.

"All right. Wait here." Will tiptoed down the hall, feeling like a criminal. Cousin Elspeth had been so kind; he really should obey her rules. She hadn't made many. . . .

He quietly unlocked the back door and went out. The gravel hurt his bare feet, and too late, he remembered his shoes.

He squatted at the door to Gormlaith's kennel and spoke quietly. "Gormly?"

There was a snuffle and a thump. Gormlaith launched herself out of the kennel, barking with wild joy, her paws heavy on his chest.

"Oof!" Will got out from under her with a sideways wriggle and rolled into the shadow on the far side of the kennel. "Quiet, girl! Shhh!"

Gormlaith subsided into muted, ecstatic whines. Will stared anxiously up at the darkened windows of the house. If a light went on . . .

But it didn't. Five minutes later, his hand on Gormlaith's collar to keep the jingling tags quiet, Will slipped up the stairs and into the bedroom he shared with Jamie.

"Oh!" Jamie sat bolt upright, and Gormlaith leaped into his arms, bowling him over in a frenzy of wild face licking. A muffled giggle emerged from beneath the squirming heap of dog, and Will closed the door quickly, grinning.

"Shhh!" He leaned over the bed, and his hands closed around Gormlaith's muzzle. "Quiet, Gormly, or you can't stay. You hear me?"

Gormlaith moaned softly in her throat.

"And, Jamie, you have to go right to sleep now. Promise?"

Jamie nodded. "Can she really stay all night?" he whispered.

"Most of it. I'll take her out in the morning before Cousin Elspeth wakes up. And it'll be our secret, okay?"

"Yes," Jamie said, snuggling down again. He pressed his back against Gormlaith's heaving flank and shut his eyes, smiling.

By some miracle, Will managed to wake up just as the sun rose and get the dog out before anyone discovered him. He stood for a moment, listening to the sweet repeated calls of what seemed like five hundred birds. In that moment, the pink-and-gold glory of the sky and the piercing sweetness of the birdsong made it possible to believe that everything would be all right. Any day now, a call might come to say that his mother was safe, and coming home.

"Please, *please* help it happen," he said with his face lifted to the sky.

At breakfast, Cousin Elspeth watched Jamie closely, the skin above her nose wrinkling in a slight frown. When Nan ran out the door for the school bus, Cousin Elspeth stood abruptly.

"Will," she said, rummaging in a corner closet, "I'll let you lads use Ewen's—that is, Nan's father's—metal detector today. You must promise to be careful with it, mind! But you can have fun looking for coins that the tourists have dropped. Who knows, you might even find something that's been buried a long time."

Jamie looked up. "Treasure?" he said, brightening.

Cousin Elspeth's face relaxed into a relieved smile. "You never know, laddie!"

ৰ৹

The metal detector was fun, Will had to admit. It had a box with a dial, and a long wand with a thing on the end that reminded Will of a ski-pole basket. Cousin Elspeth had shown him how to sweep it slowly over the ground; when it came upon something metal, it gave a high-pitched *beeeeeep*. Jamie, interested and happy for the first time in almost a week, followed with a trowel and helped dig up what they had found. By lunchtime they were richer by two crowns, fifteen pence, and a quarter.

"That must have come from an American tourist," Will told Jamie, who happily put it in his pocket.

"You had good luck!" said Cousin Elspeth at the front desk when they showed her the coins. "You could spend that in the tearoom, for pudding!"

Will grinned. Pudding, he had found, was what Cousin

Elspeth called *any* kind of dessert except cookies (which were biscuits).

"Yeah!" Jamie was beaming. "Can we, Will?"

"You'll need more than a quarter. Here." Will tipped the rest of the coins into Jamie's pocket and watched him skip down the hall to the tearoom. There wasn't enough money for Will to have dessert, too, but it didn't matter. He had done it. Jamie was comfortable in his own time once more.

Will wandered out to the old kitchen garden, where they had left the metal detector, and, by standing on a convenient bench, hitched himself up on top of the gray stone wall. It was warm from the sun, and he lay back and gazed at the clouds scudding across deep blue sky. There was a wind, high up, but here in the sheltered garden he felt only calm.

Would his father be proud of him? Would it make his mother happy, that he was taking care of Jamie? Yes, he decided . . . as long as she could forget how he had refused to hug her that last time.

He had been angry, though, so angry it was like a bitter taste in his mouth. It wasn't much of an excuse, but it was all he had. And while he wasn't mad anymore—he couldn't stay angry forever, he had found—the sadness wouldn't go away. He still didn't understand why his mother had left them.

No, he corrected himself, he could understand part of it. Those sick kids, they had needed her. He could see that. What he couldn't get was how she had put those other kids ahead of him and Jamie. That part, he would never understand.

The clouds slipped away from the sun, and Will squinted against the sudden brightness. The warmth beat against his face in waves like heat from a fire, like light from a burning castle. . . .

And what would his mother think of what *he* had done? How he had run away when Castle Menzies went up in flames, after he had opened the door to the Stewarts?

Will made an instinctive motion of protest. He had gotten his brother and cousin to safety—that should be good enough for anyone. He didn't want to think about it anymore. He would just wait here on the wall for Jamie, and they would go looking for treasure.

His eyes closed slowly as his thoughts drifted. Nan would be home from school soon, too. . . . Maybe they would find more coins, enough so he could have his sticky toffee pudding after all. . . .

He awoke with a start and sat up, dazed. How long had he been asleep? And where was Jamie? The metal detector was gone.

Will hopped off the wall to wander the grounds, calling for Jamie and whacking at bushes with a long stick, pretending they were Stewarts. He was knocking a dead branch off a tree whose pointed sharpness reminded him of Neil Gointe's face, when Nan found him. "You've got wood bits in your hair," she informed him. "Where's Jamie?"

"He's off somewhere with the metal detector."

Nan stared. "Mum let Jamie take Dad's detector all by himself? Dad's not going to like that if he ever finds out."

Will gave the branch a last whack, and it fell with a dry-sounding creak. "Do you think I should go back and warn Sir Robert?"

"I've been wondering the same thing." Nan fished in her satchel and pulled out the Magic Eyeball book, which looked a little battered around the corners. "Here."

"What's that for?"

"Just in case you decide to go." Nan gazed at him ear-nestly, her freckles standing out against her pale skin.

Will took it with reluctant fingers. "I suppose I could open a window," he said. "It wouldn't hurt to look."

"Face the castle," Nan suggested. "Go back to a time before the fire. Then we can run in quick, warn somebody—"

"Cook, maybe," said Will, sitting up. "If I told her the old pot boy was really a Stewart spy, I bet she'd get Sir Robert to listen."

"Go on, then." Nan knelt behind Will and put her hand on his shoulder. "We can nip in and come right back."

"All right." Will held out the book at arm's length.

It was easier every time he did it. Maybe everything got easier with practice. The past slid into focus, and Will could feel it there, waiting, behind the book in his hands. Only this time there seemed to be faint tracks that he could sense, too, like the fine glimmering threads of a spider's web, nearly invisible. Now that he thought about it, he had noticed something like that before. . . .

Nan shifted behind him. "Better hurry up, before Jamie decides to come find us."

"Quiet, will you? This takes concentration." Will held the focus, moved it in and out slightly, and—there! It was as if the faint threads had suddenly caught the light. He could sense them clearly now. Some were thicker, as if they had been traveled more than once, or by more than one person. . . .

Will lowered the book to reveal the gray light of dawn. Through the ragged opening of the time window they could see the castle, a smoking, blackened mass of collapsed stone walls and burnt timbers poking up like rotten teeth. Around it, people huddled, weeping. Some were poking through the ashes.

Nan took in a breath behind him. "You've got to get to an earlier time."

"I know." He shook his head to break the focus and lifted the book to try again. If he did it right this time, there would be no fire, no ruined castle, and Sir Robert would be safe. Will gazed ahead, ever so slightly beyond the book, and felt with his mind's eye for the shimmering sense that told him now, this was the right time, right *here*—

But there was a grayness, a sort of blockage, in the way. He tried to beat at it with his mind and it . . . resisted. It was as if he were pounding at a rubber wall.

He could almost feel the heat from the fire. Will tried to probe back before the warmth, before the fire had been set, but the faintly shining threads went into the gray blankness and disappeared. He couldn't follow them.

How far back in time did the gray part go? Will pushed his focus deeper into the past. He couldn't exactly tell how long before the fire he was going—days, weeks?—but it felt as if the grayness was lifting slightly. If he pushed just a little bit more—

"Hurry up, can't you? What's the matter?" Nan's voice was in his ear.

Will tossed down the book and rubbed his forehead, which had begun to ache. "Something is stopping me. I can't go back before the fire. It's all—I don't know, just *gray*. Like there's nothing there."

"Try again, okay? Maybe the fire is causing some kind of energy surge or something. Maybe it's messing up the time window. Go back farther."

"I have been! I'm telling you, it won't let me!"

"All right, all right, calm down." Nan picked at a frond

of bracken, shredding it between her fingers. "What do you think it means?"

Will gazed at the castle. It was beautiful in the afternoon sun, warm and golden. "I don't know. Maybe it means I'm not supposed to go back."

"Says who?"

Will shrugged. "Maybe there are rules to time travel; we just don't know them yet."

Nan let the bracken fragments sift slowly out of her hands. A small willful breeze stirred them up and whirled them away. "What if," she said slowly, "you can't live through a time twice?"

Will's eyebrows lifted. "But going back in time is living through something that's already happened."

"Right, but it's happened to *other* people. What if we can live through any time at all, in the whole history of the world—but we only get to do it *once*?"

"Huh." Will stared out at the castle without seeing it. "But then why couldn't I just go to the day before we first came to the past? We haven't lived that time yet."

Nan grabbed both sides of her head. "Wait a minute— I'm getting an idea—don't talk to me yet." She screwed her eyes shut and wrinkled up her mouth.

Will rolled his eyes but was obligingly silent.

"We can't go back then because we might *stay*, see?" Nan opened her eyes wide to stare at Will. "We might stay in the time we aren't supposed to live twice! Don't you think that's the reason?"

Will shrugged again. "If it's some kind of rule, then maybe when we hit the time we've already lived, we just get sent ahead to our own time. Or maybe," he added slowly, "we just go into the gray bit . . ."

"And never come back!" Nan said in a dramatic whisper.

Will had no intention of getting lost in some gray part of time. And he had thought of something else. "If we did go to a time earlier than we went before," he said, "then Jamie would still be there. We'd have to convince him to come with us all over again."

Nan's forehead ridged. "But Jamie is still here, in this time. What would happen to *our* Jamie, if we go back? Would he just . . . disappear?"

Will shrugged for the third time, though he did not feel nearly so casual about it as he had before. "I don't really know." He ran his hand along the stem of a furze bush, setting its yellow flowers trembling.

"Well, we can't do it, then," said Nan with sudden decision.

Will tried not to show his relief. "I guess not."

"And it's not as if Sir Robert didn't already know the Stewarts were dangerous. Probably people had been warning him all along."

Will crushed one of the yellow blossoms between his

fingers, and a sweet scent wafted up. "Do you think Neil Gointe Stewart would starve them? Sir Robert and that little boy?"

"No," said Nan. "Bread and water, that's what people got in dungeons. And sometimes gruel . . . that's watery porridge. Boring food, but it would keep somebody alive, anyway."

Will dusted his fingers, and bits of yellow dropped to the ground. "But they might be in chains. Fetters, you know, around their ankles, and slime on the walls, and *rats*—"

Nan clapped her hands over her ears. "Stop! We can't do anything, so it's no good talking. Anyway, it's all over now, it happened hundreds of years ago, so there!"

Will expelled his breath in a long sigh. It *was* over now. He would just keep telling himself that. It was over. It was over.

He watched as a blue car drove up to the castle and parked. More tourists, he thought bitterly. They probably thought dungeons were *fun*.

A tall man with sandy hair, slightly balding, got out of the car and stretched. He looked familiar, somehow. Will narrowed his eyes. "Who's that?"

"Daddy!" Nan jumped up and took off running.

Will watched as Nan leaped into her father's arms, and something prickled at the back of his throat. Someday Will's own father and mother might drive up to the castle, just as suddenly. For a moment he wanted it so strongly he could almost hear the car.

He followed Nan at a slower pace. "Hello, sir," he said as Nan introduced them.

"Call me Cousin Ewen," said the man. He was tall and lanky, and bent slightly to shake Will's hand. "I'm glad to meet you, Will. You have a look of your father."

Will smiled politely. "And everybody says Jamie looks like Mom." He squinted up at Cousin Ewen against the sun's light. The man's face had strong features, with kind eyes, and he looked—just a little—like Sir Robert.

Cousin Ewen looked around. "Where is Jamie, then?"

Will opened his mouth and shut it again. He didn't want to say that Jamie had run off with Cousin Ewen's metal detector, not when Cousin Elspeth had made Will promise to be so careful with it. "He's out digging holes," he said.

Cousin Ewen glanced around the castle grounds. "By himself? Where?"

Will spun slowly on his heel, looking at the trees, the rocks, the hill rising behind him, hoping by some miracle that Jamie would suddenly appear.

"There he is!" said Nan, pointing.

Jamie ran toward them, a small frantically waving figure. "Will! Nan! I found buried treasure!" He tore back up the hillside and disappeared in the shadow of the trees.

Nan and Will ran to catch up with Cousin Ewen, whose long legs were making good time up the hill.

"It's probably just more coins," said Will, panting. "Or a rusty nail."

"Once," said Nan between breaths, "I found a watch someone had dropped. It didn't work, though."

But Jamie seemed to have found something more interesting than coins or a watch. When Nan and Will came upon them at last, Jamie was watching with barely suppressed glee as Cousin Ewen knelt over a hole in the ground, enlarging it carefully with the trowel.

Will noted with some guilt that the metal detector was lying on the ground a few feet away, but Nan's father wasn't paying it any attention. His whole body seemed alert, somehow, and his eyes never left the object in the hole.

"What did Jamie find, Dad?" Nan squatted next to her father and peered in the hole. "A hunk of scrap iron?"

Cousin Ewen sat back on his heels and set down the trowel. "Iron, yes—or bronze, maybe—but not scrap. Look here." He traced with his finger the curving piece of metal, like an upside-down bowl, that showed in the small hole Jamie had dug. "Do you see this? That's a bit of a design that someone worked on. It's scalloped along this side, see—like the edge of a wing, maybe."

He scraped away some loose dirt with his fingernail, and now Will could see it, too—regular lines on a curved surface. The metal was dark, and pitted, but clearly it had been made by humans a long time ago. "What do you think it is, sir?" he asked.

"I'm no expert," said Cousin Ewen, "but I wonder if that isn't a Roman helmet. If so, it's an important find, Jamie." He grinned. "I won't even mind that you used my metal detector without permission, as long as you found something like this."

"We did have permission," Will said quickly, "from Cousin Elspeth. But Jamie wasn't supposed to go off with it by himself."

Cousin Ewen chuckled. "Never mind, lads." He stood, rocking back to stretch his legs, and picked up the metal

detector. "I'm going to get some proper tools. With a find this important, I'd better take care digging it up before I bring it over to the museum."

"But don't I get to keep my helmet?" Jamie wailed. "I found it!"

The tall man shook his head. "It's not yours, strictly speaking, Jamie—it's the property of the Crown."

Jamie rubbed his forehead. "But I don't see what King James wants with an old Roman helmet—"

"It's not King James anymore!" Will whispered urgently.

Nan took Jamie's hand. "Come on, let's help Dad get the tools. I bet they'll put your picture in the paper and everything!"

༻

That night Will and Jamie's father called. Jamie, who had taken an instant liking to Cousin Ewen, seemed unsure about who his father might be. He took the phone in his hand awkwardly, with an uncertain glance at his brother.

Will's heart sank. Jamie couldn't have forgotten his *father*—could he? But then, it had been a whole year since Jamie had seen him. . . . "Tell him about your helmet," Will suggested.

When it was Will's turn to talk, he gripped the phone with a hand that felt suddenly sweaty. "How are things going?" he asked.

"Oh, fine." His father's voice came through the line with what sounded like forced cheer. "Things are moving right along."

"Are you bringing Mom home?"

"Not quite yet," his father answered. "But soon, I'm sure. Don't you worry, son, that's my job. Your job is to take care of your little brother, and be sure to obey Cousin Elspeth. I love you—"

Will clutched the phone a little tighter. "Have you seen Mom yet? Is she okay?"

"I'm told she's fine." Will's father spoke rapidly. "Now, can you put Ewen on the line, please? I don't have much time to talk—"

Cousin Ewen took the phone and listened. Will watched his face grow serious. When he put his hand on the wall, as if to steady himself, Will turned away. Something that felt like ice water seemed to be trickling through his bones, making his legs feel weak. What was his father saying to Cousin Ewen that he wouldn't tell his son?

Someone nudged him. "What's happening?" Nan hissed.

Will flapped his hand to get her to be quiet. He was trying to listen. Cousin Ewen was saying things he didn't understand. Something about a consulate, and the American Embassy.

"Well?" Nan said, a little louder. "What did your dad tell you?"

Cousin Ewen glanced at them both and turned away, speaking more softly.

Will glared at her. Couldn't she take a hint? Now he'd lost his chance to find out more.

"Oh, sorry," Nan said, belatedly figuring it out.

A small hand slid into Will's, and Jamie looked up into his face. "What was that book you were looking at before?" Jamie asked. "About history?"

Later, Nan found them sprawled on the floor in Will's bedroom, their heads bent over the book Will had bought in the gift shop. She lingered in the doorway to listen.

"See?" Will was saying. "Here's the time you remember."

"That's King James," Jamie said, jabbing at the book with a pudgy finger. "James the Fourth. He came to our castle once."

"Yep. And if you turn the pages, you can see what happened after that. . . . And here we are at our time. You can tell because of the cars and planes."

Nan, at the door, made a sudden noise like a hiccup. "I've got it!"

"What now?" Will glared up at her. Just as he was getting Jamie to look at the book, Nan had to jump in the middle of everything!

"I know how to explain it to him! Listen, Jamie." Nan flopped down on the floor and folded her legs beneath her. "See how we're at modern times, now, on this page?"

Jamie nodded.

"Well, look." Nan stuck her finger in the book to hold the place and flipped back through the pages. "Here we are at Sir Robert's time again. Can you see the page for our time now?"

Jamie shook his head.

"But it's still there, right?"

Jamie stuck out his lower lip a little. "Of course it's still there. I'm not stupid!"

"But don't you see?" Nan leaned over the book. "It's just like going through the time window. When you were back in Sir Robert's time, here"—her finger jabbed at the picture of King James IV—"you couldn't see our time, because you weren't *in* it then. You weren't on that page."

"So to speak," Will said cautiously. Was Jamie going to get angry again? Was Nan going to confuse him more?

"But it was still there all along," Nan went on. "When you crawled through the time window to *our* time, Sir Robert's time was still going on, only now you weren't on *that* page anymore, so you couldn't see it. Does that make sense?"

"Sort of." Jamie frowned and reached for the book. "I want to look at the Romans again." He paged carefully back until he came to a picture of a soldier with spear and shield, outfitted in shoulder pads and breastplate, with an ornate red-crested helmet on his head. "Nobody could hurt some-body who had all that on, right?"

"It wouldn't be easy," Will agreed.

There was a muffled sound in the hall, and Will turned to see Cousin Elspeth, wiping at her eyes. She put on a bright smile and came into the room. "Do you like history, then, lads? Why don't you let Nan take you up to see Saint David's Well tomorrow? That's not a long hike, and it's got a good bit of history to it. It's a pretty view, too. I'll pack you a picnic lunch."

Jamie looked up. "Was Saint David a Roman?"

Cousin Ewen appeared in the doorway behind his wife. "No, he was a Menzies. But if you're interested in Romans, there are going to be some historical reenactors here tomorrow, staging a battle in the field. You could learn a lot!"

"Um—we'll go to Saint David's Well, thanks," Nan said hurriedly. "Less like school."

"What are reenactors?" Jamie wanted to know.

Nan snorted. "Grown-ups who like to play 'let's pretend we live back in the past.' They get dressed up in costumes and whack each other with swords and things."

"Real swords?" said Jamie, looking worried.

"Yes, but it's a mock fight—they don't hurt each other," Nan's father assured him. "At least not much, and not on purpose."

Will asked, "Were there really Romans here once? I mean at Castle Menzies?"

Cousin Ewen stroked his chin. "It's possible. They built

190

a fort only about twenty miles from here, at Inchtuthil. The Romans called it Pinnata Castra—fortress on the wing. You remember, Nan, you went on a field trip there once—"

Nan glanced at Will and rolled her eyes ever so slightly.

"And the Romans might have sent riders out from the fort when they were trying to subdue the natives." Cousin Ewen grinned wickedly. "They didn't succeed, I might add."

Jamie's face twisted up into worry. "Did the Romans fight people who lived at the castle?"

"No," said Cousin Ewen, "because the castle hadn't been built yet. We're talking two thousand years ago."

"Oh," said Jamie, his face clearing. "That's all right, then."

8

SAINT DAVID'S WELL

THE PATH TO SAINT DAVID'S Well wound up and up through Weem Wood; past Nan's father, who was pruning trees in the garden; beyond the historical reenactors, who were beginning to pull into the parking lot. Gormlaith yanked the leash out of Nan's hand and rocketed off to chase a squirrel ("Don't worry," said Nan, "she never catches anything.") and circled back, panting with her mouth open in a goofy grin, only to take off after a rabbit and disappear again, ears flopping.

The children passed great slabs of rock, seamed and furred with moss, and jumped over small trickles of water. Bracken crowded the path, thickly green, swishing at their legs as they trudged higher and higher. In the steepest parts flat stones had been set, making a sort of irregular stair.

Will half expected Jamie to complain that the walk was too long. Certainly the Jamie of just a week ago would have been whining already. But this Jamie trotted up the path with bright eyes, turning his head this way and that, and patting the boulders he passed as if they were old friends. "I know the way to the well," he announced. "I used to go there all the time. There's a hermit's cave there, too, close by."

"Where?" Will wiped his forehead with his sleeve.

"I'll show you. They say you can follow the cave into the hill for miles!"

"No, you can't," Nan said. "I know that cave. It's all blocked up with rubble."

"How did the old hermit live in it, then?" Jamie fired back.

But when they came to the cave, Nan was right. Jamie turned back from the choked entrance to the cave with a look of bewilderment. "I was sure this was the place."

"This *is* the place," said Nan, "but so many years have passed that it's all different."

"It looks like half the ceiling fell in." Will stepped back. He hoped the old hermit, whoever he was, hadn't been inside when it happened. "Come on, let's go up to the well and eat lunch. I'm starving."

"What about Gormly?" asked Jamie.

Nan snorted. "She'll come when she smells food."

Saint David's Well was made of flat, smooth slabs of

stone surrounding a rectangular basin of water, dark in the shadow of the overhanging rock cliff. The pool was coffin shaped, and Will felt a chill between his shoulder blades.

He turned his back and stepped out onto the wide, grassy wedge of turf, like a terrace, that overlooked the valley below. The sun was bright on the tops of trees; across the valley, the forest fit snugly over the hilltops like a thick green blanket. As clouds moved briskly overhead, the faraway greens changed from bright to dark and then back again, so that the hill seemed to ripple with light.

"Lunch!" said Nan, pulling a large packet out of her ever-present satchel.

There were roast beef sandwiches on thickly cut bread, with tomatoes and cheese. There were three apples, red and crisp with juice. There were packets of chips—Nan called them crisps—and carrot sticks, and hard-boiled eggs, and nearly half a chocolate cake. Nan cut the cake with her penknife and opened three bottles of fizzy lemonade. They sat down on a low, lichen-covered rock to eat. For a long time there was a steady sound of chewing and not much else. When Gormlaith appeared, drooling happily, Nan snapped the dog's leash around a convenient tree and gave her two sandwiches.

Jamie finished eating first. He dug inside Nan's satchel and pulled out the Magic Eyeball book.

Will slanted a look at Nan. "Did you have to bring that?"

Nan lifted one shoulder and grinned. "You never know, it might come in handy. See, I have this history project due after the school break—"

"Forget it." Will resolutely ignored her dimple. "I'm staying in my own time, thanks very much."

Jamie opened the book. "But how do you *do* it? I want to know." He faced the cliff behind them, held the book out at arm's length, and squinted. "Nothing's happening. How come you can do it, and I can't?"

A small satisfaction warmed Will's chest. Jamie had bragged about seeing the hidden pictures when his brother couldn't, but the pictures Will could see were *real*.

Jamie's lower lip pushed out. "Show me how, please? Please please *please*—"

"Go on, why don't you?" Nan began to pack up the litter from their lunch. "It's not likely he'll be able to do it, anyway," she added in a low voice.

Will didn't let himself get close to the book. Nothing would happen if he didn't touch it. "Okay," he said. "Just look at the page—only sort of gaze past it, like you're looking at something farther on, see?"

Jamie frowned. "That's what you do to see the hidden pictures. I can see those all right."

"No, you have to look past the hidden pictures, too." Will had never seen the hidden pictures in the first place, but it was as good a guess as any.

"Should I look all the way to the cliff?"

Will wasn't sure. How far away did he usually focus his eyes? He stared at the cliff face, and the crack in the rock that looked as if it, too, might be a cave if only it went a little farther in. Then he pulled his focus back a little, so he was focused on a spot of nothing in the middle of the clear air. He pulled back a little more—and a little more—

The air shimmered; the cliff face seemed subtly changed. Gormlaith whined. Instinctively Will jerked his head to one side, and the shimmer in the air disappeared. His pulse beat rapidly in his throat.

Jamie, who hadn't seemed to notice, said, "I'm going to try from farther away." He stepped back as Nan was clearing the picnic things off the rock, and looked down. Then he let the Magic Eyeball book fall. "Hey, look! Circles in the rock!"

Will peered over his brother's shoulder. Amid the dull, fuzzy lichen, the rock was dotted with small round holes, less than an inch wide, and not very deep. At first glance they just seemed like natural flaws in the stone. But some of the holes were surrounded by concentric rings, and a few of those had a straight line running out from the center. Somebody had worked a long time to pound those holes. Will squatted down to trace one of the rings with his finger. He felt strangely crowded, as if there were someone behind him, pushing. . . .

"They're called cup marks," said Nan. "My dad says people made those thousands of years ago, maybe in the Copper Age. Nobody knows why."

Jamie gave an excited bounce. "Did they leave stuff we can dig up?"

"Aye, if you want to dive for it," Nan said. "They found some dugout canoes under Loch Tay, buried in the mud, and pilings from a crannog, and they're digging up more now. But the water's cold and dark."

"What's a crannog?" Jamie was hopping on both feet now.

"It's a big sort of hut built out over the water, with a walkway to it. You can see one at the Crannog Centre, and walk right into the hut, and look down into Loch Tay—"

"Can we go? Would your dad take us?" Jamie bobbed up and down, waving his arms as if he were about to fly.

Nan sighed. "He'd take you in a heartbeat. The problem is, he'd probably make me come along and *learn* something."

"Yay!" shrieked Jamie, his arms windmilling. "Let's go ask him right *now*! Come on, Gormly!" He unsnapped the leash and tore down the path, Gormlaith galloping alongside.

Nan's dimple flitted into sight. "Back to the old Jamie."

"Yeah." Will grinned.

Nan stuffed the Magic Eyeball book into her satchel with the picnic things. "We'd better dampen his enthusiasm a bit, or Dad will have us all signed up for classes before you know it."

Will hesitated. "Go ahead. I'll come in a minute."

He watched Nan skip down the path and round the bend. Then he turned. Before him was Saint David's Well, dark and still, below the massive, looming cliff.

Had he really done it? Had he opened a window into the past, without the book? This was as good a time as any to find out.

Will gazed at the air in front of the rock, focusing his eyes in small increments forward, back, trying to sense the spot in the past where he had almost opened a window before, probing with the strange, delicate new awareness that was as sensitive as a moth's antenna. There was no thin transparent golden thread, this time—of course not, no one had gone through—but he could feel something like a little rounded dent, or a dimple, in the fabric of the past. He was almost . . . *there*. . . .

The air before him moved slightly, like a sheer gauze curtain in a breeze. Will kept his focus steady. He found it even easier than before; perhaps it was because he didn't have anyone distracting him. How big, he wondered, could he make the window?

The edges were hard to locate without moving his eyes; the cliff looked almost the same in both times. But the light on the rock, and the bits of lichen, were different. Could he lengthen the time window slightly, make it the shape of a door? He experimented, carefully.

No, it didn't change shape; it remained squarish with rounded corners. Like anyone's field of vision, it was sharpest in the center and fuzzy around the edges. But he could enlarge it, he found, by moving his focus slowly away. Now the opening was taller than he was, and touching the ground. Just a little bigger, and a car could drive through.

Will's chest expanded. He'd mastered it! He didn't need the Magic Eyeball book to open a window into time; he could do it all by himself. Anytime he wanted, he could walk into the past. . . . Where would he end up, if he stepped through right this minute? He wasn't crazy enough to *do* it; he'd probably end up in another clan war. But maybe, if he moved the window to the side, he would see a clue to how far back in the past it was.

He rotated slowly in place. The time window, large as a garage door, moved with his gaze, past the cliff, past the well, across the path. The giant window hung there, wavering slightly. If you gazed straight ahead and not off to the sides, it looked almost ordinary: just a simple trick of the light as it filtered through the branches.

Leaves rustled overhead; behind him a bird trilled. There was a muffled, rhythmic sound, like a branch knocking in the breeze, or perhaps footsteps. Suddenly a man rounded a bend in the path, lifted his hand, and walked through the window into Will's time.

Will gasped; he blinked. The time window snapped shut, and the man looked at him.

He was tall, with gray hair in a fringe around his ears. He held a cloth bag in one hand and a walking stick in the other, and he seemed to be wearing a kind of bathrobe.

"Who are you, my lad? Art from the village, then?" The man's eyebrows were thick and untidy, but his eyes were vividly green. They rested with what looked like astonished amusement on Will's shorts and T-shirt.

Will opened and shut his mouth, like a fish.

"Dumb, are ye?"

Will felt the red rise to his ears. He shook his head. He might not think of things to say as quickly as Nan, but he was far from stupid.

"If naught is wrong with your speech, why not answer my question?"

The flush left Will's face as he realized the man had used the word *dumb* in the old sense, meaning "unable to speak."

"My name is Will," he said. "William Menzies."

The man's face crinkled into a smile. "And I am David Menzies."

Will stared. "Are you the hermit? *Saint* David?"

The man laughed out loud. "Certainly not a saint yet, though the good God knows all, and he sees I try! I am Sir David Menzies, once laird of the castle and chief of Clan Menzies."

"You're not the chief anymore?" Will blurted out. "Why not?"

Sir David shrugged. "I tired of worldly things." He lifted the hem of his robe briefly and let it drop. "I wear the garb of a monk now, and it suits me. I have had enough of power and the tumults of kings." His smile deepened, and for a moment a dimple showed in one cheek, exactly like Nan's. "And what are you doing up here, young William?"

"Nothing." Will took a step back as the man came closer.

The monk put up a hand. "No fear, laddie. You can run faster than I, in any case."

Will took another look at the man leaning on his stick, decided this was probably true, and relaxed. "What are *you* doing up here, sir?" he asked. Maybe, if he kept the man distracted by talking, he could open the time window and get him to walk through it.

Sir David lifted the bag in his hand. "Gathering herbs, and roots, and things I need. This is tansy, see? It makes a lovely tea, good for the bones. And here is Saint John's wort, good for all sorts of ills." He smiled a little, and stooped to look into Will's eyes. "And what ills might you have?" he asked gently. "Did you come up to seek my counsel?"

Will frowned. "No," he said. "I'm fine."

"Truly?" said the monk.

Will looked away. The only problem he had right now was how to get Sir David back to his own time. Unless you counted worrying about his mother, but no monk from the Middle Ages could help with *that*.

Sir David nodded gently some seven times, crossed the green wedge of lawn, and seated himself on the picnic rock. "Sometimes it is good to speak of what ails you," he said mildly.

Will cleared his throat. "Do you ever think about time?" he asked.

The monk didn't look surprised. "Time present, time past, or time to come?"

"All of it." Will crossed the green terrace and looked out

over the valley. The River Tay twisted here and there, and off to the west he could see a glimmer that he thought was Loch Tay . . . but in the other direction, much farther than he could see, he knew the river flowed on and on until at last it reached the sea. "I think time is like a river," he said slowly. He broke off a stray branch and swished it in the air, watching the leaves flutter.

Sir David sat quietly on the rock, tracing the cup marks with one long finger. "Tell me what you mean," he suggested.

"Well, where the river comes from is like the past," Will said. "And where it goes to is the future."

"True enough," said the monk, smiling. "And we cannot see around the twists and turns, can we? But we ride on the current, always moving, and the river carries all souls to the sea, which is eternity."

Will whacked the tops of weeds off with the branch. "But if someone swam to the bank, got out of the river, and walked around the bend, he could get to a different time."

The man's smile made deep creases appear on his face. "Ah, I have often wished to do so, laddie. I would go back and undo all my mistakes."

"No, you can't do that," said Will, "but you can visit a time you haven't already lived. Like, way in the past. Or even the future," he added, looking sideways at the monk.

"No man knows the future, save God," said the man. He spoke gently, as if to a young child.

The breeze lifted Will's hair away from the sweaty back of his neck and cooled his skin. "You *can* do it. In fact, you just did. Sir, this is going to sound odd . . . but did you notice that you passed through a sort of shimmering in the air when you came up here? Something that looked different, somehow?"

Sir David stroked his chin. "'Tis odd that you should say that, lad. There *was* a sort of disturbance, a troubling of the air, but I held up my hand and pronounced a blessing, and stepped through. I am not afraid of the spirits of the air."

"Not spirits," said Will, "just a different way of seeing. You saw into a future time, *my* time, and you stepped into it. Just like stepping up onto the riverbank, and walking forward."

The man frowned. "I think I should give you some yarrow leaf, to soothe your mind. It is clear it is unsettled. Did you say you were from the village? Has someone been giving you black hellebore?"

"I'm not crazy." Will threw his branch over the cliff. "Come here, and I'll show you. Look there!"

The monk stood by Will and looked down. Below him, the modern town of Aberfeldy spread out in buildings of two and three stories. Roads crisscrossed, with cars on them like fast-moving beetles, and on the river a motorboat left a foaming wake.

The man clutched Will's shoulder as if to keep himself from falling. "What witchcraft is this?" he muttered.

"No witchcraft, sir," Will said. "Haven't you heard of the Second Sight?"

Sir David passed a hand over his eyes. "Aye," he said hoarsely. "My mother had it, and the good Saint Columba himself, so it cannot be an evil thing—"

"Well, this is like Second Sight, only it's Time Sight, and it just means you can see through a sort of window into another time than your own. And if the window is open, anyone can just walk right through it."

The monk's brow contracted into a mass of wrinkles. "You opened this window? You, yourself?"

Will nodded.

The man looked down again. "Know you," he said quietly, "what year it is, yonder?"

Will had been waiting for this question. "It's 2019," he said.

The monk wavered slightly, as if his knees had grown suddenly weak. Still, when he turned, his expression was as stern as the cliff's rock face. "You must know that you have brought me here from the year of our Lord 1470. How did you come to choose my time, out of all the times you could have chosen? Did you have some purpose in coming here to trouble us?"

"No! I was thinking about you, because of Saint David's Well, and so I guess the window just naturally opened onto your time." Will pointed to the rock basin of water, against the cliff.

"I told you before, I am no saint, and that is Saint Cuthbert's Well."

"People will call you a saint, though, later on. In five hundred years, people will still call this place Saint David's Well, after you."

The monk sat down abruptly on the rock once more. "So I have left something good after all, in spite of my past mistakes," he said in a low voice, clasping his hands on his knee. He looked up, smiling. "I would like to see this wonder. Can you open the window to my time again? I want to see you do it."

"Yes, sir. You'd better hold on to my shoulder, though."

The monk's grip was firm. Will gazed into the middle distance, feeling with his mind for the spot where the man must have come through. . . .

The air before them moved slightly, like a sheer gauze curtain. Behind Will, the old man gasped. Within the rough-edged opening, like a picture frame enclosing the past, they could see the figure of a boy running up the path. His hair was dark and long, and his feet were bare, but his plaid was pinned with a silver brooch, and his belt was of polished leather. He stopped to look in all directions, lifting his chin with a distinctive sideways jerk that seemed familiar.

"Robert!" breathed the monk.

Will almost lost his focus. Was it possible? He had only ever seen one person do that exact chin motion before . . . but Jamie's beloved Sir Robert had been a grown man.

"Grandfather!" the boy called, putting a hand to his mouth like a megaphone.

The monk let go of Will's shoulder to step forward. Then he whirled, his eyes wide. "That was my grandson! Where did he go?"

Will held himself perfectly still and kept his focus steady. "You have to touch me to see him," he said. "He can't see or hear you, either, unless you go through."

The monk laid a trembling hand on Will's shoulder. "Get me back to my own time, then, and quickly," he said. "This is a wonder too great for me."

"All right," said Will, "but let's wait until your grandson goes away. If he sees you appear out of thin air, he'll think it's witchcraft for sure."

They watched as the boy glanced here and there, disappointment clear on his face. He slanted his chin up, frowning, and then Will was sure. It *was* Sir Robert, only thirty years younger than when Jamie had known him. And why not? Even the grand laird of Castle Menzies must have been a boy, once.

Robert turned with a snort of impatience and trotted farther along the path, around the bend.

"Quick," said Will, "he might come back."

Sir David cast his bag of herbs through the time window. "You're a good lad," he said. "Be careful with your gift, now, will you? For it might be dangerous, indeed."

"I'll try," Will promised.

Sir David gave him a wink and a nod, and the dimple like Nan's flashed into his cheek once more. Then he stepped through to his own time, picked up his bag of herbs, and called to his grandson. In a moment Will saw the boy running back up the path, gladness on his face.

Will closed his eyes, and the picture was gone. When he opened them again, he could hear voices shouting his name. He ran down the path, where just a moment ago—no, hundreds of years ago—Sir David and his grandson had met. Will leaped tree roots like a deer and bounded farther down the hill.

"There you are! We've been calling and calling!" Nan pointed at the hole in the earth where Jamie had found the Roman helmet. "Gormlaith just dug up something else!"

The dog, dirty-pawed, sniffed at the bottom of the hole and seemed to lose interest. Her leash trailed behind her as she wandered over to a nearby bush and poked her nose beneath its branches.

Jamie, on his knees beside the hole, held out his open hand with a beaming face. "It might be another Roman thing!"

Will took the small metal object from Jamie's grubby palm and held it up away from the shadows. It looked, he thought, like a small harp without any strings. One side was curved and one straight and pointed, and there seemed to be a sort of hinge, too. . . .

"I don't know if it's Roman," he said slowly, "but I think it might be partly gold. See that spot? And there?"

Three heads bent over the object with sudden interest. There were definitely golden gleams here and there.

"Here, let me." Nan carefully picked away at the excess dirt with her penknife. "I bet it used to be covered with thin gold, only most of it flaked off. And see that hinge?" She tapped at it with the knife's point. "It might be a sort of a pin—you know, like the pins ladies wear in their scarves sometimes?"

Jamie snatched the curved bit of metal from Nan's hand. "My Roman guy wouldn't wear a lady's scarf. I bet he *stabbed* things with this."

"*Your* Roman guy?" Nan countered. "Since when?"

"Since I dug up his helmet!" Jamie's face was flushed. "And Gormly dug this up when I was with her, so I get to say what it is!"

Will stepped back, frowning slightly. He had thought his little brother was back to normal, but now he wasn't so sure. "It's all right, Jamie, calm down," he said. "It does look like you could stab stuff with it—"

"Like *cloth*," Nan said, dimpling.

"But we can show it to Cousin Ewen," Will went on, "and he'll tell us for sure."

"Hey! I have a better idea!" Nan clapped her hands, and her penknife fell to the earth. "Why don't you open a time window, Will? Then we can see the Roman for ourselves."

"Yeah!" Jamie leaped up wildly. "I want to see my Roman guy! *And* his helmet, *and* his stabber—"

Behind them, Gormlaith stopped sniffing dirt and looked up, her ears alert.

"*No*," said Will.

"Oh, come on." Nan tugged at his elbow. "It will be fun. And it will settle an argument."

Jamie stood still. "You *said* we could go back and forth. Just like the pages in a book. And I want to see my Roman."

Will hesitated. It went against his better judgment. Still, if it helped Jamie understand better about moving through time . . .

"All right," he said. "But only to look. We're *not* going through."

Nan dug inside her satchel. She had the Magic Eyeball book halfway out when Will put a hand on her wrist.

"Forget the book—I don't need it anymore. Just put the—uh, stabber on the ground by my foot, and let me concentrate."

Nan and Jamie moved close, and Will slid his foot until the toe of his sneakers touched the Roman pin. Down the hill, through the trees, he could see a bit of the castle, and the historical reenactors busy setting up awnings in the parking lot.

He took a deep breath and blocked out everything but his thoughts of the Roman helmet, and the pin, and the man who had worn them. He focused on a point in the air ahead, moving his focus in tiny increments and searching with the part of his mind he had begun to call Time Sight. He searched back, back, farther than he had ever gone before. It felt like hundreds and hundreds—no, a thousand years, *two* thousand . . .

Jamie's delighted gasp sounded in his ear.

The castle had disappeared. At the bottom of the hill, the reenactors' clean white pavilions had been replaced with soiled wheat-colored military tents, and one man in a leather tunic seemed to be standing guard.

"Can you make the window bigger?" Nan whispered. "I want to see more."

Will carefully adjusted his focus, and the scene enlarged. Men in short tunics and sandals were cutting wood, digging holes, shoving logs upright and nailing them to crosspieces.

A horse reared, whinnying, and two men shouted as they pulled on the reins. Most of the men were bareheaded, or wore leather caps, but the sun blazed off a couple of shiny helmets, and one helmet had a bright red crest.

"Romans!" breathed Jamie. "Gormly, look!"

Will sensed rather than felt the dog crowding in. "Hold on tight to her leash," he warned. Suddenly, in the foreground, a strange black-and-white animal, low to the ground, came trundling across the turf.

"Badger!" said Nan.

"Gormly, no!" cried Jamie, struggling with the leash.

And before Will could react, could even blink to shut the window, the big creamy dog leaped through, barking, dragging Jamie with her.

9
BATTLE OF THE
BLOODY HANDS

"YOU—GORMLESS!" NAN HOWLED AND jumped headfirst after Jamie. Will followed resignedly. There was really no choice.

He landed, rolling, on the dry turf and breathed in a rich scent of earth and leaves mixed with a trace of wood smoke.

The forest was different again. The trees were taller, with thicker trunks. There were leaves underfoot, golden and russet, and the air had a bite to it that spoke of fall. Will shivered in his T-shirt and looked around. At least the path was familiar, winding up in a crooked brown slash—and there, flat on his stomach a few yards ahead, was Jamie. In his hand was a broken leash.

Nan was crawling toward the little boy, keeping low.

The badger had prudently disappeared into its burrow. And Gormlaith was bounding down the hill toward the Roman camp, barking joyously. Already the Romans were looking up, and one had started toward the dog.

Will groaned. "Stupid animal."

"Too right," Nan said. "Just call her Gormless, it means the same thing."

"She's not stupid!" Jamie took in a breath. "G—"

Nan's hand clapped over his mouth before he could call out the first syllable. "Are you daft? Look at the size of those Romans! Don't let them know we're here—they might be worse than Stewarts!"

Jamie gulped. "But we can't leave Gormly."

"We won't." Will crouched behind a wide-trunked tree and peered around it. "Look, she's just making friends, okay? In a little while she'll get bored and come find us again. She's got a good nose, she'll be able to sniff us out."

"We could make friends with the Romans, too," Jamie said, but his tone lacked conviction.

Will gazed through the trees at the camp below. The Romans looked much more real than when viewed through the time window. Their voices were rough-edged and loud, and every instinct urged him to get the others back to safety. Maybe he should open a window now—he could come back later for the dog—

"They're speaking Latin," Nan whispered. "It sounds awfully forceful, doesn't it?"

Will was silent. Something felt wrong. The small hairs at the nape of his neck lifted, and he turned slowly around.

Three men stood watching him.

Their cloaks were pinned with iron brooches, their bodies were tattooed with spiraling blue patterns, and each man held a spear. One had what looked to be a wolfskin knotted around his neck, and the paws dangled against his bare chest.

Will's heart kicked into a hammering beat.

The man with the wolfskin spoke. The words were in a language that seemed oddly familiar, yet they made no sense.

Will stared at the strange, stern face and remembered a line from a movie he had seen once. He lifted his hand, palm out. "We come in peace."

The men talked among themselves in a low jumble of sound. Will listened intently. The meaning of the words seemed to hang in the air like fruit ready for picking, but he could not seem to understand, not yet. . . .

Nan slid a step closer to Will. "I don't think my Time Hearing is working. Let's run and grab Gormlaith, and get out of here."

"I thought you were afraid of the Romans," Will said out of the corner of his mouth.

Nan slid her eyes sideways. "I'm more afraid of *them*."

"They're Scots, though, right?"

"Well, probably Picts. . . ." Nan twisted a strand of hair around her finger. "I think Scots came later. I forget. Anyway, they might be our ancestors and everything, but they look *wild*."

Will knew what she meant. The three men looked fierce; clearly they were fighters. One was missing two fingers and an ear. Another held his spear crookedly, cradled in a twisted arm. And the man in the wolfskin had slashes across his bare chest that had healed unevenly, in ridges, like a plowed field.

Nan was plaiting her hair now, nervously winding the strands together. "I mean, the Romans were more civilized, right? They built roads and aqueducts and things. . . ."

Will chewed the inside of his cheek. The Romans probably had better weapons and armor; maybe the wild men were afraid of them. That might help. He slapped himself on the chest, and the Picts snapped their heads around at the sound. "WE," Will announced, "are with THEM." He pointed through the trees to the camp at the bottom of the hill.

The tattooed Picts muttered angrily. The man in the wolfskin flung out a guttural word. He shifted his spear in his hand and took a step forward.

The blood pounded in Will's ears. He had to get to Gormlaith. He had to open a time window. He had to get everyone out of here.

Jamie pressed close to Will's side. "Make them go away!"

Will forced himself to speak calmly. "Okay, let's go get Gormlaith," he murmured. "You two start down the hill, kind of wandering, like you're looking for something. But when I yell, run hard for the Romans. Got it?"

Jamie nodded, edging backward. Nan picked up a bright pebble, pretended to admire it, and turned around. She took two steps after Jamie.

The man in the wolfskin gave a signal that set his arm-band flashing. The others leaped forward like wildcats.

"Run!" gasped Will, a moment too late.

Callused hands clamped over the children's mouths. Powerful arms gripped them around the waists. Will, struggling, was squeezed sharply under his jaw and went limp. In a moment he was bundled through the woods and up onto a horse's back. Someone leaped on behind, clamped him tight with a tattooed arm, and snapped the reins.

They were riding. The animal smell of horse mingled with the odor of human sweat, and the black neck of the mare glistened beneath Will as it pumped up and down in a labored canter. Then they crested the hill and headed down through dark pine woods.

Will clutched the horse's mane to keep from sliding forward and twisted to look behind him. He caught a glimpse of Jamie's pale face and Nan's flying hair before his captor jerked him around and growled something low in his ear.

Ridged chest scars pressed against Will's back, and wolfskin paws made a hard knot between his shoulder blades.

The reins flicked again, and the black mare stretched out her canter, putting on speed as the riders emerged from the trees and racketed down the last bit of hill. Above their heads, dark pine branches changed to windblown clouds, and ahead was a wide, grassy valley. A river shone in the distance, curving and silken in the shifting light, and the horses headed straight for it, fanning out as they raced one another across the flats.

Something else was moving across the wide valley—horses, drawing behind them a two-wheeled open cart that looked like . . . Will narrowed his eyes. Yes, it was a chariot, and the driver was a girl! Her long dark hair flew in the wind, her vivid blue cloak streamed out behind her, and she was laughing. She shouted something at the approaching riders, flicked a whip with a sharp *crack,* and her chariot surged forward.

Will's captor chuckled and kicked his horse in the flank. The black mare flattened out into a full gallop and Will hung on to the mane for his life, his T-shirt rippling in the rush of wind. The other horses joined in, their paths converging as they thundered toward the bridge that spanned the river.

The drumming hooves echoed in Will's ears as if there were fifty horses instead of five. In spite of the danger and worry, his heart lifted in elation at the surging speed. It was like flying!

The girl clattered across the river bridge a full length ahead of the others. She pulled up, grinning wickedly as she let the three horses pass. As they neared her, Will could see she was a little taller than he was, with pale gray eyes and a gap between her front teeth that looked familiar. Then they were all trotting up a wide path, tossing comments that sounded like teasing as they zigzagged up another rocky slope.

It was a steeper hill than the one they had come down, but nearly treeless. Here and there, curly-haired sheep grazed with a clanking of bells. Will tipped his head back to look up. The sky was so full of movement and clouds that for a moment he was dizzy, and then he lowered his gaze to the crown of the hill, where stone walls rose grimly and wooden timbers reared up like a row of pencils set on edge. Cone-shaped roofs, thatched with dark gold straw, rose above the walls, and someone, watching from a high wooden platform, gave a shout and a wave.

The first raindrops hit then, making darker patches on the mare's neck and spotting Will's forearms. The Picts urged their horses to a canter, and clods of turf flew up from hooves as they pounded up the long track and past terraced walls of gray stone. Long before they got to the big barred gates, Will was soaked through and shivering in his thin shirt.

The wolfskin man slid off the black mare and pulled Will down with him. Someone opened the wooden gates with a vast creaking, and the children were marched through.

The huts crowding the hilltop were tall and round, with gray stone walls curving beneath thatched roofs, and the place was full of smells and noise. People stared from doorways as rain puddled on the paths the children walked. One child with reddish ringlets pointed her finger and laughed, and Jamie stuck his tongue out at her.

Will swatted away a goat that tried to nibble his shorts. "Do you know where we are?" he asked Nan quietly.

"I think this is a hill fort. There used to be one on Drummond Hill. My dad took me to see it once, but there was only a bit of rubble left." She rubbed her arms in an attempt to warm herself, and sneezed. "Wherever they're taking us, I hope there's a fire."

"We have to get Gormlaith," said Jamie, shivering violently.

"We'll get her later," Will promised. "One thing at a time." He glanced at Nan. "Any luck with Time Hearing yet?"

Nan shook her head. "Last time, it only took a few minutes to kick in. But we've been here a lot longer than that, and it's not happening."

The children were pushed toward the largest hut and

through an opening in the thick stone wall. Inside, it was dark except for small glowing lights here and there like weak candles, and a larger, brighter glow of a central fire. Above their heads, long poles rose to a peak like the ribs of a gigantic teepee, holding up the thatched roof.

Nan sneezed again, and Will glanced up at his captor. The tattoos did not look quite so frightening in the dim light. Will pointed first to his own chest, then to Nan and Jamie, and finally to the central fire. He raised his eyebrows in a clear question. Surely the man would understand that they had to get warm? The men were wearing woolen cloaks that shed the wet like ducks' backs, but the children were in thin cotton T-shirts and soaked to the skin.

His captor jerked his thumb at a furry-looking pile a few steps away.

"Sheepskins!" Jamie darted forward. The children each grabbed a pelt and draped it over their shoulders. The man with the chest scars gave them a push toward the fire and turned to join the others, who were talking earnestly to someone sitting in the shadows.

Will was too thankful to get to the fire to care. He crouched under the sheepskin and warmed his hands at the blaze. Something bubbled in the cauldron over the fire, sending forth a savory smell so good that his stomach flipped. It seemed like an age since they'd eaten lunch on the cup-marked rock.

"I'm hungry." Jamie's voice was muffled.

Nan turned her head on her arms. "Don't stick your tongue out at any more little girls, then, and they might give you something."

Will curled his arms around his knees. Voices rose in a babble of sound. The fire crackled, dogs barked, and wood clicked on wood as, nearby, an old woman wove a length of cloth on a loom. A distant *clang clang* sounded at uneven intervals. Someone was probably making horseshoes—or more weapons.

Will shut his eyes wearily. Everybody had weapons, it seemed. Stewarts had them, Romans had them, Picts had them, people in his own time had them. Did the people who were keeping his mother from going home have them? Probably.

He felt anger like a slow burning in his chest. Maybe his mother should have brought a weapon along herself. But who would have expected that a doctor would have to fight the people she was trying to help?

Nan gasped softly. "Listen," she whispered, taking hold of Will's arm.

Suddenly words came clearly out of the dark. "And they can help us defeat the Romans!"

Will jerked his head around. The words were thicker and oddly accented; still, he could understand them.

"They're only children," came another voice, scornfully.

"But children with *magic*," said the first voice. "I saw them appear, I tell you, out of the air!"

"Like they stepped out of the hollow hills," said another.

Will took in a careful breath and glanced at Nan and Jamie. Both of them were staring at the speakers.

"Time Hearing, at last," Nan breathed. "I wonder why it took so long, though."

Will had been wondering the same thing. "Maybe it takes longer, the farther back in time we go," he said, scarcely moving his lips.

Jamie pressed close to Will's side. "I don't want to fight the Romans," he whispered. "Did you see their swords?"

"These people have swords, too," Will whispered back. His eyes were adjusting to the dim light now, and he could see the glint of weapons stacked off to one side of the hut.

On the far side of the fire, the wild young men had gathered around two tall, carved chairs. In one of the chairs was an older man, broad of shoulder. He wore an armband that looked like a coiled snake, and around his neck was a thick iron chain, or torc. A scar ran from his brow across his cheek, pulling one eye down at the corner so that his frown looked very fierce indeed.

In the other chair was a woman, tall and queenly, her hair bound back from her forehead with an iron circlet. Her eyes were steady, but her face looked as if she hadn't laughed in a long time. She was speaking now, her voice high and clear. "Magic we can use."

She made a gesture, and the edge of her sleeve swept over the carved arm of the chair. "But why do these children not speak for themselves?" She gazed at the huddled group under their sheepskins; the firelight caught her cheek and made a tiny shadow along the lines at the corner of her mouth. "Come, now, surely you have voices?"

"They speak a foreign tongue, my lady Brethia," said the wolfskin-clad man. "They may even be Romans themselves, though"—his gaze swept grimly over the huddled children—"they seem to have come out in their underclothes for some strange reason."

The chieftain shifted in his chair, and his iron torc gleamed in the flickering light. "The children are not as important as the news you bring of Romans camping nearby. We knew the Romans had built a fort at the Island in the Flooded Stream, but that was a day's march away. This—this is the enemy at our very door!" He brought his fist up to his mouth as if to keep himself from saying anything else.

The man with the missing ear and fingers spoke up. "My chieftain, if the children are Romans, we can make them tell us what the Romans are planning."

The chieftain gave a short, bitter laugh. "Roman plans are always the same. Invade our lands, kill and torture, demand our young for slaves, and force tribute from whoever is left!" He gripped the armrests of his chair as if they were sword hilts. "It was Romans who did this," he said, tilting his chin to show the slash on his cheek, "and who killed my only son at the Battle of the Bloody Hands. And it was Romans who gave you the scars you carry to this day." He stared at Will, Nan, and Jamie with cold dark eyes. "If these children are Romans, they will use their magic to hurt us, not to help."

There was a sudden bustle at the entrance, and a swirl as a cloak was flung off. "Magic? Did somebody say magic?"

The girl who had raced them in her chariot entered the spacious hut, tossing her hair behind her shoulders. Droplets flung from her passing sprinkled Will as she moved toward the fire. "So, what magic? And who are these strangers?" She turned and looked them over, her mouth curving. "Surely they are dressed somewhat . . . oddly?"

"Breet," said the queenly woman reprovingly. "Where are your manners? Greet us properly."

The girl's smile opened, and the space between her teeth flashed into view. She joined her hands together into a double fist and thumped them against her chest. "Father. Mother. Your daughter returns and greets you. With greatest respect," she added hurriedly, "more respect than you would believe, truly, and who *are* these people?"

"They are Roman children," her father said. "We're deciding what to do with them."

"Probably kill them," said the man with the twisted arm.

"Oh, don't do that!" said Breet. She lifted her hands in sudden appeal, and her iron armband flashed in the light. It was coiled like a snake around her upper arm, but Will saw that its head had been worked into the shape of a strange, long-nosed beast. He stared at it and numbly hoped that the chieftain wouldn't decide to kill them.

"It's what they do to our children, after all," Twisted Arm said bitterly.

"We're not Romans," Will blurted out.

There was a sudden silence. All eyes turned to him.

"If you can speak our tongue, why did you not answer when we spoke to you in the forest?" Missing Ear sounded irate.

Will stood up and the sheepskin slid off his shoulders. "We couldn't understand it then. The language of—of our ancestors—only comes to us after we've heard it for a little while."

"Ancestors?" said Breet quickly. Her gray eyes sparked, and her chin lifted slightly. "If we had one of our druids here, he could recite every ancestor we've ever had. I do not think you are among them."

"We're not *your* ancestors," Will tried to explain. "You're *ours*."

"If you are not Romans," interrupted Missing Ear, intent on his own train of thought, "why, then, did your dog run to them? And why did you try to follow?"

"Who, us?" Will glanced at Nan.

"Don't pretend innocence!" shouted Missing Ear. "We saw you!"

Nan threw off her sheepskin and stood shoulder to shoulder with Will. "Please stop shouting!" Her voice trembled a little, and she lifted her chin. "He's told you the truth—why don't you believe him? We're not Romans. And our dog didn't run to them because she knew them. It's just that she wanted to make friends."

"Foolish of her," said Twisted Arm. "She may discover they are not so friendly in return."

The man with the chest scars hitched his wolfskin over his shoulder. "You say you are not Romans. But then who are you? We know you use magic, but you do not look like druids. Did a druid send you?"

Jamie pointed to Will proudly. "A druid didn't do the magic. My brother did!"

The chieftain's eyes

seemed to bore a hole in Will. "Then do your magic now," he commanded.

Will wished with all his heart that he had never learned to open a time window. People were never content to just *look*—they kept walking through and messing everything up. He didn't want to let a bunch of warlike Picts into some other time and then try to get them all back. He was going to have enough trouble rounding up Gormlaith—

"Well?" said the chieftain sternly. "If you truly have magic, as our druids have, you will not hesitate to show us. And if you are not Roman, then I demand to know—where did you come from? Why are you on our lands?"

Will was trying to figure out which question to answer first, when Nan swept out her arm in imitation of the lady Brethia. "We come," she said in a sonorous voice, "from a future time. We have come to visit you, our ancestors." She gazed around impressively. "Now that we have seen you, we wish only to return to our own time. And—er—take our dog with us," she added.

There was a silence.

"Ancestors you may be," said Wolfskin in a courteous, disbelieving tone, "but you still have not shown the chieftain your magic. If you are friendly to us, you will do this. If you are our enemy, and refuse, we will . . ." He glanced around the fire at the crowd that had gathered. Behind him, Twisted Arm made a motion as if he were wringing someone's neck.

"All right, I'll do it." Will jutted out his chin to hide the sudden fear that jabbed him. "But only for the chieftain. Nobody else can watch."

The chieftain raised his arm and flicked his hand. The queenly Brethia rose and took a resisting Breet by the hand. "But I want to see the magic, too!" Will heard the girl say, with a flash of temper, as her mother towed her toward the exit. The rest of the crowd followed, murmuring. Only Wolfskin remained.

"My chieftain," he said quietly, "consider that they have magic. What if they are planning treachery?"

The chieftain rubbed his chin with a callused hand. "Take the lass and the small lad out. Feed them if they are hungry, but keep them under guard while the young druid shows me his magic. He will not dare to betray me while I hold his brother and—friend?"

"Cousin," said Nan faintly.

"While I hold his family hostage."

Will could not help a small, startled jerk. Hostage. It was the same word he had heard Nan's parents using, when they were talking of his mother and thought he was not listening, and now he understood what it meant. It meant to keep someone prisoner until someone else, who cared about them, gave you what you wanted.

Jamie and Nan stumbled out, their shoulders gripped by Wolfskin's huge hands. A trickle of cold moved down

Will's spine as he realized the power of taking a hostage. Bleakly, he knew that he would do anything the chieftain asked. Anything at all.

"Now," said the chieftain, "show me your magic."

Will forced himself to breath evenly, in and out. "Take hold of my shoulder," he said. "And stand behind me, and watch."

The chieftain's hand was heavy. His body smelled of smoke and sweat, and his breath was loud in Will's ear.

The room was full of shadows. Will turned away from the glare of the fire and focused on a spot a few feet ahead. The air became lighter. He shifted back and forward, searching, groping through future ages. And then, as easily as breathing, he opened a window to the time that he knew best.

Behind him, the chieftain gasped as the sunshine of a summer's day filled a rough-edged square that hung in the air before his eyes. Above and to each side of him loomed the solid walls and sturdy beams of his dwelling place, but directly before him a vision of a bare hilltop had appeared, windswept and bright, covered with bracken and mossy stones.

"What am I seeing?" the chieftain asked hoarsely.

Will did not blink as he answered. "You are seeing the same hilltop we're standing on, only in a future time."

"It cannot be real." The chieftain's voice trembled. "This is an illusion."

"It's real enough," said Will. "We stepped through a window just like this one, and came into your time. Your men saw us."

The chieftain leaned forward. Tentatively he put a hand through. He snatched it back and turned, his dark eyes startled. "I felt the wind!"

Will kept his focus steady. "Now will you let us go? You've seen my magic, and it isn't anything that will help you fight the Romans."

The chieftain stared at the bare, sunlit hillside. "I want to go there."

"Of course you do," said Will, sighing. "Listen, can't you just look from here? It's much less complicated that way."

"I must find out for myself if it is true," said the chieftain in a low voice.

"Will you promise to come back?" Will countered. "Will you come back right away? It's hard for me to hold the window open for very long."

"I will indeed return quickly. It will not take me long to see what I need to see."

The chieftain was as good as his word. He stepped into the future; gazed in every direction; went to the edge of the hilltop and looked over; turned around, spinning on his heel.

Then Will put a hand through the window to guide him, and the chieftain came back into his own time with a face as set and hard as iron.

"Close it," he said grimly, "and open it no more in my sight. To me!" he shouted, and in a moment, his fighting men crowded into the hut, followed by the rest of the villagers.

"Arm yourselves. Paint your bodies with warrior patterns. Say your prayers to the gods and prepare yourselves; we attack the Roman camp tonight, at sundown. Mothers," he said, and his voice cracked, "paint yourselves and your children with patterns of the afterlife. What was done after the Battle of the Bloody Hands must be done here. Do not forget that we are the People—though we go down into the dark, we will go down fighting."

Bewildered, Will glanced around him. The Pictish faces were contracted in grief, as if they had all been suddenly struck with the sharpest of swords. A low sound, like a stifled groan, ran through the group like the whimper of one great, wounded beast.

What had the chieftain seen when he went through the window? It couldn't have been anything so very terrible. The scene had been peaceful—at least as much of it as Will had seen. He opened his mouth but only managed to get out a sort of protesting croak, when the chieftain whirled on him.

"GO!" the chieftain ordered. "Go where you will and trouble me no more! Your magic only brings despair!"

֍

Will sat dangling his legs on the high stone wall overlooking the river valley. Nan had brought some flatbread and a lump of yellow cheese, which she and Jamie hadn't finished; Jamie had put his head in Will's lap and was fast asleep. Though the rain had stopped, the day was gloomy and cold, and Will tucked a sheepskin closely around Jamie's shivering body. Behind them, all throughout the hilltop village, the Picts were busy sharpening weapons, checking harnesses and other tack, mending chariots, and painting themselves with spiraling blue designs and dots. Through all the preparation there came a humming sort of moan, now soft, now rising louder, but never quite going away, as if a whole people were grieving terribly, without words.

"We've got to get out of here." Nan glanced behind her. "These people are crazy."

Will didn't think they were crazy, but he didn't understand them. And he didn't know what they were intending to do. "You're right," he said thickly through a mouthful of bread and cheese. "We have to get back. But there's still Gormlaith, too."

Nan narrowed her eyes against the late afternoon glare off the river. "I know where we are. That's the River Lyon, and that's the Tay. If we were back home, I mean in our own time, all we'd have to do is cross the Lyon at that bridge and we'd be on a road that would take us straight to Castle Menzies. The Romans made their camp right about where the castle is."

"You mean, 'going to be,'" Will said.

"Right. Anyway, I know where it is, and with luck, Gormly is still there. But it's probably four miles at least, and with him"—she nodded at Jamie's sleeping form—"it could take hours."

"Not to mention the Picts might get nasty if they see us heading off in that direction," Will said gloomily.

"The Romans might get nasty if they see us, too," Nan said. "I don't know anything about the Battle of the Bloody Hands, but it didn't sound good." She gnawed on a fingernail. "They wouldn't be mean to a dog, though, would they?"

Behind them came a scraping noise, and Breet scrambled up onto the stone wall, breathing hard. "What in the name of the gods did you show my father?" she demanded. "What made him decide to sacrifice us all?"

Will gulped. "Sacrifice?"

"Yes, sacrifice!" Breet hissed. "You heard him. Do you not know what was done after the Battle of the Bloody Hands?"

Will shook his head. He wasn't sure he wanted to know.

"Two springs ago," said Breet furiously, "we had a great

army of the People, twice as many as Romans, and we met them far to the northeast, on a great plain. The carnyx blew and the druids wailed—"

"What's a carnyx?" Will interrupted, unwisely.

Breet glared. "It's a great loud beast horn that strikes the fear of death into our enemies. And so it did at the Battle of the Bloody Hands—for a while. But then the fighters came close together, so close our warriors did not have room to swing their great swords. The Romans, though, had short, sharp swords—wondrous sharp," she added bitterly, "that could stab and thrust from inches away. So many lay dead in the end that the warriors who were left saw they could not win, and fled back into the hills. And then—" She clenched her fists and fell silent.

Nan asked, "Is that why it was called the Battle of the Bloody Hands? Because so many died?"

Breet shook her bowed head, her hair a curtain that swayed back and forth. "It was because of what happened after. There were hill forts nearby, small villages like ours, too close to the battlefield. The Romans were pursuing, and our warriors could not carry all the children and the pregnant women and the old people with them. . . ." She lifted her head, and her eyes were tearless and hard, like glimmering stones. "We all know what happens when the Romans come upon defenseless villages. Terrible things, things I will not speak of. And when they are finished, they take those

237

who are still alive and sell them—like cattle—and turn them into *slaves*. Do you know what happens to slaves?"

Will looked at his hands and nodded slowly. He had learned about slavery at school. He had a suspicion, however, that he hadn't been told everything.

"Then you will know," said Breet, "that it is better to die and go to one's gods than to ever live as a slave. And that is what the People did. When the Romans came to those villages, they found only bodies and smoking ruins. We had beaten them. They found no one left alive that they could torture, or take captive as a slave."

Nan made a strange gulping sound. "Is that what your father wants to do here? Have the villagers kill themselves, just in case the Romans come?"

Breet nodded. She touched the coils of her armband and rubbed her thumb against the strange beast head, as if it gave her comfort.

"But why?" Will exploded. Jamie stirred in his lap, flinging out an arm, and Will lowered his voice. "Listen, all I did was let your father go to the hilltop in the future. There was nothing there to make him go crazy, I swear it!"

Breet leaned forward, her gray eyes intent. "Show me," she said. "I ask it as the chieftain's daughter. I want to see what he saw."

"All right." Will swung his legs out from under Jamie

and moved him carefully over to Nan. "But we need to do it where nobody can see you disappear."

Breet pointed downward. "There's nobody there but sheep."

Will jumped off the wall and tumbled to his knees on the sheep-bitten turf. Breet followed a moment after, and Will gave her instructions. Then he looked back toward the wall, now between him and the top of the hill.

He breathed in and out, slowly. He let all thoughts drop from his mind except that he wanted to find the same time as before. As he had hoped, the last opening of the time window had left a thin trace on the air—he could still almost see it, glimmering like a spider's web in the sun. He followed the trace; the window opened as before, and a patch of bright sunlit hilltop appeared in the middle of the rough stone wall.

Breet gasped softly; then she stiffened her chin and stepped through the window. Will watched her walk up to the top as her father had done. She bent down to pick up a stone and held it in her hand, seemingly frozen.

"Hurry up," Will muttered. His head was starting to ache. He reached his arm through the window and snapped his fingers.

Breet turned around and ran toward him. She took his hand and climbed through, and Will let the window close with a sigh of relief.

"Did you see what your father saw?" Nan demanded from her perch on the wall.

Breet pushed back hair from a forehead damp with sweat. "I saw."

"And?" Will asked. "It was just a bare hilltop, with some rocks on it, right?"

"Ruins," said Breet somberly. "Not one stone left upon the other. I know it was our hilltop, for the rivers and the shape of the land were the same, but our hill fort was in ruins. The Romans had destroyed it. That is what my father saw, and that is why he knows we will not defeat the Romans. They will come and destroy our village, and we must make sure that there is no one left alive here for them to torture and enslave." She bowed her head, clutching her armband.

"But that's all wrong!" Nan cried. "The Romans didn't win!"

Breet looked up, her face contorted. "The hill fort was destroyed."

"Yes," said Nan passionately, "but that's just because you saw so *far* into the future—things fall down after two thousand years, you know, even rock walls! Your people didn't lose to the Romans. They won! At least," she added honestly, "I'm pretty sure they won. Anyway, the Romans went away. And we're your ancestors in the future—your great-grandchildren, only with about seventy more greats attached—and that means you survived, don't you see?"

Breet frowned. "How do you know this?"

"It's in all the history books . . . and my class even took a field trip to—oh, I forget the name, but my dad said it was called Pinny Castra, or something, where the Romans built a fort—"

"Pinnata Castra," said Breet slowly, fingering the knife she carried on her deerskin belt. "That is what the Romans call their fort at the Island in the Flooded Stream. We call it Inchtuthil."

"Inchtuthil! Right, that's the same word my teacher used! And the Romans left it in a hurry, only I don't remember when, exactly. . . . Oh," she burst out, "if only I could ask my dad, he'd tell us everything, and then you'd *know* the Romans didn't win!"

"I wish *I* could speak to your father," said Breet darkly. "You don't seem to remember very much."

"I never thought it was important," Nan admitted. "It all happened so long ago. . . ." She trailed off. "Wait. Why don't we just go tell your father that the Romans don't win in the end?"

"We can try," said Breet, "but I don't think he would listen. He saw for himself that the fort was destroyed. I think you would have to show him a battle where the Romans were actually defeated. Can you do that?"

Will shook his head. He didn't know about any battles except for the one about to happen tonight. And if he tried to show the chieftain that one, Will suspected he wouldn't be allowed to bring the man back before that same time again. Will remembered the grayness that had come when he had tried to go back to just before Castle Menzies had burned; the time window hadn't let him through. Oh, it was all getting too complicated!

Will rubbed his eyes, frowning. "Okay, let's figure out one thing at a time. First, we've got to get Jamie home—I have a feeling he should have been in bed hours ago—and second, we have to get Gormlaith away from the Romans. But the Roman camp is four miles away. It will take us hours to walk it with Jamie."

"We've got to get Gormly before the battle tonight, or she might be killed," Nan said.

Breet frowned. "I'd let you use my chariot, only the sentries would never allow it. If they saw you so much as cross the river, you'd be dragged back by your hair. They would be sure you were going to tell the Romans exactly where the camp was, and all our battle plans—"

Nan gasped aloud. "Be quiet for a minute, let me think!" She gripped the sides of her head. "I might have an idea— it's coming—"

Will waited dully. Taking care of Jamie and rescuing Gormlaith seemed difficult enough, but that wasn't the worst of it. Now a whole village was going to die because he, Will, had shown their chieftain a vision of the future that had filled the man with despair.

A sound of two hands clapping together broke into his depression. Will looked up to see Nan's face alight.

"I've got it!" she cried. "Will, can you make the time window bigger? Big enough to drive a chariot through?"

10
FORWARD IN TIME

"BUT I DON'T *WANT* TO climb another wall," Jamie mumbled, his eyes closed.

"Just one more." Nan, perched on top of the last terraced wall, reached down her hand to the little boy.

"You said that the last time." Jamie sagged against the stone, his knees buckling.

Will shook him awake. "Put your foot in my hand—that's it—now step up."

Thoroughly grumpy, Jamie did as he was told. Nan locked her hand around his wrist and gave a mighty heave. She and Jamie tumbled over together, and Will heard a muffled series of groans.

He glanced behind. They had come down three levels

of terraced pastures, and no one had seen them. He scrabbled for a foothold between the rough stones and flung a leg over the wall. Then he was rolling on the spice-scented bracken that covered the hillside.

Where was Breet?

"Maybe she had trouble getting the horses," Nan said.

They sat shivering with their backs to the wall. The river valley was closer now, but it still looked like a long, long walk across, plus another few miles to the Roman camp.

"I want Gormly," Jamie said miserably.

"She'd keep us warmer," Nan said through chattering teeth.

Will rubbed the goose bumps on his arms in sudden irritation. "It's her own fault we're in this mess. Seriously, she has to chase *everything* she sees?"

"She's just a dog!" Nan said heatedly. "She was only following her instinct!"

Yeah, an instinct for trouble, Will felt like saying, but he caught sight of Jamie's face and didn't. In spite of his annoyance, he hated to think what might happen to the dog, especially after what Breet had said about the Romans.

There was a sound of hoofbeats, a chariot's distinctive rattle. "Oh, wow," said Nan.

Will glanced up, then took a second look. Breet's cheeks were painted with blue spirals, slanted lines crossed her nose, and patterns of dots curled over her forehead. Every visible part of her body was covered with blue designs; he wouldn't have recognized her without the flyaway hair and the deep blue cloak.

"Sorry it took so long," Breet panted. "My mother wanted to paint me with patterns of protection and the afterlife, and she wouldn't stop. Get in, hurry!"

The chariot was an open cart of wood and leather. The horses, small and shaggy, stamped and tossed their heads; Breet held them back with an effort. Nan got Jamie in and wedged against the front panel. Then, cramming herself in behind Breet, she grasped the curved wooden rim on both sides. "Come on, Will," she said over her shoulder.

Will looked at the restless horses, the jostling carriage. There was too much movement to open a time window. "I'll do it from here. Wait till I give the word, Breet."

Breet nodded, her arms tense.

Will quieted his mind. He let his eyes relax, focus on a spot that wasn't quite there, until the air began its familiar shimmer. Now to find the right era, the right day, the right moment.

He probed to locate the strongest pull, the pull of his own time. Almost . . . there . . .

He passed a sort of grayness that pushed back; that had to be the time he had already lived through. Beyond it was a mist, not gray exactly, but dim somehow, as dim as the future he had not yet lived. But in between the gray and the dim darkness was a bright sliver, thin as a bookmark between pages in a diary. That was the place. He sharpened his focus delicately and opened the window on the very afternoon he had left his own time.

Through the window it was a bright summer's day, midafternoon by the shadows. Breet and Nan, off in the chariot, could not see the window of course, but if he could just place it correctly, that wouldn't matter.

He was freezing, but he couldn't shiver; he couldn't move in any abrupt way, or he would lose the picture. Slowly, carefully, Will shifted his focus for more distance. The window enlarged the way a small picture grows if the projector is moved backward. It grew until it was higher than the horses' heads and wider than the chariot. He adjusted its position, moving his focus ever so slightly to the side. Now the window was as big as a garage door and just a few yards in front of Breet's chariot. His head began to ache, especially around his eyes; it was an effort to keep his focus steady.

"All right, Breet," he said tensely. "Drive straight ahead. That's it, keep going. . . ."

The horses' heads were through the window. It was working!

Suddenly the horse on the left tossed its head, snorting in alarm, spooked by the sudden change in atmosphere. Now the horses were trying to back up—the chariot tilted—

"GO!" Will shouted.

Breet cracked her whip over the shaggy hindquarters, and the horses bolted forward, whinnying in panic. The chariot surged ahead over the stony turf, bounced twice, hit the side of the window with a strange shimmering screech, and was through.

Will let his breath out slowly. The chariot and horses dwindled in the distance; Breet seemed to be fighting to keep them under control, but that was her problem, not his. Carefully he adjusted his focus to bring the window closer, make it smaller, until it was close enough that he could step through himself. Then suddenly the blessed summer sun of his own time was shining warmly on him. Far overhead, he saw the silver gleam of an airplane going south; over the river was a modern bridge and a paved road leading toward Castle Menzies. His headache began to recede.

Breet's whip cracked again. The horses wheeled in a circle; she pulled the reins, and they stopped, trembling. "Hurry, Will," she cried, "I can't hold them forever!"

Will scrambled to find a foothold in the back of the chariot. Breet clicked with her tongue, and the horses lunged forward.

"Ow, somebody's stepping on me!" complained Jamie sleepily.

Will gripped the sides and hung on. The chariot had a springy, whippy motion, and every so often it hit a rock and jounced up a foot or more. His insides felt like eggs in the process of being scrambled. "Head for the road!" he shouted over the rattle of the chariot.

Breet stared at the winding asphalt. "How can it be so *smooth*?"

The wooden wheels made a sound on the highway like logs rolling; the drumming hooves echoed across the river valley. "Aiii!" cried Breet, her eyes blazing. "What a glorious road! Are you sure the Romans didn't build this?"

"*Our* people built this," Nan shouted in her ear. "Your great-great-great-great-times-ten-grandchildren built it!"

"Ha!" Breet snapped her whip as the horses charged across the bridge.

"Don't whip the horses so much," Nan begged.

"I'm not touching them," Breet said scornfully. "I'm just encouraging them."

"Look out!" Will called in her ear. "Car!"

Breet shrieked. The car passed them with a smell of exhaust and a blaring red whoosh; they swerved off the road into a stand of gorse bushes, and the horses reared, rolling their eyes until only the whites showed. The chariot tipped sideways.

"Get out," gasped Breet, "tip it up again," and Will and Nan put their shoulders to the painted wooden sides until the chariot righted with a crunch. Breet flipped down a wooden lever for a brake and stared at the red car, fast disappearing down the road. "Was that a dragon?" she gasped. "Or an avenging spirit?"

"It was a—a horseless chariot," Will said with sudden inspiration.

"Your great-great-times-twenty-grandchildren made those, too," Nan added.

Breet's eyes had a strange glitter. "*My* descendants made that dragon chariot?"

A low, fretful wail came from within Breet's chariot. "I'm *tired*! I want to go *home*!"

Nan glanced at Will. "Let's put Jamie on his cot at the castle," she urged. "My mum can deal with him."

"Perfect," Will agreed. It would be far easier to accomplish

250

what he had to do without Jamie along. "How far is the castle now?"

Nan screwed up her face. "Maybe two miles? We'll have to watch out for—er, dragon chariots."

Breet was hesitant to try the road again. Every time a car came into view, she pulled off to one side, and Nan and Will jumped out to hold the horses' bridles. It took a long time to reach the castle. For the last half mile, Breet refused outright to use the road, preferring to drive the horses through a field of grain.

"The farmers are going to hate us," Nan muttered.

Will stared at Breet's blue-painted face and the designs on her arms. "How are we going to explain her to your parents?" he whispered in Nan's ear as the castle loomed.

She grinned. "I'll just tell them she's one of my weirder school friends. Here, Breet," she added, "go around to the back of the castle, okay?"

The horses, going slower now, turned in response to Breet's hand on the reins. But Breet wasn't paying much attention to her driving. She tipped her head back, staring up at the massive stone castle, and let the reins go slack. "I hear the Romans build marvelous things," she said slowly, "great fortresses, and walls that go almost from sea to sea—"

"The Romans didn't build this castle," Nan said. "Your descendants did. Come on, let's get Jamie inside."

Will and Breet took Jamie under his shoulders, and Nan took his feet. They passed the gift shop, where Cousin Elspeth was busy with a tourist, walked up the long narrow stairs, and tipped the little boy into his cot. He grunted, rolled over, and fell asleep again.

"Right, that's him sorted," said Nan. "Come on, let's find my dad."

They went out the back way. "Let's avoid the car park," Nan said quietly to Will. "Too many dragon chariots. Oh, there's Dad!" She waved at the man approaching with a ladder over his shoulder.

Breet stared out over the fields, shading her eyes against the light. Then she stiffened, her face twisted with fury. "You *betrayed* me!"

"Huh?" said Will.

Nan looked where Breet was pointing, and her eyes widened. "Oh, no, no, no—"

"Did you think I wouldn't see?" Breet hissed. "Those are *Romans*!"

Will turned. There, in the distance, the reenactors had begun their battle. Men in shiny metal helmets and tunics were waving their swords about, and wild-looking blue-painted people were brandishing spears.

"Wait!" Nan cried. "You've got it all wrong!"

Breet was already running toward the horses, reaching for the reins. The shaggy beasts sprang forward at the crack of her whip and headed straight for Will and Nan, gathering speed.

"Jump on!" Will shouted. As the chariot passed, they leaped onto its open back, cracking their heads together in the process. By some miracle, they both stayed aboard. Will saw Nan's father drop his ladder and begin to run after them.

"They're not Romans!" Nan screamed in Breet's ear over the rattling of the chariot.

"Do you think I'm a fool?" Breet shrieked. "Do you think I can't see the Roman armor, and the Roman swords, and the arrogant red Roman crests?"

"They're just acting!" Will shouted, gripping the sides of the chariot. "It's a *mock* battle, it's not real!"

"I will believe no more lies! I can die here just as well as in my own time. Look, where my people lie slain!"

Will groaned. Naturally some of the reenactors were playing dead. Some of them apparently used red dye for blood, too. In a minute, the horses were going to run straight into the crowd . . . someone was going to get hurt . . .

"We've got to do something!" Nan cried.

Will spoke into Nan's ear. She nodded and readjusted her grip.

"*Now*," Will said. Together they each raised one leg and pushed their feet into the backs of Breet's knees. The girl's legs buckled, and Nan lunged on top of her while Will grabbed for the reins, pulling back. The horses reared, squealing, as the crowd of reenactors stopped in midbattle.

Breet fought to get free, and Nan was getting the worst of it.

"Knock it off, Breet!" Will tried to control the horses as the chariot slowed. "They were just pretending to fight!" He wound the reins around his forearm and grabbed Breet, turning her to face the crowd. "Look, no one is getting hurt, they're having fun!"

The audience was clapping delightedly now, the children craning their necks for a look at the horses and the painted chariot.

Breet looked around, panting. "But—there's blood . . ." She gasped as one of the blue-painted dead bodies suddenly sat up and put on his glasses to look at her quizzically.

"Nice chariot," he said. "Hey, what language are you speaking, anyway?"

The English words sounded oddly strange to Will's ears. He glanced at Nan, who looked slightly startled as well, but promptly switched to English.

"We were speaking Pictish, of course." Nan tossed her head, dimpling.

The crowd chuckled.

The man on the ground got up, hitched his pants up around a chubby waist, and looked the children over with a superior air. "Of course, no one really *knows* the Pictish language anymore. Some people believe that the language is of Celtic derivation, but most *current* scholars hold to the view that—"

"The Picts came from Ireland!" shouted a voice from the back of the crowd.

"No, they were descendants of the original people that were here in the Stone Age—" said someone else.

"No, you're wrong, Pictish is closely tied to the Q-Celtic languages—"

"Absolutely not, it's *P*-Celtic—"

"That has been *totally* rejected by all reputable scholars!" cried the man in the glasses. "It's a Germanic language, everyone knows that!"

Breet stared at the Roman and Pict reenactors, all arguing heatedly, their mock battle forgotten. "I do not understand these people. You say they were *pretending* to fight? What for?"

Nan tried to explain, but Breet's frown only grew deeper. Meantime the argument had somehow moved on to something called the "Pictish beast."

"It's not a *real* animal; all reputable scholars agree," the chubby man insisted. "It's got a snout like a crocodile, antlers like a stag, coils like curled flippers instead of feet—" He stepped forward, jabbing a finger at Breet's armband. "*That* is only a modern imitation, not particularly accurate, of course, but still the snout indicates—"

"Stop waving your arms!" Breet ordered. "You're frightening the horses!" She broke away from Nan's restraining hand and climbed the front of the chariot to get to the ponies. She stroked their shaggy necks, crooning words Will suddenly did not understand.

The chubby man pushed his glasses up on his nose, looking angry. "Stop pretending to speak Pictish, you silly girl, and get out of here so we can continue our battle. If you wanted to be in it, you should have registered in advance and paid your dues."

Breet's eyes narrowed at the sneering tone. She tossed back her wild hair and took a belligerent step forward.

"Uh-oh." Will got out of the chariot and pushed through a group of people examining its painted sides. "Excuse me— excuse me, please—"

"This chariot is remarkable," said a woman, reaching out a hand to stop him. "And the lashings seem surprisingly authentic. Where did you get it?"

He didn't answer. Breet was saying something back to the man, and it didn't sound friendly at all. Will strained to hear the words, but nothing that he heard made sense. . . . Why couldn't he understand her anymore?

The man wiped his sweating forehead. "You've got a nerve, disrupting everything, charging in with horses and talking gibberish. We're trying to make history come alive for these people, and you—you're not even authentic! Where did you get your ideas for how to dress like a Pict, from Hollywood?"

Breet's arm went back; Will lunged for the hand that held the whip. "No! Stop!"

Breet did not take her eyes off the chubby man. "I may not know his tongue, but I understand a rude and insolent tone," she said through gritted teeth. "No one insults the daughter of a chieftain without penalty! And let go my arm!" She gave it a furious shake.

Will, relieved that he could understand her again, held on grimly. Things would get out of control fast if she started whipping anyone she didn't like.

"You'd better take your friend away." The man glared at Will. "Get her out of here before I call the police on you lot."

"No one is going to call the police. They're coming with me." Nan's father was slightly breathless from running, but his voice was calm. He gave the chubby red-faced man one brief glance, then raised his voice to address the crowd. "Step back, please, give us room to turn the vehicle around—that's right, thank you. We'll let you get on with your battle in just a moment. Nan," he added quietly, "give me the reins; I'll lead them. Is this a friend of yours?"

"Yes," said Nan hurriedly. "Dad, this is Breet, from . . . over the hill a bit. Breet, this is my father, Ewen Menzies."

Breet stared uncomprehendingly.

Will still had hold of her arm. "That's Nan's father," he whispered in Pictish.

Cousin Ewen gave her an absent smile, clucked to the horses, and walked slowly in the direction of the castle. The horses followed, and the chariot rolled behind. Nan jumped out to walk with Will and Breet.

Breet said something that sounded furious. She tossed her head.

Nan glanced at Will, startled. "I don't understand her!"

"It happened to me, too," Will admitted. "But when I got next to her, all of a sudden I knew Pictish again." He frowned, thinking. "Time Hearing worked when we were with the Picts. Now that we're back in our own time, maybe it won't work unless we're touching her?"

"But I could understand her when we first got to our time," Nan objected. "We were talking the whole way, in the chariot."

Will shrugged. "Time Hearing takes a while to kick in when we're in the past. Maybe it takes a while to wear off, too. Anyway, we were crammed in so tight in the chariot, we were always touching."

Breet muttered something again, frowning at them.

Will flung an arm over her shoulders. "Sorry. Say that again?"

Nan, on Breet's other side, reached her arm around the girl's waist.

"Those were not my people at all," Breet said, casting a last scornful glance at the crowd behind her. "Why were they pretending to be?"

"Ha!" Will grinned at Nan. He was right—touch was the key! Then, in Pictish, "Maybe they like history. You know, showing people what battles were like in the past."

"That was not a battle," Breet said, her face grim. "Do they think fighting Romans was a *game*?"

"Well, you can't expect them to kill people nowadays," Nan said. "Anyway, they probably *are* your people. They're your descendants, anyway."

"*My* descendants?" Breet flung back. "Running about on a field, pretending to bleed?" She snorted. "If they are so anxious for a battle, why don't they find a real one to fight? Or are there no enemies left?"

"There are plenty of enemies," Will said slowly, "but they aren't always close by." The thought of his mother, always in the background of his mind, came to the fore, and his throat tightened until it ached. She had gone among enemies when she had traveled to that far country, only she hadn't known it. It was hard to know how to fight enemies like that.

Breet was still talking. ". . . and I didn't like that little man with the red face and soft belly. I didn't understand his words, but I could see he thought he knew everything. And he wasn't even a druid!"

Nan suddenly spoke in English. "Will, how is Breet going to understand my dad when he tells her about Romans? He won't know her language. And she won't know his."

Will wrenched his thoughts back to the problem at hand. Cousin Ewen might develop Time Hearing if he went back to Pictish times for a while, but there was no way Will was going to let *that* happen. Having Gormlaith stuck back there was bad enough.

"Maybe," said Nan brightly, "Time Hearing will work for Breet, too, and she'll understand English all at once!"

"I doubt it." Will rubbed his nose. "Didn't we figure out that Time Hearing worked because some genes or something in our bodies, passed down from our ancestors, almost *remembered* the language? So when our bodies were actually back in that time period, the memory came back?"

"Y—es," said Nan. "Something like that."

"Well, then, Time Hearing can't work for Breet, because this isn't her past. She can't remember a language her ancestors never spoke."

Nan's forehead wrinkled. "I suppose I was hoping it would work for her, anyway. Because if we have to translate into Pictish, my dad will think we're just . . . you know."

Will knew. Cousin Ewen would think they were playing

a childish game, wasting his time. He would think they were being rude on purpose.

Nan asked Breet in Pictish, "Did you understand what we just said?"

Breet's leather boots crunched on the gravel drive. "Nay."

Nan wiped her forehead and trudged on with the others, following her father up the driveway. It was hot; whatever breeze there had been had died long ago.

Breet, sweating in her heavy blue cloak, undid the pin at her throat—a curving bit of iron shaped like a sea creature, with the same long nose—and ran forward to throw the woolen cloak into the back of the chariot.

Nan's father half turned. "I'll bring the horses around the back of the castle, where they won't be spooked by the cars," he called. "Then you can tell me what happened back there."

Breet turned to Will and Nan and said something. The Pictish words didn't make sense, since she wasn't touching them anymore, but they hardly noticed. They were each busy with their own thoughts.

Nan worried what her father would say when they spoke Pictish in front of him. Will wondered how to get Gormlaith away from the Romans.

He could not shake his dread at having to go back among real Romans and Picts, with their swords that were honed to a killing edge. *Their* blood would not be fake. And anyone who died in battle wouldn't get up after it was over and go home.

Breet rapped out another sentence, louder this time. She sounded angry. Will and Nan ran forward, each taking hold of an arm, and asked her what she had said.

The Pictish girl frowned. "Why are you always holding on to me? And why do you not answer?" She pulled away with a sharp jerk, glaring fiercely.

Nan grabbed her elbow. "Listen, you can't—"

"I can do anything I want! Loose your hold, you worm. I am a chieftain's daughter!"

"Worm, is it?" Nan's tossing hair whipped across Will's cheek. "Fine then, see if I care about helping *you*!" She threw up her hands and ran to walk by her father.

Breet said something that sounded like it might be swearing. Will gripped both her wrists and shook them. "Stop calling names, and listen for a minute."

Her gray eyes were icy as winter. "If you weren't holding my wrists so tightly," she said with dangerous calmness, "I would slap you for the insult. I am a chief—"

"Oh, shut *up*. What did you have to go and lose your temper for? Haven't you noticed you can't understand a word we say unless we're touching you?"

Breet frowned. "I am a chieftain's daughter. Naturally I will lose my temper with anyone who displeases me."

Will rolled his eyes. "Get over it. Nobody cares here if

you're a chieftain's daughter—and they wouldn't believe it if you told them, anyway. Look, if you don't want me to hold on to you, then *you* hold on to *me*." He dropped her wrists. "See? I bet you can't understand me now, you little ingrate," he muttered in English.

The blue-painted chin lifted higher, and the gray eyes stared without blinking. But Will noticed the chin tremble slightly. He looked away.

A crunch of tires sounded on the gravel drive; a car rolled past with a quick honk. Breet jumped away with a smothered cry and stumbled against Will. He put out an arm to catch her, and she clung to him, trembling.

"Everything here is so strange," she said in a low voice. "And back in my true time, my people are . . ." She swallowed. "They are preparing to die. Truly, I do need you to help me. And I am sorry."

Will gave her a fleeting smile. "That's okay. It's Nan you should say sorry to, not me."

Breet looked as Nan and her father walked around the corner of the castle. The horses' braided tails flicked, the chariot gave a last bumping rattle, and then the whole equipage was out of sight.

She took hold of Will's arm and started forward. "Is that man—her father—the one who can tell me about the Romans in my time?"

"Yes."

"But I can't understand him when he speaks."

"We'll translate," said Will, sighing inwardly.

Breet held his elbow firmly and marched him around the castle. The horses, calm now, grazed on the patchy grass beside the low garden wall as Nan stroked their necks.

Ewen Menzies bent to examine the chariot with keen eyes. "Marvelous workmanship," he muttered. "Someone put a lot of effort into making this authentic . . . wooden pegs, rawhide, root lashings! Unbelievable . . ."

He looked curiously at Breet. "You're Nan's friend from school, are you?"

"Actually, I just met her today," Nan said quickly.

"One of the reenactors, then? She's a bit young to be doing that on her own, not to mention having charge of two horses, small though they are. Or is she with her parents?"

"Um . . . ," said Nan. "I met her parents, but I don't know where they are, exactly."

"Mmm. What was all that fuss about, back there? Someone was actually threatening to call the police. What happened?"

"I'm not even sure how it started," Will said. "All of a sudden, everyone was arguing about where the Picts really came from in the first place. This one guy got really mad. And then he made fun of Breet because she was talking Pictish. I mean," he amended, "*trying* to talk Pictish."

Nan said, "She's dressed like a Pict, so naturally she's going to try to talk like one, right? But this guy thought she was being rude."

"All the arguing was frightening the horses," Will put in. "Breet tried to calm them, but the mean guy insulted her, and she got mad and raised her whip. I don't think she'd have used it," he added hastily, "but that's when you came in."

"Ah." Ewen Menzies looked at Breet kindly through his glasses. "Well, lass, maybe we'd better get you back to your parents."

"Dad," Nan said, "Breet is really interested in the Picts and Romans. She wants to know all about Pin—Pinnata something—"

"Pinnata Castra?"

"Inchtuthil," said Breet.

"That's right; good for you!" Cousin Ewen's eyes seemed to grow bluer as he gazed at Breet. "What do you want to know?"

Breet turned to Will.

"Um," said Will, "I think she's a little—er—shy?" He gazed at Breet with her wild hair, fierce gaze, and blue painted designs. He had never seen anyone look less shy in his life. "I mean, she's kind of . . ." He looked helplessly at Nan.

"Intense," Nan said at once. She stepped closer to Breet, then hesitated.

"She's sorry she called you a name," Will said quietly. "She told me."

Breet nodded. She held out her hand.

Nan's dimple showed as she took Breet's hand in hers. "See, she's really into this Pictish thing. She tries to stay in character, you know? So please don't think she's rude if she acts like she can't speak English."

Nan's father's mouth quirked at the corners, and his eyes twinkled. "But if she wants to ask me questions, how am I supposed to understand her?"

Will hesitated, feeling foolish. "I guess we'll translate," he began, but at the same moment another voice spoke over his.

"I will ask in your language," said Breet in slightly accented English. She grinned at Will and Nan, showing the space between her teeth, and whispered, "All in a moment I could understand. But keep hold of me, or it might go away."

Will nodded his complete agreement. Maybe Time Hearing was like electricity—you had to make a connection before current flowed. It made sense. After all, the others had to touch him to see through the time window. Time Hearing could work like that, even in reverse. He didn't really care why or how, just so long as it *did* work.

"What would you like to know about Inchtuthil?" Ewen Menzies asked. "Do you have an interest in Romans?"

Breet leaned forward, her whole body tense. "How long did they stay?"

"At Inchtuthil? Let's see . . . it was built after the Battle of Mons Graupius—that was a huge battle between the Picts and the Romans, about AD 84, when thousands died."

"We call it the Battle of the Bloody Hands," said Breet soberly.

Nan's father lifted one eyebrow. "Indeed? Well, it was bloody enough, according to all accounts." He gave Breet a considering look. "That's a piece of history not many learn, nowadays. What school do you attend?"

Nan cleared her throat. "She's—er, homeschooled, Dad."

"Ah. Well, you can tell your parents for me that they're doing a fine job of teaching."

Breet's eyes seemed to turn darker. "I would be without honor," she said, very low, "if I could forget a battle in which my brother died, and my father was wounded, and my mother broke her heart for weeping."

Cousin Ewen's eyebrows twisted up sharply. "And when do you imagine that this battle took place?"

"I do not imagine. It was two springs ago." Breet's shoulders rounded as she stared at her feet. "I only wish I *could* forget it, as you seem to expect."

Nan's father shot a glance at his daughter. "She does stay in character, doesn't she?"

Nan nodded fervently.

"Well, then, I'd better play along. Let's see. If the Battle of Mons Graupius was two springs ago—and this is summer, so that's, say, a year and a quarter, perhaps—then the fort at Inchtuthil must have been only recently built."

Breet nodded. "This past year they began it. It is not finished, but already it is strong, and now they send their warriors out to raid our people." She pressed her lips together as if to keep them from trembling.

"Then to answer your question, the Romans will be gone in one or two more winters. Perhaps even three, but no more."

Breet sucked in air between her teeth. "How can this be? The Romans never leave a place until they have conquered!"

"They will leave this one. They will leave suddenly, with little warning—and they will never come back. The fort will be abandoned."

Breet just stared at him. "Why?" she whispered.

"No one knows. One of the reasons, I think, was that they realized they could never win in the Highlands. Our people could not beat the Romans on an open battlefield—but in the narrow glens and thick forests, they could disappear, attack when the Romans were not expecting it and then retreat into the caves and hidden places to fight another day."

Breet smacked her palms. "This is the news that will

give heart to my father! I must tell him! I must tell all my people!"

"You do that," said Nan's father, grinning.

❧

"All right," Will said, holding tight to the sides of the chariot as they rolled across the grounds, "now to get you home. Should we go back the way we came?"

Breet shuddered. "No more dragon chariots. I'll go the long way around—up the hill, then down into the river valley."

"Can you drive uphill? Through the trees?" Will was doubtful.

Breet laughed. "This is a war chariot! And they are war ponies! They go uphill and down—and fast, too. Besides, look, the old road is still there!" She pointed to the path leading up through Weem Wood.

"It's funny," Will said, "that the path we still use is really an old Pictish road."

"What's really funny," said Nan, "is that we're riding across where real Romans are camping, right this minute."

Will looked over his shoulder. Cousin Ewen had gone into the castle. "Stop here, will you? I'm going to open a window into the Roman camp. Just to look," he added as he stepped from the chariot. "I want to see where Gormlaith is."

But the time window did not open easily. Will suddenly realized how very tired he was. He had spent many hours back with the Picts; his body probably thought it was way past bedtime. Suddenly he envied Jamie, fast asleep in his cot in the castle.

Will tried again until he got a shimmer. Then he searched wearily for the right moment in time. It was harder than he had thought it would be. When he'd gone into Pictish time before, he had been touching the ancient Roman pin. He needed a strong connection to Breet's time—oh, of course. Breet herself. He reached out to grab her hand.

The late-afternoon sun filtered through the leaves in the woods, lighting the forest floor with a shifting mosaic of greens and soft browns and bright gold. Somewhere above his head, a bird trilled, and Will breathed slowly, deeply. Gently he probed with the strange inner vision he called Time Sight for the telltale tracks that marked the trips they had taken into the past. In this quiet space, with no need to rush, he could see the faint golden threads clearly. Each one had a slightly different—color? No, not color. A different vibration? That wasn't quite right, either. It was almost as if each one had a different . . . *personality*.

His heart beat a little faster. Why not? Why wouldn't each person's track through time be a little bit different? Now that he was looking for it, he could almost tell who was who. That swooping one might be Nan—it had a sort of humming energy that reminded him of her. There were two tracks that looked almost alike, except that one had been traced over again, as if more than one trip had been made—oh, of course, that would be Breet and her father. The bouncy one that almost seemed to fizz had to be Jamie, and he would bet that the wavering, loopy one was Gormlaith. That left—

"Quickly!" said Breet at his elbow. "My people—we can't wait too long!"

Will abandoned his study of the golden threads and pinpointed what felt like the right time. There. He couldn't go back any farther, or it all turned gray on him. . . . He opened the window and found himself looking directly into the sneering face of a Roman guard. The man's fist was drawn back, and he looked as if he were about to—

"Watch out!" cried Breet.

11
ROMANS AND PICTS

WILL'S HEART GAVE A VIOLENT leap, and he ducked. The window snapped shut.

"Better try again, farther off," said Nan.

"Thank you, Captain Obvious," Will muttered. His heart raced; his headache had returned. How many times today had he opened a window into a new time? Seven? Eight?

"Well, excuse me for wanting to keep you from getting punched!" Nan said hotly.

"Sorry," Will mumbled, backing up out of Breet's way. The ponies had shied at the noise; Breet ran to calm them with Pictish endearments. Will glanced up the wooded slope behind him. "Breet, you'd better take the chariot up the hill.

Go far enough away that the Romans won't see you through the trees. I'll come up and open a window into your time in a little while."

"In a *while*?" Breet's voice scaled up fiercely. "My people need the news I bring! You know what they will do—kill *everyone*—"

"But we have to get Gormlaith," Nan soothed. "It won't take a minute."

"You'd make my people wait while you rescue a *dog*?" The color on Breet's cheeks rose dangerously high.

"No worries," Will interrupted hastily. "I can open the time window to almost the moment we left, see? Your people will hardly wait a minute."

"Then send me through now and get the dog later!"

Will leaned his forehead against the trunk of a tree. He didn't want to climb the hill to send Breet home, then have to come all the way back for Gormlaith. . . . Besides, it was completely unnecessary.

"Do as I say!" Breet shrieked. "I am the daughter of a chieftain!"

"Oh, give it a rest," Nan snapped. "And don't you dare!" She knocked aside Breet's whip, which had begun to rise. "Do you want to go home, or not?"

The blood drained from Breet's face; the blue painted spirals stood out weirdly on skin suddenly pale. She lowered her whip.

Will looked straight into Breet's gray eyes. "I *will* get you back in time, I promise."

Breet bit her lip. Without a word, she clucked to the horses and led them up the hill.

Nan turned to Will. "Are you all right?"

Will shrugged. "It's harder and harder to keep the window open. My head starts to hurt. . . . Listen, let's just get this over with. I want to go home and sleep."

He backed up, a good distance from where the angry Roman had been, and let his eyes glaze over as he stared into space. It was surprisingly difficult to relax. He could not forget that Roman fist; what if it was a spear next time?

The window wasn't opening. Will took in a breath and let it out. Maybe his eyes were focusing too sharply, watching for danger. He deliberately slackened the tension in his body and tried again.

The threadlike tracks of his passage through time emerged at last, glimmering faintly at the edges of his vision. There. That one. Will gently pushed the worry to the back of his mind, and opened the window.

There was a thick tree just ahead. Good—it would block any stray spears. Slowly Will turned until he saw the Roman tents, bright in the high afternoon sun. Some of the men were building a sort of tall fence with sharpened spikes. There was the centurion with his red-crested helmet, drawing in the dirt with a stick while two other soldiers looked on. Battle plans, maybe. Something glinted at his shoulder—a sort of curved pin, holding the folds of his cloak together.

But where was the guard who had almost put a fist through the time window? Will continued to turn his head slowly to the right. Then he stopped.

Behind him, Nan gasped. "Why is that guard hitting that poor man?"

"He must be one of their slaves," Will said slowly. "Captured in battle, I guess." He watched, feeling sick, as the spindly man on the ground wiped his bloody nose with the back of his hand and struggled to his feet.

The angry Roman guard let loose with a string of words Will didn't understand. Then, amid the babble, he heard clearly the word *janitor*.

The slave picked up a bucket at his feet and went trudging off to one of the tents.

"*Janitor?*" said Will.

"Maybe it's a Latin word," Nan said. "You know, what the Romans spoke? At school, they told us we still use a lot of Latin words today. Like, uh, *gymnasium*. And *auditorium*. And *janitor*, I suppose, and—"

"Gormlaith!" said Will.

"No, Gormlaith isn't Latin," Nan corrected.

"The *dog*, you dumbwit! Look there, by the corner of the tent the slave just passed." Will turned the window slightly.

There, in a triangular bit of shade, a large creamy dog lay with her head on her paws.

Nan's fingers dug into Will's shoulder as the angry Roman guard moved toward the dog. "If he hurts Gormly, I swear I'm going to kill him."

But the guard only stooped to fondle the dog's head. Gormlaith scrambled to her feet, pulling against the rope that tied her. The guard disappeared into the tent, laughing.

Nan made a sound remarkably like a snarl. "Right, that scunner isn't touching my dog again. Let's get her."

They moved forward slowly, Will concentrating on keeping the picture focused, Nan trying not to step on Will's heels. They reached the dog and paused, irresolute.

"I'll call her," said Nan. "Then she'll jump through."

"She can't hear us, remember? The sound and sight only goes in one direction—"

Nan suddenly stuck her head through the window.

"No!" Will protested, but Nan couldn't hear him with her head on the other side.

"Gormlaith!" Nan reached a hand through and tugged on the rope. "Come!"

Will tried desperately to keep his focus around Nan's shifting head and shoulders. He *couldn't* let the window shut when her head was hanging out there in another time.

Gormlaith's glad snuff at Nan's voice changed in an instant to a fearful whine. She backed up, pulling at the rope to get as far from the disembodied head as possible. In the distance, Will saw movement as a Roman turned toward the dog—and Nan's head.

Sweat from Will's forehead dripped down onto his lashes and hung there, trembling. He groped for the back of Nan's collar and yanked hard.

Her head came back, but her hand was still through the window, gripping the rope. Now Will could hear someone shouting on the other side.

"Let go!" he urged.

"Come on, you—Gormless!" Nan tugged at the rope, but the dog tugged harder.

"Pull—your hand—in *now*," Will said through his teeth. He kept focus with a shaking effort; it felt as if an iron band were pressing around his forehead. He couldn't hold out much longer.

Desperately Will clamped his hand around Nan's wrist and used all his strength for a last, violent yank. He fell on his back, and Nan tumbled on top of him.

"Why did you do that?" she cried. "Gormly was going to come in a minute!"

Breathless, Will pointed. Four inches of rope still dangled from her fist. The end had been cleanly cut, as if by the sharpest of knives.

"Oh . . . ," said Nan.

"It would have cut your hand right off if I hadn't pulled."

Will sat up, rubbing his eyes. "Next time, listen, will you? I can't keep that window open forever!"

"You don't have to get stroppy about it." Nan's voice was sulky.

Will glared at her. "Fine. Next time, *get* yourself cut in two, see if I care!"

Nan tried to return the glare, but her eyes filled in spite of her. She turned away, sniffling. "It's just—she's my dog, and I don't know how to get her back."

Will brushed the dirt off his knees. "Okay," he said heavily. "I'll open a window for a few seconds, so we can see what happened to her. Then I'll close it, and we can think what to do. All right?"

Nan sniffled again and nodded.

Will's head felt like a split melon, but he managed to get the window open again after three attempts. He tried for the moment after the rope had been cut and was just in time to see Gormlaith's hindquarters as she dodged through the camp and tore off up the hill, the long rope flapping and jouncing behind her. Will shut the window with relief. "No one followed her. She went up the hill—I saw where. Let's go take care of Breet and then find Gormly and go home. All right?"

Nan nodded, gulping. "But *hurry*—we don't know how fast time is moving, back there. Remember how a year went by for Jamie, while only an afternoon passed for us?"

"Only because I wasn't used to opening the window. I didn't know how to zero in on the time." Will had a feeling there was more to it than that, but he couldn't think what.

He trudged up the hill after Nan. On this very soil, two thousand years in the past, Romans were beating their slaves and preparing for war. But here in the twenty-first century, the woods were quiet and green, and the path was worn smooth by the feet of hikers. Behind him, in the distance, he could hear faint shouts from the reenactors, and the sound of clashing swords mixed with laughter and the happy shrieks of children. Everyone was having a grand time playing Romans and Picts. Will was consumed with longing to stay in this time, his own time, where things were peaceful and battles were pretend . . .

Except they weren't always. Not in the place where his mother was. Not in lots of places.

Will winced. He was so tired. He didn't want to think about the world with all its troubles, past and present and yet to come; there was so little he could do about any of it. Nothing at all, really—

No, that wasn't right. He *had* done something. And in spite of the ache that always came at the thought of his mother, the ache that never quite went away, there was a lightness in him, too. Because he had done what his father had asked. He'd taken care of Jamie.

It was a small thing, maybe, compared to all the

problems in the world, but it would not seem small to his mother or his father. And though his parents would never know how difficult it had been, Will knew. And if the old man at the well—Sir David—was right, then God knew, too. Somehow that was a comfort.

Will glanced over his shoulder. He couldn't see Castle Menzies through the trees, but it was there all the same, and his little brother was safe inside it, sleeping. Now if only Will could get Breet back to the Picts, and find Gormlaith and bring her home, he would never, ever go back in time again.

"Don't step in the hole," Nan said suddenly.

Will blinked and came out of his daydream. There, at his feet, was the hole Jamie and Gormlaith had dug, with a trowel stuck beside it in a pile of earth. Next to it was Nan's satchel where she had dropped it, with a corner of the Magic Eyeball book poking out the top. And still on the ground was the Roman pin—Jamie's "stabber"—and next to it, the penknife Nan had dropped. No one had disturbed anything.

"Look, there's Breet," said Nan, pointing.

The brightly painted chariot was screened from the base of the hill, where the Roman camp would be when Breet went back to her own time; she had chosen her spot well. The ponies whickered softly, pawing the ground as if anxious to get going. Breet left the reins looped around a tree and trotted back to grip their hands so they could speak together. "I want to go back to my people *now*."

"I'm going to send you." Will looked around to get his bearings. "Okay, the Roman camp was just about there." He pointed down the hill and to the right. "And the last I saw Gormlaith, she was running up here, but more to the left, I think."

Breet's head reared back. "My people come before your *dog*!"

"I'm just working everything out in advance," Will explained. "I don't want to keep the window open while we figure out what's next. It hurts my head if it's open too long, and it's bad if I accidentally close the window at the wrong time." Will glanced at Nan.

"Really bad," Nan agreed fervently.

"So here's my idea. Breet, you stand by the horses' heads and wait for my signal. When the window opens, lead them through—they'll go more quietly that way."

"Yes," said Breet.

Will went on. "I'm going to open a window to a few seconds after Gormlaith's rope was cut. That's as early as I can go, and it should be enough time for you to get back and stop your people from—you know."

Breet nodded grimly.

"You won't see the time window because you won't be

touching me. But I'll make it big enough for the chariot to go through, like before. When you hear me shout your name, just walk straight ahead. There might be a sort of strange look to the air; go right through it and you'll be back in your own time."

"Then drive straight over the hill and down the other side, and back to my village to tell my father all that I have seen!" Breet's face was triumphant.

"But what about Gormlaith?" Nan twisted her fingers together.

"I'm coming to that. As soon as Breet makes it all the way through, I'll turn the window to face the Roman camp. We should see Gormly running up the hill toward us. You'll have to call her—"

"What, stick my head through again?" Nan looked worried. "Are you sure? I don't want to get beheaded. . . . Anyway, Gormly didn't even come the last time I did that. I think she was scared to see my head just floating there."

Will hesitated. He did not want to send Nan into danger, but he couldn't see any way out of it if they wanted to get Gormlaith back. "You'd better go all the way through the window to call her. It won't take a minute," he added, hoping it was true. "Even if the Romans hear you, they won't be able to get up the hill fast enough to do anything."

Nan swallowed.

"Unless you have a better idea?" Will asked hastily.

"No," Nan said in a small voice. "I'll do it."

"Ah—you are brave, like my people!" The gap between Breet's teeth showed as she grinned. "I wish you could come back to my village; I'd paint you with warrior patterns. But I can give you this." She wriggled off her iron armband with a quick motion and put it into Nan's hands. "It will bring you protection."

"Thanks!" said Nan, pushing it onto her arm.

"Yeah, thanks," Will said. "And good luck!"

Nan traced the curving iron with her finger as Breet trotted off to the ponies. "Will, promise not to leave me there?"

"Of course I won't!"

"I know you wouldn't do it on purpose. But what if something goes wrong and you can't keep the window open anymore? Promise you won't just shut it and come back for me later. Promise me you'll come through right that minute."

Will sighed. Nobody seemed to really understand that he had the time window thing under control now. If something did go wrong, it would actually be better to shut the window, think up a plan, gather any weapons or whatever he needed, and then open it again to the exact second he'd left—

"Please?" Nan begged.

"All right," said Will. "But I won't have to," he added hurriedly. "It's a good plan. It ought to work perfectly."

Breet was in position, the reins in her hands and her head

turned, waiting. Will took a deep breath and allowed his gaze to blur. Now that he'd had time to rest his eyes, his head didn't hurt so much, and Nan's armband, so close to him, was a powerful connection to the past. The threadlike tracks of his passage through time became stronger, glimmering faintly at the edge of his vision. There, right *there*, was a clear trace to the moment when he had last opened the window—a jagged sort of track that felt like fear.

"Better hurry," Nan murmured at his elbow. "Breet looks like she's having trouble keeping the horses still. Why aren't you facing her?"

"Just checking to make sure I've got the right time. . . . Yes!" he breathed. "There's Gormly, see? Her rope has just been cut, and she's running from the Roman tent up the hill toward us—"

"Oh, brilliant," said Nan with fervor.

A bubbling elation fluttered in Will's chest. He had opened it *perfectly*. Slowly he turned his head, bringing the window around toward Breet; the stout trees of Pictish times moved past one by one. He was going to do it—it was all going to work—

There was a sudden movement in the window, low down. Will caught a glimpse of a broad black-and-white snout emerging from a wide hole in the ground, followed by two bright eyes. Nan gave a faint shriek and clutched his shoulder.

The picture blurred slightly, and Will made a heroic effort to snap it back into focus.

"Don't *do* that!" he said through his teeth. "You almost made me lose the window!" His headache, never really gone, grew into a dull pressure behind his eyes. The light through the window seemed to have dimmed—was his vision going?

"Sorry," said Nan. "It startled me, that's all."

"What was it?" Will stopped the motion of his head long enough to look at the hole. It was largish—over a foot wide—but the creature was gone.

"That same badger Gormly chased before, I think." Nan glanced up the hill to where Breet was waiting patiently to go back to her own time. "Never mind, it's gone. How are your eyes doing? Can you make the window big enough for the chariot?"

"Yes." Will ignored the strain in the small muscles of his eyes; he tried to forget about the pulse that was beginning to throb at his temples. Just a little more effort, and he would be done with Time Sight forever.

Slowly, with infinite care, he enlarged the window. When it was big enough for Breet to drive through, he carefully slid it through the air until it was directly in front of the girl and her chariot.

"Breet, go!" he shouted, wincing as the sound pierced his head.

The blue-painted girl looked at them steadily for a long moment. Then she joined her hands together in a double fist and thumped them against her chest.

"We'll miss you, too!" Nan called, waving.

"She can't understand you anymore," Will said.

"I don't care. She knows what I mean. Oh, good-bye!" Nan cried.

Breet raised her hand in a tentative wave, and her teeth flashed in a sudden grin. Then, calmly and without fuss, she walked the horses through into her own time and was gone.

Will pulled the window gently around in the other direction. "Your turn now, Nan," he said, holding the focus steady in spite of the pain. He could do this. It was only for a minute more.

"But where's Gormlaith?" She peered past his shoulder.

"Oh, for—" Will bit off a word and held his focus with determined concentration. The dog should have been right *there*. . . .

Will turned slowly in a circle, searching. He blinked quickly, moistening his eyes, keeping the focus intact.

"There! What was that?" Nan pointed. "Go back a bit."

"What?" Will couldn't see anything but a rock and some pine branches . . . wait. Something was sticking out behind the rock. Something pale and feathery; it almost looked like Gormlaith's tail, but it wasn't wagging. It wasn't moving at all.

"Something's wrong," Will said slowly. His eyes, already strained, began to burn. "She was running up the hill just a minute ago. What could have happened in that time?"

"Get closer!" Nan's hand gripped his elbow, urging him on, guiding his steps.

Will paced forward over the rough ground, his headache growing fiercer with every step. He longed to close the window, but he couldn't, not until they knew if the dog was dead or alive. He stepped around the rock. Nan gasped.

The rope the Romans had put on Gormlaith was tangled around the pine tree and caught in the low-reaching branches. The dog had clearly tried to free herself but had only succeeded in getting one leg caught up inside her collar, a strange, wide leather affair with metal spikes. She lay almost flat, with her head lifted slightly at a strained angle, and her eyes were closed.

"Gormly!" Nan breathed. In an instant she was through the window and ducking under the branches, crawling on her hands and knees to Gormlaith's head.

The dog opened her eyes, dull and glazed with pain. In that moment, Will noticed that the earth all around her hind legs was gashed deep, as if she had scrabbled mightily with her paws for a very long time.

Nan was having trouble. She dragged the heavy dog a few inches forward, to slacken the tight rope, but as soon as Gormly got more air, she began to struggle. Will's head felt like a gong beating, but in spite of the pain, he could see that the more the dog struggled, the tighter the rope grew and the more impossible it was for Nan to untangle.

Why didn't she use her penknife? As if Nan had heard his thoughts, her hand fumbled in her pocket, but came out empty. She looked up, despairing, in the general direction of the window. "It's gone!"

Suddenly Will remembered where it was.

Warily, slowly, he turned around, keeping his focus on the Pictish forest but losing his view of Nan and Gormlaith. He felt strangely guilty for turning his back on them, but he *was* still keeping the window open. He slid his feet forward, carefully feeling the ground ahead, never able to look down. The hole Jamie had dug should be just . . . about . . . here. . . .

He felt around with his foot for what seemed like an eternity. At last his toe dipped into a depression, and he knelt with great care to grope with his hand. He had to use all his concentration to keep the window open now. . . . His fingers closed around smooth metal, and his thumb felt a sharp edge.

He stood, he turned, barely hanging on to his focus. He had planned to toss the knife through to Nan, but he could hardly see anymore. Black dots swirled in his vision, and he was nauseated from pain. He had only a few seconds left, and he had promised. . . .

Will stepped into the time of the Romans and Picts, and stumbled toward the pine tree where Nan and Gormlaith still struggled. "Here," he gasped, pressing the knife into Nan's outstretched hand. Then he fell to his knees and was sick.

When at last he lifted his head, it was the light he noticed first. Slanting in low from the west, it furred the leaves on the hill with gold. Then, in a moment, the golden shafts were gone and the forest turned somber. Will looked to the upper branches to see the sun still lighting the treetops. That, too, would go in another minute.

How could the sun be setting? His head felt full of nails, and he was half-dazed, but he was sure it had been midafternoon when Gormlaith had run away from the Romans.

A few steps away, Nan cradled Gormlaith's head in her lap. The dog's chest rose and fell in reassuring rhythm, and her brown eyes, no longer glazed with pain, were fixed on Nan's. The rope and spiked collar lay curled in the pine needles that covered the ground.

"She's breathing fine now," Nan said in a low voice. "Let's get out of here before any more Romans come."

Will ripped up a handful of grass to wipe his mouth and scanned the surrounding forest. "Wait." He squinted at the bit of brightly painted wood showing through a gap in the trees. "Isn't that Breet's chariot? Why hasn't she gone back to the hill fort?"

"How would I know? I've been busy with Gormlaith!" Nan frowned. "Hurry up—open a window to our time!"

Just thinking about opening a window made the spots swirl in front of Will's eyes again. He couldn't do it—not yet. "I need a minute," he said, glancing again at the bit of painted wood farther up the hill. "And I want to check on something."

"Are you crazy?" Nan hissed. "Come back here!" But Will was already gone, slipping quietly from tree to tree as he moved toward the painted chariot. He was almost there when suddenly a hand was clapped over his mouth and his arms were pinned to his sides.

"You!" said his captor.

It was the tattooed man with the wolfskin cape; his chest scars were plain even in the dwindling light. "I thought you had gone," the warrior said, releasing his hold. "Have you come to bring your magic to aid us in battle?"

"Husha!" said another Pict near him. Will looked around. Hidden among the shadows and behind trees were the forms of other tattooed Picts, women as well as men. Of course. They had planned to storm the Roman camp at sunset.

Some extra time must have slipped by, somehow, when Will had opened the window into Pictish time. He remembered how the window had blurred for a moment when the badger had startled him, coming out of its hole.

Breet was speaking to her father in low but clear tones. "Yes, I saw the ruins that you saw," she said, "but listen to me. The hill fort was only deserted because our people had built bigger, better dwellings."

"And how do you know this?" the chieftain demanded.

Breet raked a hand through her hair, dragging it back from her forehead. "Will took me there, with his magic. I have seen chariots like smoking dragons, racing faster than the fastest horses, over roads as smooth as a pool of water on a windless day."

There was a low murmur from the listening Picts. Will's eye was caught by the gleam of a strange brass object on top of what looked like a pole. He squinted and decided it was a boar's head—or something like it.

"I have seen proud dwellings, towering high above the trees, many times the height of our tallest hut, built of stone squared like Roman walls, yet built by *our* people they tell me—built on the very spot of that Roman camp!" Breet pointed down the hill.

"Is this possible?" whispered the Pict standing next to Will.

"And I have spoken with a man of that time, Father. He told me—" She flung back her head, her face alight. "He said that the Romans may have beaten us on the open plain, at the Battle of the Bloody Hands, but that they could not win among these, our own hills, where we can attack without warning and retreat into hidden places where they cannot follow. They will be gone soon, Father!"

The chieftain's eyes seemed to grow darker. "And you believed this man?"

Breet clasped her hands and thumped them on her chest. "As much as I believe you. He was a wise man, a druid, I think, one of our descendants; I looked him in the eye, and there was no lie in him. He swore it, Father! In one or two winters, no more than three, he said the Romans will abandon the fort at Inchtuthil and never trouble us again!"

The chieftain's face lit up with a fierce joy. "Then we fight, not to destruction, but to victory!" He raised his spear and shook it. All around him, his warriors did the same, silently but with a sort of breathing exaltation.

The chieftain lowered his spear and looked around the circle of waiting Picts. "When the carnyx sounds, strike your blows, then disperse into the hidden glens and caves. They will follow, but they will not follow far, for they do not know this land as we do. We will meet again at moonset and strike another blow when they expect it not!"

A low, fierce growl went around the circle. The man holding the brass boar's head lifted it higher.

The chieftain turned to Breet. "Though some may die today, not all will die. Take this news back to your mother, Breet. Tell her that no life need be taken in the village. Then stay with her, and stay safely."

Breet pouted. "But I want to come back and join the battle. We are not like the Romans; our women can *fight*."

"Strong women," said her father quietly, "will always join in the fighting, if they are not caring for children or the old and sick. But you are still just a girl."

"I'm a *strong* girl," Breet insisted.

Her father's voice was stern. "You are brave, my daughter, but you have your task, and your orders. Go now, go silently—and if the gods are kind, we will meet again!"

Will hurried back to Nan and Gormlaith. He had to open a window before the battle started.

Down between the tents, torches were being lit; a Roman guard stared up the hill as if looking for someone. Will squatted behind the boulder, breathing quickly.

Gormlaith was on her feet now, whining, and Nan used all her strength to hang on to the dog. "Can you open it *now*?" she begged. "It's hard to hold Gormly, and I think the Romans might have heard her."

Will nodded. He was not exactly calm, and his head still hurt, but once he got the window open, they only needed a few seconds to get through.

He shut his eyes, took a breath, and opened them again. The trees around him blurred as he focused, not on anything he could see, but on what he *couldn't*. The air before him wavered slightly—the gossamer threads of their movements through time shimmered, faint and golden in the dusk. There. There.

In the back of his mind, he was aware of increasing

noise—a rumble, a vague sound of movement, a voice shouting—but no matter, he had the window to their own time open. There, through the window, was Nan's satchel with the Magic Eyeball book still half tumbling out; there was the hole again where Jamie had unearthed the helmet.

"*Now*," he said urgently. "Go on through."

BRRRAAAANNNGGGH! BRANG-RANG-RAAANNNGGH!

The noise, wild and brazen, bellowed through the trees like the sound of a metallic beast in a furious rage. Will clenched his jaw and stifled an almost uncontrollable instinct to turn around and look. "*Now*, Nan!"

"I can't!" Nan had both arms locked around the dog's midsection. "Gormly's scared, she's trying to run off! And I'm not touching you, I can't even *see* the window—"

"It's right in front of me. Nan, shove her *through*!"

Gormlaith squirmed as Nan tried to push her. Suddenly the dog turned around, breaking Nan's hold, and anxiously licked the girl's face. Nan laughed wildly.

"Are you *insane*?" Will demanded. "Laughing, at a time like this?"

"No," Nan gasped, "but I just figured out what to do—Gormly, stay!" she said firmly in the dog's ear. Startled, Gormlaith froze for a moment. "Fetch!" Nan cried, and threw a pinecone straight through the window that led to their own time.

Gormlaith leaped after it, her tail flying as she cleared the window.

The thunder of charging warriors was loud in Will's ears. "GO!" he shouted, but suddenly Nan yanked hard at Will's shirt. The window disappeared as she pulled him down behind the rock and a spear whizzed by where his head had been.

A man holding a long sort of trumpet that ended in a brass beast's head strode past, blowing fiercely into the mouthpiece, his cheeks distended. Will clapped his hands over his ears as the bellowing sound seemed to pierce to his bones. That had to be the carnyx—the "great loud beast horn" that Breet had described. It was supposed to strike the fear of death into Pictish enemies. Will wasn't an enemy, but he was terrified all the same.

Hooves pounded, shaking the earth; there was a whinny like a scream, rising above the brazen howl of the carnyx. Will and Nan huddled together behind the boulder as a horse reared above them, its helmeted Roman rider fighting to control it. Then, faster than Will could take it in, a spear flashed, blood spurted, and the Roman rider toppled, his cloak tearing loose from its pin. His bronze helmet fell off, hit the ground with a clang, and rolled into the badger's hole.

Nan was saying something; her mouth moved, but Will could hear nothing over the roar of battle. He pulled at her, and they crawled away through the undergrowth.

"That's the helmet Jamie found!" Nan said breathlessly. "It rolled into that hole—and stayed there for two thousand years! And his cloak pin, too!"

Will was shaken to his core. Breet had been right—the reenactors' battle was nothing like a real one. "We've got to get to a safe place," he said. "A quiet place."

Nan glanced over her shoulder. "Let's go to Saint David's Well."

"Will it still be there?" Will wondered aloud, but he staggered after his cousin up the path. The well *was* there. The flat stone slabs were not yet placed, but the water brimmed up over earth and moss, and the sheer cliff and the apron of turf were just the same. The cup-marked stone they had picnicked on was there, too, and Will sat down upon it, breathing hard, his knees strangely weak.

Nan looked nervously over her shoulder. "At least Gormly's safe. Better open a window for us now."

"Just . . . let me catch my breath."

"Do it fast," Nan advised. "I hear someone coming."

Will's hands pressed down hard on the rock as he tried to concentrate. He glanced involuntarily to one side as two tattooed warriors raced silently past them up the path. Were the Picts dispersing already?

Nan's hand on his shoulder was shaking, as if she had a chill. "Aren't you going to stand up so we can walk through?"

Will got to his feet with reluctance. He felt as if his

muscles had turned to water; he longed to sit back down on the cup-marked stone. He had the strangest feeling that the stone itself was exerting a force, drawing him back. . . . He took a few steps away from the stone and shook his head, to clear it. Now he could hear the sound of someone running—louder, coming closer, with creaking leather and the clank of metal armor—

"Hurry!" Nan's whisper was hoarse in his ear.

"I can't find the right time." Will searched frantically for the shimmering golden threads, the feeling that said "now," the sense that he had homed in on the moment he wanted, but something—something strong—seemed to be tugging him in another direction.

"It doesn't have to be the perfect time—just get us out of here!" Nan's fingers clutched his shoulder.

The air shimmered faintly. The window came into focus—faded out—came in again. There were no golden threads there, yet something dragged at him like strong hands, pulling in spite of his resistance.

"Now!" Nan squeaked as a Roman appeared at the head of the path.

Will gave in, and the window opened. Nan sprang through it. Will dived after her, rolling on the ground, and lay there, panting.

The sky above him was a dark slate-gray, with a glimmer

of pink in the east, and the earth beneath was cold and prickly with early-morning frost. He sat up and rubbed his arms, already covered with goose bumps.

And there was a boy, dressed in skins with a rough fiber torc around his neck, staring at them with his back to a tree.

12
CRAY-TEE AND POUN-KA

THE BOY'S EYES WERE WIDE, and his face pale beneath his shaggy hair, but he stayed pressed against the tree, as if too terrified to move.

Will raised himself cautiously and gave Nan a silent jerk of his chin in the direction of the path. If they could just get to a place without any people around, where he could have quiet for a minute, he could get them back home—

Tap. Tap. Tap.

The sound came from behind them. Will whirled to see a man crouched over the cup-marked stone, his back to the children. His hard-muscled arm jerked in time with the taps; he seemed to be using a rock to hammer at the stone.

A leather pouch hung at his side, and the knife in his belt was the color of a new penny.

Beyond the man, a small group of people swayed back and forth, their eyes closed. They chanted three notes in a minor key, over and over, and their voices rose and fell weirdly, with a sound like wind blowing through a hollow pipe. Standing before them was a woman with a pelt of white fur about her shoulders. Her head was thrown back, and her arms were lifted toward the faint pink tint at the edge of the sky.

Will exchanged a glance with Nan, put a finger to his lips, and took a silent step toward the path—then another. He and Nan were almost past the shaggy-haired boy. With any luck, the boy would keep still—

But Nan stopped dead, as if she had suddenly grown roots.

Come on! Will mouthed the words in furious silence.

Nan shook her head. She pointed to the fiber torc around the boy's neck.

Will rolled his eyes in a fury of impatience. What did it matter if the torc was made of rope? Maybe the kid wasn't important enough to have a better one!

Then, all at once, Will saw. Knotted around the boy's neck, the rope led tautly down his back behind the tree, ending in a knot around the boy's wrists. The rope necklace wasn't a torc at all. It was a noose that both choked him and tied him to the tree.

Nan pulled her penknife out of her pocket and flicked it open.

The boy's eyes dilated in horror. He leaned away, and the rope tightened about his neck. A sound gurgled deep in his throat.

The crouching man turned, suddenly alert. The chanting stopped.

"Hurry!" Will whispered.

Nan cut the rope from the boy's wrists with two jerks of her knife and turned to run.

The man caught up to them before they had gone four yards. Will felt a powerful hand clamp around his neck, and then his head was smacked together with Nan's. Dazed, he struggled to get away, but the fingers around his neck tightened and his vision clouded. He felt himself being dragged.

When next he could see, he was kneeling next to Nan, his arms pinned behind his back. Voices were speaking a language he had never learned. Nearby, the boy Nan had tried to rescue sat chafing his wrists; the long end of the rope still dangled from his neck.

The headman examined Nan's penknife with great interest.

"That's *mine*," said Nan, but her voice trembled.

"They can't understand you." Will's throat ached where the man had squeezed it, and he felt a great weariness. They had barely escaped a battle, only to be taken captive. Was it never going to end?

"I don't care," Nan said wildly. "My dad gave me that knife!"

The crowd murmured. It was a threatening sound.

"Don't make them mad," Will whispered.

But Nan could not seem to calm down. "It's horrible here! They tie kids up, and bash their heads, and I'm cold, and I want to go *home*!" She shivered, rubbing her arms up and down. Her hand bumped the strange beast head on Breet's armband, and she turned the coiled metal ring so that the elongated snout faced outward, away from her fingers.

The richly dressed woman moistened her lips with her tongue. Then she fingered the copper clasp at her throat that held her fur together, setting a fringe of black-tipped ermine tails swinging. "Cray-tee," she murmured.

"What's she staring at me for?" Nan flung her hair back, scowling.

"Take it easy," Will whispered. "I think she's a high priest or something."

"They called them druids." Nan wiped her nose on her sleeve and glared at the muscular man who had captured them. "And I suppose *he's* the headman. I don't like either one of them."

The headman and the druid conferred in low voices, glancing from Nan to the sky. They looked nervous, Will realized suddenly.

"Why are they pointing at me?" Nan shifted her weight uneasily.

The people *were* pointing at Nan. They were talking excitedly, repeating the word *cray-tee,* jostling to get a better view. They didn't seem nearly as interested in Will. Then suddenly he realized why. "They're pointing at Breet's armband!"

The richly dressed druid moved closer. A smell rose from her like burning leaves. She leaned in, tapped the armband with her finger, and tried to pull it off.

"Stop that!" said Nan. The woman put up her hands in a placating manner. The crowd grew silent, watching.

"I think they're afraid of it," Will whispered.

"What, like it has some sort of power?" Nan slid her eyes sideways.

Will nodded. "Remember Breet said the armband would protect us?"

"Yeah, but Breet was a Pict, in the Iron Age, right? That's way later than these people here. Pictish beliefs can't possibly affect anyone in *this* time."

Will frowned slightly. "Maybe we've got it backward. Maybe these people believed in—whatever it is—and then handed their beliefs down to the next people, and the next, until it got all the way to the Picts."

Nan chewed her bottom lip. "Could be, I suppose."

"Why don't you pretend to use it? See if you can get them to go away."

"I'll try." Nan frowned. "What was the word that leader said—*cray* something?"

"*Cray-tee*," Will murmured.

Nan pointed at the iron armband with a dramatic gesture. "Cray-tee!" she shouted. The crowd backed away; a sound like a low moan swept over them. The druid's eyes widened, and the headman dropped Nan's knife. It skidded on the frosty ground to her feet.

"That's right," said Nan firmly, "and now you can just all cray-tee away. Go on, shoo, leave us alone! Cray-tee, I say!"

The crowd seemed to be talking this over. Their breath made little clouds in the cold air.

Nan took a cautious step forward and snatched up her penknife. "Can you tell what they're saying yet?" she muttered.

Will shook his head. He could hear the word *cray-tee*, but now another word was repeated as well. "They keep saying *poun-ka*, but I don't have a clue what it means."

The druid was addressing the crowd now; heads began to nod. Then the boy with the rope around his neck was pushed forward to stand before Will and Nan. The loose end of the rope, with great ceremony, was placed in Nan's hand.

Nan's mouth fell open. "Huh?"

Will stared at the boy. His hair was shaggy, his face pale and smudged. He had a badly scarred arm—a burn, it looked like—and a twisted hand. He looked about nine years old and scared to death.

Will said slowly, "I think they're giving him to you. As a slave."

"A *what*?" Nan's eyes narrowed. She lifted her knife and slid the blade between the boy's neck and the rope. It was a small knife, but very sharp, and the cut rope fell, looping around the boy's ankles like a discarded snakeskin. "He's not going to be *my* slave," Nan said, breathing hard.

"They don't understand you," Will reminded her.

"Cray-tee, then!" She grabbed Will's shoulder, shouted, "Poun-ka," for good measure, and spoke low in his ear. "Get us out of here," she whispered. "Can't you open a window in a hurry?"

But something seemed to be happening to the crowd. Their faces, which had been so sober, erupted into glee. The druid, sweeping her fur over her shoulder with an almost royal gesture, took Nan by the shoulders and pressed her forehead against the girl's. The headman grunted an order; someone picked up the rope and coiled it.

Will, too, was surrounded by beaming faces. He was

patted, not once, but many times, on the head or on the ear, as someone might touch a rabbit's foot for luck. The shaggy-haired boy stood close to Will, and his face was the happiest of all.

"Wow," Will said to Nan. "I think you just freed him or something!"

But now the druid raised her arms and began to chant. The crowd hummed with her, swaying, and the eastern sky glowed pink. Suddenly a bright sliver of light shone over the horizon. The druid's voice rose to a piercing shriek.

The headman grabbed Will's wrist with one hand and Nan's with the other.

"POUN-KA!" the druid shouted, and the headman raised Will's arm high. Then came a torrent of more words, and the headman raised Nan's arm high.

"CRAY-TEE!" cried the crowd all together.

"I think they like us now," Nan said under cover of the noise.

The crowd quieted, watching motionless as the sun slowly heaved itself up into the sky. When the glowing ball had completely cleared the horizon, they relaxed, breaking up and chattering among themselves. The druid came to Nan, making emphatic gestures.

Nan grinned over her shoulder as the druid urged her forward, down the path. "Want to go with them? I bet they'll feed us and get us warm, anyway."

"I don't think we have a choice," said Will as the headman gripped his arm with fingers like iron clamps. The man propelled him along the path after Nan, and everyone else crowded behind.

They began to trot, a shambling sort of half run that ate up ground quickly. Will stumbled more than once, but the headman hauled him back to his feet each time.

How long had he been awake? Will's head felt strangely light and odd. He shivered violently; the headman grunted an order, and someone threw a hairy pelt from some kind of animal over his shoulders. It smelled like rancid fat, but Will was beyond caring. His calf muscles burned, and his breath came hard and fast by the time they stopped at the river's edge, where several long boats like hollow logs were drawn up on shore.

Will was thrust into one of the log boats and Nan into another. He sat on a wooden seat and gripped the edges as the boat was launched into the water. Paddles dipped strongly, and the log boats moved upriver, staying near the shore on the outside bends and traversing across when the river bent the other way. He supposed it had something to do with the fact that they were paddling against the current.

The journey went on and endlessly on. Will shivered as a cold gust slipped across the water and, with it, a few flakes of snow.

He couldn't help but notice that the people around him

weren't dressed all that warmly, yet they didn't seem to feel the cold. Maybe he was too soft for the Copper Age, or whatever this was. These people were *tough*. Will sat in huddled misery and steeled himself to endure. After a long while, the river widened into a vast gray lake; on all sides rounded peaks rose, dusted at the tops with snow.

"It's Loch Tay!" Nan's voice came from across the water. "And that's a crannog!" She frowned slightly. "It doesn't look exactly like the Crannog Centre, though."

Before them, a narrow causeway of stone extended out into the water, and at its end was a small, round island. Taking up most of the island was a large hut. Its roof was thatch, its walls looked like a mixture of mud and sticks, and sharp wooden stakes surrounded it, standing on end.

But Will was happiest to see the faint wisps of smoke rising from the huts on shore. Where there was smoke, there was fire; where there was fire, he might get warm.

The boats scraped bottom and paddlers leaped out to pull them farther ashore. Will got out unsteadily, the boat wobbling beneath him. One boat over, the ermine-clad druid got out with fluid dignity and waited as Nan struggled out. Then, with a sweep of her arm and a half bow, she motioned for Nan to step onto the causeway.

Nan grinned at Will. She made a royal gesture of her own, flinging her arm around until her hand was on Will's shoulder. "Cray-tee!" she shouted. "Poun-ka!"

"Poun-ka," everyone agreed, nodding.

Will snorted. "Ham it up, why don't you?"

"Why not?" Nan's dimple deepened, and it had its usual effect—everyone in the crowd smiled back at her. "Come on—maybe they'll feed us. I'm starving!" She ran along the causeway toward the crannog and disappeared into the hut, followed by the druid.

But Will was not allowed to go with Nan. Before he could protest, two paddlers steered him toward a huddle of huts on the shore. He was thrust through a low entrance into a room lit by a small, smoky fire in the center. Someone pushed him down onto a pile of furs.

Will was too tired to wonder why he and Nan had been separated, or even to care. The furs were soft and warm, and he was exhausted. He slept.

When he woke up, there was a rope around his neck.

ତ୬

Time went by. How much time, Will did not know, for the small room had no windows to let in daylight, and the door was covered with a deerskin. People came and went, but always there was the shaggy-haired boy nearby, watching him. The first time Will's fingers went to the knotted rope to try to untie it, the boy said something sharply and pushed his hands away.

Will tried again when the boy was looking the other way. But others must have been watching from the dark corners of the hut, for in a moment he felt his wrists yanked around behind him, and the rough end of the rope being looped around them.

"No!" Will cried, struggling. Instantly he was surrounded. Someone threw him onto the pile of furs; someone else put a knee on his chest to hold him down; the hands at his back continued to work busily.

The shaggy-haired boy jumped to his feet, pouring out a torrent of words. It was not in a language Will knew, but the tone of pleading was unmistakable.

The hands at Will's ankle paused. The knee on his chest was removed. But the people around him did not move away. The shaggy-haired boy shook his finger at Will. "NA!" he said. "NA!"

Will sat up slowly. "All right. I won't try to untie it anymore."

The boy looked blank.

Will spread his hands wide, as far from the rope as he could get them, and shook his head. "*NA*," he repeated with emphasis. "Na, na, na."

His captors walked away, but not before each one slapped the side of his face—a last message, clear in any language. Will watched them go, his cheeks stinging. Fine, then. He would escape some other way. He was strongly tempted to open a time window for himself and step through into freedom, but it was tricky with so many people around. Besides, he had promised Nan that he would never leave her alone in the past.

Had they put a rope around *Nan's* neck? Somehow he doubted it. Nan had the armband; they seemed to fear it too much to make her a slave. He hoped she would come looking for him soon, wave the armband around a few times, and get them to set him free. The rope rasped the skin of his neck, and in spite of the warmth from the fire, he shivered.

Only, *was* he a slave? No one was making him do any work. He was given food—a hard, flat piece of bread, fish stew in a wooden bowl—and there was a clay jar of water within arm's reach. But there was no sign of Nan. And although he listened carefully to the conversations he could overhear, he still couldn't understand. He heard the word *poun-ka* now and then, as people glanced at him, and he guessed it was their name for a special kind of slave. But he didn't know for sure.

Why was it taking so long for Time Hearing to kick in? Were they back so far in the past that it wouldn't work anymore? He must have been here for hours and hours already.

Will hugged his knees to his chest. He didn't have much chance of finding Nan if he couldn't figure out what they were saying. He glanced anxiously at the door.

The shaggy-haired boy, squatting nearby, watched Will out of the corners of his eyes. He moved a little closer.

"Nurth," he said, patting his chest. Then he tapped Will's chest and raised his eyebrows.

"Will. My name is Will."

Nurth reached inside his belted shirt, pulled out something small, and dangled it in front of the fire. It was something small and round, on some sort of string. . . .

Will laughed. So they played conkers in the Copper Age, too, did they?

Nurth took out another cobnut and handed it to Will. It was not on a string, as he had first thought, but a thin, twisted cord of some sinewy material.

Conkers was a good game to pass the time when there was nothing else to do. It took Will's mind off his troubles to aim the conker and flick it out, trying to hit Nurth's and break it. After a while the two boys were laughing, and Will had almost forgotten the rope around his neck. But Will's conker broke first.

Nurth started to raise his fist in triumph, but stopped midmotion, as if remembering something. He shrugged an apology. Then he put his conker in Will's hand.

"No, that's okay," Will said. "I've got lots of games at—at home."

Nurth reached out and closed Will's fingers over the cobnut. He pushed Will's hand away and said something gently in his own language.

"Okay, thanks, I guess." Will put the conker in his pocket

and wondered how to get across his own, rather urgent, message. He jerked his chin toward the door. "I need to go out," he said, hoping Nurth would get the idea.

The boy's eyebrows pinched together in perplexity.

Will stood up, crossed his legs, and joggled from side to side. Then he pointed at the door again. "I—need—to—go—OUT."

Nurth's face split into a grin, and a bubbling laugh escaped him. He said something to one of the men, who unhooked the rope's end from a beam and led Will outside.

It was bitter cold. The sun was a blear of red above a lowering rack of cloud; he must have been in the hut the whole day. Will did his business behind a bush and looked around him. Smoke rose from the hut on the small island Nan called a crannog, and as he watched, villagers began to gather at the shore and get into the log boats again.

Will's guard spoke—and for the first time, the meaning of the words felt tantalizingly near. Maybe Time Hearing was going to work, after all!

The guard jerked at the rope. It chafed Will's neck, and a sudden fury surged in his blood. It took all his self-control to unclench his fists.

He was tired of being treated like a dog on a leash. The minute he could speak the language of these people, he would demand to see Nan. She would arrange for them to be alone in a quiet place, and he would open a window. And once he got home, he would never, *never* use his Time Sight again.

The guard pushed him into one of the log boats. Will sat in the center, behind a man with a paddle, and looked about for Nan. The boat was shoved off, and he lurched backward; a thump and wobble told him that his guard had leaped in behind him. Paddles dipped, water droplets splashed on Will's arm, the log boat rocked unsteadily, and Will hung on to the sides, shivering in spite of the pelt that covered his shoulders.

The boats clustered near the crannog as the paddlers kept them in position. The druid appeared in the doorway of the crannog hut with a lighted torch in hand; behind her came Nan, wearing a long, belted dress and a wreath of leaves in her hair. Her armband gleamed dully, and over her shoulders she wore a small cape of fur like the druid's. She looked like some ancient princess, and she was carrying an armful of what looked like greasy cattails.

The druid walked to the island's edge. One by one the boats came in close and Nan handed out the cattails. The villagers lit them from the druid's torch and set them upright in hollow tubes at the front and back of each log boat. Then the druid stepped carefully into Will's boat, sitting at the very front with her torch held high; Nan climbed in behind her. Only one paddler was between Will and Nan, a man with broad shoulders. Will leaned to one side to speak around him, but the paddles dipped again and the man's elbow knocked into Will's head as the log boat moved out into the loch.

The sun slipped behind the rack of clouds and the sky turned purple, like a bruise. The loch gleamed violet and indigo in the dim light, and stones rose wetly out of the water, smooth as dolphins' backs. The torchlight gleamed and flickered on the wavelets made by dipping paddles as the boats swung into formation.

Will leaned to the side again. "Pssst! Nan!"

Suddenly something broke the surface of the loch. It was gray, like a stone, but it was oddly shaped, and it was moving.

The crowd gasped.

"Cray-tee!" cried the druid, high and thin.

"CRAY-TEE!" roared the crowd.

The light from the blazing cattails shone on the thing in the water. It was the head of some kind of water beast with an elongated snout. It seemed to be smiling. Then the waters closed over the head and the loch was as still as if nothing had happened.

Singing with joy, the paddlers skimmed the boats strongly down the loch toward the river. The sky was gray and the sun was hidden behind a bank of cloud, but the torches sent out a warmth Will could feel on his skin. They were going with the current this time, and moving quickly.

He gave up trying to talk to Nan—the paddler's elbows were too energetic—but when the boats grounded a mile or two downriver, he had his chance.

"Poun-ka," said the druid, nodding at Will as she got out of the boat, and Will's guard pushed him into line after Nan. The villagers beached their boats and took up torches as the druid headed for a path that led up a hill.

Nan hadn't seemed to notice the rope around Will's neck. He leaned forward as he walked behind her, and the rope pulled and rasped until the guard gave him a little slack.

"Your hair smells smoky," Will said.

Nan half turned, still walking, and Will could see the faint small shadow of her dimple in the outline of her cheek. "She had me burning stuff in a little stone pot while she chanted and danced around. First a pinch of some dried-up old weed, then a little pile of grass, then some seeds and fluff. And I had to cut a bunch of reedmace—my penknife stays a lot sharper than her copper one, by the way—and melt this white slippery stuff and soak the reedmace heads in it. I think the white stuff was some kind of animal fat, because it smelled like pig. I must absolutely stink."

"What's reedmace?" Will glanced back to see villagers falling into line after them.

Nan pointed. "The druid set hers on fire."

"Oh, a cattail."

Nan's dimple deepened. "They're fuzzy enough to be cats'

317

tails, I suppose, but in Scotland they're reedmace. Anyway, she lit one of them in the hut, and it lasted for *hours*."

"Do you know what's going on?" Will lengthened his stride a little. It felt good to stretch his legs. "I've been stuck in a dark hut this whole time, and they put this *rope*—"

But Nan was already answering. "I can't understand the language yet, but it feels sort of close, you know? Anyway, I think they're performing some sort of ceremony."

Will refrained from saying that he could have figured out that much on his own. The air was colder than ever, and his legs were bare, but as long as he kept moving, he thought he might not freeze.

Nan said, "Did you see the water beast?"

"I saw something, but it was gone so fast."

"I think it was the Pictish beast. You know, the one on Breet's armband? My dad says people used to draw it all the time—you know, long-ago people. But he said it was probably imaginary."

"That thing in the water was real enough," Will said, "except I couldn't see more than its head. I think you're right, though—they used the same word for both."

"I wonder if they worship it?" Nan said thoughtfully. "The cray-tee, I mean."

The guard behind Will jerked slightly, and the rope pulled at Will's throat. He pried his fingers between the rope collar and his skin, giving himself room to breathe. "I don't care what they worship," he said, coughing. "I just want to get out of here. Like, *now*."

"Okay," Nan said, "only I'm having fun being an assistant druid, or whatever they think I am. I'm going to write a terrific school report! We're supposed to do an era in history, and I won't have to look anything up at *all*."

"Good for you," Will said bitterly. "Just make sure you put in how they tied me up with a rope around my neck and choked me every so often."

Nan swung around. She stared at Will's neck, and her mouth went straight and hard.

"Go on, keep going, or they'll be all over us," Will hissed, pushing her.

Nan marched forward, her breath whistling through her nostrils. "I didn't know," she said at last.

"Never mind."

"But we've got to get out of here!" Nan whispered.

"First chance we get." Will rubbed his arms and flexed his hands. His toes were starting to go numb. In fact all his reactions seemed to be slow, for when a large shadow broke out of the woods, he stared at it, unable to make his feet move.

"Aurochs!" came the whisper behind him, and the rope's end dropped limp at his feet. The line of villagers scattered in a silent flurry.

Frozen in place, Will took in the great slobbering jaw,

the splayed front hooves, the wide horned head taller than a man. The creature snorted, tossing its head, and then wheeled as a wildly thrown spear hit a horn and glanced off. In a moment the swishing tail and rank smell were gone, and several spearmen slipped away from the line at a nod from the headman and ran swiftly after the lumbering creature.

The line had dispersed, and Will found himself next to Nan. "Seriously? Was that a giant *cow*?"

Nan's giggle was a little shaky. "I think I read about them at school. They're extinct now. . . . They're called—"

"Let me guess. Aurochs."

The line re-formed, and the villagers continued up the woodland path. It was darker under the trees, and the torches streamed flame and smoke. Now the chanting started up again, more joyous than ever. Will put a hand on Nan's back and found that snatches of meaning were beginning to come clear, like voices on a radio turned to almost the right frequency.

He tapped Nan on her spine. "Can you understand them yet?"

"A little." She turned her head, frowning in concentration. "They're happy, I think. Food . . . they're saying something about food, meat to eat . . . and of course they hope the hunters are going to catch the aurochs. And then there's a bit I can't understand, about giving something to some god, something to strengthen him. Some of the meat, maybe?"

"Makes sense to me," said Will, who had heard pretty much the same thing. Listening, concentrating hard, he didn't notice where they were going until all at once a cliff rose on his right and the trees opened overhead. At the base of the cliff, water brimmed among stones and mosses. They were at Saint David's Well again.

The sky showed a thin slice of the sun now very low in the sky, peeking out from beneath the thick shelf of cloud. The people made a semicircle around the cup-marked stone, its newly chiseled cup showing white against the lichen.

"Light, quickly," the druid said, and all at once, Will could understand every word.

"O Great Sun," the druid chanted in a high, keening voice, "we have carved your image again on the sacred rock. Now we light the sacred fire."

Will watched, fascinated, as a village woman took solid white fat from a beaker and pressed it into the small round depressions in the cup-marked stone. Then she pushed in bits of what looked like braided twine, so that one end was in the fat, and the other end trailed out along a carved line in the stone. Flaming reedmace was lowered and held until the wicks caught, and in a moment the cup-marked stone danced with flickering light; each cuplike depression a candle, each candle ablaze.

Now the sun's lower rim was almost touching the horizon. It blazed out, red and baleful, like an angry eye. The

crowd hummed three repeated notes, like a hive of swarm-
ing bees, growing louder and louder until Will felt the hair
stand up on the back of his neck. There was some kind of
power here—he could feel it. Perhaps this was why he had
almost felt dragged back to this time when he opened the
window in a hurry. He had been too close to the cup-
marked stone, a place where people had performed this ceremony for years uncounted.

"O Great Sun," the druid chanted again, "we have lit
the sacred fire. Now we offer the power of blood, to give
you strength to rise higher."

"Higher! Higher!" chanted the crowd, and suddenly the
druid shrieked, her arms raised to the sun. "Poun-kaaaaa!"

"POUN-KA!" shouted the crowd, and Will's guard thrust
him forward, holding the rope tightly. Choking, Will tried
to claw at the rope, but his hands were gripped and pulled
behind his back. Someone grabbed his hair and forced his
head back until his throat was exposed. Now the druid was
pulling out her copper knife.

"Poun-ka," the druid said again, and her eyes turned to
Will, gleaming like polished stones.

Now, too late, Will understood. *Poun-ka* did not mean
a slave. It meant a sacrifice.

13
Almost Home

It was strange the way time slowed down. Will could see everything clearly, more clearly than he had ever seen anything before. He had time to take in Nan's face frozen in horror, and the strange mixture of guilt and relief on Nurth's; he saw the hooded predatory eyes of the druid, and the thick, frowning brows of the headman, and the last rays of the sun on every frosted blade of grass and the rough hard edge of the cliff and the cup-marked stone with its flames rising. It was as if a whole hour went by between the drawing of one breath and another, and he felt his blood pumping hard through his veins and thrumming in his ears. There was time for everything—thoughts of Jamie, of his father, his mother—

And suddenly he was filled with an overwhelming

revulsion for the violence he had met everywhere in time. The Stewarts killing and kidnapping; the Menzies fighting back. The Romans invading with sword and spear; the Picts driving their war chariots to battle. In this ancient time, killing children to sacrifice to a sun god—and in modern time, wars and savagery and his own mother taken hostage for reasons he did not understand.

Had it always been so, from the very beginning? Was it never going to end? He was so tired of it all that he felt it like a sickness inside him. And then, as the druid lifted her knife, time suddenly snapped back into its normal pace and he saw Nan react in swift fury, chopping her arm down hard so the copper blade spun out of the druid's hand and stuck, point first, in the frosty ground.

Nan yanked off Breet's armband and held it high above her head. "CRAY-TEE!" she shouted, waving it in the druid's face. "NO poun-ka!" She fumbled in the pocket of her dress, yanked out her penknife, and sawed through the rope around Will's neck.

The druid muttered something, and the headman gave a hand signal. Two strong-looking villagers took hold of Nurth at once; the boy looked suddenly sick with fear.

"Explain yourself," said the druid sternly to Nan. "You came to us with power and strange metal, and cut through the rope that held our sacrifice." (Here she glanced at Nurth.)

"You told us that you had brought a new sacrifice instead, a better and stronger poun-ka for our sun ceremony."

Nan's mouth fell open. "That wasn't what I meant at all!"

"Nevertheless, we must make the sacrifice to our Great Sun *now*. If you will not let us use your poun-ka, then we will use ours."

Nan bit her lip as two men dragged the terrified Nurth forward. "But why do you need a sacrifice at all?" she pleaded.

The druid frowned. "Surely you know that the sun loses strength as the year grows colder. It drops lower and lower in the sky each day, until sun-stand, when it must somehow gain the strength to begin its climb back up once again. We offer a sacrifice of blood to give it strength."

"Sun-stand?" Nan repeated blankly.

"The winter solstice, I bet," Will whispered.

"Oh." Nan twisted her hands together. "But why sacrifice a *person*? Can't you use a bird, or a sheep, or maybe the aurochs?"

"We rarely see the aurochs anymore. It was a great good fortune that we came upon one today—a sign that the gods are smiling on our sacrifice. And we saw the cray-tee as well, so it is clear that luck is with us and we are doing right."

"You are *not* doing right!" Nan cried. "You can't just kill one of your people every winter!"

The druid looked distinctly annoyed, and her voice took

on a frosty tone. "Most winters, we sacrifice an animal, and the sun is well pleased. But this has been a year of poor harvests and too much rain. The sun is weakened and needs extra strength. And this boy"—she nodded at Nurth, whose face had gone chalk-white—"has a damaged arm and can be spared."

"But you *can't*—"

"Enough talk!" shouted the druid, pointing to the sun. "The sacrifice must be made *now*, while the eye of the sun can still see it! So choose which poun-ka will die!"

Nan looked desperately at Will. "Can you open a window?" she whispered. "And bring him through with us?"

Will glanced at the sun. It was cut almost in half by the horizon now and going lower every moment. He might be able to open a time window before the sun set, but if he brought Nurth through, the druid would only grab someone else to kill; that old woman, perhaps, who had trouble keeping up, or that man with the swelling on his neck. Will's mind was moving smooth and fast now, like a river in a narrow place between high cliffs. A hand still gripped his hair, and he jerked his head to free it.

Now what? Will's heart pounded like a mallet against his ribs. If he was going to pull this off, he could not sound afraid. He had to act like someone with authority, someone whose ancestors had lived on this land, who had a right

to speak. He whispered a one-word prayer in his mind—
Help!—and took in a breath.

"Listen!" His voice wavered slightly, but at least it
was loud. "The aurochs and the cray-tee are signs, but what
they *really* mean is that next year's harvests will be better"—
he devoutly hoped this was true—"and that the sun doesn't
need any sacrifices. It's going to come back every year,
anyway!"

The druid looked suspicious. "I am usually the one who
interprets the signs. How can we know this is true?"

Will shot another rapid look at the sun. "I'll prove it by
showing you an even greater sign. When you see Nan—er,
the assistant druid—and me disappear right in front of you,
you will know that means the sun is strong enough already
without any sacrifices."

The druid's eyebrows twitched down. "A sacrifice would
make *sure*, though."

"No," said Nan hurriedly. "Don't sacrifice anyone, ever
again, or the sun god will punish you! Terribly!"

"Are you," said the headman, "messengers of the sun?"

"Er—yes," said Will, and at the very same time Nan said,
"No."

The druid and the headman looked at each other.

"*He's* a messenger of the sun," Nan said, "but *I'm* a messenger of the cray-tee. And," she added with a sudden burst of

inspiration, "I'll give you my cray-tee power if you promise never to sacrifice anyone again." She slid off Breet's armband and held out the beautiful coiled iron.

The druid looked at the armband with covetous eyes. "If you truly perform the great sign you spoke of, then— yes. I will vow."

"I'd rather have your knife," said the headman, who had picked up the rope and was examining the cut ends with admiration.

"You can have it," said Nan recklessly. "But you have to promise, too."

The headman nodded. "You have my sacred vow," he said, "and all of us here say the same."

"All right, then," Will said. "Everyone stand back. Keep still, and watch."

From the corner of his eye, he saw that two men still held Nurth; the druid had her copper knife ready. There was only a quarter of the sun left above the horizon.

He had perhaps one minute left. Will resolutely turned his back and stared at the cliff face as Nan took hold of his shoulder. He took a deep breath, willing his mind to calm. He didn't dare take time to search for the precise moment, but he couldn't just go blindly into any time at all—not after what had happened the last time he'd tried that.

The last gleam of the sun caught the cliff and edged it with pink. Behind him someone rustled; a throat was cleared;

there was the rasping sound of a foot scraping on gravel. Will's breath made frosty clouds in the air. It was hard to relax when he was freezing. It was doubly hard when there were people with knives behind him, who might decide to sacrifice him after all.

No. He couldn't let his mind go there. He had one chance. In spite of everything that made him want to tense up, he had to calm himself. Maybe if he thought of something happy, something peaceful? He stared vaguely into space, letting his vision blur. An image of Jamie, running through a field with the sun on his hair, entered his thoughts, and suddenly the air before him shimmered. Will realized with excitement that he had stumbled upon the golden thread of Jamie's track, a little bouncy, almost seeming to fizz.

It didn't matter if the time wasn't exact to the minute; if Jamie was there, that was good enough. Will opened the time window quickly, and on the other side it was summer.

"Now," he said, and Nan stepped forward.

The villagers gasped aloud as she disappeared. Will heard a clatter, as if someone had dropped a knife. And as he went through the window, he thought he heard Nurth laugh for joy.

❧

Nan, breathing hard, lifted a pale face as Will emerged on the other side. The wreath of leaves, still in her hair, was slightly askew, and her fur cape hung to one side with a bedraggled air. She showed him her quivering hand. "Look, I'm still shaking."

Will jammed his hands into his pockets. Now that it was all over, he was shaking a bit himself.

Quick, light steps pounded up the path, and Jamie burst into the clearing.

"You're here!" Jamie cried, his small face elated. "I knew I could find you if I tried! I found your backpack, and the Magic Eyeball book, and—"

Nan grasped Jamie's hands and began to dance him around in a circle, the hem of her dress swinging. "We're home again, we're home again, we're home!"

Will leaned against a tree and watched them, grinning. He *was* home and he was not going into the past again if he could possibly help it.

Another boy came running into the clearing in front of Saint David's Well—a strong-looking, dark-haired boy a little bigger than Jamie, dressed like a reenactor in a belted tunic with a plaid flying over his shoulder. Jamie greeted him with a happy roar. "I beat you, Robert!"

"I gave you a head start," said the boy, grinning. "Isn't that right, Grandfather?" he called over his shoulder.

A slower, heavier step sounded on the woodland path, together with the rhythmic thunk of a walking stick. Will caught a glimpse through the trees of a long brown robe and a man's bald head with a fringe of gray hair.

Will's heart skipped a beat. He looked at the sturdy dark-haired boy again.

"Race you to the top!" the boy said, laughing as he dashed up the path.

Jamie made a move to follow, but Will grabbed his arm. "Did you say that boy's name was *Robert*?" he asked hoarsely.

Jamie's cheeks bunched in a grin so wide his eyes nearly disappeared. "Yeah! It's Sir Robert, when he was a little boy! And the old hermit is his grandfather!" He dug in the waistband of his shorts and pulled out a somewhat grubby Magic Eyeball book. "I woke up, and you weren't in the castle, and Gormly wasn't anywhere, so I went up the hill to look for you, but I only found Nan's backpack and the book. And then I wished I could see Sir Robert again, only before the Stewarts came. So I looked at the book the way you showed me, and after a while, the air got all funny, and I knew it was him on the other side so I went through, and we've been playing ever since. *Now* will you let me go?"

Will's grip had slackened as Jamie talked. The little boy shook off his brother's arm and tore off after the young Sir Robert.

Nan dropped her heavy fur cape on the ground. "I'll keep an eye on Jamie," she said, and sprinted after him, her Copper Age dress flapping around her calves.

The old man came stumping into the clearing. "Well,

lad," said Sir David, his green eyes twinkling, "I see you are still splashing about in the river of time!"

ᴏᴌᴏ

"So that's all, sir." Will let his gaze drift from Sir David's face to the castle beneath him, with its fields of grain spread out like a green-and-gold plaid. He had told the monk everything; it had taken a long while. He knew he should be anxious to get back to his own time, but now that he had landed here, he was strangely reluctant to leave. There was something deeply comforting about Sir David. And it had been a relief to talk to a grown-up about what had happened.

Of course Will could talk to Cousin Elspeth and Cousin Ewen about all sorts of things. But they would think he was pretending if he told them about traveling through time. The monk actually believed it was true.

More than that, Will was grateful for a sort of *pause*. The past had been so packed with action and danger that he still felt a little breathless. As for the future, something inside him shied away from going there just yet.

He would only be going back to anxious, endless waiting to hear news of his mother. And a deep part of him feared that the news, whenever it came, might be bad.

He didn't mind putting off that moment at all. As long as he stayed in this time, nothing could happen to his mother; she hadn't even been born yet.

His gaze strayed to the cup-marked stone. He put his hand in his pocket and pulled out Nurth's gift, swinging it lightly.

The monk laughed. "I used to play with those when I was a lad, too. One nut would be the Roman, come to conquer, you see, and the other would be one of us, fighting back. We won in the end," he added thoughtfully. "We will not see the Romans come again, God willing, though we have other difficulties to conquer now."

Will set the cobnut in one of the cup marks on the stone and curled the sinewy string around it. *Conker—conquer—* he hadn't gotten the connection until this moment. He leaned back on his elbows and let his eyes linger on the far hills. Somewhere above him the laughing voices of Nan, Robert, and Jamie echoed faintly. The monk sat in thoughtful silence, his gnarled hands clasped around his knees.

"There's one thing I still don't get, sir," said Will, turning toward the monk. "Why does time seem to go at different speeds? I mean, okay, at first I was new to it and didn't know how to locate the exact times. But how could Jamie live through a whole *year* in the past, when only a couple of hours went by for Nan and me?"

The monk's eyes crinkled at the corners as he smiled. "If time is like a river, as you told me once, it makes perfect sense."

"What do you mean?" Will asked.

The monk shrugged. "If a riverbed is shallow or narrow, the stream rushes along in a great hurry. If the riverbed widens or deepens, the stream slows. Who is to say that time, like a river, must always move at the same speed no matter where you dip into it?"

Will frowned, thinking this over.

"Have you not noticed this yourself?" the monk went on. "When you are dreading something, does not the time seem to hurry by far too quickly? Or, if you are waiting impatiently for something good to happen, does it not seem that the moments lengthen into hours, and the hours into days?"

Will nodded. The last week of summer vacation always

sped by in a heartbeat, but the week before Christmas seemed to last forever.

"For me," Sir David went on, a shadow crossing his face, "my life went by like a slow trickle of water, the year I was a hostage."

Will stared at him. "You were a *hostage*?"

"Indeed, yes." The monk's mouth tightened slightly.

"But why?"

"It began because our King James, when he was just a boy, was taken by pirates."

"Pirates." Will stared at the distant river. Once, Will had thought of pirates as fun and adventurous, but now he knew what it felt like to have a knife at his throat. "Was that King James the Fourth?" he asked.

Sir David shook his head. "It was our first King James. After his capture, pirates brought him to England, where he was held hostage for many years. To get our king back," the monk went on, "Scotland had to pay a ransom—and when we could not pay the whole amount, we sent Scottish nobles to be hostages in his place, until the ransom was paid in full. I was one of the nobles who went."

"You *volunteered* to go to prison?"

Sir David nodded, a little ruefully. "It was my duty to my king. But when at last I was allowed to come home, little wonder that I soon tired of being the Menzies chief and passed that title on to my son. I have a great need for peace now . . . and I have a great desire to serve God. So, as you see, I became a monk."

Will sat up and curled his arms around his knees. He could understand the longing for peace. His eyes moved slowly over the battlements and brave towers of Castle Menzies.

It had been just a few days of his own time since he had first climbed the hill, looked through the time window, and seen the Stewarts murder two men and kidnap a little boy.

They had met the village girl, Morag, down the hill to the right. Not far away, Ranald had tossed him in the mud. Will had been shocked, then, that a grown-up would lay hands on him, actually *throw* him through the air and laugh when he hurt himself.

But Ranald's violence had been nothing compared to that of the Stewarts, who had set the castle ablaze and carried off Sir Robert. The same dark-haired boy who was playing now with Jamie and Nan would grow up and be taken hostage someday by brutal men.

There, at the bottom of the hill, the Romans had once made their camp and sharpened their weapons. Will remembered the fist almost coming through the time window, and the way the Romans had beaten an old man who was their slave.

Not far away was the hill fort of the Picts. It was only

338

rubble now, but it had once held real people, people like Breet, people who were ready to die before being enslaved, who knew that they had to either kill or be killed.

Will stood up restlessly. Somewhere in the woods, a bird called low and soft with a repeated *coo, hoo*, but in his mind he heard the clash of iron weapons, the rattle of chariots, and the screams of horses and humans piercing through the dust and noise of battle.

He moved off, hardly looking where he was going, and bumped his foot against the cup-marked stone. Immediately he saw it aflame with light, heard the druid's chant rising to the sun, felt the rope on his neck, pulling tight—

Will's throat contracted with a low, protesting note. The monk looked up.

"I don't understand," Will blurted out. "Every place I've been, every time, people have been violent. They've taken hostages. They've fought and killed and set things on fire. You'd think people would have learned something over all those years, but they're just the same as they've always been! Even in my own time, they're still doing it!"

The monk nodded somberly. "Each human soul must learn these things all over again, for themselves. Love and mercy are gifts of God, but they are gifts that can be discarded."

Will picked up a fallen twig and broke it. The small snapping sound was loud in the stillness. It seemed to him as if far too many people had discarded love and—what was it? Mercy. "My mother is a doctor," he said, without knowing why. "A healer. She went to another country to help some kids there who were sick."

A slow smile spread across Sir David's face. "Wherever there is healing, and rescue, you can be sure people are using the gifts of God to bring hope to the world. Each one lights their own small candle from the greater light."

"Yeah, well, I wish she wouldn't have left us," Will said before he could help himself.

"Perhaps she felt she had to go," the monk said gently.

"But why didn't she let someone else do it?" Will blurted out.

The monk's brows twitched slightly. "Sometimes," he said, "you are drawn to do a particular task, in spite of personal hardship. You feel it in your heart and mind, like a strong hand, pulling. We monks say this is a calling."

Snap. Snap. Snap. Will broke the twig into ever smaller bits. He didn't understand what the monk was saying, and he didn't want to.

"Think of it this way," the monk said, clasping his gnarled fingers together. "You are sitting by a good fire, warm and safe, but all around you it is dark. And you hear someone crying. Would you not pick up a candle, and light it from that fire, and go out into the dark, searching for the one who needed you?"

Will flicked away the twig fragments. *WE needed her*, he thought with a spurt of rebellion. Aloud he said, "Some of the people where she went didn't even want her to come. They—" He gulped and went on, his voice harsh with his effort to keep it steady. "They took her hostage. My dad is trying to get them to let her go."

The monk's gnarled hands tightened on his walking stick, and the lines in his face deepened. "I shall pray for them," he said simply.

Will didn't want to seem ungrateful, but he couldn't help a small, cynical shrug. "It isn't even going to happen for hundreds of years. So thanks, but I don't suppose your prayers now are going to do much good."

The monk looked thoughtful. "I don't think time matters much to God. The Maker of time can certainly pick up a prayer from one bank in the river, and apply it to a spot farther downstream, if it is his good pleasure."

Will stared at him. "Are you serious?"

The monk chuckled. "If I can believe that you can travel through time, why can you not believe me?"

The voices of children grew suddenly louder, and Nan came running across the green turf. The boys followed, laughing and half wrestling as they came.

"Robert says he has to go down to the castle," Nan said, breathless from running. "He's got to do sword practice or something."

"He'll need it," Will muttered. "Considering that the Stewarts are going to burn the castle."

Sir David turned quickly, his eyebrows shooting up. "Burn the castle?"

Robert came quickly to his side, all laughter wiped from his face.

"Not for a long time," Nan assured him. "Not until Robert's all grown up and kind of old."

Jamie caught the tail end of this as he came up. "You're going to be awfully nice when you're grown up," he said earnestly to Robert. "But watch out for those Stewarts!"

Robert looked at him in surprise. "The Stewarts aren't so bad," he said. "It's the Campbells I worry about."

"The year?" Sir David said quietly. "The year when it happens, do you know it?"

Will looked at Jamie. "Do you?"

Jamie shook his head.

"I'm sure it's in all the Menzies history books, at home," Nan said mournfully. "But I never read them."

"Grandfather," broke in Robert impatiently, "this is only a play, a pretend, of theirs. Jamie has been talking silliness all morning. Surely you don't believe any of it?"

"Oh, I am pretending with them," said Sir David absently. He folded his hands in his sleeves and stared, frowning, at the castle. Its stone walls looked stark and gray in the morning light, and impossibly strong. "Will they destroy the kirk as well?"

"I don't know," said Will uneasily.

Sir David cleared his throat. "Well," he said huskily, putting his hand on young Robert's shoulder, "you may have to fight, but you don't have to hate. And we can always rebuild. Remember that, my boy."

Robert tossed the dark hair out of his eyes. "Vil God I Sal," he said.

"Huh?" said Will, but Robert was already vaulting down the path to his sword lesson. Nan and Jamie followed for a few steps and stood, waving.

The monk smiled kindly down at Will. "He said, 'Will God, I Shall.' It means that if God wills it, I shall do it. It's the Menzies motto. Didn't you say you were a Menzies?"

Will nodded.

"Then it is your motto as well. Now I must go, my son, but take my blessing with you." Sir David made the sign of the cross on Will's forehead. "Be strong," he said, "and very courageous. I am glad to know that the Menzies have such descendants as you!"

Will watched until both Robert and Sir David were out of sight. He was thinking hard. Of course they had to go back to their own time now, but he wanted to be careful. He couldn't make any more mistakes.

Nan came back, pulling Jamie by the hand. "What are you waiting for? Open a window, why don't you?"

Will started down the path. "I want to open it at the same spot where you threw the pinecone and Gormlaith jumped through—you know, where the Roman's helmet fell off. If I open a window to a second after that, and if I'm in the right place, we should see Gormly running away. Then we'll know it's the exact right moment, see?" Will started down the path. "Where was that big rock we hid behind?"

The rock, when they found it at last, looked just the same as it had five hundred years before. Will faced in the correct direction, took in a long breath, and began the careful, precise search for the time he wanted.

It wasn't difficult, now that he wasn't hiding from soldiers or afraid for his life. Will probed delicately, and after a minute, he gave a little grunt of satisfaction. There was Gormlaith's track, faint but unmistakable, doubling back on itself. He allowed the shimmering window to open and turned his head slowly from side to side, scanning.

Jamie gave a little crow of excitement. "Look, there's Gormly!"

It *was* Gormlaith, plunging down the hill toward the castle, ears flapping and paws thumping in the goofy, lolloping gallop that was all hers.

Will took in a breath. "All right, let's go through."

The children stepped into their own time, one after the other. Last of all came Will, his knees weak with relief. He had brought everyone safely home at last.

They collected Nan's satchel and picked up the ancient Roman cloak pin to show to Nan's father. At the bottom of the hill, Gormlaith sent up a sudden loud barking, and a plump figure came hurrying across the parking lot.

"That's Mum!" Nan struggled out of the long Copper Age dress that covered her shorts and T-shirt, and ran down the hill.

"Why is Cousin Elspeth hurrying?" Jamie asked.

Will hesitated. "Maybe she has news."

Jamie's eyes flew open wide. "About Mom?" He bounded after Nan like a rabbit, in great leaping springs.

Will followed more slowly. And as he came closer, his footsteps dragged still more, for he saw that Cousin Elspeth was crying.

"Oh, Will!" she sobbed, enfolding him in her arms. "I just heard from your father, and—oh, children, your mother is all right, he's got her, and they'll be here the day after tomorrow!"

Supper was shepherd's pie, and Will stuffed himself to the brim. Cousin Elspeth declared her intent of taking them someplace special the next day.

"You deserve a holiday," she said, "and since tomorrow

will be your last day before your parents come, I thought we could show you a bit more of Scotland. I'll get Callum or some other lad to watch the desk at Castle Menzies. What would you like to do? Visit some ruins? Or, say, the Crannog Centre—it's this marvelous hut built out over water, you know, showing what it was like in the Bronze Age, or even before—"

Will suppressed a shudder as a breeze from the open window wafted across his neck like a thin blade.

"Can we let you know, Mum?" Nan said hurriedly, after a glance at Will's face. "Somehow I don't think we'd fancy the Crannog Centre."

"It's wonderful history," said her father reprovingly. "I wish you'd take more of an interest in that, Nan—there's so much that's happened in the past, right here on this land. For instance, take this fibula you dug up. It's not just a piece of bent metal—it once held together a real cloak, worn by a real Roman centurion. If you use your imagination, you can almost see him!"

The Dimple flitted into Nan's cheek. "As a matter of fact," she said, "I *am* interested in history. Mum, can you tell us what happened to Sir Robert Menzies after the Stewarts burned his castle? I saw—I mean, I was telling Will and Jamie about the fire, but I might have gotten some of the details wrong."

Cousin Elspeth launched into a delighted—and lengthy—

explanation. Jamie paid close attention at first but was yawning openly before she was done.

"So they held Sir Robert at Garth Castle?" asked Will, who had followed her narrative closely. "Did they ever let him go?"

"Yes, but not until they had starved and mistreated him, and made him sign a 'paper of forgiveness' so he wouldn't try to get revenge on them for burning his castle."

"Did the Stewarts burn the church?" Will asked.

"Oh yes, the kirk and the whole town of Weem."

Will toyed with his fork, making patterns in his mashed potatoes. "Was Sir Robert the only one that the Stewarts put in their dungeon? I mean, did they take anyone else in the family, like—oh, I don't know, maybe a nephew?"

Jamie stopped yawning.

"History doesn't say," said Cousin Elspeth briskly. "Sir Robert seems to have been the only one released, at any rate."

"Oh," said Jamie.

"I wonder if we could see Garth Castle tomorrow?" Will said suddenly.

⁂

"It's going to be dangerous," said Nan. "Don't pretend it's not."

"I'm not pretending anything." Will paced the floor in Nan's room, then stared out the window into darkness. "But we can't leave him there. He's just a little kid."

"Who?" said Jamie from the door, wide-eyed.

Will frowned. "You're supposed to be asleep."

Jamie bounced onto Nan's bed and showed every evidence of staying. "Are you talking about Sir Robert's real nephew? The one they thought was me?"

Nan twisted a lock of reddish gold hair around her finger and then untwined it again. "I don't think we should do it."

"You were the one telling me not to be a chicken before!" Will's neck grew hot.

"I know. But we keep getting in trouble when we go back in time! And it just gets harder and harder to get home again!" Nan's chin turned square, and the Dimple was nowhere to be seen. "Only I think we should let someone else rescue him, that's all."

"Who else even knows he's at Garth Castle? Everybody thought *Jamie* was the real nephew, for a whole year. Nobody was looking for the real James, and the Stewarts kept him all that time—I heard Neil Gointe Stewart say it."

"Well, someone must have found out where he is by now," Nan said stubbornly. "Didn't you say he was in the dungeon with Sir Robert? Sir Robert will know."

Will leaned against the windowsill and folded his arms. "They might be in different cells. Anyway, you don't have to come with me."

Nan made an exasperated noise. "What makes you so

brave all of a sudden? I mean, we just found out your mum's okay, so now you're going to go get lost or maybe even killed? There are Stewarts back in that time, remember?"

"*Stewarts?*" Jamie whispered.

"The same ones who burned Castle Menzies," Nan said mercilessly.

Jamie butted his head against his brother's side. "Don't go," he begged.

Will bit his lip.

"*Please* don't go," Nan echoed.

"Your mom's already set it up for tomorrow," Will said slowly. It had taken several phone calls and a bit of arm-twisting for Cousin Elspeth to make the arrangements for them to visit Garth Castle. He didn't want to tell her it had all been for nothing.

"We can still go to see Garth Castle. We just don't have to go back in time to find a kid who's been dead a long time already." Nan tossed back her hair and stood up, taking Jamie by the hand. "Sorry if that seems harsh, but I think your first job is to make sure you and Jamie are here, and safe, when your parents come."

Nan was right, Will thought later as he lay awake in the darkness. His first duty was to his own family. His father had trusted him to take care of Jamie, after all.

But the thought of Sir Robert's little nephew wouldn't leave him.

On the way to Garth Castle, they stopped at Castle Menzies to drop off Gormlaith. "She won't be allowed at Garth Castle," Cousin Elspeth explained, "and Callum doesn't mind having her here. I'll be just a minute."

The children got out to stretch their legs. Cousin Ewen stayed in the car, reading the paper.

Will turned around slowly, taking in the castle, the hill, the woods, the fields, and the castle again. It was hard to believe everything that had happened in this place. He remembered the flames licking from the windows the night Sir Robert had been kidnapped and wondered suddenly if Ranald had survived.

Nan moved close to him. "You're going to stay with us, right? Because if you try to go back in time, I'm going to scream or something."

Will jammed his hands in his pockets. "I haven't decided yet."

"You *can't* go," Nan said earnestly. "We can't keep messing about in time. Sooner or later, something really big is going to change. I mean, look what happened with Nurth!"

"What? We saved a kid's life!"

"Yes, I know," said Nan, "but think about it. Somebody didn't die who was going to die, and maybe when he grew up he had kids and *they* weren't supposed to exist, either. All those extra people had to change what happened, later on."

"So what did you want us to do?" Will demanded. "Let Nurth get murdered?"

"No . . ." Nan picked at a bit of skin on her thumb.

"Anyway, I haven't noticed any big changes," Will said.

"But we wouldn't notice, would we?" Nan shot back. "We would think everything was the same as always, because that's how we would remember it—oh, I can't explain it, but what if some people weren't even *born* just because we went back? What if we ended up actually doing harm while we were saving Nurth?"

Will stared at the castle stones, one on top of the other, and tipped his head back, following the blocks all the way up to the sky. "It's the same as now, though, isn't it?"

"What do you mean?"

"Every single thing we do now affects what's going to happen next. We can't stop doing stuff just because we're afraid of the future. We just have to pick, you know? We have to do the best we can, in the time we're in." He gazed at the blue-and-white flag of Scotland flapping briskly at the top of the castle, and suddenly realized he had already made his decision. "I'm going back."

"But how are you so sure it's the right thing to do?" Nan demanded.

"I don't know." Will frowned. "I was the one who heard where they were taking James—I mean the real nephew. So that makes me responsible."

"*You're* not responsible," Nan said furiously. "The Stewarts were!"

"I hate the Stewarts," said Jamie, coming up suddenly.

Cousin Ewen had gotten out of the car and was following. "Why is that, then?"

"He means Neil Gointe Stewart," Nan said. "The one who burned the castle. Jamie doesn't like him."

Cousin Ewen grinned. "So you *were* listening to Elspeth's history lecture last night!" He ruffled Jamie's hair. "Ah, lad, don't tar all Stewarts with the same brush. Neil Gointe Stewart was a nasty piece of work, I admit, but there are plenty of good people among the Stewarts. In fact, you probably have a bit of Stewart blood yourself. See?" He pointed to the heraldic panel over the ancient castle door. "There's the joined coat of arms—the Menzies and the Stewarts, together. That was put up after they rebuilt the castle, when a Menzies laird married a bonnie Stewart lassie named Barbara."

"So there *was* forgiveness?" said Will slowly.

"Enough, anyway, to be going on with," Cousin Ewen said cheerfully. "Neil Stewart came to a bad end, of course, but the Stewarts who came after him were better."

Jamie pointed to the motto inscribed above the coat of arms. "What's that word—*Vil*?"

"Vil God I Sal," said Cousin Ewen. "It's the old spelling for the Menzies motto, 'Will God, I Shall.' It means that, with God's help, the Menzies can tackle anything that needs doing, and do it no matter what."

Will was silent.

"Whoever wrote that spells like I do!" Jamie said brightly.

"Come on, if you're coming!" Cousin Elspeth called, appearing from the castle door, and in a moment, they were in the car and rumbling off over the narrow road to Garth Castle.

14
GARTH CASTLE

GARTH CASTLE WAS A PLAIN, square tower, much smaller than Castle Menzies, and as Will followed the caretaker up the long, straight stairs, he wondered if Neil Gointe Stewart had been jealous.

Suddenly he thought of something. "Time Sight might not work here, anyway," he whispered to Nan. "We're not on Menzies lands anymore!"

Nan rolled her eyes wearily. "Actually, we probably are. The boundaries in the Highlands shifted, my dad says— the clans kept fighting back and forth over lands—and we're only about five miles from Castle Menzies. I'm pretty sure our ancestors lived on this land, too, some time or the other."

"I guess we'll find out," Will muttered.

They emerged at the top of the tower into the shifting light of a half-cloudy day. Will walked to the edge and looked down. His stomach gave a sudden turn. Far, far below was a stream—no, a burn—noisy with water and full of rocks.

"It's a long way down, isn't it?" The caretaker leaned his elbows on the parapet. "The laird who built this castle used to tie people up and throw them off when they displeased him. The Wolf, he was called."

"Not—Neil Gointe Stewart?" Nan asked in a small voice.

"Eh? Nay, the Wolf was Neil Gointe's great-great-great-granddad, or something like that. But I hear as Neil Gointe was near as bad. He murdered his own wife as she was strolling down by the burn. Dropped a rock on her head, he did—or paid to have it done."

Jamie's cold fingers stole into Will's. "Let's go down," he urged.

಄

They were in the dungeon. The owners of Garth Castle had turned it into a wine cellar, but the stone walls were still there, rough and stained, and even in summer the stone floor breathed cold.

It was the last part of their tour. The caretaker had shown them around the whole castle, and there had been a few snatched moments when Will had told Nan his plan. She had argued, and reasoned, and finally agreed to help him. Now she was using her persuasive powers—and the Dimple, of course—to get the grown-ups to leave them alone in the dungeon.

"For the experience, see?" she said, tilting her head adorably. "You told us we should use our imaginations with history, Dad. And we want to imagine what it must have been like, to be locked up here so long ago. . . ."

The adults exchanged indulgent smiles. "All right," said the caretaker, "but don't touch the wine bottles, and climb back up as soon as you get bored. That won't be long," he added in an aside to Nan's parents.

"I want to stay, too," said Jamie.

"Are you sure?" Cousin Elspeth smoothed his hair. "It's cold down here, and there isn't much light. You might get frightened."

Jamie held up the Highlander toy, grubby beyond all recognition. "Vil God I Sal," he said.

Cousin Ewen chuckled. "He's a Menzies to the bone. Come, Elspeth, let's leave our budding historians to soak up the atmosphere."

The door at the top of the stairs shut with a hollow *boom*. Will backed up to a corner, away from the wine racks. "Stand against the wall—there isn't much room, and we don't want to get stepped on. Nan, warn me if you hear your parents coming."

Will stared into the middle of the room with unfocused eyes. "I'm going to try to find the time when they let Sir Robert out," he said quietly, as the air before him began its familiar shimmer.

"Why then?" asked Nan.

"Then we can see if they let out the nephew at the same time," Will answered. "We might not need to rescue him at all. Quiet, now—give me a second."

In fact it took almost two minutes of careful probing. Will went back first to the time of the fire—he couldn't go beyond that; it turned gray on him—and then he pressed forward in time until he sensed the disturbance when Sir Robert was brought into the dungeon, a prisoner. He inched ahead—it felt like months, not years—until he felt Sir Robert's presence leaving the dungeon. Then he went back just a hair. There, that was as close as he could come.

Carefully, quietly, he opened the time window. Nan and Jamie crowded close over his shoulder to peer through.

Before them was a vaulted space that had been closed off by a wooden door. The only light came from an arrow slit, high above. A shadowy form hunched in the corner; a bucket gave off a foul smell. A thin beam of flickering light shone into the cell through a grated window in an iron-studded door.

The shadowy figure moved, and the light fell on a gaunt face, deeply lined.

Jamie gasped. "Sir Robert!" he cried.

It *was* Sir Robert, looking sick with misery and far thinner than a grown man should be. Will felt a pang, remembering the bright-eyed, laughing boy who had run down the path to sword practice.

Nan grabbed Jamie's collar with her free hand. "Don't go through. Just watch. He can't hear you if we're on this side of the window."

"But they're *starving* him," Jamie said, his voice trembling.

There was a sound of footsteps. Sir Robert's eyes flickered, and he turned his head. Then he rose, straightening his shoulders. A panel in the door slid across, and a man's hairy face showed briefly, peering in.

The heavy door opened with a creaking of hinges.

Armed men appeared; a small, narrow-lipped man with a squint was at their head.

Jamie pressed closer to Will's side.

Sir Robert, a look of deep disdain on his face, reached into his sleeve and pulled out a rolled-up piece of parchment. Neil Gointe Stewart took it with a thin, malicious smile, unrolled it, and ran his finger down the lines. His smile stretched wider, showing his teeth. "How pleasant that you've decided to be reasonable."

Sir Robert said nothing.

"It's too bad you're not reasonable enough to ransom your little nephew, though," Neil Stewart added, tapping his fingers together.

Sir Robert snorted. "You sent your first ransom demand over a year ago, telling me you held the boy captive. And all the time he was safe in my castle! You will have to find someone else more simple than I, to pay you. *I* am not so great a fool."

Neil Gointe Stewart shrugged and made a gesture with one hand. The armed men stood back to let Sir Robert pass out of the cell.

One guard went up the narrow, steep steps. Sir Robert followed, moving stiffly, and with another guard at his back. Last of all, Neil Gointe Stewart swept the dungeon with his cold gaze. For the briefest of moments, his eyes seemed to look directly into Will's. Then he turned to speak to the hairy-faced man.

"I think that's the dungeon guard," Nan whispered.

"Shh! I want to hear what they're saying."

The guard jerked his head at something beyond Will's field of vision. Neil Gointe Stewart grinned on one side of his mouth, like a dog snarling. "No, we'll leave him there for now. He's got parents in France; we might get a ransom out of *them*." He chuckled. "Anyway, I hear that the other lad—the one Sir Robert had at the castle all this time— went missing the night of the fire."

"Should I search for him?" The guard's feet scraped on the floor, as if impatient to get moving. "There are woods and caves where a lad could hide. I could smoke him out."

"Perhaps." The Stewart laird tapped his fingers together again, as if thinking. "One or the other of them must be the real nephew. We'll find out. There are ways."

"What will you do with the false one?" the guard asked eagerly.

The laird laughed softly. "Garth Castle has a high parapet, and it's a long way to the gorge below. I don't think it will be hard to get rid of one small lad, when the time comes."

Jamie's hand gripped his brother's shoulder convulsively.

Will could not recall ever hating anyone as much as he hated Neil Gointe Stewart. He watched grimly as the Stewart laird mounted the stairs, followed by the guard.

When the door banged shut at the top of the stairs, Will moved slowly out of Sir Robert's cell and then turned, keeping his focus.

The window to the past showed another wooden door. Will moved forward and shifted his focus slightly, and the door melted away to show a boy.

He lay on a dirty mattress atop a rough wooden bench. Bits of straw stuck out here and there from the ticking. His face was turned toward the dim light that shone palely through an arrow slit high above, and his arms were folded about himself. He looked like a grubbier, more hopeless version of Jamie, and Will felt a lump rise in his throat.

"Still think we should let someone else rescue him?" Will whispered to Nan.

"Hold your whisht, will you?" Nan wiped the back of her hand across her eyes. "Of course we have to get the poor wee lad. I'll do it; you hold the window open for me."

But Jamie had already scrambled through.

"Oh, brilliant," Nan muttered. "Now I have to bring two of them back."

"Quick, Nan," said Will tensely.

Nan lifted her foot to follow Jamie, but suddenly a small shape scuttled across the wine cellar floor and ran over her foot. She shrieked and fell backward, knocking Will sideways. The window snapped shut.

"What did you do that for?" Will shouted.

"It was a mouse!" Nan said hotly. "I'd like to see *you* hold still if one ran across your foot!"

The door at the top of the stairs opened. "Is everyone all right down there?" Cousin Elspeth's voice floated down. "Only I heard shouting."

Will and Nan stared guiltily at each other.

"We're fine, Mum," Nan called up. "We're just play-acting."

"Are you sure? Maybe you'd better send Jamie up to me."

Nan opened her mouth and shut it again, like a fish. She looked at Will.

Will never knew where the words came from, but suddenly he found himself speaking. "We're reenacting history, Cousin Elspeth. Jamie is locked in a cell, and he wants us to rescue him. Can we have a few more minutes?" He moved to the bottom of the stairs and produced what he hoped looked like a carefree grin.

Nan's mother chuckled. "All right, then. Far be it from me to discourage an interest in Scottish history!"

"Oh, well done," breathed Nan.

Will didn't waste any more words. His brother was back in Sir Robert's time, locked in the dungeon at Garth Castle; seconds counted. He stared into the middle distance and concentrated. He couldn't mess this up.

"Hurry," said Nan. "What if another whole year goes by, like before?"

"It won't," Will said shortly. "I'm getting so I can find the exact time—almost." He swallowed. It was that *almost* that had him worried.

"But what if the guard comes back before you get there?" Nan whispered. "What if he looks in the cell and sees there are *two* boys?"

The air, which had begun to shimmer, went flat at Will's anguished jerk. He turned on his cousin and shook her by the shoulders. "Stop *saying* that!"

Nan's face crumpled. "Don't be such a bampot. I'm worried about Jamie, too."

"*Talking* about it isn't going to do any good," Will said, his own face scrunched with the effort to keep himself steady. "I know it could happen, do you think I'm stupid? I'm better at Time Sight now, but it's hard to get the exact moment, and if I'm too late—or if a whole year goes by, like before—"

"Then you just try again and go back a little earlier," Nan said in a soothing tone.

"But I *can't* go back earlier. Not once I've been there. There's this grayness there, remember? It won't let me live the same time over again." Will's voice broke.

"Okay," said Nan, "but what if you just open a window, and *look*? If you just look, and see that it's too late, it won't count as *living* the time, right? I'm pretty sure you can still open a window to an earlier time, it just makes sense—"

"You don't *know* that!" Will said in a whisper so fierce it was almost a shout. "We don't understand how Time Sight works, not really. We're playing around with something as dangerous as lightning, and I don't know all the rules, and I'm scared!" He scrubbed at his eyes furiously. "Go ahead, call me a chicken like you did before, I don't care! It makes *sense* to be scared sometimes! And I can't do anything to rescue my mother or help my dad, but I can try to get Jamie back, so will you just shut up and let me *do* it?"

Nan's eyes were wide, and her mouth was a small, round shape, slightly open.

Will pressed his fists to his chin to hold it steady. "If I don't get the time right," he whispered, "if the guard has already come back and seen the two boys and brought them to Neil Gointe Stewart—oh, God." Will shut his eyes, and a small, keening note came from him, like a bird singing sorrow, or an animal with a wound.

Nan put a timid hand on his arm. "I'm sorry I called you a feartie chicken. I think you've been really brave all along."

Will gulped, shook himself like a dog coming out of water, and took a deep breath.

"Vil God I Sal," said Nan, patting his arm.

Will nodded. He breathed in deeply. His head ached and his eyes were hot, but he had a job to do, he was a Menzies, his brother was waiting. His thoughts swarmed and rose like a cloud of buzzing insects. *Vil God I Sal*, he repeated in his mind, and the buzzing swarm subsided. He gazed into the middle distance, relaxed his focus until the air changed and moved, found a thread, and followed it. Inside himself he became aware of a still point of calm, a strength that flowed in from somewhere else, a clear path to his goal if only the window would open *now*. . . .

It opened on a boy very like Jamie, but thin, terribly thin and dirty, as if he had been ill-treated for a very long time. Will's heart seemed to stop in his chest. He lunged through the window, forgetting about Nan, forgetting everything but the need to get to his brother—

Jamie popped up from a shadowy corner of the cell, his round face beaming. "What took you so long? I had time to teach James all the verses to 'Flower of Scotland'!"

⁂

Will sat in a corner of the cell with closed eyes, half listening as Jamie talked on and on. Will's other ear was cocked for any noise outside the cell that would signal the guard's return. If only he would stay away just a few more minutes. He wanted to rest his eyes, and they had to get James to trust them enough to step through the time window.

"—and so James thought it was witchcraft at first," Jamie was saying eagerly.

"But then he told me he was an angel." James, the real nephew, looked doubtfully at Will. "You keep your wings hidden, mayhap?" he added politely.

"I said we were *like* angels," Jamie corrected. "Angels are helpers; I learned that in the Menzies kirk, and we're here to help you."

"The Menzies kirk?" said the boy slowly. "You are not Stewart children, then?"

Will shook his head. "I'm William Menzies. This is Jamie—James Menzies. We're your . . . cousins. Distant ones."

The boy rubbed his forehead. "My name is James Menzies, too."

"We know that already," Jamie said.

Will put a hand on the boy's shoulder. "Listen, James," he said. "We're going to get you out of here. Just do what we say, all right?"

The boy looked at them from beneath straight brows. "Be you honest men?"

"Well, honest, anyway," said Will. "Now, listen. I'm going to open this sort of door in the air, and I want you to walk through. We're taking you to your uncle, Sir Robert."

The dim light shone on the boy's uncertain frown. "My uncle does not want me. If he did, he would have rescued me long since."

Will gripped the boy's shoulders. "Sir Robert *does* want you. We'll explain later. But for now, you've got to trust us. Will you do what we tell you, no matter what?"

The boy lifted his chin. He was so like Jamie, and yet

there was something different about him, too. He looked as if he had suffered, and been alone, for far too long a time. But still—"I am a Menzies," he said. "Vil God I Sal."

"Good lad," Will whispered. "Hold on to my shoulder and don't be afraid."

The air glimmered like a pearl seen through water. Will searched, gently, for the right moment. He was close. . . . He sensed the familiar tracks of their passage through time—

There came a muffled thud from somewhere outside the cell and a clatter of boots on stone. Jamie gasped.

The wavering air opened onto a stone cellar stocked with bottles of wine. "Okay, Jamie," Will breathed. "Go through, and don't make noise."

"But I don't see Nan!" Jamie whispered.

"It doesn't matter." Will fought to keep a steady focus. "You have to get out *now*."

Jamie cast a frightened look behind him and dived through.

That was one safe. "You next, James," said Will, very low.

Sir Robert's nephew stood as if in a trance, staring at the time window. Then he turned his head, listening.

"The laird wants the lad brought up?" said a voice outside the cell.

"Aye." There was a clinking sound, as if keys were being pulled from a belt. "Sir Robert's men came to escort him home, see? Then they told him that his nephew disappeared the night of the fire and hasn't been seen since. So Sir Robert changed his mind. He wants to see this lad we've been keeping safe for him, after all."

Will's heart beat against his ribs. "*Now*, James!"

"But—my uncle wishes to see me! You heard it! Surely I should let the guards take me to him?"

Sweat broke out on Will's forehead. He could walk through the time window right now and be safe. He could leave James behind, and the guards would take him to Sir Robert.

But did James look enough like Jamie? Would Sir Robert believe he was his real nephew? Unlikely, when James wouldn't be able to answer the simplest question about anything that had happened at the castle in the past year.

And after Sir Robert rode away, what would Neil Gointe Stewart do to James then?

The metal key made a *snick* as it was inserted into the lock.

There was no time to argue. "Do you trust Neil Gointe Stewart?" Will asked. "Or me? Choose!"

James bit his lip. He stared up at Will, trembling.

"Vil God," Will whispered as the key turned in the lock.

James plunged forward blindly. "I Sal!"

The heavy door swung open. There was a shout. Will sensed a burly shape coming at him from the side.

James's heels cleared the window. Will sprang after him.

Something grabbed at his foot, but he kicked, hard, and heard a bellow of rage. There was a sudden flash to one side, as of reflected light, and then the bellow cut off as the window snapped shut. Will stumbled forward onto a cold stone floor, and something bounced behind him with a metallic clatter.

"There you are!" Nan cried, rushing forward. "I've been standing at the bottom of the stairs—my mum's been *calling*—"

Jamie picked up a shard of metal off the floor. "It's the tip of a sword," he said breathlessly. "You almost got stabbed."

Will couldn't speak. His head rang and his eyes burned, but something fizzed through his veins like soda pop as he saw the others safe around him.

He had done it. He had stolen back what Neil Gointe Stewart had taken. He only wished he could see the laird's ferret face when he heard that little James Menzies had escaped from a locked cell.

"And who are you?" demanded the caretaker of Garth Castle, staring at the oddly dressed small boy who tagged after Will, Nan, and Jamie.

They had made it up the stairs and out of the castle before being spotted. The grown-ups were talking around the corner, though, and before the children knew it, they had blundered straight into them.

"He's a friend of mine," Nan said at once. She smiled at the caretaker. Then she aimed the Dimple at her parents. "Can we give him a ride to Castle Menzies? Please?"

"But what's he doing here? He's too young to be on his own," Cousin Elspeth protested. "And he looks terribly tired."

"He got lost from his—er, group. He needs to find his uncle. And Castle Menzies is the meeting point. Right?" she said, turning to James.

James nodded, his eyes widening as he took in the modern clothing, the cars in the driveway. "My uncle, Sir Robert, the Laird of Weem, is at the castle, and I must go there without delay."

Cousin Ewen chuckled. "You're another young reenactor, I see. But your clothes look a little ragged for the nephew of a laird. Well, climb in, all. We'll make some phone calls and get it all straightened out when we get to the castle."

But they did not get far before the car gave a sudden lurch. James, who had said little but was staring at everything with awe, clutched the edge of the seat and went pale.

Cousin Ewen said something under his breath as the car bumped unevenly to a pullout at the side of the narrow road. "Got to change a blasted tire," he muttered, rummaging in the boot for his jack and spare. "Get out, all of you—run around, stretch your legs. This will take a while."

"Don't go out of sight, though," Nan's mother warned.

Cousin Ewen sweated and strained; Cousin Elspeth hovered around, giving advice; the children walked down a hedgerow full of ripening gooseberries. James went slowly, on shaky legs.

"This is joy," he said fervently, lifting his pale face to the sun. "The Stewarts scarce let me outside—only under guard, for an hour at a time. And these berries! I haven't tasted gooseberries for a year." He popped one in his mouth and began to hum the song Jamie had taught him, an expression of bliss on his face.

"You'll get lots of berries when we get you back to Castle Menzies and Sir Robert," said Jamie earnestly. "Cook makes the best gooseberry tarts ever." He put three in his mouth, and his cheeks distended like a chipmunk's.

James stopped humming, and his face took on a look of

uncertainty. "Are you sure that my uncle wants me? He did not pay the ransom to get me out."

"He would have," Jamie said indistinctly through a mouth full of gooseberries, "but he already had a boy at the castle he thought was his nephew. So when the Stewarts said they had you in their dungeon, he thought they were lying."

James frowned. "This false boy, who was he? I must smite him!"

"It was a mistake!" The red mounted in Jamie's cheeks. "I was the one Sir Robert thought was you. I looked like you, see, and he hadn't seen you for a long time. Go ahead and smite me if you want, but I'm going to hit you back if you do."

James stared hard at Jamie. "I thought you were an angel. Why did you not tell him you weren't his real nephew?"

"I did try. I told him and *told* him. But he told me I was—um—befuddled, because the Stewarts had hit me in the head."

James frowned. "So he still thinks you are his real nephew?"

"Probably." Jamie kicked a little at the earth.

"Well, then." James shrugged as if he didn't really care—but he turned his face away. "I do not know where I should go if my uncle won't have me."

"He might, though." Will put his hands on the boys'

shoulders and stood them side by side. "What do you think?" he said to Nan.

"They're the same size," said Nan. "The hair's the same color. And their faces—well, they *do* look a lot alike."

"They could be brothers," said Will thoughtfully. "Except that one of them looks like he's been half-starved and locked up for way too long."

Nan chewed on her lower lip. "Maybe Sir Robert will think that's the reason for the difference—that he was held captive for all the months since the fire. That would change anyone."

Will nodded. "You won't remember anything they'd expect you to remember from the past year," he told James, "but maybe they will think you're in shock or something."

"I can tell you some of the things you should know." Jamie began to talk eagerly as James listened, nodding.

Will stared out over the fields to the hills beyond as Jamie went on and on, and Nan picked more gooseberries. The sun was warm on the back of his neck. Unaware, Will let his eyes glaze over. The air shimmered. . . .

Nan looked at Will's face. "What is it?"

"Shh."

"Don't open a window now!" Nan said urgently. "Wait until we get to Castle Menzies, so we can find Sir Robert."

"But Sir Robert's *here*, he's passing over this road, I can feel it. Hold on to my shoulder. See? I told you!"

The others got behind Will, peering through the time window at a group of men on horseback. Jamie sighed with relief when he saw Sir Robert. "They really did let him go."

"He looks even paler in the sunlight," Nan said critically. "And sicker."

"I thought Sir Robert's own armed men came to get him," Will said. "Aren't those Stewarts?"

James looked carefully through the dust kicked up by the horses on the road. "They must be seeing him off Stewart land."

Now the Stewarts were wheeling their horses away from Sir Robert and his men, not without a few catcalls and jeers. The Menzies rode off slowly, supporting their laird in the saddle, their faces grim.

Suddenly Will realized the Menzies horsemen were almost past him. "Nan, are your parents still busy fixing the tire?"

Nan glanced over at the car, where her parents were bent over the wheel. "Yes."

"Okay, listen. You and Jamie cover for us. Wave at your parents if they look this way. I'm taking James back to his own time now."

"Why not wait until we get to Castle Menzies?" Nan objected.

"Castle Menzies was burned, remember?" Will did not take his eyes from the horsemen. "They'll take Sir Robert somewhere else to live, but I don't know where that is. This is our best chance."

"I wish I could go," said Jamie sadly. "I miss Sir Robert."

"You can't," Will said, "not if we're going to convince him that James is really you. Now, James!"

James clapped Jamie on the shoulder, snatched Nan's hand and kissed it, and then stepped carefully through into his own time. Will followed, and the window closed behind him, leaving them in a field of standing oats.

Will pushed James down and knelt beside him, peering through the slender stalks at the passing horsemen.

"Jamie did not explain everything I need to know," James whispered urgently.

"Just tell them the truth. Say you were captured by Neil Gointe Stewart and he kept you captive. You won't remember everything that Jamie did at the castle in the past year, but that's all right, just tell them you got hit in the head—"

"The Stewarts did hit me in the head," James said seriously. "Many times."

Will's heart gave a painful twist. He did not regret coming back to rescue James, not the least little bit. He cleared his throat hurriedly. "You'll know all kinds of things Jamie didn't, though. Like—don't you speak French?"

James shrugged. "Of course. English and Gaelic, too. But what if they ask me how I escaped from Garth Castle?"

"Just tell them you were rescued by three kids. Call us angels if you want. They'll just think you're—"

"Befuddled!" James's eyes were bright with laughter. "And truly, I do not understand at all what has happened. You might be angels, in truth."

"Kind of grubby ones," said Will, brushing off his knees. "Anyway, you've got to go *now*. They're only walking the horses—can you catch up to them? Or are you too weak from prison?"

James tossed his head, and his gaze was suddenly proud. "I am a Menzies, and the nephew of a laird," he said. "I am as strong as I need to be."

"Go, then, and—good-bye!"

"God be w' ye, too," said James, flashing a weary grin.

For a moment Will caught a suggestion of a dimple—it was in almost the same place as Nan's—and then James was staggering forward, calling, waving.

The group of horsemen stopped—turned in the saddle—and then one came riding back. Will didn't recognize him.

"What is it, lad?" the man demanded. "Do you have some message? Be quick about it!"

"I must speak with Sir Robert," James said grandly. "Take me to him, if you please."

The horseman stared—and then laughed. "Fine airs, from a dirty beggar's brat!"

James threw his head back, flushing. "I am Sir Robert's nephew. Take me to him at once!"

The man leaned over the saddlebow, his face threatening. "Sir Robert's nephew died in the fire. And even when he was alive, he wasn't such a starveling skint creature as you. Now, be off with you, before I teach you some manners!"

"I—I have been a captive in Garth Castle!" James stammered. "That is why I'm thin."

"Oh? And how did you get out, then?" The man grinned, showing two blackened teeth. "Neil Gointe Stewart escorted you to the gate, did he?"

"Angels!" James burst out angrily. "Three angels let me out!"

Another horseman detached himself from the group and came riding back. With a sudden lurch in his stomach, Will recognized the burly shoulders and broken nose of Ranald.

"What's the delay?" Ranald demanded. "Sir Robert is weary, and we must get him to a place of rest!"

"Nothing much," said the first horseman. "A gowky brat with a daft tale. Says he's Sir Robert's nephew, just escaped from Garth Castle."

Ranald gave the little boy a careless glance. "Aye, that's likely!" He snorted and jerked on the reins, wheeling his horse around. "Neil Gointe Stewart's been trying to tell Sir Robert he has his nephew for over a year, and now he sends the false lad after us. Begone, brat, and bother Sir Robert no more!"

The two horsemen trotted off to join the waiting Menzies band. James stood with his hands dangling helplessly at his side.

Will clenched his fists. They had to take James—they had to! Where else would he go? "Call to them again!" Will whispered through the standing oats. "Shout out something that only the real nephew would know. Like—I don't know, say something in French?"

James stared at him, his shoulders slumped. "That would not convince him. Many in Scotland speak French," he said dully.

Ranald and the other man had reached the knot of Menzies that surrounded Sir Robert. There was a brief exchange of words across the tossing manes of the horses. Any moment now they would turn and go—

Suddenly Will smacked his forehead. "James!" he hissed. "Sing 'Flower of Scotland'!"

James looked at him, startled.

"The song Jamie taught you in the dungeon, remember? He sang it for Sir Robert the night of the fire!"

"O flower of Scotland," James began obediently, his voice thin and wavering.

"Louder! Put some muscle into it!" Will urged. "It's practically your national anthem—in my time, anyway!"

James took a deep breath. "O flower of Scotland," he began again, more strongly, his clear voice piercing through the air like a bugle. "When will we see your like again? That fought and died for . . . um . . ."

"Your wee bit hill and glen," Will whispered, watching the group of horsemen. They had not ridden off. One or two had turned their horses' heads and were staring in James's direction.

"Your wee bit hill and glen," James shouted lustily. "And stood against him, proud Edward's army—"

The horsemen were coming now, all in a group, with Sir Robert in their midst. But one man came more quickly than the rest, his thick shoulders and belligerent expression seeming to urge his mount on.

"And sent him homeward," James shrieked, "to think again!"

Will crouched, his legs tense and ready to spring. He should have waited until he could find Sir Robert alone—was it too late to grab James and try to escape somehow? But no, he would never make it, never stand a chance against Ranald, who had already leaped off his horse and was running toward James, boots pounding heavily on the earth. Will watched anxiously from between the oats, his forehead damp with sweat as the guard grabbed James beneath his arms—swung him up—and embraced him, tears streaming down his grim bull-dog face.

"Forgive me, lad; I didn't know it was you," Ranald said brokenly. He set the boy down and looked him over. "And no wonder, you've gotten thin as a twig! Your face is different, too, not so full of laughter." He looked up as Sir Robert approached, frail but upright in the saddle. "But there, it's the same with the laird," Ranald went on. "Months of abuse at the hands of that twisted, bitter weasel of a Stewart have changed him, too, almost beyond recognition. Eh, lad, but it's good to see you again!"

Sir Robert checked his horse and looked down, his eyes large and burning in his too-thin face. "Is it truly you, James? They told me you were dead. . . ." He raised a hand to his eyes as if to shade them from the light. "What happened? Where have you been since the fire?"

James looked up at Sir Robert and told the truth. "I don't remember the fire. I remember riding to Castle Menzies, but then I was attacked, my men were killed, and the Stewarts took me away. I have been their captive for long and long. But I have seen wondrous things!" he said, his eyes brightening. "Carriages that move without horses! And angels! Though without wings," he added doubtfully. "They brought me away from Garth Castle, and I stepped through a sort of window in the air—"

The Menzies men exchanged glances. "It's the same nonsense that he was spouting before," one of them muttered.

"Hit on the head again, no doubt," said another.

James swallowed hard. "I *was* hit," he admitted. "Many times."

"But you are back with us now, dear lad, so never fear." Sir Robert's voice, which had been so weak, rang out now with new strength. "Lift him up to me—he shall ride on my saddlebow. We will get well together, with food and rest, and soon his mind will return to him, as it did before."

Ranald hoisted James gently in his big, rough hands. "Would you believe, laddie," he said, "that Cook made gooseberry tarts this very day?"

James laughed out loud, his face alight, and leaned back against his uncle's enfolding arms as they rode away.

Quietly, amid the oats, Will opened a window to his own time and went through.

⁂

The flat tire was fixed. Nan told Cousin Ewen that the little boy had found his uncle on the other side of the field and gone home with him.

Will sat between his brother and cousin in the back seat with his eyes shut. He was tired—he had never been so tired—but it was all over now, all the time travel and the worry about his mother and father. They would be here tomorrow, and meantime he would figure out what he wanted to say to his mother—

"Goodness!" cried Cousin Elspeth, sitting bolt upright as the car rumbled down the castle drive. "Is that Andrew?

And Margaret! Oh, thank God, thank God, they're here, I don't believe it—"

"They must have caught an earlier plane," said Cousin Ewen, his voice rasping as if suddenly hoarse. He turned in the seat, his eyes bright. "Do you see, lads? Your parents are here, safe and sound!"

രശ

At first it was just a babble of greeting—jumbled arms and laughing voices and cheeks wet with tears—and it was all so confused, like happiness multiplied until Will hardly knew who he was holding on to or who was holding him. But although he grabbed his mother and squeezed at least five times, it didn't count, not really. He was hugging everyone, and so was she. She wouldn't know, from that, how sorry he was that he'd refused to hug her before. She wouldn't know how he wished he hadn't turned away from her at the airport, when she'd said good-bye. But he was shy of saying anything about that now, in front of Cousin Ewen and Nan and everyone.

There was one moment when he could have told her—when his mother drew back a little and just looked at Will, smiling—but he wasn't ready for it, and he couldn't think what to say. Then Gormlaith came galloping up, barking madly, and Cousin Elspeth herded everyone to the castle tearoom to give the travelers a quick bite, and everyone began to exclaim how big Jamie had gotten, and the moment was over.

They all sat crammed around one table in the tearoom, talking and talking. Will said little, but he watched as his mother—thin, pale, but smiling and alive—pushed the hair back from her forehead in a gesture he had known all his life, and he had a sensation of lightness inside like a balloon expanding.

He watched them all, his gaze going from face to face. It was strange but he could see glimpses of Sir Robert in both his father and Cousin Ewen. Cousin Ewen had the same kind, serious eyes; Will's father had the laird's strong, beaky nose and sudden flashing grin.

Jamie leaned against his father's chest, holding his Highlander toy in his right hand while his left reached down to play with Gormlaith's ears. Nan was charming everyone, telling of their games in the woods and throwing in bits of history that made the grown-ups smile.

Will smiled, too, but he was beginning to feel odd, as if there were a thin veil of gauze between him and the others. He wanted to be with everyone, but at the same time he felt the need for a breathing space. . . .

Gormlaith padded over and licked his hand anxiously. "Good dog," Will said quietly, stroking her smooth head. She wagged her big, plumy tail and opened her jaw in her version of a laugh.

She *was* a good dog—a very good dog, Will thought as she left him to snuffle at Nan's knee and receive a caress.

Then, satisfied that everyone was happy, Gormlaith flopped down at Cousin Elspeth's feet with a deep sigh, laid her head on her paws, and closed her eyes.

Will slipped away, mumbling an excuse. Once around the corner he leaned against the wall, his palms pressed flat on the cold stone. He was glad his parents were back again—he was overflowing with gladness—but everything had happened so fast, and now they would be leaving for America soon, perhaps the very next day.

If this was his last visit to the castle, he wanted to walk its halls one more time.

He mounted the circular steps slowly, memories rising at every turn. Here he had staggered up with a bushel basket of bread; there Ranald had tripped him. In this very hall he had first seen Sir Robert, and Jamie had sung "Flower of Scotland."

Sir David, the old man by the well, had been the laird in this castle once, too. He had gone away to be a hostage for his king, but then he had come back to be a monk. And even Breet had left the Picts and her own time to come to the castle—to see with her own eyes the proof that her people would outlast the Romans in spite of everything.

They were still here, still part of him. Even the people from the Copper Age, perhaps more than all the rest, had had their effect on the people living now.

He had reached the top floor. Will paused in the south tower to look through the window at the stone carvings on the castle face, and then out over the fields, golden and green. It hardly seemed possible that, just yesterday by his time, the ground had been covered in snow and he had almost been sacrificed to the sun.

A soft step sounded behind him on the stone, and the clean scent of his mother's shampoo drifted past his nose.

"It's a beautiful view," his mother said, standing next to him. "I loved it when I was a little girl. I'm glad I got to see it again."

"I'm glad I got to see *you* again," said Will, very low. He stared through the window at the stone pediment he had noticed before, with its carved hand pointing. *IИ OWR TYME*, it said with its backward *N*. It seemed oddly right, somehow; after all, he *had* gone backward in time. . . .

Margaret Menzies took his hand and squeezed it lightly. "I'm sorry, Will." Her voice held a ragged edge. "I'm so very sorry that I worried you. It must have been so hard not to know what was happening, and to wonder—to wonder if—" She faltered into silence.

Now. He had to say it now. Somehow, Will forced the words past the ache in his throat. "I deserved it, Mom. I wouldn't hug you when you went away, I wouldn't let you kiss me, I wouldn't even say good-bye."

"Oh, son." Her hand came up to stroke his hair. "You were angry with me."

Will nodded wordlessly.

His mother fumbled for a handkerchief and pressed it to her face. "I shouldn't have gone," she said in a muffled voice.

Will did not look at her. Instead he traced with his eyes the stone pediment with its carved letters and the hand, pointing. The letters at the very bottom were discolored with lichen and with time, but he could still make them out. *PRYSIT BE*, he read, and then the letters blurred.

He rubbed his arm across his face. "It's okay," he said, not sure if he believed it or was just trying to make her feel better. And then all at once he was sure.

"It's all right," he said. He curved his arm around her back and hugged her to his side. "I know why you had to go."

His mother laughed a little, wiping her eyes. "Why is that, then?"

Will frowned in concentration, remembering how he had felt when he went back for Sir Robert's nephew. "It's because you knew something had to be done, and you thought you were the one who was supposed to do it."

"Yes," said Margaret Menzies slowly. "That's exactly how I felt. But now I wonder if I should have ignored that feeling. You needed me, too—you and Jamie and your father."

Will leaned his cheek on her shoulder as if he were a small child again. "You couldn't have known what was going to happen. It wasn't your fault."

His mother was silent.

"It's true, Mom. Look." Will pointed to the pediment. "Can you read that? It says 'in our time.' You know what I think that means?"

His mother shook her head.

"I think it means you can't worry too much about the future. Because nobody knows what's going to happen, anyway. We just have this one time, see? Our time. And we get to choose what we're going to do in it."

Margaret Menzies blew her nose. "We can light a candle in the dark," she said at last. She tilted her head until it rested against his.

"That's right." Will saw in his mind's eye a thin, cruel face, a night sky bright with flame and filled with the sound of screaming. "Some people like to hurt, and destroy, and make everyone afraid of them. And others," he added, "like to heal, and build, and keep people safe."

It wasn't that simple, he knew. Some people were just mixed up. Like those from the Copper Age, who wanted more light but didn't understand it. Still, they had been trying to figure it out. Will smiled at his mother. "I'm glad you're the kind who heals."

A heavier footstep sounded at the threshold, and Will's father entered with a sleeping Jamie on his shoulder. "When did you get so wise, son?"

Will grinned at his father. "When you made me responsible for Jamie."

Andrew Menzies laughed and shifted the sleeping boy onto his other shoulder. "He's a heavy load, I know. But thank you for taking such good care of him. I'm sure it wasn't easy."

Will gazed at Jamie's small fist, still clutching the Highlander toy. "Not always," he admitted.

His mother pointed out the window. "I've never noticed those letters before. What does that say, below the 'in our time'? 'Prysit be God—'"

"'For evir,'" finished Will, squinting. "Oh—they must have meant 'forever.' What does *prysit* mean?"

His father said, "It must be an alternate spelling of *praised*. People used to say that word with two syllables, 'prais-ed.'"

"Prysit be God for evir," read Margaret Menzies slowly. "I like that. It goes perfectly with 'in owr tyme.'"

"How so?" Will's father boosted the sagging Jamie higher on his shoulder. "I don't get it."

"I do," Will blurted without thinking.

His father looked at him, waiting.

Will hesitated. "I don't know if I can say what I mean,

exactly. But it's like, in our own time, we can only see the one little piece—just the one thing we can do. We can . . . how did you put it, again?" he asked his mother.

"We can light a candle," she murmured.

"Right. But it's only a little candle, and there's a lot of dark."

"Sometimes there's a great deal of dark," his father said, very quietly.

"Right. In our time, there is." Will looked out at the stone carving that had already lasted almost five hundred years. "And in their time, and maybe in the times to come, too. But the next line says that the dark isn't going to win in the end. Not when you think about forever. Light wins."

"Ah," said his father. "Light wins. That's good to know."

Afterword

This story takes place in the area surrounding Castle Menzies in Scotland, both in the present day and far into the past. Some of the people described really lived, and some of the events really happened; others could have happened, based on what we know about past ages.

Castle Menzies is a real place, and you can visit it if you take a trip to Weem, Scotland. You can go to the kitchen where Will worked, and stand inside the fireplace. You can run up the winding staircase to all the rooms Nan showed Jamie, and climb into a turret on the top floor. You can look for the joined coat of arms of Barbara Stewart and James Menzies over the ancient door, and if you stand in just the right spot, you can see the carved window pediment that reads "IИ OWR TYME." If you are tired, you can have a fizzy drink and a biscuit in the tea room, and then you can go outside and explore until you find the iron gate and the walled garden. Oh, and don't worry if you hear people calling it "Castle Mengis"—

this is just the way Menzies is pronounced in Scotland. If you ask at the front desk, they will tell you the reason!

Just across the car park is the entrance to Weem Wood. Along the path, there are stones and trees carved with faces, dragons, and fanciful beasts. These are modern carvings, but they are still very fun to see, and I hope you find them all.

If you walk up the path to Saint David's Well, you can look out over Aberfeldy and sit on the cup-marked stone just as Nan, Will, and Jamie did. There is a carved stone cross and a cave there, though the cave is full of rubble, and the carved cross is a replica. The real stone cross—very old, in two pieces, and said to be carved by St. Cuthbert himself—can be seen in the Old Kirk at Weem, now the Menzies Mausoleum. If the mausoleum is closed, you can peek through the window, as I did.

Across a wide river valley—a strath—is Drummond Hill. If you don't mind a hike, you can walk up another trail to the site of an Iron Age hill fort. Be careful how you place your feet when you cross the small valley to climb up to the stony hilltop—hundreds of years of fallen branches and covering bracken have created foot-traps for the unwary. There is not much left of the hill fort except for a stone wall, but when you get to the very top, you will be able to see a long, long way across two river valleys. This is where Breet raced her chariot. Then, if you walk to the other end of Drummond Hill, you can stand at Black Rock Point and look out over Loch Tay.

On the southeast shore of Loch Tay is a crannog, built on stilts out over the water. This is the Crannog Centre, and you can run along the wooden walkway and go right in. You can see how the ancient peoples used to live, and even try making fire and operating a primitive lathe yourself. They won't let you paddle the dugout canoes, but you can see them drawn up at the water's edge, and sit in them, too, if you don't mind getting a little wet.

The Battle of the Bloody Hands (history books call it the Battle of Mons Graupius) was a great Roman victory, and the Picts really did kill their own villagers near the battlefield rather than let them fall into Roman hands. After that, though, the Picts changed their tactics. They did not try to battle the Romans again in the open, but switched to night raids and surprise attacks, quickly disappearing into the folded glens and hills they knew so well.

The Romans called their fort Pinnata Castra, which means "Fortress on the Wing," but the Picts called it Inchtuthil, which can be translated as "Island in the Flooded Stream." If you visit, at first you may think it is only a few long ditches and low mounds. But if you look carefully, and compare it to diagrams of Roman encampments—they were all pretty much the same—you will be able to see just where the buildings were, and how big it all was. The Romans did mysteriously leave this fort even before it was fully completed, and never came back. They retreated far to the south, built a wall, and stayed behind it. This was called Hadrian's Wall, after the Roman emperor, and you can still see parts of it today.

If you want to see Garth Castle, you will probably only see it from the outside, because at the time of this writing it is privately owned. But you can walk around it, look up, and see the high square parapet from which, legend has it, people who displeased the Stewart laird were thrown off. And you can walk by the stony burn beneath the castle, where Neil Gointe Stewart's wife met her death when a rock was dropped on her head.

If you would like to hear "Flower of Scotland," the song Nan taught to Jamie, you can find it online. It was written by Roy Williamson of the Scottish folk group The Corries. Since it was first performed in the 1960s, it has become an unofficial national anthem of Scotland.

Why did I write about Castle Menzies? Well, my grandfather was a Menzies (though in America he dropped the *s* at the end), and when I was a little girl he showed me a picture of Castle Menzies, and told me it was the castle of our clan. I wanted to go and live there!

Then one day, many years later, I saw a picture in my mind of an acorn rolling out of a stone wall. I didn't know why the acorn was doing such a strange thing, but I had a feeling that the stone wall was a part of Castle Menzies. It was clear that a story was stirring in me somewhere. And so I wrote it. I hope you like it.

Here are some more detailed notes about the book, starting with the different ages the children visited:

COPPER AGE

The Copper Age was a narrow time period between the end of the Stone Age and the beginning of the Bronze Age. In the Stone Age, people used stone for weapons and tools. In the Copper Age, people learned how to mine copper and make it into edged weapons, tools, and beautiful objects. In the Bronze Age, people learned how to mix copper and tin together to make bronze, a much harder and more durable metal. We know that copper was mined near Loch Tay in historic times, and it could have been mined there in prehistoric times, too.

AUROCHS: An aurochs was a huge wild ox, fast and aggressive, as tall as a grown man. They became extinct in Scotland during the Bronze Age, but they lasted longer in Europe. The very last aurochs died in a Polish forest in 1627.

LOCH: This is a long, narrow, often very deep lake in the Scottish Highlands. There are many stories about unusual creatures that swam in from the sea and might still live in lochs today.

CRANNOG: This is a man-made island in a loch. Some crannogs were made by piling up stones, with a narrow stone causeway leading to it that could be easily defended. Others were built on tall stilts over the water, with a wooden walkway. It is believed that they were used in the Copper, Bronze, and Iron Ages. The Crannog Centre near Aberfeldy, Scotland, shows how archaeologists discovered timber and canoes from thousands of years ago, buried and amazingly preserved in the peaty mud of Loch Tay.

CUP-MARKED STONES: These are stones that have been marked with small, circular indentations, like little cups; some of the cups have rings around them, with one line leading out straight from the center. No one knows why the ancient peoples made them, but one theory is that they had something to do with worship of the sun. They are found all over Scotland, and there is one at Saint David's Well in Weem Wood.

IRON AGE

The Iron Age came after the Bronze Age; this was when people learned to make things out of iron, which was the strongest metal anyone had yet known.

PICTS: These people were descendants of the very first people to come to Scotland (probably from Scandinavia), and so they called themselves *Pecht*, a word meaning "the ancestors" or "the people." Later on, the Romans took that word and changed it to *Picti*, which means "painted people," because of the blue painted tattoos on their skin. They loved bright colors; their chariots were painted, their shields were enameled, and they wove vivid checkered cloth for clothing.

The Picts lived in northern Scotland, in what we now call the Highlands. Though they were made up of many different tribes, with different names, they would band together to fight a common threat. They were tall, fair- or red-haired, pale-eyed, and very strong and hardy. When the Romans invaded Scotland, they were astonished at the Picts' ability to run fast and long and hard, even uphill, and to fight in the cold without letting it slow them down.

The Picts did not have a written language and so there is much we do not know about them. But they left us clues, in ancient burial sites and in carvings on stones. The mysterious designs under each chapter title in this book are Pictish. What do they mean? Even experts are not sure. Historians and archaeologists are still finding things out about the picts—and arguing about them, too!

PICTISH BEAST: This is a strange, some say mythical animal that shows up over and over again in Pict carvings. No one knows what it is supposed to represent. Some think it might have been a real sea creature, since it does not have hooves or paws but rather curled-up appendages that could be flippers of a sort. If it was a real creature, why don't we see it today? Maybe it is extinct, like the aurochs.

I liked the idea that the Pictish Beast was a realistic drawing of a sea creature that once existed, long ago. So I gave it a name—"Cray-tee"—and had it appear in the Copper Age, to bring good luck.

WOMEN: From what we can tell, Pictish women were strong forces within their community, farming, fishing, raising children, and sometimes fighting. Burial sites show that virtually all of the men and some of the women were warriors, for they were buried with their swords and spears.

CHARIOTS: Picts were using war chariots well before the Romans arrived. Their chariots were open, two-wheeled, made of painted wood, probably held together with root lashings; they were pulled by two horses side by side, with braided tails. The horses Picts used were smaller than modern horses, and shaggier—the Romans called them "ponies"—and Picts in war chariots charged up and down hills with great daring and speed as they raced to attack.

HIGHLANDS: The northern part of Scotland where the land is seamed with long lines of high steep hills and mountains, with rivers and lochs stretching out in the valleys between. It is difficult country to travel, and the Romans found it was difficult to conquer as well.

HILL FORT: Hill forts were small groupings of huts built on the tops of hills. The huts had stone walls and tall pointed thatched roofs like wizards' hats. The little village was protected by an encircling wall, and there were often several terraced walls farther down the hill as well, which may have enclosed areas for farming and grazing.

ROMANS: The Roman Empire started in what we now call Italy, and grew and grew until it seemed the Romans were out to conquer the world. They managed to conquer a great deal of it, but when they got to Scotland they tried—and then they stopped. One reason was that the Roman Empire had its own troubles, back home. Another reason was that, although the Romans could beat the Picts in Scotland on an open battlefield, they had a lot more trouble fighting the Picts in their mountainous glens. The Picts' method of fighting, then retreating into the hidden valleys and caves of their homeland, then coming out when the Romans least expected it to fight again, told the Romans that they would never truly conquer this last bit of land. In the end, they decided it wasn't worth it, and went home.

FINDING TREASURE: All over Scotland, people find treasure every day. The freeze-thaw cycle of that climate makes sure that ancient metals keep thrusting up through the earth, and when a farmer plows a field, treasure-seekers with metal detectors often go prospecting. There are so many artifacts from ancient times to be found that there are very specific rules about who gets what share of the treasure!

MIDDLE AGES

The children visited Sir David Menzies and Sir Robert Menzies in 1470 and 1502. These years were at the very end of the Middle Ages in the Scottish Highlands.

BURN: The Scottish word for a small stream.

CASTLE MENZIES: This is not one of the big, grand, endless castles that take a whole day to tour, nor is it one of the small, ancient, crumbling castles. It's a Z-plan castle, meant for defense but also for family living, and is a nice size for children to explore. It was built after the previous castle was burned by an enemy in 1502. In 1746, Bonnie Prince Charlie rested in it two nights on his way to the fateful Battle of Culloden.

FOSTERING: In the Middle Ages it was a common practice for nobles to send their sons to the castle of a relative, to be trained as a page, then a squire, and then a knight. The boys could have been trained at home, of course, but it was thought they would learn the necessary toughness better away from their own parents, who might tend to spoil them.

LAIRD: Scottish pronunciation of "lord." The laird was the chief of his clan; he was the lawgiver, the fighting leader, the one to whom land was granted by his king.

NEIL GOINTE STEWART: This Stewart laird was a descendant of "The Wolf of Badenoch," another wild Stewart laird who was famed for brutality, treachery, and murder. Neil seems to have been much like his ancestor. He was given the nickname "Gointe," meaning "bitter and twisted," by those who knew him. When Neil Gointe Stewart's father died, Neil came into the lairdship as a young, angry man and he gathered lawless men around him who made a habit of stealing and murder. He burned Castle Menzies, kidnapped Sir Robert, and it is said that later on he killed (or paid someone to kill) his own wife by dropping a stone on her head from the ramparts of Garth Castle as she walked by the burn below.

SAINT CUTHBERT: Cuthbert was a Christian monk from Ireland who came to Scotland in the seventh century to preach and teach. He lived for a time in a cave on a hill near a natural well, and built a small church at the base of the hill, at "The Place of Weem" (*weem* is a word that means "a cave"). The village there is called Weem to this day. It is said that Cuthbert carved a stone cross that stood near the well for many long years.

SAINT DAVID'S WELL: Originally this was called Saint Cuthbert's Well, after Saint Cuthbert, who lived and taught there about eight hundred years before Sir David Menzies. When Sir David became a monk and lived at the well for a time, it began to be referred to as Saint David's Well. If you walk up the path through Weem Wood, you can still see it today, a rectangular pool of water below the stone cliff.

SIR DAVID MENZIES: There really was a Sir David Menzies, a knight and laird who, in 1424, volunteered to go as a hostage to England for his king. He was imprisoned in the Tower of London, among other places. When he came back at last, he felt the need to live as a hermit in peace and holiness. He gave up the title and responsibilities of laird to his son, John, became a monk, and later an abbot. One of John's sons was Robert, who eventually became the laird in turn.

SIR ROBERT MENZIES: There really was a Sir Robert Menzies, too, and he was laird at the time there was a bitter fight with the Stewarts. Neil Gointe Stewart was jealous of Sir Robert, and angry that the king had granted the Menzies some lands that Neil thought should be his own. Neil Stewart and his men came to the castle in the dead of night, set it afire, and took Sir Robert hostage. They held Sir Robert in the dungeon of Garth Castle for months, mistreating and starving him and demanding that he sign over the disputed lands. Sir Robert refused. Finally, when the Stewarts heard that the king himself was coming to set matters straight, Neil Stewart got nervous. He told Sir Robert that, if he would sign a "paper of forgiveness" promising not to take revenge on them, he would be set free. Sir Robert signed and was released. Within a few years he rebuilt the castle and the kirk (church) that had been burned. The Castle Menzies that you can visit today is the very one Sir Robert built.

"MENZIES" OR "MENGIS"?

If you are in Scotland, you might hear people pronounce the clan name so that it sounds like "Mengis" (or "Meng-yis"). This is how the clan members have always pronounced it. Why is it written with a z, then? Well, hundreds of years ago, the Scots used an old-fashioned letter called *yogh* to represent the sound of a *g*. This letter looked almost like the number three, and so the Menzies name was written like this: MEN3IES.

Unfortunately, the yogh wasn't usually in the fonts that early Scottish printers used. The yogh did look a lot like a cursive z, though, so the printers substituted a *z* in script for the yogh, and the clan name was printed like this: MEN3IES.

You can guess what happened! After a while, people who were not in the clan forgot that the cursive *z* was supposed to represent a yogh. They thought it was just a *z*. They printed it without using the cursive script at all, so it became Menzies, and this spelling was copied over and over in many official documents. By the time someone realized that they probably should have used a *g* instead of a *z*, it was impossible to change all the documents throughout all of Scotland and everywhere else!

When my great-grandparents came to America, they decided to pronounce their name the way it was spelled, with the *z* sound. Later on, my grandfather and one of his brothers decided to drop the *s* at the end and became the Menzie brothers, to differentiate their dairy from the Menzies dairy across town.

TIME TRAVEL

Is time travel possible? Some of our greatest scientists think so . . . in theory, at least. Eminent physicist Michio Kaku, cofounder of string theory, puts it something like this: If you have a radio in your living room, you have all the radio frequencies in the room with you—the BBC, Radio Moscow, ABC, and many more—but your radio is only tuned to one frequency. Still, those other frequencies are vibrating all around you, ready to be picked up if only you turn the radio dial just a little bit.

What if there are other times, past and future, all around us? We can't see them because we're only tuned to the present. But what if we could tune our perceptions to a different time? And what if that ability was stronger in a place where connections to the past went back for many generations?

That is what happened to Will. He discovered that ability, and experimented until he knew how to use it. I don't see why it couldn't happen . . . someday.

❧

We now believe that the universe is vibrating . . . probably there are other parallel universes in your living room and believe it or not this is called modern physics . . . get used to it.

—Michio Kaku

Acknowledgments

I am deeply thankful for the interest and advice of the representatives of the Menzies clan. Special thanks go to Robin Menzies Bentzen, Executive Director of Development for the Menzies Clan Society of North America, whose counsel helped at numerous points, and whose enthusiasm extended even to trekking about the castle grounds with camera and notebook to answer some final questions. I am also truly grateful to George Menzies, Esq., Trustee and History and Legal Advisor to the Menzies Charitable Trust, for checking the manuscript for historical accuracy and discussing some thorny points with me; to Rory Menzies, Menzies Clan Society President and Chairman of the Menzies Charitable Trust, and Neil Menzies, Secretary of the Menzies Charitable Trust, for kind permissions and approval of the project; and to David Henderson, Castle Menzies Manager, who cheerfully poured information into my head during my visit to the castle.

Many thanks also are due to the late Drue Heinz for the Hawthornden Castle Fellowship. A month in a castle in Scotland with nothing to do but write, research, and nurture the muse was a gift beyond all praise, and laid the groundwork for this book. And I also warmly appreciate Kathleen Coskran and the Malmo Arts Colony for providing a winter retreat where further progress on this book was made.

My heartfelt thanks to my perceptive editor, Christy Ottaviano; my terrific agent, Stephen Barbara; to friend and colleague Heather

Bouwman for her excellent critique; and, as always, to my dear husband, Bill, first reader and most enthusiastic of supporters.

Finally, and most of all, I remember with profound gratitude my beloved grandfather, James David Menzie. He took me on his lap when I was small and told me enthralling stories; he read me poems from his worn copy of Robert Burns; he showed me a picture of Castle Menzies and said, "There is the tree under which Bonnie Prince Charlie once played." He fired my imagination and planted the seed for a story. It sprouted and grew, and half a lifetime later this book is the result. Under this tree, I played for many years.

CASTLE MENZIES.

CASTLE MENZIES
AND SURROUNDING LANDS

Garth Castle

the River Lyon

Drummond Hill

the Crannog